THE CARETAKERS

THE CARETAKERS

WILLIAM T. DELAMAR

OPEN ROAD
INTEGRATED MEDIA
NEW YORK

ISBN: 978-1-5040-8256-3

This edition published in 2023 by Open Road Integrated Media, Inc.
180 Maiden Lane
New York, NY 10038
www.openroadmedia.com

This book is dedicated to my wife, Gloria Delamar, who stood by me through all the turmoil of my hospital experiences.

THE CARETAKERS

CHAPTER ONE

Doug pulled past the emergency room and swerved to miss a large police van with BOM3 SQUAD written boldly on the side. It stuck halfway out in the lane.

What the hell! He zipped into the parking garage and nosed into his space.

"Mr. Carpenter!" Bill Hanes, the safety officer, came running and huffing up the ramp, his fat face and bald head pointing like a warhead. "I had you paged. We've got a problem in the labs."

"Got anything to do with that bomb squad truck parked by Emergency?"

"Yes, sir. The bomb squad is here." He took short side steps, dancing back toward the hospital as though to pull Doug with him.

"What the hell for?" Doug moved with him and Bill walked faster.

"Well, I . . ." his voice trailed away, "called them."

Doug ran to keep up with the big man.

"Why?" *With everything else, what now?* "Was there a bomb threat?"

"No, sir. Maybe. Yes, sir. Dr. Snowden has stuff on the fourth floor that could blow up any minute and take the hospital with it. I mean the *whole* hospital." He gestured with his arms, making a large circle.

Doug nearly ran into him as he followed him across the short stretch of lawn. "What stuff?"

"Picric acid, and it's been there a long time, and you know what happens to that stuff when it gets old."

"No, I don't know. What happens?"

"It crystallizes, and that's when it's ready to explode. Anything will set it off and he has big jars of it sitting in the hallway."

Bill gestured and jabbered, and Doug felt like an idiot chasing after him but followed him through the side door of the main building, into the clinging hospital smells. He clanged up the metal-stripped steps, not waiting for the elevator.

"How did you discover it? And why didn't you work it out with Snowden? Why call the bomb squad?" He strained to catch his breath. "And what does Snowden use it for if it's an explosive?"

"I don't know what he uses it for, but I picked up one of the bottles to tell him he couldn't store stuff on the hall floor when I saw the name on the label. I started to unscrew the cap, but then I saw the crystals. And you know what that stuff can do."

The big round man strained up the steps ahead of him like Humpty Dumpty.

A wild goose chase to start the day? Was this guy's brain a wad of waste? But sometimes he was right. Snowden had been a pathologist forever. Certainly, he would know. He'd been chairperson of the labs for over twenty years without blowing up anything. Three more flights of clattering stairs. Gasping for breath, they burst out of the stairwell into the hallway to find Cliff Toliver, the Chief of Security, all five foot four of him, talking to Dr. Snowden. A police sergeant and two other officers, covered with body padding, stood listening.

Doug and Hanes stopped for a moment, perspiring and panting. Ben Snowden bent down, scooped a half-gallon glass container from the floor, tossed it in the air, then caught it with one hand.

One of the officers threw himself flat on the floor. The other officer and the sergeant backed against the wall.

"Idiots." Snowden tossed the container to the surprised sergeant who managed to clutch it to his chest, mouth open. "I was using this stuff when you were in diapers."

The sergeant straightened up, his eyes like stones, and turned, handing the container to the officer standing next to him. The officer squatted and placed the container in a padded steel box. The other officer got up from the floor and stared at Snowden.

The sergeant turned to Snowden. "No disrespect intended, sir. You may be a doctor but you're a damn fool, sir." He looked at Bill. "Any more of this stuff? We've got seven containers."

"No, sir. I've checked everywhere. That's all there is."

"You're sure? If there's more hidden away, I'll have the building evacuated."

"Sergeant, I'm Doug Carpenter, the administrator. Can you tell me what's going on?" *Little martinet, he's not about to close down this hospital.*

"There's not much to tell. We received a phone call from Mr. Hanes at 6:35. We proceeded here, arriving at 6:40, and found twenty-six half-gallon containers of what used to be picric acid and is now a highly explosive salt. If all of this blew," he waved his hand at the steel boxes, "none of us would live to tell about it." He glared his contempt at Snowden.

The other two officers snapped a series of latches shut on the steel box.

"Doug, all these idiots have to do is add water to restore it. This is stupid." Snowden laughed, but he didn't look happy.

Doug turned to the sergeant. "What are you going to do with it?"

"We're going to take it out into the north rock quarry and detonate it."

Ben Snowden planted his fists on his hips, his mouth twisted to one side, white eyebrows raised in disbelief.

The sergeant kept his eyes off Snowden as though he didn't exist. "The point is, in its crystallized form it's explosive. If you'd like to come along and see what could have happened in this building, you'd be welcome."

Doug shook his head slowly. "No, thanks, but Bill, I think you should."

"I'm going, too," snapped Dr. Snowden. "I want to see these toy soldiers blow up this harmless material. It might be enough to pop corn."

"Okay." Doug turned to Bill. "I'd like a complete report as soon as you return. Maybe you ought to go, too, Cliff."

Toliver was already moving to a hall phone to have a car brought around.

"Ben, give me a call later." The old man just distorted his face in disgust. Doug felt like apologizing for being in a hurry. He waited for the elevator to drone to the fourth floor. He had told Dr. Whyte he would meet him at seven. Doug looked at his watch—ten after. Whyte was not a man to be kept waiting. *What the hell? Who was?*

He hurried into the administrative reception area. Whyte, his eyes, hair, and face, all the same putty gray, was sitting, quietly, in one of the soft, upholstered chairs.

"Been waiting fifteen minutes for you, Doug. Have trouble getting up early?" Ed Whyte unfolded out of the chair, mouth clamped into a thin line.

"Wish it were so." Doug unlocked his office door. He decided not to tell Whyte why he was late. He didn't want to embarrass anyone. "We need to talk about the plan to take over the Highland Hospital obstetrical patients."

"No, Doug. We need to talk about *implementing* the plan."

Doug settled behind his desk and watched the prima donna select a chair by the window.

He heard the police siren as the bomb squad headed toward the old rock quarry north of the city. He could imagine Snowden in his white lab coat, his arms folded, lips twitching.

"Well?" Ed Whyte's voice vibrated through his anger.

"Ed, there's reason to think the plan's just not to the best interest of the patients."

"How can you say that? Highland does a lousy job with maternity cases. They want to close their delivery rooms. The patients will get better care here at Eastern."

"*If* they get here. Are you aware Highland had worked out this same plan with Community Hospital two years ago?"

"No, and it doesn't interest me."

"Maybe the reason it failed will."

"Spare me the details."

"It's short. I can put it into one word. Perez."

"For Pete's sake, talk about the program. I don't have time for games."

"I'm talking about the program. Ester Perez was a sixteen-year-old in her eighth month."

Whyte sighed and looked at the ceiling as though searching for divine intervention.

Doug realized he was wasting his breath but went on. "Late in the night, she went into labor. Her husband was at work twenty blocks away. By pay phone at a gas station, she reached him. Buses running once an hour, he called a taxi, in excited Spanish, in the Hill District, in the middle of the night. Taxis, in this city, don't answer to Spanish, rarely go to the Hill District in broad daylight, and never in the middle of the night."

Whyte studied his fingernails.

"On icy streets, he ran, slipped, and fell for twenty blocks, trying to stop cars, but none would pick up a wild man in such a place. He finally got home. No Ester. He called the hospital. No Ester. He woke up all the neighbors. None of them knew where she was." Doug paused. "To cut the story short, she gave up on her husband and panicked. With labor pains close and her water already broken, she tried to walk. Not to Highland Hospital. They had closed their OB department. She tried to walk all the way to Community."

Whyte's face was like an ice sculpture. "And I suppose she died in a snowdrift."

"They found her unconscious on the sidewalk, about twenty blocks away. She was holding her baby. It was dead."

Whyte gave him a dead-fish stare.

"Ed, she wouldn't have made it here, either. We're farther away than Community. And she's not the only example. With all your plans and prenatal classes, less than half of them would make it. We're all the way on the other side of the city. Why not let our residents rotate through Highland, improve their OB skills, keep the patients where at least they'll get some care, instead of none? Many of them are high-risk mothers."

Whyte gazed out the window.

Doug recognized the political power of this man, that he would go around him, discredit him with the medical staff, the Board, his boss, and jeopardize his job. His stomach tightened like a vice had clamped it. "The best thing for those patients would be for us to work with Highland. Help them with their training programs, give—"

"And occupy the beds there." Whyte cut him off. "You keep after me to bring up my census, fill the beds." He waved a hand. "Now, you want me to help fill Highland's beds. They no longer have any obstetricians. I've arranged for Highland's general practitioners to refer cases here. It'll bring our census up to sixty-five percent. Now, tell me . . ." Whyte's putty face shifted, shade by shade, to blood red. He took a deep breath, obviously fighting his temper. "You tell me why should I bust my ass to bring in patients if you're going to say 'no' anyhow? And who cares if some Rican lost a baby on the sidewalk? That's one less Spic in the world."

It felt like someone had given a full turn to the vice clamping his stomach. He hated this man and everything he stood for. But if he went up against him, he could lose his job.

"Ed, we do need to bring up the census. We need the money, but to—"

"How long have you been on the Board, Doug?" Dr. Whyte interrupted. "A year? A little more?" He didn't wait for an answer but leaned forward and stared into Doug's eyes without blinking. "That's not much of a commitment. You haven't been here long enough to learn how we do things." His voice dropped as he added, "There haven't been many administrators around here that made a commitment." His voice rose again. "I've been here thirty-two years, and seen dozens of *administrators* come and go." He enunciated "administrators" with a tone of disgust. Then another thought seemed to strike him. His face got even redder and he almost lost control. "I've made commitments based on this program. I'll be damned if I'll let you screw them up because of some Rican whore."

Doug's right hand quivered. He pressed it down on the desktop. "She was just a young Puerto Rican woman trying to survive in a tough world." Anger clawed at his self-control. *Did Whyte's commitments include a boat or summer home?*

"Bullshit. They're all whores and their mothers are whores. And we have to pay their damn bills. They get what they deserve."

"Ed—"

"I didn't think you'd be able to see the sense in this." Whyte stood. "I'll go see Stan."

The door closed. Doug shut his eyes and clenched his fists, blood pulsing through his head. He took a deep breath to relax.

Ed Whyte had been born into money and had married money. He had little concern for the poor. They were the great unwashed. The fact was he didn't know how to deal with them or even why he should deal with them. He used the poor for training residents but kept them away from his private patients.

And now that he was being pressured to bring in more patients. The only ones he could find were the poor, and he had no plans to give them anything resembling decent service.

Doug gazed out the window that framed the blue sky. He concentrated on the cumulus clouds, gigantic floats in a parade across the sky. He thought of his childhood days in the South where this same sky was so common, clouds like cotton for miles in all directions. No hard decisions.

His hand continued to shake. *Ed Whyte. All the Ed Whytes. A damned army of Ed Whytes. They cared only for themselves, using patients to collect fees.*

And administrators went along in an effort to survive. The administrator might be number one in the hospital, but not in the college it was part of, and the Board was the final authority. They hired and fired administrators, and the medical staff influenced them. But in all fairness, there were more good physicians than bad. It was just that the bad ones were somehow more interested in running things.

He bowed his head and rubbed his neck. *How much longer will I be at Eastern? What can I do to survive and not give in to their greed?* He couldn't play the game. He wasn't a taker. He hated takers. But the tension and bad dreams of unemployment every night . . .

He leaned on the windowsill and gazed over the western section of the city—mixed business and residential all the way to the river. The blossoms on the cherry trees caught the sunlight and filled the air like a million butterflies.

April. Some of the women would deliver in November, some in December, then January and February. The days would turn dark earlier. Cold. Ice. Snow. No taxis. Whyte would go over his head to Stan Boswell. And Boswell would side with the bastard. He didn't have the strength not to. Stan needed Whyte as an ally. As college vice president for Health, he had to fill the beds to justify a new building to the state. Plans were already under way. As administrator, Doug had to run the hospital, but Stan was his boss in the college structure. Doug wished the man had his office somewhere outside of the hospital.

He fingered the stack of correspondence left over from yesterday and the day before. *How the hell do I keep Boswell from screwing the patients in order to build a bigger building?* He felt like he was trying to block a river. And if he lost his job for interfering, it would be difficult to get another. He thought of Bess. When he'd left the house, she was still asleep. A strand of amber hair lay across her nose. Even her hair was asleep. Her cheek was soft to his kiss, and somewhere deep in a dream world she had stirred. Her lips moved a slow-motion kiss. Forty-four. Only a year younger than he was, but she looked twenty-five. But in his dreams, he had failed her, making her a bag lady rooting through garbage cans; old and cold and afraid, alone on a sidewalk grate on a deserted street.

The bomb squad must have reached the rock quarry by now. He focused his attention on the correspondence. Another day was beginning.

CHAPTER TWO

The intercom scratched and Ann's voice announced, "I brought you some coffee from the cafeteria."

He stepped into the reception area to her smile.

"How was the meeting with Dr. Whyte?" She took the lid off and handed him the cup.

He held the cup up and inhaled the steam. "About as expected."

"That bad, huh?" She whisked around to unlock her desk. "Didn't get to you, did he?"

"No more than usual. I've still got my perspective." He sipped the coffee.

"Good. Then I won't quit today."

He ambled into his office, calling back, "Thanks for the coffee."

His schedule book was clear until nine-thirty. Maybe he could get some of the correspondence out of the way. *Won't quit today.* Everyone underestimated how much secretaries knew about the goings and comings around them.

Ann Wheeler had been there four years and was working for her third administrator. Frequently, when administrators were fired, their secretaries were displaced. Not Ann. Everyone liked her, not only for her incredible smile but her complete competence. And it hadn't hurt that she had jet-black hair and electric-blue eyes.

Again, the intercom scratched. "Don't forget you've a nine-thirty appointment. Is there anything you need for the meeting? The file's on your desk."

"Thanks. I've got it all."

"That's more than most of us can say."

Halfway through a letter of complaint from the wife of a patient, and once more, the intercom.

"Mr. Carpenter, Mr. Boswell wants to see you in his office."

"Okay, Ann. Tell him I'll be right there." He frowned, the tension spreading again to his neck. He glanced at a picture on the desk of Bess and himself. Her face gave him some reassurance. Hanging on the opposite wall was an enlarged color photograph Bess had taken, a scene of a country road in September outside of Williamsburg, Virginia. He had grown up there and wanted to sink back into it, inhale the odor of fall, relax to a chorus of crickets, and absorb some of the sleepy sense of peace. Instead, he pushed back from his desk. *What now?*

Stanley Boswell's office was one door down the hall. He was eight years younger than Doug and had been with Eastern Medical College six weeks.

Doug had been administrator under Stan's predecessor, George Brown, and knew the job well, but his relationship had started out poorly with Stan, who trusted no one. And it was no secret his main contender for the vice president job had been Doug. They both had good credentials: master's degrees in hospital administration, experience in complex medical centers, demonstrated abilities.

"You lost out by a whisker," a Board member had told him, but he knew the reason. He hadn't placated the more demanding physicians. He put the hospital first. He didn't play the game.

And now, Stan played it as though it were the only game, promising large chunks of hospital money to the more influential doctors for office space and equipment.

Stan Boswell didn't look up from the conference table that he preferred to a desk. "Sit," he said.

Doug sat, feeling a wave of disgust, and waited. On a credenza behind Stan was a framed picture of Stan and his wife—his third wife. No one at the hospital had met her. She hadn't come to any hospital functions. Liz Racoda, Stan's secretary, always came in her place.

Stan raised his eyebrows, but his eyes squinted as though he needed glasses. His eyes never seemed to open, but his mouth usually hung slightly open almost as though to compensate. He held his hands up, gesturing a question. "Doug, what's the matter with the Highland Hospital plan? I ran into Dr. Whyte downstairs and he was upset. Says you won't cooperate with him because of someone named Perez."

"Stan, there are serious problems with the plan."

Stan held the edges of the table as though he might jump up at any minute.

"Ester Perez was just an example I used. She was a young Puerto Rican girl who lost her baby."

"Who cares about another welfare patient? If there are problems, work them out. I don't want Whyte going to the dean and lining up sides. I need his help on other things. Work it out." He picked up his phone and waved his hand to dismiss Doug.

"Stan, the plan won't work."

"I don't care if it works or not." He slammed the phone into its cradle. "Do it. If it fails, then he can come up with something else, but don't put him in the enemy camp." He leaned forward as though he were coiled, ready to strike, still holding his hand on the phone. "Okay?"

"There are patients who stand to get hurt by his plan."

Stan kept his voice low, as though to confide. "You don't know that. No one's going to get hurt," he explained. "Do it. If anyone gets hurt, I'll be responsible. There." He smiled. "Does that make you feel better? Come on, Doug. From what I'm told, this is the first time this guy has tried to raise his census in ten years. Get on with it."

"The patients will never make it to this hospital because of the distance."

"Hey," Stan waved both hands in the air. "Get Social Service to work with you. Work it out. That's a detail. Now, I'm done with that subject. I don't want to hear any more about it.

"Let's talk about your relationship with the medical staff. How good—let me change that—how acceptable do you think your relationship is with the doctors?"

"It's good with some, not with others. It depends on whose greed hasn't been satisfied. A few of them are greedy bastards and are never satisfied, like Whyte."

"I don't care about greed. Give him what he wants." Stan clenched both his fists and aimed his face at Doug as though locking in for an attack. "I care about political impact. He can stand between a new hospital and me. The Board brought me here to build a new hospital because this one is about to fall on our heads. It's your job to run the hospital and keep the peace."

"To run the hospital and please the doctors."

"Exactly!" shouted Boswell, slamming his fist on the table. "And if you can't do it, tell me, and I'll get someone who can."

Doug forced himself to stay calm. "Stan, I know your charge. I know there are fleas biting you."

"Fleas, hell. I've got alligators." Stan swiveled in his chair and shook his head at the wall. He turned back around and his face was red. "You don't know anything."

Doug took a deep breath. "I know Dean Shocks wants to control the hospital division of the college. He's working on the president. We'd just be middlemen."

Stan let his hand move slowly to the table surface, his face still directed at Doug.

Doug continued. "The college vice president of finance sees the hospital as a money cow he could milk for the college. He's just looking for a way to get control."

Boswell rubbed his temples with the palms of his hands.

"Hell, Stan, I know these things."

"Well, at least you do understand *that*." Stan paused then took a deep breath. "But then you ought to." He folded his hands in front of him. "You didn't answer my question."

"What was that?"

"How do you think you're doing with the medical staff?"

"Stan, a few of the staff are lazy, a few others are incompetent. A few are greedy. It'll never be a hundred percent."

Boswell gripped the edge of the table again and leaned forward. He spoke slowly. "It will have to be a hundred percent. And, incidentally," he added, "I'm not sure it's fifty percent. You work on it." He prepared to leave. "I'm sure you can do it because you have to. Your job depends on it."

Doug avoided a staring contest. He wanted to reduce conflict, not increase it. "I'll give it my best shot, Stan, but you're going to have to work with the dean to get some people replaced." He moved to the door, then he remembered Ben Snowden. "By the way, we may have a problem with Dr. Snowden."

"Forget Snowden. He's an old man. A has-been. He doesn't matter. Don't waste time on him. Put your time on the Highland Hospital plan. See me later." Stan waved his hand to dismiss Doug once more. "Oh, and another thing, your request for $40,000 for renovations to meet the state's requirement for fire partitions above the ceilings. We can't afford it and never will. Tell them we did it. Fake the drawings. Do what you have to."

Doug wrestled for words. "Stan, that's fraud." He ran his fingers through his hair. "And they'd find out anyway. They aren't stupid. Besides, this portion of the building's a potential firetrap." He shook his head. "Stan, let me get this straight. Are you saying lie to them?"

Stan pushed his intercom buzzer. The door opened and Liz Racoda slinked in carrying a cup of coffee. She was the inventor of slink. Her blood-red fingernails stuck out like rakes. Doug wondered how she managed to use the computer keyboard, much less wipe her ass.

Stan smiled at Liz and then frowned at Doug. "It's your job to handle it. When they come back to check for compliance, do it."

"They're due here now. Stan, I've too much respect for those people and for myself to do such a thing."

"I don't want to hear it. I'm busy." He motioned to Liz, who leaned over the table, placed the coffee in front of him, then sat to take dictation. "And no more Ester what's-her-name," he called after Doug as he shut the door between them.

Doug stalked back to his office, hate churning in his stomach, but he maintained a noncommittal expression, a tight face, something he did automatically. No sense upsetting the rest of the staff when he and Stan had problems. The guy wasn't even a turkey. Turkeys were good for something.

He interviewed a candidate for the food service manager position, talked with a financial consultant about the HMO and Medicare payment system, and dictated letters. But, throughout the entire morning, he wondered about the picric acid and Ben Snowden. And Dr. Whyte. Dr. Whyte. *"They're all whores and their mothers are whores."*

Damn the man. He's the whore, chasing after money.

The call from Bill Hanes came when Doug was at lunch. Ann transferred the call and he had to strain to hear Hanes's nasal voice over the clattering of dishes and talking.

"Mr. Carpenter, they blew a hole must've been six feet wide and three feet deep at the quarry. Dust everywhere. It nearly blasted my ears out. They're still ringing. Must've been a twenty on the Richter scale." He laughed, then went into a coughing fit.

Doug said nothing for a moment. "And Snowden was there?"

"Yes, sir, he sure was. Bet he won't store no picric acid in the hall no more."

"What did he say?" Doug wondered if Hanes was exaggerating.

"He didn't say nothing. Not one word the whole way back."

Snowden would have been embarrassed and mad as hell at himself—at the world. Doug liked Snowden, but this was not excusable. A pathologist should know his chemistry, and this had to be basic chemistry. Picric acid really does crystallize and becomes explosive.

It could have made a mess of the labs and the building. No telling how many people might have been killed. Doug left the cafeteria and took the elevator up to the labs, but nobody had seen Snowden, so he went back to his office.

"Ann, see if you can find Dr. Snowden. Try every place you can think of until you find him." He told her about the crystal-lized picric acid.

"What a shame. He's such a nice guy. What's going to happen now?"

"I'm still processing that one." But things would *never* be the same for Snowden. "He has to be going through some trauma. When you get him, tell him I want to buy him a cup of coffee and ask him to come down here."

"If you're talking about me, no need to call," said Snowden, coming through the doorway. "I take it black."

"How are you, Ben?" asked Doug.

Snowden managed a thin smile. "I'll complain if it'll help. On the other hand, let's skip the coffee. I've had enough excitement for one day."

Doug ushered him into the office. Snowden crossed the room and stood looking out the window. He shrugged his shoulders but said nothing. Held his hands up as though to gesture to Heaven, then dropped them, slapping his legs. Turning around, he faced Doug, shaking his head.

"When that damn stuff blew, I couldn't believe it." His hands were reaching to the sky again. "I thought those cops had planted a stick of dynamite in there. I couldn't believe it would do such a thing." His voice rose. "And then, as I watched all that . . ." he gestured, arms flapping like wings, "that . . . damned dirt in the fucking sky! It was everywhere!" He sank into a chair, deflated. "I knew they hadn't planted it. Doug, I could've made a shambles of the laboratory." He gazed across the room as though seeing the lab falling apart. "I could've . . ." he shook his head. "I could have killed some of my people." He pushed up from the chair and turned to the window.

Doug didn't know what to say but sensed it was best to say nothing.

"I've been here a long time, Doug."

The calm statement, the quietness of his voice surprised Doug. *Where had the feisty old man gone?*

"I didn't want to go like this," he said, as though talking to himself, "but I've seen it coming." He locked eyes with Doug. "Five will get you ten, you have, too." For just a moment, he looked both angry and hurt.

Doug shifted uneasily. "I guess you had a pretty bad moment."

"A bad moment." Snowden's eyes welled up like blue ink. "A bad moment." He put his hands to his face and turned to the window, put his head back and dropped his hands, then took a deep breath and managed to squeeze out the words, "I'm tired, Doug, and I've gotten old." His voice cracked. "We all get old, eventually, all of us." His shoulders shook, and he sobbed openly.

Doug moved to him, but the old man turned and held up his hand.

"I remember when I came here in my forties." He wiped his eyes with a handkerchief. "Still young, still anxious. Hell," he shouted, "in my prime!" He sank into the chair, propped his face in his hands and cried, "In my damn prime, and it's gone."

Doug pulled a chair over and sat facing him.

After a while, Snowden leaned back and wiped his eyes. "You'll have to excuse an old has-been." Some of his natural humor showed through. "It was good, Doug. Boy, was it good." He smiled. "It was so good, I never thought it would end." He took a deep breath, as did Doug.

"Ben, you've given a lot to this place."

"Yeah, I know," said Ben, "picric acid and all."

Again, Doug didn't know what to say.

"I think I'll go home for the rest of the day, and then, tomorrow, I'll come in and maybe we can talk, and maybe I can put a few mementos in some boxes for the pasture."

"Tell you what, Ben, why don't you take a month's vacation, and then let's talk. God knows you've earned it."

Ben thought for a moment. "No, let's make it a clean break. Everyone knows I'm past time to retire. But thanks for the thought." He left quickly.

Doug remained seated, still surprised, feeling drained. He looked at the empty chair and imagined thirty years of dedication, thirty years of one contribution after another, of helping an institution grow, of merging mind and body into its works, and then passing on into obsolescence, the forgotten past, a faint echo in a long, dark hallway.

CHAPTER THREE

After a quick tap on the door, Dr. Charles Ellington Smith III walked in.

"Doug, I need to talk with you."

"What can I do for you, Charles?"

Smith strolled over to a chair and sat down. His tweed jacket smelled of stale pipe tobacco, his trademark. He placed his pipe on an ashtray, crossed his legs, folded his hands across his stomach and eyed Doug. His face was permanently frozen in a bad-smell expression. His eyelids, rusty awnings over raisin eyes, gave him a lizard-like appearance.

"I want your concurrence in something before I discuss it with Stan Boswell."

"What's that, Charles?" Doug watched him select his words carefully.

"Nursing in this hospital is unacceptable. My staff is hampered in caring for their patients by incompetence at all levels, and it starts at the top. I want you to fire Kay O'Connell."

"Charles, she's been here for less than a year. The department was a shambles when she started. You're not giving her a chance."

"A chance? She's had every chance. I've given her my full support. I think it's time we give the patients a chance. In a year's time, if she's worth anything, she should have made significant improvement." Smith gazed at Doug and picked up his pipe. "I don't see significant improvement."

A dull ache began to spread in Doug's temples. Smith was a brilliant diagnostician but had a narrow mind that matched his small, bald head.

"What's happened?" Doug asked.

"Has anyone talked to you about Mr. Bergman?"

"No. Who's Mr. Bergman?"

"I thought not." Smith eyed him questioningly. "You should ask Kay O'Connell. In the meantime, I'll give you the story minus any cover-up attempts."

Smith sat motionless as he talked. It was as though a ventriloquist were throwing the words but forgot to manipulate the mouth. "Mr. Bergman is a quadriplegic. He's been in and out of the hospital for both medical and surgical services. He has many problems. He's diabetic. We have to watch his diet, blood sugar, kidneys, and circulation closely."

He paused and focused on Doug as though to impress the importance of that point. "He's incontinent and is, consequently, catheterized." He paused again. "He is, supposedly, under constant observation. Twice, we have nurtured him through heart failure in this hospital. Nursing has written a careful and thoughtful care plan for him. The 'care plan' is one of the 'improvements' Kay O'Connell initiated here, oh, six months ago."

Doug hid his impatience.

"Last Wednesday at nine a.m., Mr. Bergman was taken to the amphitheater for grand rounds."

Smith's voice rose and Doug knew he was nearing the point.

"When his case was finished, he was pushed into the exit room to the rear of the stage. And there he was forgotten. No one came to get him. He was there until seven p.m. in that isolated amphitheater where no one could hear him calling. He was not missed on the floor until six p.m., and, finally, someone had the sense to check there for him."

His voice became singsong like a recitation. "He was not missed at lunch. He missed medications. His urine bag was filled and backed up. He has since developed a urinary infection, requiring adding more drugs to a complex balance of medications." He tilted his head to one side. "I think it was nice that Kay O'Connell introduced the new nursing care plan. When is she going to introduce nursing care?"

Doug tapped his fingers on the desk, Smith watching, eyes unblinking as though searching for flaws he could carry off to share with others.

"Two different nursing shifts failed to miss him?"

"Two shifts."

"How is he, other than the urinary infection?"

"No visible marks."

Doug picked up the phone and dialed Kay O'Connell. "She's in a meeting, Mr. Carpenter."

"What kind of meeting is it?"

"She's counseling an employee, Mr. Carpenter."

"How long has she been in there?"

"About fifteen minutes. Do you want me to interrupt?"

"No, but have her call me the minute she's done." He turned back to Smith. "She's counseling an employee. Charles, I'd appreciate your holding off on this to let me check it out. I want to find out what she's done about it."

"Doug, she's been here almost as long as you. Between the two of you, I had hoped things would show more improvement."

"It's a complex set of issues, Charles."

"So it is, but I'm bringing patients into this hospital who are receiving poor nursing care. Something's got to be done."

"Something will be. You have my word. Let me get back to you."

"I won't wait long, Doug." He paused at the door. "And there's another matter. You need to do something about these HMOs. They're taking medical care out of our hands. You're the administrator. You are supposed to be in control." He closed the door quietly behind him.

HMOs. Like I could control them. Like any administrator could control them. And Kay O'Connell. Charles Ellington Smith wouldn't wait long. He would go to Stan. Doug was surprised he hadn't already. Then he remembered. *Stan's out.*

Smith had a powerful technical mind. He analyzed everything—facts about the human body, ideas about diseases, human behavior. He processed information thoroughly, taking inventory, chewing each bit carefully and digesting it before the next bite.

He was a brilliant diagnostician with an encyclopedic mind. He knew he was brilliant and had long exceeded the point of being simply arrogant. His arrogance had become an art form. The hospital was there to serve him. The hospital was his learning lab. The patients served him for studies. He demanded deference because of his importance. He had gained an international reputation. He attracted more research grants and top physicians than anyone else on staff or in any of the hospitals in the city or state. In fact, he was one of the top grant earners in the country. Consequently, he competed with Administration in running the hospital—his hospital. He was all the more arrogant because he had come from middle-class roots. His superiority was earned and proven.

The damned intercom buzzed. Doug paused before answering. Doctors were ganging up on him. *What now?*

"You back from lunch, already, Ann? You went late."

"The cafeteria was closed. I got something from the vending machine. Kay O'Connell is on the line. She says you wanted to talk to her right away."

"Right." He switched to the waiting Kay. "Can you come over for a minute? I need to discuss a problem with you."

Within three minutes, Kay O'Connell was there, the essence of a professional, of being in control. *How could anyone be that good and be so young? She couldn't be thirty.* Even so, her hair was turning slightly gray. She threw herself into her work completely.

He told her Smith had given him the details about Mr. Bergman.

"I thought that was what it was about. I wanted to give you a full report on it myself, but before doing that, I had to investigate." She shook her head. "I knew the arrogant son-of-a-bitch would jump at the chance to find fault. It would be nice to have his help."

"I agree. It would be nice. But it's not his nature for whatever reason. What's been done to prevent it from happening again?"

Kay slipped into a chair. "The head nurses on both the day and evening shifts have been counseled. I put one on probation. One more mistake, and out she goes. I don't know what I'll do in that case." She sighed and sucked on her lower lip. "You know what our salaries are?"

"Yes, I know." He studied her, knew she could do the job, but negative circumstances surrounded Eastern like a black fog. The salaries were not just low, they were incredibly low . . . and the college kept them that way.

Doctors frequently sabotaged directors of nursing at Eastern. Nurses didn't give in to them. For example, the accident cases.

Several doctors were bringing in patients with minor accident problems, calling them severe, and collecting fees from
the insurance companies. The nurses blew the whistle, not the
other doctors.

"Another corrective measure we've taken," Kay continued,
sounding irritated, "is that the Transportation Department is
setting up a system to show where any patient is that they've
transported. There'll be a card in an out-rack until the patient is
returned, from wherever."

"What happened, Kay? How could two shifts of nurses over-
look a patient?"

Kay's hands dropped to her lap. "Anything I say will sound
like excuses. The census on the unit was eighty percent, but the
staffing was at sixty. We had three code blues, one at shift change,
and everyone was running. These aren't acceptable reasons," she
explained, "but, coupled with the fact the residents had taken
him, the head nurse on the day shift had put it out of her mind,
thinking the residents would bring him back when it was time.
They have in the past."

"The residents took him?"

"Yes, that's not unusual for grand rounds."

"And they were supposed to bring him back?"

"It's been an unwritten agreement, but my nurses should
have been on top of it."

"Kay," Doug put his hand on her shoulder, "you've taken
some appropriate measures, but I wish I had known about this
when Smith came to see me."

Kay took a deep breath and tilted her head toward the wall.
For the first time, she looked tired, even old.

"I'm sorry. The next time there's a problem, I'll tell you about
it even if we haven't resolved it." Then she added, "You know
Smith is one of the docs that dumps on the nurses. He treats

them like something in a litter box. He's one of the reasons they leave."

"I'm not surprised to hear it. Let's take it a step at a time." Doug walked over to the window. "How can some of these guys be so rotten and others so good?"

"I don't know, but I wish they were all like Garland Riggely."

"Garland. Yeah. In fact, almost all pediatricians are good people. Maybe it's because they deal with the untainted and see the world's potential at its innocent best . . . but that's too deep. Garland's one of the best."

"That reminds me. I want to start a Death and Dying Committee. I've a nurse who's gung-ho on it, and I've already talked to Dr. Best. She said if I hadn't called her, she would have called me."

"That's good. Psychiatry should be involved. Julia Best is always up-front, completely honest. The medical staff respects her."

"What reminded me was this crap about Smith. He's one of those who needs it, and he'll oppose what we want to do."

"What do you want to do?"

"We want patients who are dying to be told they are dying. Too many doctors refuse to tell them, maybe because they can't deal with it themselves. But the patient should be told, and there should be no tiptoeing around it. Usually, the patient figures it out, but the family, the doctor, and the nurses avoid the subject. The patient, undergoing the most incredibly lonely experience in life, has no one to talk to about it."

"Kay, most hospitals are already doing this. Why aren't we? I could understand if this were fifty years ago."

"Many of our doctors are handling it right, but we have some, Smith included, who refuse, claiming the patient should be allowed to die in peace. He misses the point. Anyhow, will you endorse it by being at the first meeting?"

"Count me in." Then a thought hit him. "In two months, you will have been here a year. I want you to prepare a report describing the improvements you've made. It's time we had some horn-tooting." He crossed the door to the office. "Come on, let's walk and talk. I've got to make rounds, but I've got some ideas, and I want to discuss them now."

They squeezed to the back of the elevator. The doors opened on the third floor and two surgeons got on having an angry discussion.

"Why did you do it?"

"Hell, she was on the table, open, and it needed to be done. It was no big deal."

"No big deal. It's my specialty. It's my procedure. It was my fee."

"What was I to do? Sew her up and reschedule her to be cut open again so you could have your fee?"

"You had no business doing it. You should've closed and rescheduled her. You owe me the fee. I'm more qualified than you." The door opened on five and the two got off.

"You're crazy. What about the patient?"

"The patient? You just earned yourself an extra . . ."

The door shut.

"Have mercy," commented an old lady near the front of the car. "Who said leeches aren't used in hospitals anymore. They just give them a diploma and call them doctor."

Someone laughed and there was a lot of head shaking. Kay looked as though even she didn't believe her own ears.

Doug leaned to her ear. "That's how many seconds it takes to destroy our reputation."

"Yeah. Must've majored in financial extractions."

Doug closed his eyes. One more problem in the parade. He'd have to start numbering them just to keep track.

CHAPTER FOUR

It was four o'clock when Doug returned to his office. In the hallways and offices that afternoon, he had dealt with purchasing problems, a possible narcotics theft, a laboratory staffing change, and three nursing problems that Kay couldn't tackle alone. One of them was like a whole keg of picric crystals.

Al Robinson, the chief anesthesiologist, had been drunk, and a resident took over in the middle of a surgical case when Robinson couldn't control the gas flow. The resident refused to acknowledge there was a problem. No incident report from him.

Robinson was a young man, competent and well-thought-of, but alcoholism wasn't uncommon among anesthesiologists. And, once again, it would be the nurses who would blow the whistle.

Damn. The docs protect each other blindly and hurt themselves and the patient in the process.

"Wow, I don't usually see a scowl on your face," said Ann.

Doug stopped and leaned against the doorjamb. "Guess I have to watch that. I'll find something good to think about."

Ann raised both eyebrows. "The only problems while you were gone were things I could take care of and you don't want to know about."

"There's a nice world out there after all." He rubbed his neck. "I'm going to the cafeteria for a cup of coffee. You want one?"

"No, I'm much too busy running the hospital."

"Sounds like a good deal to me," said Doug, heading into the hallway. "I'll be back in a few minutes to relieve you of the helm."

Coffee took longer than planned. Doug ran into the manager of the Rehab Unit and discussed refurbishing the occupational therapy kitchen.

Upon his return, a stack of phone messages awaited on Ann's desk and in his office, he found Herb Cline, hospital attorney, leaning over the desk.

"Just leaving you a note." Cline straightened up and stretched his back. "I'd given up on you."

"What's the note say?"

"Says I'm disgusted. Says you got a dumb doctor. Says you better do something to control him or you are in big trouble here."

"Reminds me of the Sid Caesar routine. A guy in front of a firing squad spits on the commander who screams, 'Now you in big trouble.' Besides, that piece of paper's not big enough to say all that. What's the problem?"

"Woman suing your friend the doctor. I'm reviewing the case. Reading physician progress notes. Progress notes, standard hospital form, revised. Revision date printed on the bottom of the form. Woman discharged from hospital one year earlier than date form revised. Dumb doctor rewrote progress notes after suit filed. Mistake number one." Cline held up one finger. "Now comes mistake number two." He held up two fingers. "Old progress notes not removed. Left in patient medical record. Copy of medical record already sent to woman's attorney. Dumb, dumb doctor. See woman win. See doctor lose case."

"Damn! You can lay the case out by just comparing the two versions." He couldn't believe it. "Easy enough to prevent it in the future. When litigation is filed, we'll pull the original patient chart so the docs can't tamper with it. Let the doctor have only copies. But, what do we do on this one?"

"I don't know, Doug," He sounded weary. "Sad part is we would have won the case. He overreacted, tried to remove anything that could be questioned. Her lawyer will expose it as a cover-up. I'd love to be on the other side of this one. If we can settle out of court without losing the building, that's what we'll do." He crumpled the note and looked for a trash can. "Just thought I'd let you know. I've already talked to the doctor, but you might want to reinforce it."

Doug took the note from him. "Thanks. If you find any more jewels, let me know. By the way, you didn't say who the doctor is."

"Mulstein. Mark Mulstein. How well you know him?"

"Not too well. One of Smith's boys. Been here two years. Must've been one of his first patients. Good way to start."

The phone rang. It was the nurse supervisor.

"Mr. Carpenter, I just got a call from the emergency room. They're working on a patient who jumped from the fourth floor. He landed on the pavement beside the emergency room entrance. I'll let you know more when I know more."

Cline remained in the doorway, apparently detecting something by Doug's expression.

"I'll be here," Doug told the nurse supervisor, then explained everything to Cline.

"Psychiatry patient?" asked Cline.

"Don't know yet, but he didn't jump from the Psych Unit." He picked up the phone again.

Herb Cline sat. "This sounds like the best show in town."

Doug got the charge nurse from the fourth floor. "Miss Henderson, did a patient jump from a window on four?"

"Yes, Mr. Carpenter," came the frightened voice.

"Can you tell me about it? Who is the patient?"

"He's Jerry Brownstein, nineteen years old. He has all kinds of medical problems and threatened to kill himself. We kept asking for a psych consult and, finally, one of the residents ordered one." She paused and Doug heard a sob. "Dr. Afton came in for the consult. He didn't think Jerry needed to be transferred to the Psych Unit. Said to have the window nailed shut and keep an eye on him."

"To have the window nailed shut?"

"We had maintenance do it." She paused then added, "Several days ago."

"It didn't seem to stop him."

"No, sir, it sure didn't. And his brother had just left, about ten or fifteen minutes before."

"Had anything happened to upset him?"

"Not that we know of. We stopped letting his parents in. They always upset him." She paused a moment. "He did a lot of weird things. He ate garbage. He didn't wash. Never changed clothes. His parents always argued with him."

"Have the parents been notified?"

"No, sir, not yet."

"Get ahold of his attending physician or the house staff officer and make sure they notify the parents."

"Yes, sir."

"And, thanks, Miss Henderson."

Doug dialed public relations.

"Henry? Glad you're still here. Better be alert for a call from the press. We just had a patient jump from the fourth floor. Better get the details. He's in the emergency room. Went out a window."

34

Doug slowly cradled the phone and turned to Cline. "The psychiatrist said there was nothing to worry about. The psych staff never wants medical/surgical patients on their unit."

"Hope I don't hear about this one through the mail." Cline got up to go. "See you later. Have a nice day."

Doug sat at his desk, alone, staring at the stack of mail, then decided to dial the page operator. "Get Dr. Best for me."

"She's not in today. She's at a psychiatric symposium in Dallas, but she's due in late this evening."

Doug looked at the messages Ann had left. The stack seemed to have morphed. *What hidden treasures lurk among them?*

The evening nurse supervisor called to let him know the Brownstein boy died. She filled him in on her investigation.

Doug leaned back and stared at the ceiling. The carpenter hadn't wanted to damage the window, so he drove in two nails, one on each side, leaving enough of them exposed so he could pull them out later.

The boy had relieved him of that job, worked them loose, probably in the middle of the night when staffing was low and he would not be seen. He put the nails partially back in, so the window still looked nailed shut, and he could open it whenever he was ready.

Doug could just see him in the middle of the night working the nails loose, while the carpenter slept, while the psychiatrist slept, while the hospital slept. *Do they think two little nails can stop me? I'll just play their little game with them. And we'll see who wins.*

The psychiatrists never wanted patients with tubes sticking out of them and devices supporting them. They said the psych nurses weren't trained to handle such cases. *Was it the psychiatrists who couldn't cope? Trained to work with the mental, had the physical become taboo?* It was a problem that existed in every hospital he had worked in. The answer wasn't a prescription for nails in a window frame. Hell, he could've gone *through* the glass. The system failed Jerry Brownstein and his brother who cared and his parents, forever smothered by feelings of guilt.

Doug started going through the stack of mail but then looked at his watch and picked up the phone. "Bess, I'll be later than usual, or maybe later as usual. Anyhow, you better eat without me."

"No way, I'll snack and eat with you. I've made some Brunswick stew so you won't forget the South."

"Is it the way my mother used to make it?"

"No."

"Does it even have squirrel in it?"

"No squirrel."

"In that case, I'll be there as soon as I can clean these old dogs off my desk."

"Doug," her voice sounded worried, "don't speed. Okay?"

He promised. She always made him promise to be careful driving. She knew his habit of rushing to the safety of home.

CHAPTER FIVE

Interruptions crowded the morning schedule to the point that there was no schedule. Nothing on his list of to-dos had been touched. The intercom buzzed again to emphasize the point. "Mr. Carpenter, there's a Miss Simba Agiza here to see you. She's with the Hospital Workers' Union."

Simba Agiza? The Hospital Workers' Union? Half-hearted attempts had been made to organize the employees, but never with any steam. He opened the door.

"What can I do for you, Miss Agiza?" He tried not to stare. Beautiful. Dress hardly there. Tight. Form-fitting silk. Legs forever.

She turned, displaying her body like a model mincing on a runway. "Nothing, honey." She stood by Ann's desk. "I'm replacing Harrington, the albino turd, as union organizer for the employees in this so-called hospital." She smiled, faint crease marks like dimples at the corners of her mouth. "Because blacks understand the issues. The rest is garbage, honey." She leaned forward and spoke like a close friend confiding. "I just wanted to see the man who sucks the doctors. And now that I've seen you, I'm even less impressed than I thought I would be."

She arched her body and her smile seemed to say, "I dare you."

Doug concentrated on her face. "It was nice talking to you, Miss Agiza."

"It's not Miss Agiza. It's Simba Agiza. That's my name. Remember it. I'll remember you as the whore of the rapists." She turned, glanced at him from the corner of her eye, and bumped her rear end in his direction. Then she was off, down the hall, head up, looking through the ceiling.

Bitch.

"Hurray!" Ann's eyebrows arched. "You made a hit with her. Good luck."

Doug retreated into his office, pondering over whether his reaction was anti-union, sexist, or racist. He hadn't thought, "black bitch," but she was black. He thought he had left that behind in his early teens in the South. And it worried him that the possibility had even occurred to him. Had something just been released from the hidden night of his past? And he was worried by the pleasure he felt looking at her.

Damn her. Damn me.

Ann buzzed again.

"Mr. Carpenter, Simba Agiza is here to see you again."

"Have her come in."

Doug remained seated as she came in the door. "What can I do for you, Miss Simba?"

"Oh, you're cute, honey." She shut the door and leaned over his desk, planting her hands on each side of his desk blotter. Her face was only a foot from his. She smiled and said, "You may know we're organizing the employees here. You may not know how the effort has been going." She took a deep breath and it was hard to tell where the brown silk ended and the skin began. "I just wanted you to know, honey, now that I've taken the white-ass's place, the effort is going to pay off. To him it was a job. To me it's a cause. This hospital will be unionized or I'll see you on the picket line, honey."

She stood, pressed her hands across her breasts and down her blouse as though to iron it out, smiled at him, and then reversed the process. She turned sideways, emphasizing her protruding nipples.

Doug thought for a second, then said, "Miss Simba, are there any issues other than the fact you have a nice body?"

"Oh, you noticed. I'm so proud."

"It would be hard not to. What did you come here for?"

She sat on the corner of his desk and hiked her skirt to reveal smooth thighs. "You know as well as I—"

"That you have a nice body," interrupted Doug. "I've already said it, but I hope there's more to you than that." He leaned forward and folded his hands on the desk.

She stood, in slow motion, and faced him.

Deliberately, she pulled the Velcro apart from the neckline down. "Oh, there's a lot more of me."

She opened the dress all the way. Nothing underneath. Nothing but her. And she filled the room. She let her dress slide off her shoulders and caught it in one hand. She turned and walked away from him, dragging the dress behind her. She stood for a moment with her back to him, then turned. She walked toward him, out-slinking Liz Racoda, and pushed her nakedness at him.

"A lot more." Her seductive voice mesmerized.

Doug took a deep breath and stood slowly. "Miss Simba, any normal male would salivate. But maybe we should discuss some issues. I mean, there's no issue about your body. It's one of the wonders of the world."

He moved sideways to the door and opened it, returned to his chair, and sat. He glanced at the open doorway. Her lilac scent was sweet and heavy.

She slinked the dress on and carefully lined up the Velcro at the top and pressed it against her body. "Tell me if I get it straight." She knew he was watching her every move, and parted her lips enough to show the tip of her tongue.

"Right now, I wouldn't know straight from my Aunt Minnie."

"Then, let's discuss the issues."

"Fine. Is it safe now to close the door?" He tried to keep his breathing normal as he moved to the door and back.

"The issues? Salaries are low, and don't tell me they aren't because you'd just be telling me what I expect to hear. There's discrimination against minorities, blacks in particular. There's not one black department head, and this city is over forty percent black. Only four percent of your professional employees are black, and don't tell me there've been no black professionals apply. We've sent them in, ourselves."

The change from vixen to all business was seamless. She was a threat, no question about it.

"Employees are fired for 'insufficient cause.' That translates to 'their bosses don't like them.' We have two cases—one black, one white—where secretaries were fired because they wouldn't fuck their bosses. And we can prove it."

She leaned back and looked at Doug. "What it boils down to is your employees need protection from you." She pointed at him. "And when I say you, I include all the doctors whose asses you kiss for breakfast, lunch, and dinner. They are all bastards. They get everything they want, have food served to them in meetings, get new furniture, new offices, secretaries they can fuck when they get tired of the nurses' twats or the nurse aides, social workers, or clerks. They are all big pricks walking around shooting whoever they want, and you're their pimp, whore-master, and whore all rolled into one." She paused and seemed to be surveying Doug.

"I guess that's pretty good for starters," Doug made an obvious observation.

"Good lord, man," she quipped. "I don't know. Maybe I'm wasting my time. What does it take to get you riled?"

"The prospect of a worthwhile solution," answered Doug, working hard on his composure.

She looked at the ceiling and mimicked, "The prospect of a worthwhile solution. Oh, Jesus, take me now. My time has come."

Doug suppressed a laugh. He appreciated the show, all of it. "Simba, if anyone could organize this hospital, you could. But, if there are inequities, they can be resolved with or without a union. I won't support a union."

"Big surprise, honey. I thought you would agree right away. Mr. Carpenter, can I call you Doug? That's your name isn't it? Doug, why discuss issues unless you're at a bargaining table? Are you going to resolve all those issues I just mentioned, forgetting your sex life? No, and you know it. You don't even accept the fact they are issues. So why waste time?"

"Simba, I'd work with you toward their resolution if I thought you wanted to. The fact is it wouldn't be to the union's advantage. The real goal of the union is to get members and more dues. After that, you'll be glad to discuss and bargain, so your union gets the credit. You said for Harrington this was a job, but for you, a cause. I think your cause is to help the union, not the employees."

She walked to the door. "I've got the right idea about you, honey." She ran her hands down her front, took a deep breath and gave him a best-friend-in-the-world smile. "But you've got some twisted notions about me, and you'll just have to learn the hard way."

She changed to slow motion again, turning around, swishing her hips. "Too bad you didn't tumble with me. I could have won it all and you could have had some fun."

She left, still smiling. Doug knew the hospital was in for a fight. He combed his fingers through his hair. *What a show! And this is just the beginning. The union now has a leader.*

One more problem on top of everything else. He made his way down the hallway to the Quality Assurance Committee meeting. And he knew this meeting wasn't going to improve anything. The agenda included the suicide case. This whacko committee blamed everyone but the doctors.

He winced when a dietary helper preceded him into the room with a cart of beverages, cream cheese, bagels, and fancy cookies. More favors for the doctors. He found an empty seat between Dr. Joe Goldman, a friendly face, and Harvey Shocks, Dean of the School of Medicine, believer in the divinity of doctors. Kay O'Connell sat on the same side of the table. Doug couldn't see her face without leaning forward.

Goldman started the meeting. "This is an item that's not on the agenda. It was just brought to my attention. Our death rate has been showing an increase over the last few months—actually, over the last six months. It is now double what it was this time last year."

"We're getting sicker patients," said Jack Apple. "The HMOs won't approve admissions as easily as they did in the beginning, so the patient can't come in until he's damn near dying."

Kay broke in. "It's true, our patients are sicker, but that's taken into account in the tallies. We've been aware of it, but no one has died who wasn't already terminal."

"Okay. It's something to keep an eye on though." Joe made note.

The suicide case came up, and Dr. Smith raised his hand.

"The hospital didn't take precautions. The carpenter barely drove in the nails. The patient pulled them out with his fingers. And nursing didn't watch the patient. Doctors can't do everything.

I move this committee place responsibility for this suicide on Kay O'Connell and Doug Carpenter."

Doug stifled a surge of anger as his stomach vise started tightening again. He wondered how Kay was reacting.

"Charles, that's unproductive and inaccurate," declared Goldman.

"I second the motion." Ed Whyte held up his hand.

"Charles," said Harvey, "I sympathize with your concerns, but from a litigation point of view, it's better not to place blame. The lawyers are privy to our minutes, you know."

"That's why I want it on record. If there's a suit, I don't want the medical staff blamed." Smith knew how to play the game.

"If there's a suit, let's address it then." Joe Goldman wanted this meeting over.

"It would be more effective if we did it now," argued Whyte. "We should censure Administration now, not when we're suspect."

"That's probably true," said Harvey. "It wouldn't appear objective. But censure and blame are harsh terms. Why not just say it appears that Administration and Nursing didn't take all the measures they could've."

"I'd like to make a few comments." Doug bit at each word. "And I'd like the first one to be off the record because I don't want to place blame. Psychiatry doesn't want Med/Surg patients because . . ."

"We already know that and that's already a matter of record," interrupted Smith.

"I want it on record," continued Doug, "that we have a meeting scheduled with Dr. Best, Kay O'Connell, myself, the chief medical resident, the chief surgical resident, and Dr. Elmer Jackson, the attending physician for the Brownstein boy. We're going to review the current policy to see what changes should be made."

"Administration's approach to solving a problem is to have a meeting," Smith stated. "That way, the blame can be spread to everybody. If Administration wants to practice medicine, then you guys should get medical degrees. If it's not one thing, it's another. Like this Death and Dying Committee Kay O'Connell is talking about." He waved a hand in Kay's direction. "Like we need another committee. People can die without a committee, and this Juanita Martinez is certainly no expert in dying. She's a nurse. That's all."

Doug hadn't realized Juanita had come to Eastern. She was a Hispanic nurse at Solstory Hospital, a place he would just as soon forget. But her, he would remember always. She was truly dedicated. Hard not to remember.

"Let's stick to the subject," Joe reminded all those present.

"It's germane. Doug wants to tell doctors how to handle dying patients." Smith gave another fish stare at Doug. "Anyhow, we will take that up another time. Right now, he and our director of nursing have shown they can't handle the simplest of problems."

"Why don't you just tell the carpenter to drive the nails in further?" asked Whyte. "That's simple enough, isn't it? I call for the question."

Doug gave up. It was a lost cause to start with. He glanced past Goldman and could see Kay's red face. She was exercising remarkable restraint.

Only the physicians vote on medical staff committees. Smith and Whyte voted for the motion, Goldman against. Shocks abstained, saying, "I'd rather see the motion toned down, but I'm with you guys in principle."

Doug tasted stomach bile. The committee's recommendation would be presented to the Medical Staff Board. It would get voted down, but not without discussion. And Boswell would view it as Doug's and Kay's failure.

Juanita Martinez. In a large place like Eastern, I couldn't possibly know all the nurses. But was it the same Juanita Martinez? Solstory and Juanita. He couldn't forget either.

Smith raised his hand and spoke without waiting to be recognized. "There's something else that should have been on this agenda. HMOs."

"We can't cover everything in one meeting, Charles," Joe told everyone. "Anyhow, that's a subject for a special meeting."

"We have to talk about it now. Doug is here and he's not doing his job. He has to stop them, and the hospital's management is the place to start."

"Charles, there's no way you can lay that atrocity on Doug or one single person."

"He's the administrator and he's not doing anything about it. I've got a young boy waiting for a bone marrow transplant. The HMO is delaying it, classifying it as 'investigative.' It's not investigative. We've been doing it for years. It's standard treatment. It's also expensive. I know their doctors are paid bonuses for holding down costs. Calling it 'investigative' is an easy out. That's another way of saying it costs too much, that the patient isn't worth it."

"Charles, I promise you we will set up a special meeting to discuss it, but not now. I know it's important, but we have other agenda items that have to be covered."

Doug pondered over what he could do against the HMO monolith, the giant octopus sucking health care out of existence. Maybe if all the administrators teamed up. Not likely with all the competition for patients to keep afloat with the tight reimbursement. They all faced the same problem, keeping a high census to make expenses. He wondered if they all faced the problem of an increase in death rates. Was that associated with HMOs?

The committee, small as it was, had censured him. Through the rest of the meeting, Doug kept seeing Boswell's red face and squinty eyes. A later agenda item dealt with Al Robinson being intoxicated while administering anesthesia. Tabled pending investigation. Doug made no comment. Goldman volunteered to pull together an ad hoc committee to review the incident.

When the meeting was adjourned, Doug didn't wait around. He wanted to talk to Kay, but he needed to separate himself from the group.

He passed Ann's desk, but not without her scrutiny. "Are you all right?"

"Sorry. I guess my feelings are showing. Whyte and Smith ganged up again. They dumped on Kay and me. I don't know how much more Kay can take. I'll have to keep her busy so there's no time for it to get the best of her."

"How about yourself? Are you all right?"

"Yeah. I've got a new secret weapon. I'll sic Simba Agiza on them."

"You just be careful. That woman's bite may be worse than her bark."

CHAPTER SIX

Doug was so tired he could barely press the accelerator. He drove this route every evening on the way home and back again in the morning—the Solstory section. Every day, he was reminded of his first job as an administrator. Solstory Hospital, his crushing failure. He should have stayed an assistant somewhere and not tried to be the big decision maker.

Out of sight, but always in mind, six blocks south was the locked, shuttered, boarded-up Solstory Hospital, like most of the houses he was passing. Everything in this neighborhood looked like something washed out of a storm drain. It had been a year since he had seen the place, even passing this close, day after day.

"Damn."

He cut to the right and headed south toward the hospital, past Emiliano Apata's house, past the old house the street people slept in with the homeless whores—the House of AIDS—and past the park the drug dealers had taken over.

When he had worked in this area, he was safe. He had belonged. They protected him. Would they now? He parked in front of the hospital. It looked like a dead animal sitting stiff on its haunches, as if a taxidermist had stuffed it.

The boarded-up windows looked like eyes sewn shut, and Carlotta's sad and accusing face hovered behind every one. Carlotta, the aged Hispanic activist, had trusted him, put her faith in him, helped get the community to back him, introduced him to Emiliano, the state legislator, and had gone with them to the capitol, talked to the Lt. Governor, the Secretary of Health, and the Secretary of Welfare.

They had managed to get the state to shake loose enough money to keep the hospital afloat in spite of the fact that ninety percent of the patients were on low-paying Medicaid and the rest paid nothing.

He had let her down. He had let them all down. He had thought he could make a difference. But in his trusting eyes, doctors were there to help the patient. They were his partners.

The dead building squatted in judgment. The doctors hadn't been gods. Some were good, even messengers of God. But others were messengers of Satan. And those were the ones with power, power he had given them. He had given them the opening to take over, and they had. Dr. Jeep, in particular. In the beginning, he had had trouble remembering the man's real name. Everyone did. It was a long East Indian name. Jiparmalanaron. He had introduced himself as Dr. Jeep. He was an Indian doctor who spoke no Spanish in the middle of a Hispanic community.

The building was not empty. It was full of ghosts. And Juanita Martinez. Nurse Juanita. Always crusading. Crusading to make things right, whatever the things were. She taught an English class for the whole neighborhood. She led a neighborhood march against drugs. Got dealers off the street. Always doing something.

He turned off the motor and stared back at the building. He'd been lucky to get the job at Eastern after this experience. This time he mustn't fail. It was dumb luck or circumstance or the work of some guardian angel that had arranged his escape from Solstory, an interview at Eastern.

George Brown was vice president for Health at that time. For some reason, he had impressed Brown, who was recognized throughout the profession, the king of some mythological hill of wisdom, Mount Helicon. He had drawn applicants from all over the country.

Brown had looked at him across the desk and insisted on first names. "Why do you want to join us at Eastern, Doug?"

"For two reasons, George. First, I think I can help you reach your goals, and second, I think I'll get experiences here that'll last me for my entire career."

Brown was an educator as well as an administrator. It was the right thing to say. "How do you think you can help us?"

"I understand the workings of medical centers. I've worked as a department head. I was assistant administrator in a large general hospital. I was administrator of a small hospital. I've learned from my successes and my failures. Some people don't learn from either."

"Tell me about your failures."

The minute Doug had mentioned failure, he knew Brown would ask about it. Mistake. But he released it all, bit by bit—how he had saved the little hospital from bankruptcy—how the community and the employees and the doctors had worked with him—how they had set up outpatient clinics throughout the area. He had trusted the doctors only to discover they were admitting patients who didn't need care just for the fees. The doctors set up their own outpatient clinics in competition with the hospital. They even hired a fake counselor on their own payroll to comb the neighborhood buying drinks for alcoholics so he could drag them in for admission to the Drug and Alcohol Unit.

He poured out how they controlled the admissions. They could send their Medicaid patients to other hospitals, including Eastern, and close Solstory if he didn't agree to do whatever they wanted him to do. And the Board always sided with the doctors, the gods. They gave one a job in charge of intensive care for a fat salary, and another a job in charge of drug and alcohol, and on and on.

Brown, a squat man, nodded in sympathy. "You've learned about that side of the business. You'll find it in most hospitals to a larger or smaller degree. How would you cope with it here?"

"Build a mantle of ethics with the concerned members of the medical staff . . . and pray."

"Yes. Pray. And hope for miracles."

Doug figured he had blown it, even though Brown shook his hand and said he liked Doug's honesty. Doug knew he had violated a basic rule of job-hunting. Don't knock your former employer.

The next day, Brown called and offered him the job, and Doug accepted. Brown must have surmised Solstory was on the verge of closing, and Doug might be considering other offers. He wasn't. There weren't any.

But a week later, Brown asked Doug to come in.

Doug knew something was bothering him. Brown hovered behind his desk, framed by his bookshelves. The titles of some of those books still glared through memory. Mocking.

"Doug," he talked as though his throat wouldn't cooperate, "I have to rescind my offer. The Board has told me to hold on filling the position. The assistant administrators will report straight to me. No administrator in between. I'm so sorry. Just so sorry."

He looked so miserable, Doug reached over and touched his arm. "George, these things happen. Don't worry about it. I under-stand. I'm honored you would consider me for the job."

Doug left with the world spinning around him. He didn't know what he was going to do. Bess was depending on him and he was failing her. Unemployment. They could lose their home. They could lose everything.

And sitting in front of Solstory now brought it all back as though he had just lost his job and faced disaster.

All because of the greed of some bastard doctors with rat brains.

Doug squeezed the steering wheel. The bastards. He would never be able to wipe that memory out. They had milked the hospital dry with the Board fooled into backing them every step. The Board wouldn't listen to him, but they blamed him when the hospital could no longer meet its meager payroll. Solstory stopped admitting patients. Patients were discharged. Over the next week, the staff was severed. People who had been there most of their working lives were gone. Then he thought of Juanita Martinez again, dedicated to the community. She had called Jeep a "filth snake" one day. She was still learning English at the time. Jeep had backed away from her, obviously afraid—something about her eyes when she was mad. The girl was pretty, spirited, and bouncing full of energy. She energized everyone. And she could scare hell out of Jeep because she could move from pretty to clawing in the same breath. She had cried when the hospital closed.

Finally, only he and his secretary were left. And she already had another job lined up. She was typing his last correspondence, the last piece of work he was to do before he became a job beggar, when Brown called again.

"Doug, we've decided to fill the position after all, and if you're still available, I'd love to have you join us."

Doug tried not to sound anxious but accepted quickly.

Even now, he could feel the surge of relief spread through his body. *Thank God or the Angels or time and chance.*

That evening, he had locked the doors and walked around checking the corridors and rooms, but didn't know what he was checking for—maybe just a last look. He made his way to the clinic exit closest to the parking lot.

Someone was trying the door. One of the rat-doctors, Muala, a little man inside and out with a face like a ferret. Doug always knew, looking at the man's quick eyes, that he had never been acquainted with the truth. He was sure if reincarnation really happened, Muala would come back a vulture. His only hope of ever being honest was if honesty could be swallowed in a pill.

"Why, hello, Doug." The words slid out. "I just wanted to come in and pick up a few things." Oily smile. Oily eyes.

Doug stepped out, shut the door, and locked it. "Sorry, the place has been picked clean." It was his last official act at Solstory.

He wondered if he could ever drive through Solstory again without feeling hate for rat-doctors.

"Damn, damn, damn." He wished he could replay all the events over and change them. Not all doctors were rats. But at Solstory, the rest were weak. He had been, too. At Eastern, it was different. Some of the good doctors were strong, like Joe Goldman.

He couldn't let himself stop trusting. It would be better to trust rats than not to trust those he should.

He pulled away from the curb and headed north again. He had no fear of the heavy crime zone he was passing through. His fear was job insecurity. He had always hidden that, even from himself. Now, he faced it. Or it faced him. He felt the fear, yet he had to do the right thing. He hadn't been able to go along with the rat-doctors after he had wised up to them. He partially blamed his father for that. His father had drummed it into him. Do the right thing; fight the wrong thing.

But it was his mother who built it into him by her own

actions. He remembered one event, in particular from his child-hood. He and a friend, Frank, had raided Dr. Cooper's back-yard filled with daffodils. Dr. Cooper was a botanist and had what appeared to be several dozen varieties planted in different beds—beds and beds of them. They had picked an even fifty bunches of twenty-five each and taken them to a complex of apartment buildings and knocked on doors to sell them for a quarter each. Two cute kids with a wagon of flowers. They sold out in no time and he went home with a pocket full of quarters. He bragged to his mother about having the quarters.

"How did you get them?" she asked.

"We picked daffodils from Frank's uncle's farm and sold them at the Markham apartments."

"You sure they weren't Dr. Cooper's?"

She didn't punish him. She just left him feeling guilty, rotten, a thief and a liar. If only she had punished him, but she just let him feel it himself, and he punished himself for the act. After years of not being punished for things he knew were wrong, it got to the point that he couldn't do anything he knew was wrong. Maybe his conscience was there all along, but she wound it tight and set it loose.

But now, he had a job to worry about, Bess to take care of, and two kids in college. Doing the right thing and job security clashed. It's easy to be righteous if you're secure.

Six blocks north, he turned right and headed for home.

CHAPTER SEVEN

Lucien Samuelson stood before the Physician Planning Committee, giving a dry run of the presentation to the state justifying the new building. He was trying to get through the slides showing the physicians' estimates of the number of patient admissions over the coming several years. The hospital had no business making a presentation to the state for a new building. Many of the doctors were grossly exaggerating their future admissions.

Charles Smith closed his eyes as though tired of everyone in the room. The reddish tinge of his eyelids made him look even more like a lizard. Maybe he could see through them. But he was not a liar. He was self-serving and arrogant, but not a liar.

Lucien articulated with an air of such authority Doug couldn't imagine the state rejecting the plan. He almost wished he weren't so good.

"Please note that on the space relationship diagram we stress the need for efficiency in movement that only a new hospital can give us. We have to show we're behind the times."

When Doug hired Lucien, Boswell had objected. "Do you really think a black man will fit in?"

It was obvious he did.

Doug glanced at Kay O'Connell across the table, and she slid an envelope to him. She looked solemn as he opened the envelope. Inside was a note.

"The attached was handed to me by Joy Coleman, one of our ward clerks. She attended the meeting."

The note was clipped to a notice—big red letters on yellow paper:

"Valued Eastern Employees! In spite of how you are treated by the bosses, you are somebody! Strategy meeting tonight at 7:30, 22 Sharp Road. You need a union to protect you from the money-takers at Eastern. This meeting is not open to everybody. Keep it secret or they will try to stop you from coming."

Kay mouthed something at him that might have been, "I'll fill you in later." Simba wasn't wasting any time. On top of everything else, a union drive.

"Gentlemen," Lucien continued, "it's my job to convince the state that Eastern needs a new building. That won't be difficult since the Health Department has condemned parts of our antiquated complex. The question is, how large and how expensive a complex can our argument support.

"This slide is pretty routine. It gives the census and patient days for ten years." He reflected for a moment. "They won't question this. Cut and dry."

Dr. Whyte looked at his watch and the clock on the wall. He crossed his arms and tapped his fingers on his coat sleeves.

"What we'll have to address," asserted Lucien, "is why we're projecting an increase when our current patient days have declined."

"Since that's to be the major focus, skip to the slides showing the projections," Doug instructed with a nod of his head.

"Right," said Lucien.

Just then, Liz Racoda slinked in carrying a cup of coffee, a tablet, and a pencil. She set them at the far end of the table and left—a signal that Boswell was coming. Only slightly less subtle than a king's trumpeter.

"Do you think anyone would notice if I drank that cup of coffee?" asked Joe Goldman, President of the Medical Staff. A tall man with silver hair, he looked like the Secretary of State.

"I can think of one person who might," warned Harvey Shocks, who was almost the total opposite of Joe. Short, fat, redheaded, and sloppy; he also had the distinction of having a Ph.D. in science as well as an M.D.

"What's the projection for OB?" asked Dr. Whyte.

"That's about four slides further in."

"Well, skip to it now. I have to leave. I want to be sure it's right."

"Come on, Ed," Joe threw up his hands, "the rest of us have patients to take care of, too. We'll get to your slide in a minute."

"Let's get moving. These meetings take too much time."

"Go ahead and skip to his slide," said Harvey. "His might as well be first as anybody else's."

"Good grief!" exclaimed Jack Apple, Chair of Surgery. "Let's take them in order. Why should Ed's be first any more than mine?" He looked at Ed, making a sound like a pump gone dry. He shrugged his narrow shoulders. "I'm due in surgery."

"Go ahead, Lucien. Let 'em roll." Joe waved him on.

Stan Boswell came in, smiled at everyone, and sat at the end of the table. "Is everybody happy?"

"No," complained Whyte. "This damn meeting's taking too long."

Stan's smile was tight as a fist. "Alright, Doug, let's get moving. You Southerners always move so slow." He looked around the room for approval.

The first slide gave the Department of Surgery projections

of 49,990 patient days for the first year after the opening of the new hospital.

"That's okay." Jack's head bobbed with approval. "With the new Heart Unit, we'll make that number. No sweat."

Doug figured it was within the realm of possibility, but just barely with shorter stays as HMO restrictions grew tighter. "Move on to the next slide."

The projections for Internal Medicine and Psychiatry drew no objections, but Doug couldn't keep quiet. The physicians would have to increase admissions by thirty percent.

"I just want to point out to you guys that we can't support these figures by longer stays. We won't be reimbursed."

"Doug," said Whyte, "we've heard that administrative smoke-screen before."

"Don't worry about it, Ed," Stan jumped in and answered through his smile. "We'll work it out."

"Doug is right," Joe pointed to the administrator, "but we've got to go ahead with these figures because we need the beds for teaching. Besides, we're state-subsidized and the state won't let us go down the tubes. If we get in trouble, they'll bail us out."

"Heck, Joe," Harvey said, "all we've got to do is bring in a few hundred lawyer-generated motor vehicle accident cases." He laughed and gave Doug a sideways glance. "Not anymore, we won't. Nursing blew the whistle. No more MVAs. Thanks, Kay."

Kay's hands went up in despair, but Joe winked at her.

Tapping his pen on the table, Ed was condescending. "We're wasting time again. We already know the nurses are out to get the doctors."

"Let's get on with it," chuckled Stan, a bit too loudly. "Nurses can't get doctors. Rock breaks scissors."

Doug glanced at the wall clock and motioned to Lucien to continue. *Rock breaks scissors. And paper wraps rock. Guerrilla warfare in the hospital.*

Lucien showed the OB slide. "We're planning thirty beds, an eighty percent census, and 8,760 patient days the first year."

Joe whistled. "What is it now, thirty percent? Will the state buy that?"

"It's not thirty percent," said Ed. "And it'll be obvious to everyone the plan is a good one if Doug ever gets it implemented." He stared at Doug. "Isn't that right, Doug?"

Doug didn't change his expression. "We'll have to be sure we've ironed out all the bugs. For planning, we'll use these figures."

"Let's just not take so long to iron out those bugs, shall we?"

"I can guarantee you it will be no longer than necessary."

"There's no necessity for any delay!" exclaimed Ed, standing.

"Sit down, Ed," ordered Joe. "You're taking up valuable time."

"Time!" Ed angrily responded. "He's the one taking time. The plan should have already been implemented."

"He said it would take no longer than necessary," reiterated Joe. "That's good enough for me. Besides, if he can implement that plan and get your census to eighty percent, he could go on TV with a magic act that would burn all the ratings."

Doug felt grateful to Goldman, and in another half-hour, the meeting was over, and the doctors scurried out the door. Stan asked Doug to remain behind with him, and Kay left them alone.

"Why didn't you tell me about Ben Snowden resigning?"

"Yesterday, when I started to tell you about Snowden, you said to forget him, he was an old man and didn't matter."

"Well, why—"

"Excuse me, Stan," interrupted Doug. "You can't have it both ways. If you tell me you don't want to be bothered, that's fine. But don't accuse me of not telling you what's going on. Anyhow, there's a memo coming to you regarding his leaving and the Search Committee to find his replacement. I'll fill you in on the details if you want me to."

"Never mind." Frustrated, Stan turned abruptly and stepped into the hallway.

Doug tried to put Stan out of his mind. The hospital should be decreasing the number of beds for the new building. A building too large would be a costly anchor. There would be empty beds, which they would still have to staff and maintain. There would be no revenue earned to pay the salaries. Stan was giving away everything to the doctors just for their support.

But any attempt to stop it could result in his dismissal, termination. Stan would get him. The Board wanted the new building. There was a groundswell.

Doug closed his eyes. *Stan's a fool; irrational, psychotic, even. The lunacy's pouring into his sinkhole of greed. How can I pull the plug? It's an anchor, drowning me, pulling me to the bottom.*

He found Dr. Julia Best, Chair of Psychiatry, waiting in his office. "We need to talk, Doug." She motioned to a man standing off to the side. "This is Dr. David Afton, our psychiatry fellow. David was the psychiatric consult for Jerry Brownstein."

Afton was a tall somber man. His hair was plastered straight back, painted on black, just like his eyes.

"Glad to meet you, David. Hope you're getting the experience you expected at Eastern." Doug waved them into his office. "How was the conference, Julia?"

"Good for a change of pace, but I wish I'd been here last night. David and I haven't talked about the Brownstein boy. I asked him to meet me here." She looked at David sympathetically.

"You mustn't feel bad about what happened. It could have happened to any of us."

Doug controlled his reaction. "I think we should review the circumstances to see if there's anything to be learned for handling future cases."

"A lot of depressed patients threaten suicide but have no capacity to follow through. We can't put them all in the Psych Unit. Our nurses are trained to handle psychological problems, not medical or surgical. In addition, our residents would be cheated of the right experience."

"We have a problem, Julia. This Brownstein case was almost predictable."

"We can't know those rare cases." She turned to David. "You handled the case correctly. I don't want you feeling bad."

David was expressionless and Doug wondered if he felt anything at all. "I don't see how he could help feeling bad. I do. It shouldn't have happened. But I don't blame David. I don't blame anybody. But if we don't change the system, we are all at fault."

"I understand," said Julia, "but the Brownstein boy could not have been transferred to the Psych Unit. Maybe we need to develop a high-security Med/Surg Unit."

"Maybe, but we ought to use what we've got before developing a more expensive facility. Our psych census isn't all that high."

"Ah, there you are. If you're not willing to spend the money, you won't solve the problem."

"Julia, when we meet, what would you say to our asking the chief residents to come up with recommendations to tweak the system and improve the odds?"

"Of course, I'm willing," she stood, "but I question how productive it'll be. What do you think, David?"

"If you get too many people involved, you won't reach any decisions," he said.

"We'll keep the number down," promised Doug. "And with Julia and me facilitating, it should be productive." Doug saw a glimmer of anger in Afton's eyes, but only for a moment. "On a different subject, Julia, I understand you're working on the Death and Dying Committee. What's the biggest obstacle you'll be facing?"

"Roadblocks by doctors who still haven't accepted the death of their patients without a sense of failure. Fallibility and a god complex are contradictory."

"Don't the med schools address that subject?"

"They do now. But that doesn't help the older doctors. Nursing is playing an aggressive leadership role by talking about death with the patient while the doctor is there. They handle it as something natural. Juanita Martinez is especially effective. She seems to be everywhere."

"She must be. Her name keeps coming up."

"You should have heard her at our last committee meeting. She even had me crying. Her father died of lung cancer, but they didn't tell him he was dying. She and her mother gave him shots of morphine to ease the pain. The narcotic kept him sedated and pretty much out of it, drifting in and out of sleep, sometimes incoherent. She would feed him baby food spoonful by spoonful. He never questioned anything. He never asked when he would get well. After a few months, he stopped eating. She used a dropper to get water into him. Then he began to hallucinate. He asked what the huge black balls were that were floating in the air. He was frightened. Actually, it was the lining in his eyeball coming loose and floating inside his line of vision. He began to talk to people who had been dead for years. At times, he would cry. That bothered her more than anything. She had never seen her father cry. He was an iron man.

"One night he whispered to her that her mother was trying to poison him. He begged for her help, but Juanita insisted that everything was okay. Her mother loved him too much to do such a thing. And he cried. She wondered if she shouldn't tell him what was really happening to him. Wouldn't that be better than the confusion and the loneliness of having no one to talk to about it? He thought the person he had loved all his life was killing him.

"Then one night, as she gave him a shot, he told her he knew what she was doing to him, as though she, too, were involved in the killing. That night she cried herself to sleep and woke up with tears still wet on her face and pillowcase. She can't get it out of her mind."

For a psychiatrist, Julia was surprisingly emotional.

"She felt that she and her mother had deprived them all of the experience of facing death together, loving and sharing through the process. She knew, instinctively, they had done the wrong thing, but the doctor had not wanted to tell him. He wasn't dying in peace and now it was too late.

"I'm still reeling from the agony she went through and is still reliving. She inspired us all to end this practice by any doctor at Eastern, and that is our resolve."

Doug was touched. "I may know her from the staff at Solstory, if she was over there."

"She was over there. She's called on to go anywhere in the hospital where there's a Hispanic patient."

Julia had become more animated than Doug had ever seen her. "You've really gotten to know her."

"I spent an hour with her after that last meeting. She struck me as so outstanding I had to get to know her. She's a real good addition to this hospital."

"She sounds like the right person for Death and Dying."

After they left, Doug reflected on Afton's reaction. *He seemed unmoved, mute, except for the anger. The man hides his feelings. Not healthy.*

Julia's reactions were more overt. *If only more were like her. Honest. Not greedy. Actually, more are honest than not.* He had to keep reminding himself of that.

He massaged his neck.

"If I get fired," he said out loud, "at least I want this place to be better than it was when I came."

Was he tilting at windmills? If he were honest, he would flat-out tell the political doctors and the Board they were wrong. But that would be suicide. He'd for sure be fired. What would he do then? Whyte breathing down his neck was enough.

"Damn, if the public only knew what the hell goes on in a hospital." He sat there for several minutes, then fairness set in. "A hell-of-a lot of good happens, too. But sometimes it's hard to keep track of that. The greed does so much damage. It was greed that brought on the HMOs as a cure to start with, and now everyone is suffering, including the greedy ones."

Something had to be done. But what?

CHAPTER EIGHT

Doug closed the front door by leaning on it and resting. He called, "Bess! I'm home!"

She ran out of the kitchen, slung her arms around his neck and kissed him. "You're on time. Must've remembered the meeting at the church. You look drained." She caressed his cheek. "I hate to rush you, but dinner is on the table. They start the meeting at seven-thirty, and you have to change out of your suit." She started for the dining room, but came back and caressed his cheek again. "I know you're expected to be there as a hospital administrator, but if you're tired, maybe . . ."

"I'm not tired. I'll change later. Lead the way. Nursing home abuse has to be curtailed, and if this group is interested in doing something about it, I want to lend my support."

The dining room had double French doors on both sides, opening to a terrace on one side and to woods on the other. He looked out at the woods and felt its peacefulness contrast with his daytime world of wobbling insanity. Its coolness reached out, its stability, its safety. It represented the world before greed. He wanted to walk into it, lie in it, and wear it.

"You going to sit or stand?" She pushed the rolls toward his plate and tilted her head to one side when she laughed, which seemed to ask a question.

He sat at the table and felt as though he were noticing her for the first time since coming home. His mind hadn't entered the house when he did. "It's good to be home."

"Yes. It's only home if we're both here."

"Bess, do you have any idea how much I love you? You reach out and melt my soul."

She smiled, stuck a bite of mashed potato in her mouth and pulled the fork out as though she were conducting the Boston Pops. "Of course, that's as it should be."

He laughed and felt the tension drain away.

"It's good to hear you laugh, honey. You haven't done much of that lately."

Her coloring went with the room. Blue-green eyes, always wide open, amber hair swept up clean, a few freckles highlighting a reddish complexion.

He took a deep breath. "You're right. I haven't done much of that lately. Laughing ought to be a part of our world." Then he added, "If I can't laugh with you, I've lost the last refuge."

"Sounds ominous. Have you reached that point yet?"

"No. It's not that bad." But he wasn't sure.

She played her fork at the edge of her potatoes. "It gets difficult for me. I can see the difference in you since Stan Boswell came. It's affected us, you know." This time her inflection made a wistful question.

He reflected for a moment. "We have our own telegraph system. Like identical twins."

"When you have fantasies from hell, so does your wife."

"Don't worry about our future, Bess. If things don't work out at Eastern, I'll find another job." He broke a roll in half and looked at it. "We'll never go hungry."

"That sounds trusting. Don't you think you're presuming on fate too much?"

"No. I'm competent and knowledgeable and people know it."

"I know. But the point is, if it doesn't help you in your own hospital, you can't count on it for elsewhere." She stirred her coffee. "Anyhow, it's more than just the security angle."

He waited.

"It's what it's doing to us." She looked across the table at him. "Have you noticed we don't see each other much these days?" Her laugh was almost a cry, a punctuation in the silence. "I spend hours thinking about it. We're not as happy as we were. You work every night and every weekend."

"Yeah, don't I know. It's become a habit." He picked up his fork and stabbed at his green beans.

"Our children were both here from college Saturday."

"Sammy and Janey were here?"

"They came to see us, but they only got me because you were slaving away at Eastern. I called your office but got no answer. I didn't want to page you. I knew you were out in the building. I tried until seven o'clock and they had to leave. You came home at eleven-thirty." Her voice cracked, whimpered. "I cried. I'm such a baby. I couldn't talk about it until now. We get to see them individually every month or so, but this time, they were together."

"Bess, I'm sorry. I promise you it'll pass."

"Oh, don't apologize for things you can't control. I just want this to be temporary. It's not a way of life. Not for us. Okay? Please do something."

He laid his hand on hers. She was his partner in life. He had known almost from the moment he met her. And this was no life. "It'll change. I'll make it change." But he didn't have an inkling of how.

He stood to gather dishes, and she suggested, "Leave them. I'll do them. You have to get changed."

"You know, the funny thing is all the extra work is political or piecing things back together. It's for survival, not to produce a damn thing."

"I know that must be wearing on you."

"If only we had more givers and less damn takers."

"Give everybody a white hat. Get changed. We've got to leave." She stacked the dishes on a tray. "How 'bout that! When I do go out with my husband, it's to a church meeting."

In the car, they talked about the meeting. Doug had received a notice at the hospital. He assumed all administrators had. Someone was making a presentation to the church council to ask for support. Obviously, the church was interested. They mentioned setting up a committee to visit patients, especially those who had no relatives.

"I wonder how many of my fellow administrators will be there."

"I wonder if any other churches are involved."

Doug was silent for a moment. "You know, Eastern gets a number of nursing home patients. They come in dehydrated, covered with bed sores, emaciated, and sometimes you can see they've been tied to their beds."

Bess was startled. "How can you tell?"

"Their wrists are rubbed raw."

"Oh, my lord."

"If Eastern gets them that way, so do other hospitals."

"How do they get away with it?"

"Hospitals that blow the whistle get fewer referrals."

"Not if they all blow the whistle."

"Yes, but who's going first?"

"It all comes down to the dollar, doesn't it?"

"You better believe it. But if enough administrators show up, maybe we can get something going."

Bess was silent for a moment. "I would think Stan would be concerned about this. Isn't his mother in a nursing home?"

"Yeah, he transferred her into one here when he came to Eastern, so he could be close to her, but that's a private nursing home with a high price tag. They take care of their residents. The only thing he has to worry about is paying the bill."

"I guess that's one thing in his favor. You think he would support such a move?"

"It'd be something of a first if he did."

The church parking lot was almost full.

"Oh, my!" exclaimed Bess. "Must be a lot of people attending."

In the church community room, Doug saw a few faces from the hospital, but not the administrative staff. They seemed surprised to see him. Concerned might be the word. Then he spotted Simba Agiza.

"I don't believe it. This couldn't be a union organizing meeting."

Simba came toward him, smiling. She was wearing a green tailored suit. "My, my," she said softly, "for a moment, I didn't recognize you. You all look so much alike, you know. What's a white racist doing in a place like this?"

"Why, Miss Simba, how nice to see you again. Of course, I've been seeing visions of you ever since our meeting."

Bess looked back and forth between the two of them.

"You couldn't be here because you heard of our meeting?" she asked, as though he were her best friend.

"Simba, you have my number." Doug turned to Bess. "Bess, I'd like you to meet Simba Agiza, hospital union organizer. Simba, my wife, Bess."

"Bess, I'm so glad to meet you." She shook her hand and held on while she talked "We have a lot in common. You're probably here to watch nursing home administrators and I'm watching hospital administrators, and Doug here has seen both of us bare-ass naked."

Bess jerked her hand back and looked at Doug. Again, her laugh was a question.

The word "bitch" crept into his mind again. "I'll tell you what that means later." He squeezed her hand.

"I've got to get my meeting rolling. How nice to see you again, Doug." Simba swished her way to a group of employees.

"Okay, Mr. Administrator. This is one I've got to hear," Bess whispered. "Did she say 'bare-ass naked'?"

"Right now, she's on her good behavior." Doug told her what happened.

"Goodness! I never knew anybody who could do that." She looked across the room, and Simba, who had been watching, smiled and blew her a kiss.

They entered the meeting room and Doug looked around for other administrators. None. But there, beaming at him, was Juanita Martinez. She sat in the front row next to Brad DeVasey, the minister. Juanita waved.

Brad DeVasey stood and introduced himself to the small group and ran his long fingers through waves of bright red hair. "This could be the most meaningful project this church has ever pushed."

They heard cheering and shouting from the other meeting, and the mesmerizing voice of Simba Agiza accompanied with podium pounding. They caught some of the words, "lewd lords," "medical masters sucking us dry," "time to show we are somebody."

DeVasey introduced Juanita to say a few words about the project. Apparently, she had taken a lead position. No surprise.

"What a gorgeous woman," said Bess.

"I'm not surprised she's here. This is the kind of thing she gets into."

Juanita plunged right in. "Six weeks ago, a young mother with limited means managed to get her eighty-one-year-old mother into a nursing home. She worked two jobs to support her fatherless family, and there was no one to take care of her mother. She believed her mother would be taken care of better by trained professionals.

"Two days ago, just six weeks after her mother went into the nursing home, this eighty-one-year-old woman was admitted to a hospital in this city." Juanita looked at Doug but didn't mention Eastern. "Dehydrated with flesh rubbed raw around wrists and ankles, showing she had been tied to her bed. Covered with bedsores, showing she had been left in her own urine and feces for days on end. Malnourished to the point of starvation, eyes sunken into their sockets, incoherent, she came into the hospital unable to talk. She couldn't cry anymore. She couldn't move. She could only stare. She was dying. That's why the nursing home sent her to us. To revive her, so she could be returned to the nursing home to be tied again to her bed, to be ignored again, crying through endless days and helpless nights, flesh burning on urine-soaked sheets."

Doug counted about twenty people in the room. They sat, paralyzed by Juanita's words.

"Therefore, the nursing home could collect its Medicare or Medicaid fee, keep the beds full and the overhead low, give no care, just pain and pain and more pain. Every day, in this city, dozens of elderly men and women, people who have worked through their productive time and are fading with the years, are admitted to hospitals to be retrieved from death and returned to a living inferno of burning pain so some nursing homes can make money, so some nursing homes can feed on them like leeches and maggots for the rest of their agonizing lives. They are our forsaken, our forgotten, our invisible mothers and fathers."

Doug thought of what Dr. Best had told him about Juanita's father. *Is she doing this out of guilt? No.* No, he thought not.

"This morning, when you had your breakfasts, in the light, the clean, the warm, reading the paper, talking to someone you loved, hearing their voices—this morning, easily hundreds, thousands, of these lost souls were burning in their beds, dying and whimpering alone, so our governments, federal and state, would pay the nursing homes. Pay the nursing homes to painfully abuse the tired bodies and forgotten minds of our fathers and mothers."

Juanita had to stop to regain control of her voice. She was speaking from her heart.

"I had hoped to see a room full of administrators here tonight, but there is only one. However, he may be the best one. I know him. I know he cares. I know he will do what's right." She pointed at Doug. "Doug Carpenter from Eastern. Doug, please stand up."

Doug half stood, waved, and sat. A few people clapped, but most of them still looked stunned by her message.

Juanita continued, "Hospitals won't expose the nursing homes because the nursing homes won't send more patients to them, cutting their revenue. That way, the hospitals play along, becoming party to mass torture."

Doug closed his eyes. He had been an assistant administrator farther north when he became aware of the abuse, and his boss told him to keep quiet. Do nothing. Instead, he had contacted the State Health Department and one nursing home was closed. His boss never forgave him and a few months later, Doug accepted an offer from a different hospital.

"This is caveman behavior. It's not even that. The caveman killed outright. He didn't drag his victim through acid to burn off the skin. He didn't tie him and starve him. He didn't revive him to torture him again. He just killed. He killed out of fear or for protection or for survival, but these nursing home people"— her voice broke and she closed her eyes for a moment—"suck them dry of life and then revive them. Suck them dry of life and then revive them again. And again and again until the spirit, deprived, broken, unloved, cut loose in a whirlpool of agony, finally reaches the dark moment alone."

And this time, Juanita didn't wipe her tears. She just let them run.

"It's happening right now. Right now. They are crying and dying right now, and tomorrow they'll be brought to life again so they can die again."

Bess was sobbing. Surprised, Doug looked at the faces of the others. Men and women, they had tears in their eyes or on their faces. He felt like saying, *Thank God, they heard her. And thank God for Juanita.*

Juanita sat down and Doug became aware of the noises outside again. The union meeting was over. There was a lot of shouting down the halls and out the doors, car motors starting in the parking lot and horns blowing in unison.

Brad DeVasey ignored the noise. "Those of you who know me know I don't get emotional as a rule. But this is the most hypocritical assault on human beings I've witnessed in my lifetime. And it's been legalized for money." He said it matter-of-fact, quietly. "They are being tortured, and if we don't do something about it, we are guilty of letting it happen." He nodded at Doug. "Thank you, Mr. Carpenter, for being here. It's good to know someone in the healthcare industry cares. I thank all of you for being here. We have a nursing home watch program in this church. People are captured by nursing home terrorists. We need you. They need you. We want all of you to write your state congressional representatives. We want to flood those nursing homes with visitors. Our guests are welcome to stay. The committee will now plan its next move. Thank you, Miss Martinez."

Doug and Bess didn't move for a few minutes. Juanita met with the committee. She was intent on listening and making suggestions.

The church outside the meeting room was silent. The union had met and left. Silent except for the echoes of the loud meeting still lingering in Doug's mind.

And in that silence, Doug knew Simba would not lose.

CHAPTER NINE

Ann handed Doug a letter received by employees that Joy Coleman had brought in.

"Dear Employee," read Doug. "Are you tired of low salaries while the doctors and administrators get fat off of your hard work?" He scanned the rest of it. "Announcement for their next organizing meeting is at my church."

"The employees received them at their homes. How did they get the addresses?"

"Probably got help from everyone who showed up at previous meetings. Not too difficult."

"Mr. Carpenter." Bill Hanes stepped into the office. "Somebody's been putting these leaflets all over the building, even the patient floors."

Doug read the scrawl on the bright yellow flier. "The hard-earned dollars you should be getting are buying new cars for the doctors and Mr. Carpenter. Is this fair?" He skipped the rest of it. "Huh, guess I'll go look in my parking space. Somebody gave me a new car."

"Why are they picking on you instead of Boswell?" asked Ann.

"My title is administrator. That says something to the public.

Stan's a vice president of the college. And even though he has little to do with the college, the public wouldn't view him as a hospital lead."

"We've been picking up the leaflets and putting them in the security office," said Bill. "If we put them in the trash cans, they'd take them and put them around again. And look at this." He handed Doug a small newspaper, *The Eastern Student Future*. In small print under the banner it announced, "All the news that will happen tomorrow."

"Oh, for Pete's sake!" Doug's neck hairs were up. "It says our nurses were all fired from other hospitals for browbeating and stealing from patients. These are students learning to be journalists? Bill, you and Cliff Toliver make sure they don't get to the patient floors. Just what sick patients need, an additional worry that their nurse is an ax murderer."

"We've already taken care of it," said Bill. "Cliff took eight bundles to the incinerator. They dropped off more, and we burned them, too."

"They had all those on the floors?"

"No, they were in the front lobby."

"Don't burn any more of them. Ann, call the dean's office and tell him the newspaper can't be put in areas where patients or visitors go because they would cause mental anguish. Tell him any more will be confiscated and delivered to his office."

The phone rang. Henry Sims. "Doug, in five minutes the morning talk show will be featuring the new organizer for the hospital union, Simba somebody."

"Simba Agiza. I'll be right over. Keep the set warm."

He got there just as the program started.

"Our guest today is the stormy Simba Agiza, the stunning new organizer for the hospital workers' union. I might add that in Swahili, *simba agiza* means 'black lion.' Simba, welcome. I must say there's some mystery as to where Simba comes from, but I did learn she is a graduate of the University of North Carolina and that she went on to Yale and got her law degree. Simba, isn't the University of North Carolina where Mr. Carpenter, the Administrator at Eastern Hospital, went to school?"

"No," Her voice sounded like sugar. "He went to Duke, twelve miles away on the banks of Durham's ditches. There's a song about it. 'Sons and daughters of the riches, they call themselves Duke.'"

"Simba, let me say, after meeting you, I'm ready to join the union."

"Thank you." Her warm smile was catching. "And let *me* add that if you go to work in Eastern Hospital's Dietary Department and serve the doctors rich food you are too poor to afford, I'll take care of you."

"Just tell me where to sign."

Stan Boswell strolled in and sat. "Um-hunh," he groaned. "Tell me where to sign, too. I might kick her out of the hospital but not out of bed. Whew. She could eat crackers and drop her crumbs all over me. I could use a change of luck. Henry, you're the PR director, see what you can arrange." Stan smiled and closed his eyes.

"Sure, Stan, sure," said Henry. "But something tells me you better be certain, first. Her name is Black Lion. She might have claws."

Doug didn't mention his meeting with Simba but wondered if she wouldn't have come away with a prize if the meeting had been with Stan.

Simba announced, "Employees are joining by the hundreds. We have another meeting tomorrow night, but the press won't be admitted because there will be strategy discussions, and I'd rather the hospital masters didn't have the details. It's interesting, though, at our first meeting, the hospital administrator, Mr. Doug Carpenter, just happened to appear for 'another' meeting at the same time and place."

Doug felt as though he had been kicked in the stomach. *Lying bitch.*

Stan frowned at him.

"You had a spy in the audience?" asked the talk show host.

"No. He wasn't admitted."

"Good Lord!" shouted Stan.

Doug felt heat rising to his scalp. Typical Boswell support.

"This is a racist hospital." Simba wasn't smiling. "Doug Carpenter is a southern redneck, a cracker, an alligator in sheep's clothing. And I mean a w-h-i-t-e sheep, white all the way.

"The employees are underpaid and overworked while the doctors make $400,000 a year just for starters, and everybody serves them. When they drive to the hospital, somebody parks their cars for them. They are constantly catered to. Trips to Aspen, Colorado, or the Bahamas or wherever in the name of conferences. They get their own libraries, leased cars, new furniture, offices with their own interior decorators, residents, and interns to carry for them and look after their patients, nurses and secretaries to do whatever they want, people running after them, bowing and scraping. When they go into a meeting, they are served food and drink, even if it's immediately after lunch. They are served, served, served, and it's all arranged by their puppet, Doug Carpenter."

"Damn! How did she get on this show?" asked Doug.

"Simba. You don't have a high regard for Mr. Carpenter. Maybe he's not the right man for the job."

"I think I should let you and the audience decide that. If employees are discriminated against, if they are abused and defiled, no matter how good and god-fearing they are, their motivation and productivity will drop. That hospital requires a leader with vision, compassion, honesty, and deep understanding."

"Do you think Mr. Carpenter is such a leader?"

"What do you think?"

"Simba, it strikes me maybe you are such a leader."

"No. No, not me, but I'm sure there are others."

When the program was over, Stan grunted, saying, "She really gave you a going over."

"Better me than you, Stan. Better me than you."

"Maybe it's getting out of hand. What do you suggest?"

"Stan, this is just the beginning. What I've seen them do in other cities makes this look mild so far. We can expect a rough time."

Stan's face was plastered with disbelief.

Doug pretended not to notice. "At the department head meeting this afternoon I'll stress the manager's role, including that of conveying the hospital's feeling about unions to all employees, but with no threats." He knew Stan needed instruction, too, but it would be wasted. "We'll also develop the strike plan."

"Doesn't sound like enough."

"It isn't. We've got to counter the claims. Their biggest issue is salaries and ours are simply not that low. In the city, we are just below average."

"What the hell?" asked Stan. "What's a few bucks? Let's offer them an across-the-board raise and put that one to bed."

"Can't. Unfair labor practice. The organizing effort has already begun."

"You have to do something to stop that woman's mouth. Why don't you meet with her?"

"She dropped by and made it clear she was going to organize.

We could agree to unionization if it's what you want. It would save us a lot of friction. But if we do, we would have to negotiate a strong first contract."

"No. I want no union. There'll be no union. But you have to do something about her."

"You're right about that. Henry, see if you can arrange for me to go on the same program. But our most effective tool is the middle management group. They've become an effective team. We'll put our greatest emphasis there. They can talk sense to the employees."

Henry's secretary cracked open the door. "Mr. Sims, the press is on the line. They heard the hospital suppressed the news by burning all copies of the student newspaper."

"Henry," said Doug, "tell the press the students were told that any papers claiming unsafe care in this hospital would be turned over to the Dean's office because we don't want the patients agitated. Tell them you don't know any more than that."

Henry passed that information on, listened for a long moment, then replied, "I don't know. I'll get back to you." He hung up. "They plan to run a story about our suppressing news by burning the paper unless we call by one o'clock to refute it. They're less concerned about the content of the paper than the fact we suppressed it. The press is sensitive about that."

"Okay, prepare a release telling them the initial papers were thrown in with trash and incinerated because they threatened patient peace of mind, and no more were delivered after our contact with the Dean's office."

Doug left the meeting stiff with tension, Stan by his side, saying nothing, but casting sideways glances and shaking his head. Anger sloshed like lava in Doug's stomach.

"Doug, it looks like one snafu after another. I can't believe you showed up at their meeting. Better get your act together.

And the middle managers are just another committee. Don't depend on them. Do it yourself."

"Stan, they met at the same church where I was attending another meeting. There's no way to control these people. They're free to organize. They're protected by law. And they can distort the truth as much as they want to as long as they stay within the law. We can't shut Simba Agiza's mouth. You can count on it getting worse."

He stepped into his outer office but stepped back out again. "And, by the way, the middle managers are more than a committee. They're a team. There's a difference."

Stan looked away and continued down the hall.

Kay was waiting in his office. "Can't stay. Got to run, but I wanted you to know the union is asking employees to sign membership cards."

"How do you know?"

"Joy Coleman told me. She's going to the meetings to let me know what's going on."

"Kay, don't ask her to. That would be an unfair labor practice."

"I know. Purely voluntary. She's a good sort. Came to me."

"Looks like we're in for a real drive. Better be thinking what you'll do if there's a strike. Their first demands will be excessive to impress the membership."

"I'll turn Bull loose on them."

"Your husband's a cop. They haven't broken the law yet."

"I'll get him to plant some drugs on them."

"You're giving him a bad name."

"No. His parents did that already. What can you expect from a cop named Bull O'Connell?"

"Remind me not to cross you."

By himself in the office, Stan's reaction replayed. But it wasn't healthy to store up so much hate for the man. He pushed him

out of his mind and focused on Simba. *A law degree from Yale.*
Law grad makes big time as union representative. Yale would be
proud. If only I had taken pictures. Great alumni news stuff. 'Law
grad makes clean breast and everything else as union organizer.'
University of North Carolina. Rival school. Well, here she was,
in a sense, his rival at Eastern. *The rivalry at UNC and Duke had*
been better. Good, clean fun.

No sooner had Doug settled into his chair than Cliff Toliver
called him.

"Mr. Carpenter, we have demonstrators along the Main Street
side of the building."

"Employees?" asked Doug.

"No, sir. They're students. I went out to talk to them. Group
called Students for Human Growth."

"From Eastern?"

"Yep."

"Sounds like some student activist group out of the sixties.
What do they want?"

"They're carrying signs saying 'For Humane Purposes, We
Support the Hospital Union.' They're being orderly, blocking no
entrances, getting in nobody's way. They're handing out leaflets saying they support decent wages, quality care, and good
administration." He sounded like he was reading it.

"Who can argue with that?"

"I told them if I found any of their leaflets on the ground, I'd
have the whole bunch of them removed as a public nuisance,
but they'd already been picking up any that people dropped."

"Sounds like they've been coached," Doug told him. "Let's
try to wait them out. They may get tired and move on if we
don't overreact."

But they were still there when Doug left at six o'clock.

* * *

Bess was waiting for him, a newspaper in hand. "I want you to see this before you eat so you get upset on an empty stomach. It's cleaner that way."

"Must be about us suppressing the news."

"There's that, but it's not the grabber." She held up the second section and there on the first page was a picture of Simba Agiza.

"Holy shit!" he shouted. "I'm getting the dry heaves."

"Wait until you read it."

He took the paper and she picked up a small tray from a table. On it was a dry martini. "Is it that bad?"

"I've already had mine."

"It's that bad." He drained the glass. "Thanks for preparing me." He went into the living room and sank into the chair cushions.

"'The mysterious Simba Agiza proves beauty and brains do mix. But she downplays her importance. When asked where she came from, she replied, "The jungle." This new and warm community leader has dedicated her life to improving quality of life for others.'" He shook his head. "I don't think I can take anymore. Does the rest mention me or the hospital?"

"No," consoled Bess, "but I predict there'll be more in the days to come. It does mention Simba is as glamorous and sensuous as she is mysterious and if she ever gets tired of her grueling schedule, she could make a living just posing. So, tell me how you felt when she posed in front of you bare-ass naked?"

"Hum," Doug teased, "I do believe I hear the agitated squawk of the bird of jealousy."

"I'm jealous all right. If I did what she did, I'd just get a laugh."

The phone rang and, grinning, she picked it up on the first ring. "Carpenter residence."

The smile disappeared as she handed the phone to Doug. "Dr. Smith."

"Doug, thought you might want to know. The little boy who needed the bone marrow transplant died waiting for the HMO to make up its mind."

"Damn."

"Get off your ass and do something." Smith hung up.

CHAPTER TEN

Doug woke at five-thirty. He kept imagining demonstrators picketing the hospital. He called the security office.

"No, Mr. Carpenter. Nobody was out there last night."

"Good." But he knew they'd be back. And *The Eastern Student Future* would carry more stories. He dressed and made coffee. In the dining room, he opened the French doors to let in the air, still cool from the night.

He looked at the woods, just turning light, and stepped out onto the grass. The silent trees seemed to blend into the vibrations of morning. He wanted to bathe in the quiet peace, but the hospital wormed its way in. The birds calling through the morning haze became strange beepers reporting problems. The crickets were Boswell blaming him for something, anything, whatever. He forced himself to think of the people who really did care, the good doctors. They just went about their business, taking care of sick people and learning more about medicine. And the nurses. So many good ones. Thank God. And all the people behind the scenes, in the labs, Physical Therapy, Dietary, Housekeeping. The hospital was full of them. They cared about the patients. The patients were why they were there.

Somewhere, from deep in the woods, a bird called through

the distance. He couldn't tell which kind of fragile messenger was sending such a gentle sound, a sweet sound.

Thank you, little bird.

He stepped back into the house.

Driving into the city at a funeral pace, he rolled the car windows down, and propped his arm on the window frame. The sun warmed his coat sleeve. It was too early for much traffic, and he wasn't anxious to get to the hospital.

That damned Simba. He kept thinking of her as a bitch. But it wasn't a sexist thought, any more than calling someone a jerk. It was a title she had earned. He worried that it could be racist. *Damn her.* Had she clawed into his brain to dig up something he purged years ago? Do past beliefs, purged or not, stay on, lurking like a hidden personality? *No.* He hated racism, whether it was white against black or black against white.

He hated Simba for what she was doing. She was too intelligent to think she was right. She used her body as a tool. She had purpose, a cause, just as she had said. *Maybe I should call her "Super Bitch."*

He rolled up his windows as he drove through Solstory. To the south was a mixture of black and Hispanic. Right here, all black. He felt out of place. He worried about blacks who were racist. They should fight against racism, not practice it themselves.

Doug stopped off in the cafeteria for a donut but gave in to the smell of bacon and eggs. One of the dietitians was eating alone and he sat with her.

"Hi, Kathy. Don't you dietitians always eat together? I always wondered if that was for protection against people with indigestion."

"Cute," she smirked. "Normally, we do, but this morning, we're taking turns. Had a lot of sick calls."

Doug was only mildly surprised. "Think it's a sick-out?"

She nodded. "The ones who are out are the ones who've been going to the organizing meetings."

"How do you know?"

"The loyal ones tell us."

"If you had to guess, what percentage of your employees would you say plan to join the union?"

"It's hard to say. Two-thirds? Some of them are being pressured by others."

"The food's good this morning. Are the cooks here?"

"The cooks are all here. It's the aides who are out, so the bosses are filling in."

"Good practice for a strike." Doug shook his head.

"I hope it doesn't come to that."

They finished their coffees.

"Time to get to work," declared Kathy.

It was seven o'clock. The day shift was starting. Doug made rounds through a couple of patient units. He approached the fifth-floor nursing station and saw Charles Smith and a half dozen interns and residents walk down the hall into a patient room. Joy Coleman, the ward clerk, watched them with open hostility.

She saw Doug looking at her, glanced down in embarrassment, and then looked up at him with a slight smile. "Good morning, Mr. Carpenter."

"Hi, Joy. Having a bad moment?"

"Oh," she leaned back and looked down again, "I was just getting the business because some of the other clerks are out today."

"Don't let it get you down," encouraged Doug. "You're better than the system. Although, I'm not sure what that means."

"Thank you anyway," she said, filing charts and still looking angrily down the now empty hall.

Doug put the scene together. Smith had been annoyed on one of the other floors because a ward clerk failed to show up, and probably had to find a chart for himself. Joy was the next ward clerk he saw, so he dumped on her. And she was one of the more responsible employees. *Way to go, jerk.* He just had to show how important he was. Power-hungry people are always self-important. Wrap that in with greed for dollars, it's an offense hard to defend against.

Doug knew the employees were aware the doctors received privileged treatment. Many of the employees trusted him, but he was associated with the doctors. And Doug didn't "control" the doctors' greed. That gave Simba a wedge. Doctors weren't controlled. At best, they were influenced.

Maybe the union exposure of the greed would force the doctors to curb it themselves. No, he knew better. It was too bad those particular doctors were needed to keep the beds filled. Sometimes, the heavy admitters demanded the most favors.

He pushed through double doors, past a poster of a nurse with her finger to her lips and the caption, "QUIET." The floor was dirty. The fresh linen hadn't reached the unit, but a dietitian pushed a cart of breakfast trays down the hall.

He worked his way to the Intensive Care Unit. A stack of cartons sat on the floor in the hallway. IV solution.

The head nurse came over. "Hi, there. You want an IV?"

"Hi, Frances. You haven't got one with enough dextrose to fill my needs. Are you short of storage space?"

"No, not really. These are sitting here because our orderly didn't show up this morning. But I'll find some Brunhilda to put them away."

"Any other floors having problems with sick calls?"

"All of them. But we're getting by. Why would they want to have a sick-out?"

"They want us to be aware of their impact."

"Hell," stated Frances, hands on her hips, "we'll do okay without them."

At Med/Surg South, Doug introduced himself to Mr. Bergman, the quadriplegic patient who had gone unattended for almost twelve hours.

"I understand you had an unhappy situation on grand rounds here a few days ago. How are you feeling?"

"Oh, I'm all right, Mr. Carpenter. I don't blame nobody for that. It happened. That's all. I'm okay." His eyes pleaded for Doug to believe him.

Bergman's head, sunken into a pillow, was anchored by his unresponsive body. Doug just then realized he was young, in his early thirties. He had appeared old, with deep wells around the eyes giving the appearance he was way down there inside somewhere.

"Mistakes do happen, but we don't want that kind, and I want you to know Nursing has changed a lot of procedures to prevent it from ever repeating."

"Mr. Carpenter, it wasn't the nurses' fault." The deep eyes closed and it was as though he had gone away. Then he was back. "It was the doctors. The nurses are great. But don't get me wrong. The doctors are great, too." The pleading eyes looked at the ceiling. "They've saved my life time after time." He paused and seemed to be struggling. His eyes focused again on Doug. "It's just they don't care about me. They just care about my body. I'm a piece of meat they're keeping alive. And they do." He paused a moment and his eyes looked out the window. "They do."

When he looked at Doug, his eyes were wet. "I don't want to criticize them. My life depends on them. But on that grand round?" He began to cry. "When it was my turn, the doctor said, 'Bring in the quad.' Not 'Mr. Bergman,' or 'Bergman,' or even 'dumb ass.' 'Bring in the quad.'" He sobbed quietly. "And then they left me." He turned his eyes to the window and whispered softly, "They never asked me in the first place if I even wanted to go on the grand round, to be put on a stage in front of all those people."

He stared at the ceiling. "But they keep saving my dumb ass. And the nurses? They care. They were short that day and busy as hell. I couldn't do without them." He looked anxiously at Doug. "I hope you're not going to fire anybody."

"No. Nobody will get fired, Mr. Bergman. I promise you. Nobody will get fired."

Doug left Mr. Bergman's room, leaned against the wall outside the door, and found himself face-to-face with Charles Ellington Smith. "Been here a while, Charles?"

"For a while," and he turned to move down the hall.

"Charles."

Smith paused without turning around.

"Kay has made some significant changes to keep this from happening again, but you need to make changes in the Department of Medicine. I'm going to make suggestions in my memo to you, and I'll be ready to discuss them with you. Nothing complicated. Just simple, basic, human concern. But, knowing how thorough you are, I suspect you'll take care of all the problems on your end."

Smith nodded and walked away.

Doug stopped by the security office.

"Cliff, any demonstrators yet this morning?"

"None yet. No, sir."

"We might start to get tic-tac'd with nuisance type things. When this union strikes, there may be hallway trash cans set on fire, flat tires in the parking—"

"We had a trash can fire this morning," interrupted Cliff. "At 6:25."

Doug nodded. "Alert your men to expect more of the same. Put a few more hours on the payroll if you need to, but beef up the parking lots and the main building."

Doug got to his office by nine o'clock, and immediately buzzed Stan, but Liz Racoda answered. "No, he's not in. I think he may be late today."

Doug knew Stan wouldn't return his call. His charge was to build a new hospital, not worry about the old one.

Doug called out the open door, "Ann, ask Personnel to check every department to see how many people called out sick. Ask them to call us by ten o'clock with the numbers."

Joe Goldman peeped around the doorjamb. "Can I come in?"

"Sure. What's new?"

"Unfortunately, nothing. You know the publicity we've been getting about our medical staff being greedy? Well, we have our Medical Board meeting next Tuesday night, and I polled the members about cutting a little on the dinner menu. Cut out the champagne, the fancy cigars, and eliminate the lobster because we don't need both lobster and prime rib. I didn't even mention the hors d'oeuvres. They voted to leave it the same, twelve to eight. The good news is we've got eight good guys on the Board. The bad news is the others have mouthed off about it and now the word is out they voted to stay greedy. I should've left well enough alone." He leaned against the doorjamb.

"What flack did they give you other than a simple no?"

"There's no such thing as a simple no from that bunch." Joe tipped his head toward the hallway. "They used a lot of other words, many of the four-letter variety, and suggested that we deny we are always being served. They forget the Dietary employees are the ones serving it, so we can't deny it. One suggested we have it catered, bring it in from the outside, and nobody would know. Can you believe it?" Joe obviously couldn't. "Sometimes I wonder if lives should be trusted in their hands."

"Don't let Simba Agiza hear you," warned Doug.

"Boy, she has a mouth on her, hasn't she? She's working you over. Oh, be on time tonight for the dinner. We want everyone there before Ben arrives. He's really going to be surprised. He thinks they're having dinner with just Dottie and me."

Ann overheard and asked, "A surprise dinner for Dr. Snowden?"

"Yes," answered Joe. "And I don't believe the word has leaked out."

"That's nice. I like Dr. Snowden. He deserves a nice retirement party."

"Yes, and we've invited all the employees from the labs and a number of the Medical Staff. I hope this union business won't be a problem."

"What about all the cars around your house? Won't he be suspicious?" asked Ann.

"This girl thinks of everything." He hiked his thumb at Ann. "We've told everyone to park in the church parking lot across the street. I've an arrangement with them."

"By the way, Joe," said Doug, "the Search Committee for Snowden's replacement is ready to go and Ben has agreed to serve on it."

"That's a nice finishing touch. Really gotta go. Be there at seven-thirty. Oh, I almost forgot. My partners and I have decided to make a gift of new monitors in the I.C.U. to the hospital."

"Joe, are you aware of the price tag on that project?"

"We know. One million, four hundred forty-five thousand for the whole system. The hospital's done a lot for us over the years. We owe you." Joe clamped his big hand on Doug's shoulder and shook him. "Besides, we're the biggest users. Will you let the Equipment Committee know so Purchasing can get moving?"

Ninety-six employees called out sick, and Doug considered requiring each to have a doctor's excuse. He decided to do it if they were out another day. Even then, he told the department heads to use their own discretion. He figured it was a one-day sick-out to demonstrate there would be enough employees to support a union. They made their point. They also built tension between those for and those against the union because the latter were doing more work during the sick-out. But the work was getting done. Nonessential matters were ignored. Many of the employees wondered, "Who needs them?" A good attitude for now, but not for when the union members returned.

Doug and Bess arrived at the Goldmans' home on time and found the library already full of people. The huge drapes were drawn tight. Soon, Ben and Joan Snowden walked into the library and were so surprised Ben couldn't talk and she cried. Then Ben saw people he hadn't seen for years and he cried, too.

The dinner was catered to include everything but the cook's teeth. Joe told Doug he had been continually indebted to Snowden over the years for his quick responses and accuracy while patients were still in the operating room. Snowden had saved hundreds of lives, and when the speech-making part of the evening started, Joe even named the patients.

Prominent pathologists paraded up front and gave testimonials. He was a resource. Many had done their residencies under Ben Snowden. He had guided them in their careers "sometimes like a shepherd, sometimes like a sheepdog" as one described it. He had taught them to be caring, and they cared for him.

The Laboratory Department head, Mary Jane McCarthy,

talked about what it was like to work for Ben Snowden, who always saw the mistakes but always saw the quality, too. He was her mentor, her patron saint. And then, this lady who was always firm and calm—the one everyone else turned to when conflict and anger took over—this lady knelt by Snowden's chair, threw her arms around his neck, and wept. When she wept, every lab employee cried. It was a signal, and Snowden, who had already been reduced to pastry dough, struggled to his feet, clung to her, and cried. It was a catharsis. When it came time to give him the plaques and gifts and to hear him say a few words, a few words were all he could wring out.

"Every person ought to have some part of his or her life that stands out in memory as being that which made it all worthwhile," he said. "I've been blessed with more than any man deserves." He looked at his wife. "Joan and I have shared a lifetime of love that exceedeth all understanding." He put his hand on her shoulder. "It's been a wonderful relationship and it'll continue, getting mellower but never rotten. But then . . ." and here he had a catch in his voice. Joan Snowden put her hand on his. "But then, there's Eastern and all the people," he gestured at them, "now and over the years, and most of them, by themselves, made it worthwhile. Added together," he paused, "it's overwhelming. We've been swimming in the same space and breathing each other's air for a long time. And that air carries a lot of good echoes for me. I hope it does for you."

Everyone stood, clapping and crying. All the lab employees had come. They crowded around Ben Snowden. It looked like a pep rally with tears.

Bess sniffled and wiped her eyes.

"I think that says it all," said Doug.

CHAPTER ELEVEN

Days hustled by with union charges of profiteering, patient abuse, and employee exploitation. The union claimed low salaries amounted to employees paying for patient care while the hospital and doctors made huge profits.

Simba Agiza monopolized TV and the newspapers. She was everywhere, and every reporter wanted to interview her. Henry's efforts to get Doug on the same talk show failed. Simba was news, not him.

They told Henry, "We're booked solid for two months. We'll be glad to have him as a guest then."

To Henry's question, couldn't they do better than that, they'd replied, "We'll cancel something else if Carpenter will debate Simba."

The hospital declined the offer. Doug could hear his father drawling, "Never get into a pissing contest with a skunk." The hospital took out full-page ads in the newspaper, refuting all charges.

The middle managers learned labor rules. Doug warned them not to threaten the employees.

"You can't hold organizing against them, but any mischief, before or during, you can." He coached them on how to keep the employees feeling like team members.

A week after after Simba Agiza threatened to see him on the picket line, Doug came out of the stairwell and found himself facing a hoard of employees crowding down the hall, shouting, "Administration stinks! Doctors care for doctors! Eastern doesn't give a damn!" He stood anchored. In front of them, as though being herded along, was a security guard trying not to get stepped on. Angry faces jeered and hands pushed. When they saw Doug, they began to chant, "Strike! Strike!"

Doug braced himself, but they split, brushing past on both sides. Fists punched the air in time with the chanting. "Strike! Strike! Strike!"

Near the end of the train came Joy Coleman, the ward clerk Charles Smith had dumped on. Her face was strained and angry. She didn't look at Doug. "Strike! Strike!"

The stairwell door slammed against the wall and they poured down the steps. Their clattering and shouting blasted like an aftershock. The door closed, muffling the sound as the horde echoed and reverberated down the steps into the front lobby. When the bottom door closed behind them, the noise was gone. The hall was empty.

Ann was standing in the corner behind her desk as though expecting an attack. Stan Boswell ran out of Doug's office and pointed at him, shouting, "I don't want that to happen again!"

The word "again" echoed in Doug's mind like spurts of anger.

"I don't want those idiots in this building ever again. I want you to fire them all." Stan stuttered, "You fire them, or I'll fire them and you." He gulped air, trying to catch his breath. "Come into my office," he blurted. "I want to talk to you." He grabbed Doug by the arm as he moved down the hall.

Doug jerked his arm free. "I'll be there as soon as I've talked to Cliff Toliver. Call security," he told Ann.

Doug stood by his desk talking to Toliver. Stan came back into the outer office. He hovered in the doorway listening.

"Cliff, I'm sure you already know. I want to be kept informed about what's happening. Give me a rundown."

"We're in the thick of it now, Mr. Carpenter. We're about to have a walkout or a strike. The crowd in the lobby split and went in different directions. I think they went to their own places of work and told everyone to clear out. We're having a mass exodus right now."

"Alert the city police, but don't do anything else. It could be a short demonstration. Keep me posted."

Doug scrutinized Stan. "Was that a delegation that wanted to see you?"

"I'm not going to talk to that mob." His voice raised an octave.

"You could've agreed to talk to a few of them."

"What the hell for? Are you crazy?"

"If you want to talk to me, do it here. I'm busy."

"Mr. Carpenter," called Ann, "there are three department heads on three different lines waiting to talk to you."

"Tell them to stay in their areas and be prepared to initiate the strike plan. Tell them to list who's gone out, but do nothing else. Call the other department heads and tell them the same thing." He glanced at Stan. "If you had talked to them, you might've diverted this."

Stan's eyes bulged. He opened his mouth and for a moment, nothing came out. "I don't have to talk to *them*." He punctuated "them" by jabbing his finger in the direction of the hallway.

Doug shrugged. *Actually, Stan would have blown it. Just as well he didn't talk to them. Idiot.*

Kay O'Connell rushed in out of breath.

"What the hell are you doing here?" shouted Stan.

Before the shocked Kay could respond, Doug said, "I asked

her to come here. Kay, I want you to have your head nurses check each unit to see if any nurses have left."

"They're checking now. Last week they all said they would cross the picket line in case of a strike."

"That's not what I heard," alleged Stan. "I heard they were sympathetic."

"They are," Kay nodded, saying, "but they also said they didn't like the idea of a strike. The RNs, not the LPNs."

"Kay," asked Doug, "how about the ward clerks, aides, and orderlies?"

"The head nurses are calling their counts into the office, but I think they all went out."

"I—" Stan stuttered in anger and frustration. "I don't understand you two. Fire them all."

"Stan, we're not going to fire any of them," said Doug.

Stan spun around full circle, mimicking disbelief.

Doug ignored him. "Kay, yours is the most critical area. In one hour, if they're not back, start calling in extra nurses. Personnel will be setting up a labor pool of volunteers to help with paperwork. We may have to send out the lab work, but hands-on care must remain as good as ever."

Doug dialed Henry Sims, and Stan, gritting his teeth, stated, "There'll be no curtailing of admissions."

"Henry? Do you know what's happening?"

"Just got word. I understand they're congregating in Alumni Park and making speeches. Channel 2 is covering it. Want to come over and watch it?"

"No, but fill me in later, and if you get any calls from the press, tell them as far as you know, it's a demonstration. You don't know if there's going to be a strike. And that's it."

"I want to know why you aren't going to fire any of them. Whose side are you on, anyhow?" Stan vehemently asked.

Doug picked up the phone. Deliberately, he dialed security. He shook his head at Stan, now hunched in a chair staring at his fingers. "Read your labor law. Hello, Cliff? Are they picketing, blocking entrances, or just congregating in the park?"

"They're all in the park."

"Let me know if that changes."

"Doug, I'm giving you a direct order to fire them all!"

"Dammit!" Doug jumped up from his chair and slammed the phone in its cradle. Then he checked himself.

Kay looked like she was searching for a way out of the room. Stan stood there, mouth open.

Doug moderated his voice. "Stan, if we fired them, we would be subject to legal action and would lose. To put it bluntly, Stan, I refuse to fire them. Now, if you're going to fire me, do it." Doug took a deep breath, and as he exhaled, the fear of losing his job was gone. "And if you're not, leave and let me get my work done."

Stan walked toward the door. His neck was turning a flaming red. His lips barely moved. "We'll talk later."

Doug and Kay looked at the empty doorway and then each other.

"Doug, we'll be okay. Our RNs are on the job and our supervisors are on the floors to help out. So what if the aides, orderlies, and LPNs went out? And who cares if all the ward clerks went out? The noon meals have already been served, and by dinnertime, we'll have everything under control even if I have to do the cooking myself. We'll make it." Kay paused and tittered. "Your statement to Stan was beautiful. It made all this trouble worthwhile.

"I've got to get back on the floors."

Doug listened to her footsteps as she marched out into the hall. She had come to life, and he had the feeling they were going to need all the life they could generate.

"Ann," he called, "go get something to eat. You may not have time later."

She came in carrying a tray of sandwiches. "A couple of dietitians brought these." She smiled. "I think the A-Team has taken over."

Kay reappeared in the doorway. "By the way, thanks for lying and telling Stan you called me."

"My pleasure. I'm always happy to lie to Stan."

"You did such a good job, I forgot the real reason I came down here before all this mess."

"I'm glad it was because I'm such a good liar and not because you're getting senile."

"That's debatable, too. Anyhow, assuming there's not going to be a strike, we need your moral support in the Death and Dying Committee. Can you come to the next meeting and give a pep talk? Smith and Whyte and Jack Apple have been vocal in opposition. They've been telling the nurses not to talk of death to their dying patients."

"Sure. Just say when, but from what I know about Juanita Martinez, you don't need me."

"She's great, but we need you. Some of the others on the committee would feel good about you taking a position for them."

"Get Joe Goldman, too. Support from the president of the medical staff should help, and he's completely in accord with the goals."

"I've already asked him and he said yes."

"I should have known you'd ask him first. You like doctors better than administrators."

"No, it's not that. It's just that he's taller, better looking, and smarter than you."

"Don't you have a patient that needs you?"

"I'm going."

The phone rang. Doug picked it up.

"Mr. Carpenter, Cliff Toliver. They're on their way back from the park."

CHAPTER TWELVE

Doug stood off to the side in the main lobby with Cliff Toliver, watching the employees filing in, orderly and quiet.

Henry Sims joined the two of them. "Ann said you'd be here. They don't look like they're about to explode."

"No. Their fuses aren't lit. They're going back to work, but they've given us a message."

"I got a message from one of the TV reporters. It'll be on the evening news. The union has petitioned the NLRB for an election. They say they have signatures from over half of the employees in the bargaining unit."

"Like it or not, guess I better call Frank Street," said Doug. "He's the college negotiator and it's time to work out a plan of action. Facts of life. We're about to have a long, hot summer. See you guys later." He headed back to his office.

"Frank Street called," said Ann. "He wants you to call."

"Right on target. Get him." He shut his door.

Street's silky voice goaded Doug. "Looks like that black bimbo's got a few things stirred up."

"I can guarantee you she's no bimbo. I wish she were. As it is, she's definitely got the pot stirred and she's getting ready to serve us as the main course."

"Nothing we can't handle, Doug. How about I drop in tomorrow and get the lay of the land and then we can make our plans? I want to bite her ass."

"She may give you the opportunity. When will we know the NLRB's decision?"

"Soon. I hear they have over fifty percent. Only takes thirty."

"No point challenging. From what I've seen, they've got the required thirty. The election will tell us if it's more."

At the Death and Dying Committee meeting, there were no distractions by the labor strife. Juanita Martinez shined life on everybody in the small conference room. She poured her warmth on Doug. "You were our savior at Solstory. The community does not forget. The nurses do not forget." She pointed to herself. "I will never forget." Her English had the perfection gained only by one who studied it totally.

"Here is an example of why this committee is needed. Two weeks ago, Mr. and Mrs. Boyer were admitted to the hospital—she, to the sixth floor; he, to the second. They were both dying of cancer. Alone. They had no other relatives, only each other. They lay separated by floors and a policy against mixed-sex occupancy. Loving partners in life for sixty years, dying alone. We moved them in together. They held each other and cried. A week later, he died first, in her arms." She pointed at Kay. "Kay O'Connell allowed us to do the right thing."

Doug was only vaguely aware of the others in the room representing Social Services, Admissions, Nursing, Medical Education, and Quality Assurance. Dr. Best and Joe Goldman were there and seemed mesmerized by Juanita as well.

"Dying can be beautiful. It's part of life. It can be tender, the culmination of everything from birth on. It can be the final statement of our lives. It can be the wonderful conclusion, the essence of our lives, if we let it, if we don't deny it." Her voice was like a song, soft and persistent as rain. "Some of our physicians are threatened by death. All of us are if we react to it and fear it rather than embrace it. Dr. Smith, Dr. Whyte, Dr. Apple are, and they aren't the only ones. Mr. Carpenter remembers Dr. Jeep, who was previously at Solstory. Dr. Jeep is like a god to some of his patients, and he enjoys that role. He denies death due to any illness he is treating. He resists even admitting a dying patient into the hospital. They can only die if he wills it, and he doesn't will it. There are others like him."

Doug endorsed the committee's action plan, which included a written policy that doctors should discuss patient status openly with the patient and relatives. When the meeting was over and everyone was thanking him for being there and supporting the committee, he realized all he had done was nod in agreement. He had given no pep talk. Juanita was the committee.

Kay sat down on one side of him and Juanita on the other.

"She keeps calling me Kayo, and now she has everybody calling me that."

"But she is Kayo. She's such a winner. We all love her." She put her hand on Doug's arm. "Mr. Carpenter, when Solstory closed, we thought the world had ended, but it was a good thing. There is so much more here. And everyone knew you were so honest. I'm so glad you are here. I know you will only do good things. It is who you are." She squeezed his arm and whispered, "I need to talk to you." She stood to go. "Thank you."

He wondered what she wanted to talk about. *HMOs?* That's what everyone wanted to talk to him about. She would be concerned about patients getting stiffed.

The election was scheduled at the armory, and Simba stepped up the campaign.

"If only I were glamorous," Doug lamented to Bess. "I could twitch my way onto TV and smile the hosts into mental oblivion."

"No, you couldn't," she retorted. "You're too honest. Besides most of the TV hosts are already in mental oblivion."

"Carpenter. The pimp of the whoremasters. Don't look for a square deal" leaflets appeared on desks, steps, taped to windows, even taped to Doug's car.

Ann was incensed. "They don't know what you do for them."

"They have to vilify someone. It's part of the game."

"Why don't they pick on the doctors? They deserve it."

"There's only one administrator. Easier target. Besides, they figure I'm supposed to control the greedy bastards."

"Sure. Good luck."

Doug felt eyes of anger on the back of his neck as he walked through the hospital. But he didn't feel alone. Wherever he went, department heads joined him. They walked with him until someone else appeared, almost like it was planned.

Whenever he called Stan's office, Liz would say, "He's busy. He told me to take a message."

It had been a stressful weekend. Ann brought in a cup of coffee for Doug. "Today's the day, boss."

"Yep. We'll know the results by one-thirty."

"How do you think it'll go?"

"They'll win."

"I don't know. A lot of people like you."

"It's not a popularity contest, and if it were, I'd lose out to Simba."

Department heads dropped by one-by-one or in groups to ask if there was news, then stayed. No one felt like working.

At two o'clock, the word came: 467 yeses, 313 nos.

"Okay, time for the next stage."

The next stage came quickly. Loud shouts filled the hallway. Doug darted past Ann's desk and into the hall in time to see a large delegation of employees walking past, away from Stan's office. "No talk. No work. No talk. No work," they chanted as they tramped down the hall.

No, not again. Why did they go to him? But he knew why. They saw Stan as a figurehead who would do nothing. Simba wasn't stupid. She wanted to justify a strike.

They turned the corner of the hallway as Stan charged out of his office, carrying a sheaf of papers. He threw them at Doug.

"I told you. I told you. I told you." His face twitched and glowed. "You. You. You." He turned and ran back to his office, slamming the door behind him.

Doug bent and picked up the papers.

Union demands. Crazy way to present them. "Call Street."

He walked into his office and stared at the list. *"Twenty percent pay increase."*

Ann buzzed and Doug picked up the phone.

"Frank, we got the demands. They dropped them off in Stan's office. He wouldn't talk to them and I think we're about to have another walkout."

"Well, they aren't playing by the rules. They're not supposed to strike until there's an impasse in the negotiations."

"They want to strike, Frank. They knew Stan wouldn't see them. They may not be coming back in at all. I'll let you know."

"Shit. In the meantime, I'll see if I can schedule something with the union."

Doug ran down the steps to the main lobby. Cliff Toliver, grim and tight-faced, walked over to him.

"I called the labor squad. They're on the way."

Doug watched the employees gathered outside the door. Signs and placards appeared.

The strike was on.

"Let your men know the strike plan's in effect."

Cliff used a walkie-talkie while he ran over toward the main entrance.

Doug picked up the phone at the information desk to tell Ann to alert the department heads.

More employees appeared with belongings from their lockers. They smiled and laughed as they joined the crowd outside. Soon the entrance was blocked.

"Cliff, let me know about every incident. I'm going back to my office. Get your camera. Document cases where anyone trying to get in for care is blocked. We'll need it for the injunction."

In his office, which was now the command center, Doug called Henry Sims to have the photographer help Cliff. He talked to the labor attorney so the judge could be contacted and the injunction enforced. He phoned Frank Street.

"Frank, the strike has started. I'm sending a list of the demands to your office."

"Don't bother. The union just delivered it."

"Set up a meeting at a neutral location. You, me, and their representatives."

"Doug, you're the administrator. It's best you stay out of it. You can object to any agreement after the negotiations and still effect change."

"I know, but this union is different. I've done negotiations before, and I want to get them back to work. I don't think it's to our advantage to play that game. And besides, I don't want you negotiating the salaries too low."

"Shit fire. I'll let you know when."

In rapid succession, Doug received three phone calls. One was from Henry Sims reporting that they had documented three cases of patients being blocked from entering the hospital, including an ambulance with a heart attack victim. The labor attorney was on the way to see the judge for the injunction.

The second was from Cliff Toliver. Dozens of cars in the parking lot had been vandalized, with tires slashed and windows broken.

"Itemize the damage. We'll replace the tires and windows. Let the employees know that, and beef up the guards over there. Hire some off-duty city cops."

The third call was from Bess. "I just got a strange phone call. A male voice asked if this was Bess Carpenter. I said yes. He asked if I was the wife of Doug Carpenter, the administrator at Eastern. I said yes. Then he asked if the dining room had French doors that could be broken into easily and if I was going to be here alone tonight. When I didn't answer, he hung up."

Doug gripped the phone and gritted his teeth.

"So, I got an idea," she continued. "I'm going to call the Youngs and the Millers, tell them what's happened, and ask if they would like to keep me company. It'll be fun having them, and besides, they're pro-union. It'll give them a chance to see the seamier side."

"You could also go to a motel, or you could stay with the Youngs or the Millers. For that matter, you could stay here. We could use some volunteer help."

"I'm not going to be threatened out of my own house by some goon. No thanks."

"Okay, but I'm posting a guard for the duration. This bunch plays rough. You're a target because they can get to me through you. And they know I'll be staying here."

Doug called Cliff to make arrangements and learned there had been three more fires set in the building.

"Two were in trash cans and easy to put out, but one was in a storeroom in the sub-basement and could've gotten out of control. I wish I could get my hands on the bastards who did it."

Ann stuck her head through the door. "Every nurse on the day shift has agreed to stay over. We're going to have a full house. All the department heads and non-union day-shift employees are staying." She arched her eyebrows. "Hope there are enough beds for everyone."

"All of them?" He knew the department heads would stay, but the others weren't pressured. The department heads had handled things well with their people.

He heard shouting outside and went to the window. On the lawn were two nurses and two aides fighting. One of the aides looked big as a mountain. She grabbed the smaller of the nurses, one huge hand around her throat the other clamped between the legs. In an instant, she jerked her into the air holding her high, at arm's length, shouting at her and shaking her like a pillow. Her neck was bent and her throat was squeezed shut. Her legs kicked against the air. The giant slammed her to the ground, jumped on her, knees first, and crashed heavy fists, left, right, left, right against the sides of her head. She jumped up from the limp body to help her partner.

The other nurse was good with her fists but it was now two against one. And such a two!

The goon lifted the second body, kicking, into the air. In panic, Doug left the window and grabbed the phone.

"Cliff, there are two nurses trying to get in and two aides are beating them to death on the west lawn. Get out there quick to help them."

He rushed back to the window in time to see the large aide stalking away from the second body. Her partner kicked the nurse, who moved from the force of the foot, but there was no other response. The larger aide grinned, and as though to demonstrate how it should be done, rushed like a place-kicker toward the smaller nurse, caught her in the side with a pile-driving foot that lifted her off the ground and flipped her on her stomach. Then they both stepped on her as they walked away.

Doug stared at the two ragdoll figures until three security guards rushed out of the building. One had a walkie-talkie, and Doug guessed he was calling for litters.

He pulled himself away from the window and called the emergency room. "Get litters out to the west lawn and pick up those two nurses." He shut his eyes and saw the girl's legs kicking in the air, then, thud. She hit the ground.

"Be careful. The way they were slammed, they may have broken necks or backs." *Oh, lord. They could be dead.*

He put the phone down and lay his head on the desk for a moment. Others could get the same treatment. He called Kay O'Connell.

"Kay, if any nurses call to see if they can get in, tell them to wait and you'll call them when the picketers disperse and it's safe. Two just got badly beaten on the west lawn. They're being picked up by emergency. Find out how they are and let me know."

"Doug," Ann informed him, "there's a fight in the lobby. Cliff's on the line."

Cliff was stuttering. "Doug, Dr. Whyte tried to force his way in by pushing some of the picketers. Some goon just beat the hell out of him and threw him into the lobby. It wasn't one of our employees and whoever he was, he's long gone. I swear, from the way it looked, they were just waiting for him."

"How is he? Is he seriously hurt?"

"They're taking him to the emergency room right now. He's unconscious."

They could hear what sounded like a PA system outside.

"What's that noise?" asked Ann. "I've been hearing it for the last ten minutes."

"It's a police bullhorn." Doug opened the window to hear better. "Wish to hell we were at the front of the building so we could see what's going on."

The riot squad gave the picketers instructions to disperse. "No more than five picketers at a doorway," came the loud voice. "Nobody is to be stopped from going in or out. I repeat. Five picketers to an entrance and block nobody."

It wasn't a peaceful interchange. Sirens, shouting, glass breaking, thumps, and crashes created a chorus of chaos.

"Oh, my lord," whispered Ann, "the patients are going to love this."

"Good point there. Tell you what. Call Kay and tell her to get all her people on the floors to maintain a calm atmosphere. Call Dietary and have the dietitians get up there, too. Then the labs, and then Housekeeping. Call Social Service, Rehab, Cardiology, and anybody else you can think of."

Soon the floors were full of quietly concerned personnel. The patients remained calm through it all.

Cliff Toliver brought Doug up to date. "The picketers refused to break up. They linked arms and the police used force. Fights broke out all over the street. They carted off over seventy of them in a bus. The police used their sticks, breaking noses and busting heads."

Ann interrupted, "Dr. Whyte has a concussion, a broken nose, and some loose teeth."

"Oh, no!" exclaimed Cliff. "What's the world coming to that they'd do that to a doctor?"

Doug tilted his head and arched his eyebrows. He caught Ann's eye, and neither of them smiled.

"He'll want me to fire everyone who joins the union. This bunch plays rough. You don't just push into them."

"I guess he knows now," said Cliff.

"Anyhow," Ann went on, "the nurse said he's mad as hell. And they're keeping him overnight. He'll be a model patient."

"Yeah, the nurses will be fighting over who gets to wait on him. What about the two nurses who were beaten?"

"They were just bringing them in."

"I'm going to make rounds," said Cliff. "I'll check back later."

The phone was ringing and Ann had already moved off to answer it. Doug thumbed through a copy of the strike plan to be sure he wasn't overlooking anything. His head throbbed. He looked up to see Ann standing in the doorway.

"It's . . . Bess," she could hardly get the words out.

"Oh, okay." Nonchalantly, Doug began moving toward the phone, wondering at the strange expression on Ann's face.

"She's not on the phone."

He froze, not moving even to breathe.

"They just brought her into the emergency room."

"Oh, no!" Doug ran down the hall and stairwell to the ER and there was Bess on a litter, red from head to foot. He could see a cut above her right eye. "Bess! Bess!" he cried.

"Doug," she called and reached out her hand.

"What happened?" He clutched her sticky hand.

"I'm going to be all right," she said without opening her eyes. "So don't get excited. It's paint."

The panic changed to rage. She was cut. He could see it. "A paint bomb?" They had bombed her. He looked down at her. She didn't have a thing to do with all the crap going on in the hospital. "Don't open your eyes. You might get paint in them." He wanted to hit somebody. He wanted to hit and hit.

A nurse placed a basin beside the litter and began to swab the skin around the left eye. "We're going to clean you up so we can get a look at you." She raised her voice as though the paint made Bess hard of hearing. "This may sting a little. We're trying an alcohol mix to thin it and clean it away."

"Why don't you get some old newspaper," suggested Bess. "That's what I clean my paint brushes with." She winced.

"You have a little cut here, and I'm going to clean it out."

"And I thought paint brushes couldn't feel."

A resident came over and helped. Another nurse unbuttoned the torn paint-soaked blouse, and Doug moved aside, still holding her hand.

"We'll get her face cleaned and these clothes off so we can see if there are any more cuts. She's lucky she wasn't seriously hurt. Oops, here's another nick." There was a cut just below the left rib on her stomach. "A little peroxide to clean that out and we'll bandage it."

"You can open your eyes now," the resident instructed.

Her eyes were inflamed. Doug saw she was crying. He stopped thinking. He wanted to hurt someone or something, but the enemy was invisible.

"I guess I knew I had been unconscious."

The nurses peeled off her ripped jeans. There on her left hip was a gash about three inches long and an inch deep. They poured peroxide on it and cleaned it with gauze.

"Uh-huh. A little glass in here. We'll just pick it out. You relax."

With tweezers, the nurse picked out a chunk of glass as big as her thumbnail. Doug winced, but Bess didn't seem to feel it.

"I guess that explains the ringing in my ears."

The resident checked the pupils of her eyes. "That's right, you keep crying. It'll help clean out your eyes. I think we'll keep you here tonight so we can check on you every so often. You're going to need a few stitches."

The nurses cleaned her arms and hands.

"Actually, I came in so that I could check on him. It's bad enough he has to be around that beautiful secretary all day, let alone all night." She forced a smile.

The resident looked at one of the nurses and winked. "She means Ann."

"Not to worry," Doug clutched her hand tighter. "I only have eyes for you. You have no idea how beautiful you are, lying there without your clothes. Eat your heart out, Simba."

"Mrs. Carpenter, we're going to wash your hair out because if the paint dries it'll have to be cut."

"By the way," asked Doug, "where are the Millers and the Youngs? Had they arrived yet?"

"No, but they should be getting there soon."

It was too late to get them by phone. He imagined their surprise when they arrived at the house. They would be rushing to the hospital soon.

He stepped out to see if the police who brought Bess in were still there and found them drinking coffee and looking out the emergency room entrance at the pickets. The hospital security guard had found her when he went to the house. He had called for help and remained at the house.

"The paint bomb had a small charge," explained one of the police officers, a short, stocky black man. "It smashed against the dining room wall and exploded, and your wife was in the room. She was lucky. She could've been blinded."

Doug could see the scene in detail.

"That dining room is one hell of a mess."

Two nurses wheeled Bess out of the exam room. She was now wearing a hospital gown.

She looked at Doug and forced a faint grin.

"We did a little stitching on her side. We're taking her to room 604, Mr. Carpenter."

"I'll be up soon, honey, after I've talked to the Youngs and the Millers. As I said, we can use some volunteer help." He couldn't make himself sound upbeat. Helplessness wrapped him like a glove.

He walked back into the ER and found the two nurses from the west lawn in the same exam room. The smaller one, Isabel Eaves, was unconscious. The other, Jean DeVries, was wide-awake and mad as hell.

"I'll get her for this," she moaned to the resident. "I'll get them both." Her face was swollen and purple.

"Any broken bones?" asked Doug.

"Looks like they each have a couple of broken ribs. Isabel has a collapsed lung. Jean's hurting, but she's so mad she's not feeling it yet. We may have a couple concussions."

A resident checked Isabel's pupils.

"Jean, who was that big aide. I don't remember her."

"I don't know her name. Just started here. Fourth floor. I'll get the bitch."

Doug guessed she wouldn't be around to be gotten. A union plant. Lady goon, brought for just this purpose. He called Cliff to have him check it out, then decided to call his kids, Sammy and Janey, to let them know what had happened.

Janey was calm, so like Bess.

"Which one of you got hurt the worst?" she asked.

"Right now, it's a crap shoot. I'll let you know when I figure it out."

Sammy was different. Doug could hear him sobbing on the other end of the phone. "She's all right. You don't need to come home. Everything's under control. Call her. Then you'll know she's okay."

But Doug wondered how often Bess would replay that explosion in her mind. Again, he wanted to hit somebody.

Instead, he called Cliff. "Check with the police and see if they arrested that big aide when they carted off a busload of them. If they did, tell them to hold her. Jean and Isabel will press charges, and I'll serve as a witness."

CHAPTER THIRTEEN

Doug sat on the edge of Bess's bed. She wanted to go home, but the resident gave orders for her to stay put. He was worried about a concussion.

"My head's clear. There's no vertigo. No aching. I'm okay. I'll stay until tomorrow, but I'm going home to clean up that mess."

The paint bomb had crashed through the glass door, hit the wall, slamming, splashing, exploding, hitting everything . . . everything . . . including her. The image blanked out. His mind wouldn't play it.

"You don't have to rush back. There's a guard there, and the dining room door has been covered with plywood. The damage will still be there when you get home."

"Cute. I know. And the quicker it's fixed, the quicker it's out of my mind. It's bothering me. It's not our place as long as that intrusion is there." She pulled her hand away and smoothed the sheet across the bed. "Don't bug me about getting out of here, and I won't even mention getting the strike settled so we can get back to what some people might call a 'normal existence.'"

"Aha, somebody's feeling her oats. What do you remember about what happened?"

"Not much." She finished straightening the sheet and gave

it a pat of satisfaction. "I was in the dining room. I heard glass break, and I think there was a dull thud. I can't be sure." She folded her hands across her stomach and looked thoughtful. "That's all I remember until the police were carting me out of the house." She reflected. "It's as though my body was clinging to me like wet plastic. Strange." She smoothed the sheets some more. "You're not just dealing with a union. You're dealing with criminals."

He placed his hand on hers, felt its warmth, and squeezed.

"They're a bunch of goons, and they'll do anything to win. The police think a dynamite charge was taped to the bottom of the paint jar. Thank God you weren't hurt more."

"Did it hit the dining room wall?"

"It was thrown through a pane in the French door and smashed against the wall. Explosion on impact." He was beginning to feel better, seeing her so anxious to get up.

The phone rang and Bess grabbed it. The way she answered it, with the lilt in her voice, sent a warm current through him, and happiness pushed his anger out.

"It's for you. I should've known."

He took the phone from her hand, but grabbed her fingers and kissed them.

"Mister," gruffly but playfully Bess addressed him, "that kind of demonstration in a patient room won't be tolerated."

"Hush. If the other patients find out, they'll all want the same treatment."

Ann's voice came over the phone. "I don't think I want to know what's going on there."

"There's no telling what would be going on here if this phone didn't work. What's up?"

"Frank Street just called. He wants to know if you can meet with the union this evening."

"Tell him yes." He dropped the phone in its cradle. "Duty calls. I've got to get to the office, too much going on. But I'll be back." He kissed both her hands and got up.

"I may not be here," she called after him.

In the office, Doug found a cot made up next to his desk. He leaned on the windowsill and looked out at the late afternoon shadows stretching across the lawn. Scraps of paper and trash lay scattered, peeping through grass like a strange garden.

"How's Bess?" Ann stood in the doorway.

"She's okay. Better. Thank God." He shook his head. "The union management should all be thrown in jail."

"I have a feeling it wouldn't be the first time."

Kay O'Connell squeezed past Ann, looking angry and shaking her head. "Oh, Doug!" She flopped into a chair and leaned back, closing her eyes.

"What's the matter?"

"We just had a death in the delivery room."

Doug waited. Kay pushed herself upright, her eyes brimming with anger. "A twenty-four-year-old mother of two in a perfectly normal procedure was just . . ." she spread her hands, "wiped out, erased, ended." She spread her hands again. "The drunken fool killed her and her baby." She rocked forward and back.

"What fool? What's happened?"

"Dr. Robinson, Chair of Anesthesiology."

"What!" exclaimed Doug. "How did it happen?"

"He was drunk, as usual. He'll get no protection from the nurses. The incident report will be candid enough to convict the bastard of manslaughter."

Doug put his elbows on his desk and cradled his head in his hands. He felt submerged and struggled to take a deep breath. "Simmer down, Kay."

"I can't simmer down, and what's more, neither can you. We've got to get him out of our hospital."

"Yes, but we've got to do it without destroying the hospital. What's that old nurse's saying? 'Don't throw the baby out with the bath water.'"

"Can't you bar him from the hospital?"

"Yes, according to the bylaws. But that's only temporary until the Medical Staff Board votes on it. And they'd overturn it."

"Damnit, then," she cried, wiping her runny nose and face with the back of her hand, "the nurses are going after him." Kay's face was turning redder by the second. Her whole body seemed on fire.

"No, no." Doug took her hand in his. "Calm down." He was afraid she was having a stroke. "I agree with you, but we have to get rid of the garbage without touching the good."

"The only way's to nail his ass with a lawsuit."

"Kay, you know the incident reports can be used against both him and the hospital in court." He shook his head. "We've got to be fair to the patient's family. But we've got to protect the hospital and we've got to get his . . ." he struggled for the right word, "ass out of here."

"The nurses are going to walk. They are tired of doctors who don't care." She leaned forward and ran her fingers through her graying hair, shaking. "She was such a sweet person. Her husband and two little girls were in the waiting room. They didn't know she was being killed." She seemed exhausted and visibly worked to regain control. "The nurses are beginning to feel like accomplices."

Ann handed her a tissue and Kay blew her nose.

"Doug, I'm not kidding. Something has to be done *now* or the nurses are going to walk."

"Ann, see if you can get Robinson and ask him to come up here." He turned to Kay. "Who was the obstetrician?"

Kay struggled to her feet. "Bob Salerno. They'll whitewash this. Wait until you read the surgical summary and the anesthesia notes. Her family will certainly have plenty of witnesses in court."

"Ann," Doug called after her. "Get hold of Salerno, too. Kay, instruct the delivery room nurses to keep the incident reports factual. They're to keep their emotions out of it. We don't want what they say to be used in court against the hospital. Tell them they are to report only what happened with the patient."

"I can't believe this." Kay wiped her face, then stood with her hands on her hips in defiance.

"In other words, they can't say 'Dr. Robinson was drunk.' They don't *know* that. If there was too much anesthetic, and they know it for a fact, they can say it. Otherwise, they have to stick to such statements as 'the patient died on the table.'" He paused and leaned forward for emphasis. "But I want them here in my office, one-by-one, to describe their roles and what they saw."

Kay was beside herself. "And you're asking them to cover for this bastard. What do you mean 'patient died on the table?' She was Jean Daniels. And she was killed in the act of bringing her third redheaded baby into the world. A redheaded girl who'll never grow up. *She* was canceled, *too*." She blubbered. "I saw her husband in the waiting room. He was crying and hugging his two little girls." Her anger overcame her grief. "The nurses will *never* cover for that bastard!"

"We'll get him, Kay. But the nurses must protect the hospital."

"Yeah? Well, who's protecting that family?" Her voice quivered as she fell back into the chair, overcome, shaking hysterically.

Doug moved to her, speaking softly. "Kay, we'll do whatever we can for her family. There'll be a settlement, believe me. But

I don't want the hospital destroyed in the process. Yes, he is a bastard. We've got to get him out of our hospital. But let's not destroy the hospital to do it."

He knelt in front of her and held her by the shoulders. "Kay, the hospital has a purpose to fill. Now, help me."

Ann swept in with an air of urgency. "No one knows where Dr. Robinson or Dr. Salerno are. Neither has answered the page."

"You see?" cried Kay, coming to life again. "They've taken him somewhere to get him sober."

"Doug," continued Ann, "there's a lot of smoke out in the hallway. I called Code Red."

He dashed out of the office with Kay stumbling after him. The elevator doors slammed open at the far end of the hall. The Code Red team piled out pushing a red cart with fire extinguishers, axes, and other equipment with members from Accounting instead of Maintenance.

Doug sprinted, reaching the side hallway before them. He could see smoke coming from the conference room and pointed. The team and cart swung in that direction. The lead man, in his three-piece suit, grabbed the fire extinguisher as he ran into the room.

"It doesn't smell like paper," cried Kay in alarm, sprinting along behind him, still wiping her eyes. Ann had stayed behind so she could hear the phone.

Doug watched the team put out the few remaining flames on a burned-out chair.

"Someone set fire to a chair. All that's left is a charcoal frame. They definitely started it with gasoline." The odor was obvious.

"Even the ceiling is singed!" He turned to the man who had been in the lead, Gordon Albright. "Better get someone here to clean up the mess. Call Housekeeping. And I guess you'd better get a report written."

But Gordon had already removed a clipboard from the cart and his stubby fingers filled out the incident report. "Gotcha, chief. Glad you weren't in that chair."

Doug and Kay walked slowly to the office.

Kay stopped at the door. "Okay, dammit, I'll talk to the nurses."

Doug called Stan's office.

"He's out of the building," Liz replied, having rehearsed. "I don't know when he'll be back, but I'll tell him you called."

Frank Street scheduled the meeting at the Parkside Inn because it was close by. Frank was tall with red, curly hair. His skin was freckled into a permanent tan. His light blue eyes seemed to jump out at you through the framework of red and tan. He and Doug walked into the large lobby a few minutes to seven.

"I forgot to mention," Frank looked around for closer ears, "most of the union delegates will be hanging out. I told Simba they couldn't sit in. That accounts for all the jungle bunnies you see."

Doug always expected racism from Frank, but it still annoyed him. He curbed his feelings but felt like it was becoming a habit. "It's a good thing they aren't all going to be in the meeting."

"No, but they want what they call their senior delegates to be there. I don't care. Do you?"

"No. I'm just interested in seeing what the lay of the land is. That's what the first meeting's all about anyhow."

They walked down the corridor to the meeting room and Frank muttered, "Sure are a lot of black asses in this place. Looks like a damn NAACP meeting."

They entered the small conference room. It was full. People stood against the walls. All the seats were taken. Simba Agiza sat at the head of the table. The room grew quiet.

"Aha!" Simba announced. "The white masters are here."

The one white delegate, a lab technician, didn't seem to notice the slur.

"Are we going to have a serious meeting?" asked Frank. "We need to talk about demands, if there are any."

"Bring an end to twentieth-century slavery."

Everybody shouted, "Slavery!" They stood, and clapped, facing Doug and Frank. They stomped on the floor in time with the clapping. The noise bounced off the walls. They sang, "We Shall Overcome."

Doug and Frank patiently waited through all the verses. They cheered, clapped, whistled, and beat on the table. Someone bellowed, "Stamp out slavery!" and soon they all chanted, swaying from side to side. "Stamp out slavery!"

Frank turned to Doug. "Let's go."

"Right."

They left in the midst of jeers.

"Mr. Big! Mr. Big! Mr. Big!" They stomped and clapped in time.

A TV reporter with a camera operator blocked the hall.

"Mr. Carpenter, are you walking out of the meeting?"

"The hospital sees the need to meet with the union if there is ever to be a settlement. We called for this one, but they don't want to talk. This isn't an atmosphere for discussion."

"So you're walking out. Sir," turning to Frank, "do you think walking out is constructive?"

"Do you think staying would be constructive?"

Frank shoved the man against the wall and pushed past. The hall filled with rank-and-file union members.

"No more slavery!" someone screamed. "No more slavery!" chanted the crowd. They clapped in unison with the chant and opened a pathway through the middle of the hall for Doug and Frank. "No more slavery! No more slavery!"

"Let's go get a cup of coffee and talk about this," proposed Doug.

They sat in the hotel restaurant. It was quiet, the first peaceful moment of the day.

"This isn't unusual, Doug. They're not in a hurry. They think we're anxious and want us to beg. I say we let them ask for the next meeting and we give specific conditions for it. To hell with them."

"Agreed. If they want a fight, they've got one."

The hotel manager came over. He knew both men from previous hospital conferences. "Looks like you had a short meeting. The union delegation just left."

"Sorry for all the racket," apologized Frank.

"Actually, they were quite orderly, coming in and going out."

"Yeah," sneered Frank, "but what happened in between qualifies them for the Stage and Screen Actors Guild."

Simba Agiza came in alone and headed for their table.

"I think I'll just run along." The manager tapped their table.

"May I sit for a moment?" asked Simba, sliding into a chair.

"Suit yourself," nodded Doug.

"Is this a sample of how you plan to negotiate?" asked Frank, leaning forward to stare into her eyes.

"We wanted you to experience the same rejection the employees experienced when Mr. Boswell refused to see them." She folded her hands in front of her and looked directly at Doug. "We wanted you to know we mean business. This will be a long strike, long enough to get all of our demands. And we are now ready to negotiate. The three senior delegates and our attorney are waiting in the conference room." She smiled.

"Why don't you run along," recommended Doug. "We'll finish our coffee. We know where the conference room is."

"I'm sure you do," said Simba, adopting the tone of a mother soothing a child. She pushed up from the table slowly. "We'll be waiting." She walked casually out of the dining room.

"I could stand another cup of coffee," said Frank.

"Me, too . . . and a piece of pie."

CHAPTER FOURTEEN

Doug and Frank entered the conference room to find Simba talking quietly at the far end of the table to a little fat man with a bald head, no doubt the union attorney. There were also three young women, obviously union delegates.

Frank selected chairs midpoint on one side of the table.

"If you care to sit across from us, it might make it easier to talk." Frank looked straight ahead.

When there was no movement, Doug added, "Of course, we could move to the other end of the table so we have the full length between us. But I was under the impression you were ready to talk."

Simba stood and the rest of her team rose in unison. They moved around to the opposite side and sat with Simba across from Doug. They stared daggers at Doug.

"Here are our demands." Simba leaned forward, folding her hands on the table. "We want a twenty percent pay increase. The workers are so underpaid it's clear the hospital is exploiting them." She pointed her finger at Doug. "We want a three-year contract that guarantees them a nineteen percent increase each year."

Neither Doug nor Frank made a response.

"We also want a prior-practices clause that guarantees no change that would place an existing job in jeopardy. We want a grievance procedure that guarantees worker protection against improper management activity." Simba was brisk and business-like. There was no smile. The absolute self-assurance was the same as when she stood in Doug's office.

She continued with a litany of demands more like mandates. "There will be a shift differential of seventy cents an hour for all full-time employees working a shift that begins after twelve noon and before 6:00 a.m.

"There will be three weeks paid vacation accrued in the first year of employment. Any employee in the bargaining unit will receive four weeks vacation after five years of employment."

Not once did she remove her fixed stare from Doug.

"We demand check-off." She paused. "For your information, Mr. Carpenter, since you may not know, check-off means you will deduct union dues from the members' paychecks and pay it to the union each month."

Throughout the monolog, the union team focused on Doug as though he were the only one there. Doug glanced at Frank and saw he was ignoring the tactic, watching Simba like he was a snake ready to sink into a bird.

"I want you also to know that what I've mentioned so far is a representative sampling of our demands. Mr. Wichard, our attorney, has a complete listing."

Mr. Wichard slipped a copy of the demands across the table to Doug, who pushed them over to Frank.

"We've already seen the list. Perhaps it would be more productive if we started at the beginning," said Frank. "And the beginning has to do with the fact you're already on strike and there's been no discussion of the demands. This shows bad faith." Frank leaned forward focusing on Simba.

Simba did not shift her gaze from Doug. "I believe there should be one spokesperson from each side at this bargaining table."

"We'll both speak. If you want to be the only spokesperson from your union, that's fine."

"Would you clarify why you've gone on strike without discussion? How can you justify a strike when there's been no deadlock in negotiations?" asked Frank.

"I imagine you two gentlemen now understand we mean business," Simba turned her gaze to Frank. "I would also imagine you realize the quicker you give in to our demands, the quicker the employees will be back on the job."

Frank smiled. "I imagine even you can figure out we can permanently replace every employee who walks off the job without legal justification." His grin showed a barricade of white teeth. "If you want to bargain in good faith, get your members back to work. Then we'll talk." He nudged Doug and they both pushed from the table and stood.

Simba stared straight ahead. She didn't change expression. "We have time, Mr. Big Deal. We'll wait until we hear from you." She stared at Frank, ignoring Doug as though he were a nonperson. "The strike will continue until you are willing to bargain and agree with our demands. We strike until a satisfactory agreement is reached on the employees' behalf." She stood and extended her hand to Frank. "Thank you for coming."

Frank ignored her hand. "We'll consider whether or not we want to deal with someone who doesn't bargain in good faith."

For just a moment, Doug could see a spark in Simba's eyes. "Good night, Miss Simba."

Outside, Frank shook his head, saying, "That's some bitch."

"Yeah, she's an effective choreographer. Let's go to the hospital and study their demands. I think we ought to solidify our position."

* * *

Ann and a half-dozen department heads and nurses were congregated in the outer office. Most were wearing shorts or jeans. Ann was wearing a light blue running suit. They had all brought in overnight bags days ago, anticipating the strike.

"How did it go?" asked Ann.

"At least the demands were mentioned. We're going to study them now. Any coffee around?"

"In here," said Frank, already in Doug's office.

"There's a whole urn in there," Ann called after him. "I don't know how much Dietary expects you to drink."

"Maybe they thought I would share a few cups with others. Let's move it out here. We're going to hole up and someone might have a caffeine fit while we're secluded." Doug did so, then closed the door.

"The wage ultimatum is more out of sight than usual," said Frank. "We're going to have to counter with a cent an hour increase and stick with it for a while, so we have room to negotiate. We can give on other things. They aren't going to be satisfied with reasonable demands." He leaned back in the chair he chose and laced his fingers behind his neck. "I can't get over that black bitch."

"Don't underestimate her, Frank."

"Face it, right now we're dealing with a black slut leading a nigger union."

"They're representing white employees, too, Frank."

"Oh? How many whites were there tonight? Don't kid yourself. This is a black union. To my knowledge, all the superstructure is black. There's one white delegate. They'll be glad to take dues from whites, but they're representing blacks, the spear chuckers and alligator bait. Don't kid yourself. And let me tell you something else. They don't give a damn about your hospital or your patients, just their own pocketbooks." Frank seemed about to explode, having to explain something so obvious. "If it's not a nigger union, why isn't there any white leadership in it?"

"Maybe the blacks are the ones that need representation right now."

"Shit. They're all on welfare, whether they're working or not. You can't walk the streets without being mugged. They don't work so they can live off welfare, get unions to back them when they do work so they can get as much as possible for as little as possible, and they have the blue-nosed liberals to back up their rights." Frank's forced smile was like a picket fence of hate. "Well, they picked the wrong guy to mess with. What increase were you going to give them this year? Five percent? They'll be lucky to get more than one."

"I think I could settle for five or six."

"Shit, no. We'll give them one or two, even three, maybe. Give them anything else, but keep the increase down. That way the union looks like the loser. We don't want the rank and file to think they won."

"No, Frank. If you give them anything else they want, they'll be the winners. Make no mistake about it. The past-practices demand could kill us. We wouldn't be able to make any improvements resulting in man-hour savings. No. We bargain on each issue and we do what's fair."

"'We do what's fair,'" Frank mimicked. "Had you planned to give them all those demands before the union came along? Bullshit, Doug."

"I'm going to get another cup of coffee." Frank's distortions had made him argue against his own side. "I don't agree with your racist views."

"Of course," Frank called over his shoulder as Doug went into the outer office. "Who do you think bombed your wife? Albert Schweitzer?"

After another thirty minutes, Frank was ready to leave. "I could handle this a lot better without you, Doug."

"We'll both be there for every session, and you know why. I can't trust you. You'll give them everything except salary, just to make yourself look good."

"Shit."

Doug asked Ann to stay in the command center while he made rounds to make sure everything was in order. He dropped in on Ed Whyte, who was being kept overnight.

"I'm expecting the hospital to find the goons that did this to me."

"The police are on it, Ed. How are you feeling?"

"Not good. And the nurses aren't checking as often as they should."

"I thought they would be fighting over you."

"Yeah," Ed smiled grimly, "and the loser gets to take care of me. I hope you aren't going to give in to this gangster union. We won't be able to tell these people anything. It's bad enough as it is."

"By law, they have the right to organize. We can't control that."

"That's what Administration is supposed to do. That's your job. I don't know who to blame for my being confined here, the union or you. I should sue the hospital for maladministration."

A nurse came in to check Ed's eyes, and Doug used that as an excuse to leave.

Doug made another trip to check on Bess. In the hall, he saw Kay O'Connell bustling in his direction. Juanita glided along beside her. Kay seemed flustered, more than normal even for her job as director of Nursing at Eastern.

"Doug, we've got problems."

"No kidding."

"No, I mean we've got even more. We just had two patients die and Dr. Smith is saying it's abnormal."

"You already know we're abnormally high in deaths."

Juanita placed her hand on Kay's shoulder to soothe her. "We are, but these were both terminal cases. They were expected to die. It's good that their suffering is over."

"Is Smith the attending?"

Juanita hugged Kay by the shoulders. "No, Jeep."

"Jeep?" Doug had a bad taste just from saying the name.

He hadn't hidden his reaction, and Juanita nodded as though in agreement. "Yes, Jeep, in both cases."

Kay pulled away, taking charge again, or maybe for the first time. "Juanita found them. She and two staff nurses took them to the morgue."

Doug nodded in recognition. *No orderlies. They're all out on strike.* "Have the families been called?"

"Neither of them had families." Juanita bowed her head slightly. "They were both dying slowly and alone."

Kay was fidgeting again, and Doug knew there was more.

"Doug, that's not all."

Doug waited.

"The nurses are walking out."

"Are they honoring the picket line?"

"No. They're protesting the fact that Robinson hasn't been dumped. They won't work in a hospital where murder is condoned. At twelve midnight, they're walking out."

"Is everybody walking?"

"We'll have the head nurses, the clinical nurse specialists, and the supervisors. In all, we'll have forty-nine nurses, which amounts to a skeleton crew, to take care of the house. Right now, we have five hundred and six patients. And spreading forty-nine nurses over three shifts is thin coverage."

"Okay." Doug settled down. "What's your game plan?"

"We're splitting into uneven shifts. We'll have thirty-two on for sixteen hours, seven a.m. to eleven p.m., and seventeen covering the night shift. We're already lining up agency nurses to help us out. But a lot of them won't cross a picket line."

Doug glanced at Juanita, who seemed so calm and in control. "Is—"

"No," said Kay, anticipating his question. "Juanita has functioned more as a roving head nurse than a staff nurse. So we've given her that title. She's staying."

"Is the Nurse Association buying that?"

"Doesn't matter. There are head nurses in that group, too. And anyhow, this walkout isn't sanctioned by the association."

Doug didn't like to think the enemy had expanded to include Nursing. He was glad Juanita was staying, not that her being there diminished the problem. "Get hold of Personnel and draw from the labor pool for help with non-patient functions."

He moved over to the nurse's station and picked up a phone. Kay and Juanita were already moving toward the elevators.

"Oh, and Kay, you have to leave yourself free for other things as well."

"I'll be doing patient care."

"Not the whole time. Keep yourself free."

The elevator doors opened and Kay moved out of sight. Doug became aware the nurses on the floor were rushing through their routines. The evening shift personnel were still there even though it was now after eleven-thirty. He called his office.

"Ann. Get ahold of Henry. He may be in the pressroom or over in PR. Tell him to be on the alert. The nurses are walking out in about thirty minutes. He may get some calls from the media.

He's to tell them some nurses left, but we have enough staff to provide necessary care. Essential activity will not be affected."

"Good grief! Why are they walking out?"

"Robinson. And we have to guard against the press getting hold of that. I don't know if they're going to demonstrate or not. If they do, the word will get out. Explain the whole thing to Henry. Is Stan around?"

"Ha. Are you kidding? He and Liz left around six o'clock. They said 'good night,' though."

"Okay. I'll call him at home when I get down there. Right now, I'm going to see Bess. Call Cliff to let him know he'll see a bunch of nurses leaving at midnight, and tell him to let us know if they hang around, if they join the picketers, or what. Let as many department heads know as you can get hold of."

"Most of them have been wandering in and out of here the whole evening. What are we going to do?"

"We've got it under control with the nursing management staff, for the time being."

Bess was wide awake, propped up and reading a book. "Get me out of here," she said.

"You're beautiful," he crooned, and meant it.

"What's going on in this place? I've never seen so many nurses. See, here's one now."

A young nurse swept in, fresh and crisp. "I just want to check your eyes again, Mrs. Carpenter."

"For the nine hundredth time this evening," said Bess, smiling at Doug.

"Oh, don't say that, Mrs. Carpenter. It's only the eight hundredth time." She focused a small beam of light into the pupils one after the other. "Uh-huh, yep. They're okay. Are you having any headaches, any dizziness?"

"No. Can I go home now?"

"That's the same question she's asked everybody all evening. You'd think she didn't like us."

"Think what it'd be like if she thought you would abandon her," said Doug.

The girl turned to him. There was purpose in her expression that outweighed her youth, her amber bangs, and light brown eyes. "We're all concerned about quality." Leaving the room, she paused in the doorway. "And we're going to protect that quality." Then she was gone.

"Did I miss something?" asked Bess.

"Some funny things happened on the way to disaster." Doug sat on the bed, holding her hand. He told her about Simba's antics, Frank Street's love for his fellow man, the two deaths, Ed Whyte's usual condemnation, Robinson, and the nurses' walkout.

"Poor baby. Sounds like I'm not the only one who got bombed." She squeezed his hand. "Outside of those few trifles, it's just been another day in the salt mine." She raised her hands toward the unseen sky and exclaimed, "Let's both get out of here."

The nurse returned and stood in the doorway for a moment. "We're leaving, now, Mr. Carpenter." She straightened her blouse and seemed to be fumbling for words. "I'm sorry."

Doug raised his hand then let it drop as she left.

Bess grasped his hand again.

"You know," he uttered, "this is beginning to feel like an invasion from Mars. The war of the worlds."

"It's ugly. Doug, I know Frank Street's a bigot, but maybe he's right about the union not caring about others."

"I hate for him to be right."

* * *

When Doug walked into his office, Mary Jane McCarthy, the laboratory director, was talking to Ann.

"Everyone's been informed," said Ann.

He noticed a cot behind her desk. "You're going to sleep there?"

"It's just for tonight. I have a bed upstairs. After things settle, I'll be up there."

In the office, Doug dialed Stan's home number.

"Stan, so you don't get blindsided by the press, our staff nurses walked out, but things are under control."

"I told you they wouldn't cross the picket line!" he shouted.

"They're protesting the Robinson incident. We've talked about him before, Stan, but now we've got to *do* something about him."

"I'm not going to let a bunch of smartass nurses blackmail me. He stays. They go. Replace them. I want it done right now."

"I'll talk to you tomorrow, Stan." He could hear Stan still shouting as he dropped the phone back in its cradle.

CHAPTER FIFTEEN

He missed his bed with Bess beside him. Thoughts tumbled like a cluster of leaves and swept away sleep. He fought the discomfort of the flimsy cot, the noisy street, and the harsh lights from the city. The air vent in the ceiling carried the same monotonous tone as during the day, a continuous syrup of sound. His imagination tried to convert it to the soothing sound of the ocean, then the wind off the coast.

"They go. Replace them. I want it done right now."

He needed sleep. Tomorrow would be another tornado. *When will it end?* Bess was sleeping floors above him. A heavy truck jolted by on the street. The cot was narrow and hard. City lights flooded through the Venetian blinds.

"We're leaving, now, Mr. Carpenter. I'm really sorry."

His pajamas were twisted around his leg.

"We're dealing with a black slut leading a nigger union." Why couldn't Frank Street be on the other side?

Then he saw Bess, who never hurt anyone, unconscious and covered with paint.

He worked at relaxing his fists, his arms, his shoulders, remembering soft white clouds in a Virginia sky, tall pines with breezes sighing through needles, mountain laurel and nandina, the sweet odor of straw and clover, jay birds calling and flashing through the thicket.

An ambulance wailed through the night to the emergency room. From the light through the window, he could read his watch. *Three o'clock.* He might have slept a little. He felt more relaxed. He rolled to his other side.

He thought of Doris Headerman and John Lutz, classmates at Duke. He hadn't written to them in six months. Both had problems in their hospitals. He could let them know they weren't bad off by comparison.

This time he knew he had slept. *Five o'clock.* He swung his feet to the floor, stood, stretched his shoulder muscles, and breathed deeply to clear his head, then opened the blind. The west lawn was quiet and dark, but in the east, the sun was beginning to creep into the edge of the sky.

He sat at his desk, turned on the lamp, and took out some paper.

Dear Doris and John,

I can't remember which of you is to receive the Xerox copy this time. I'll flip a coin, but I just want to let you know things are running at such a normal pace my life has become routine.

The vice president for Health here at Eastern College Hospital is a psychopath and wants to fire me and everybody else. I believe he had a nut case working for him at his previous hospital and wants to bring him in to fill my job. This tends to create a high energy level that causes me to rise earlier in the morning and allows me to function far into the night, a condition for which I am extremely thankful. I now know what 'grateful dead' means. Speaking of which, we have a higher number of deaths than the acceptable average, complicated by the fact that we have doctors who won't tell terminal patients they're dying.

A little over a week ago, we narrowly missed an opportunity

to gut and renovate the main hospital building when we discovered that a large quantity of picric acid in the labs had crystallized, which I believe is one of the elements in T.N.T. or one of its first cousins. If you discover some in your labs, and you've wanted to start a building program, you might be able to avoid some of the red tape associated with approvals. If not, call the bomb squad and don't touch the damn stuff. By the way, an excellent pathologist caused the problem. It just shows the best of us can become complacent and go astray.

The Chair of Medicine has demanded I fire my Director of Nursing. The pathologist has resigned. The Chair of Anesthesiology has been drunk during procedures several times and has killed at least one patient. Nursing has demanded his firing (and rightly so) and last night, all but their supervisory staff walked off the job to protest his continued presence. The Vice-President of Total Destruction and the medical staff continue to sit on their hands and tie mine. It's reached a point where I'm going to have to bring it to a head and place my own job in jeopardy, but, since it already is, that may not be a factor.

This all tends to imbue me with a sense of discipline, for which I'll be forever indebted because I no doubt needed it, having grown up in a slow and easy place where I was misguided by the idea that *people count.*

The Chair of OBGYN wants to inaugurate a program that will raise his census and place the patients in jeopardy, and the VP and medical staff support him. They all want to doctor the figures to 'prove' the need for more beds in the new building. There's the usual power and dollar reward motivating them.

This has taught me to see the other guy's point of view, even when he's wrong. And that's certainly a valuable lesson in survival.

In these same routine days, the VP has instructed me to develop a false set of drawings to show firewalls have been installed above the ceilings so we can avoid spending big bucks to keep the building safe.

It's obvious I have some misplaced values. I don't know why we didn't all discover that at Duke. I've certainly learned a lot since then. As ignorant as I was, how could you guys have nominated me for class president?

Oh, I didn't mention the suicide. The Chair of Psych didn't want a medical patient in the Psych Unit. The patient dived out the window. I just keep forgetting it's an imposition on the psychiatrists and psych nurses to give care to anything other than the brain.

I seem to have developed this notion that hospitals are for patients.

The mental fog from fettered sleep lifted as he wrote:

Maybe I should be a dictator, maybe I should knock heads. The hospital workers' union thinks I'm in it for the big bucks and power. In these ordinary days, we've had a strike and I'm sleeping in my office from which this letter is being written as the sun threatens the eastern horizon.

Some interesting encounters with the union have raised some self-doubts about racism. I'll tell you more about that when I've figured it out myself. The union publicity has made me look like a smacked ass. All the greed and incompetence is my fault.

If I were a man of great courage (instead of great wisdom), I would stand before the masses and proclaim all I know and take my lumps. I had a job pumping gas when I was in high school. Maybe it's still open. Or I could get a job working for an HMO, screwing the doctors out of their fees. That might work, except they are screwing the patients, too.

All of this has done a lot to help me determine what I want to be when I grow up. It isn't often one gets such good vocational guidance. I'd be a clod not to be grateful.

But I've been saving the best for last. Bess, who is my whole life, and who sends her love—just as soon as she finds out I've written to you—Bess was injured by a paint bomb thrown into our home by a union goon. She who loves so much and would die before hurting anyone.

Doug stopped, laid his head on his hands, and cried. His shoulders shook as he sobbed out loud. Then, just as quickly, he sat erect, took a deep breath, and picked up the pen.

You can tell by my wording I've still not learned to completely control my emotions.

She's okay now and is upstairs here at Eastern. All the paint is washed off and the cuts cleaned and bandaged.

He paused again.

There are only a few visible marks, and most people won't even notice them.

So, it's easy to see I've received some gifts of rare learning. Well . . .

Light tapping on the door broke the silence.

"Come in."

Ann opened the door. She looked half-asleep, her hair wisping across her face. "Are you all right?"

She had heard him crying. He felt his face flush in embarrassment. "I'm okay. I guess I woke you." He laughed nervously. "Sorry about that."

"I wasn't sleeping all that much. Is something wrong?" No sooner was the question out of her mouth than she lifted her arms toward the sky and repeated, "Is anything wrong? What a stupid question!" She sat and looked across the desk at him.

"Doug, if there's anything I can do, let me know. And you know that everyone in this building right now would do whatever you asked—well, almost everyone. So, if you need any heroic efforts from any of us, just say so."

"I think that's what everybody's doing. Especially you. I can count on you. Bess calls this place a pool of viciousness, and she's right, except for you, the department managers, and some of the staff. We know who they are. I often wonder why you stick it out here, but thank God you do."

"If you left, I would, too." She blushed. "Don't forget what I said." Ann headed for the door.

"Ann."

She stopped in the doorway and hugged the door frame waiting for him to speak.

"I'm glad you know I was that upset. It helps. But don't let the others know. Wouldn't help morale."

"Got it. I'm glad, too."

He slapped his pen down on the desk. "If you want to use the shower in the executive bathroom, you better get down there, because after I've used it there's going to be water dripping from the ceiling and pouring out from under the door."

"You do a good job of covering your feelings." She started to move, then paused. "Sometimes I wonder what makes you stay on here, but things are better because you do." Pushing away from the door frame, she declared, "Time to get started."

CHAPTER SIXTEEN

Back from the shower, Doug felt refreshed. He needed normalcy, centering, and Bess could give him that. He dropped his toilet kit off in the office and headed for the elevator as Kay O'Connell glided down the hall, smiling.

"Things have taken a turn for the better. You'll be glad to know the nurses are back. The day shift just arrived in full force."

"They're back on the floors?"

"Yep, right on time."

"So, the only ones who walked out were the night shift."

"Right. They all agreed to this to voice their objection to Robinson. There's a letter signed by all of them coming to you."

"Am I supposed to get it today?"

"From what I hear."

"That's good because the night shift personnel aren't going to be allowed back."

"What?"

"Come on in. We'll talk."

Kay followed him into the office. "What do you mean they can't come back?"

"They abandoned their patients."

Kay dropped into a chair as though dazed. "I don't believe what I'm hearing."

"Do you feel they should just walk back in?"

"We need them. If the night shift can't come back, the rest will leave. You can't do this."

"Think about it. They took matters into their own hands. We can't let them sacrifice their patients to emphasize a point."

"They didn't sacrifice the patients. They knew all the patients would get good care because it was only for the one night and the supervisory staff had agreed to fill in for them."

"They agreed to fill in for them?"

Kay, near tears, admitted, "All right, we all agreed to it. It was the only way to make the point."

"Kay, you and your supervisory staff conspired for them to walk off the job? Do you realize you promoted a lawless strike? What example have you set?"

She wiped her eyes and sniffled. "Doug, it was the only way. They were all going to walk out. We talked them into the token gesture of a one-night walkout, at a time when no patient would suffer. We told them we were on their side and we would support them." She leaned forward. "Doug, if they had a mass walkout, it would've been a disaster. And think what the newspapers would've done with it."

"Do you think this won't get into the newspapers?"

"How will the newspapers get it?"

"For one thing, everybody on the picket line saw the nurses walk out last night. For another, don't think there aren't some union plants still working in the building. One of your own nurses could be a strong union sympathizer and tell the whole story."

"And what would have happened if everyone had walked out and stayed out?"

"We would've coped with it, just as we are going to cope with this. Thing is, we've got to be able to trust each other."

A well of tears on the verge of spilling out did just that as she looked at him, waiting for instructions, or the next shoe to drop.

"Sorry to put you through that, Kay. But in the far recesses of my mind, I thought you might have arranged the whole thing. It was the only way I could know for sure."

Kay's face turned on like a flashbulb. "You son-of-a-gun. You had me going. I thought you meant it. I could see them all walking out. Please don't ever do that to me again." She looked relieved, hand clasped to her chest.

"I do mean it, but at the same time, I don't."

Kay stopped laughing abruptly. "I better let you explain that because I don't know where this conversation's going."

"While we're talking about not ever doing that to you, don't ever do that to me again either. I can think of more appropriate ways for the nurses to make their point. I've got to talk to them about the seriousness of what they did, and they've got to recognize it before they come back."

"Doug, you're going to make things worse. They're all keyed up about Robinson, but he's just a symbol of the worst doctors." Kay was almost shouting. "If you go up against the nurses, you'll bring it to a head and destroy the image of this hospital forever."

"I know that. You know that. I'm hoping they know that. Schedule a meeting with the night shift in Cannon Hall for eleven p.m., and have your supervisory staff work in their place—for the whole eight hours, if necessary."

Kay sighed and pushed out of the chair. "Okay. We'll call them all and tell them to go directly to Cannon Hall, but you're going to ruin everything." She paused, having opened the door. "By the way, just to make things interesting around here, we had another terminal patient die last night. We'd already arranged for her admission to a nursing home, but—"

"This had nothing to do with our being shorthanded, did it?"

"No, the staffing level was normal last night."

"That's right. I forgot you knew there was only one shift to cover."

Kay winced a little at the slight jab. "It does look bad from the point of view of our averages, but she was terminal, no surprise."

She hesitated for another moment, and Doug asked, "Was it one of Jeep's patients?"

A little puzzled, she replied, "As a matter of fact, it was. He's been notified." When Doug said nothing else, she reminded him, "Got to go get people on the horn."

When Ann returned from breakfast, she told Doug, "I asked the Dietary A-team to deliver a breakfast tray for you to Bess's room. It's on the way now. Better scoot. I'll call you if anything out of the ordinary happens."

"Out of the ordinary. Right."

When Doug walked out into the hall, he could smell paper burning. He stuck his head in the office, but Ann anticipated him.

"Someone set a trash can on fire. Security already put it out. That's not 'out of the ordinary.'"

When Doug arrived in Bess's room, the tray was set on a bedside stand adjusted for a chair next to her bed. She was smiling and waiting for him.

"It was so like you to have your breakfast sent here. Hurry and kiss me. I'm hungry."

Doug pushed her tray aside and blended his mouth into hers. "It looks to me as though you are ready to go home."

"Is that how you guys tell if your patients are cured?"

"Only the pretty ones. What do I have to eat?"

"Whatever you ordered, dummy."

"Actually, I have to confess, Ann ordered it. It was her idea."

"Hmm. Sounds like a smokescreen to me. What'd you two do last night?"

"We made love all night. What would you expect when two innocent people are thrown together by fate?"

"Don't give me two innocent people. Tell the truth. Haven't you ever felt attracted to her? She's beautiful, you know."

"Yes, she is beautiful. And I've noticed. But I've got you and you're a unique combination of everything I've ever wanted."

When he leaned over his plate to scoop some egg, he grinned at her in that boyish way she so loved. "Ann slept in her office, and I slept in mine. But if we had slept in the same office, in fact, if we had slept in the same bed, nothing would have happened." He gave an exaggerated sigh. "Besides, she's taken."

He winced as Bess slapped him on the head with the morning newspaper.

"It's a good thing she arranged this breakfast or I just might have been worried."

"Hmmm, smokescreen worked."

Bess finished her coffee. "Speaking of smokescreens reminds me of a paint screen. I guess I'll go home and start scraping paint."

"You'll do nothing of the sort. The hospital's insurance will cover the damage. We'll call Eastern contractors, get a bid, and let them do it. You rest. Read a book. Talk on the phone. Call and tell me you love me so I don't get swept away by Ann."

Bess pushed the call button.

"Yes?" came the response.

"Tell Dr. Hoozits—" She looked at Doug. "What is the name of that resident who admitted me?"

"Hoozits?"

"Oh, I can't remember because the paint blotted out my memory. Anyhow, tell him I'm recovered and I'm going home to see if paint got on anything but me."

Doug leaned over the bed and kissed her. "If he decides to discharge you, let me know. I'll drive you home. I think we ought to see it together." Going out the door, he paused. "By the way, his name is Prince Manuel Frobischer."

Bess reached for her newspaper.

Doug walked through the main building. From the top floor down, everyone was busy—rushing, more like it—but they were cheerful.

"Hi, Doug," said Mary Jane McCarthy.

"How's the lab doing?"

"Everything's fine. Some of our billing may be late getting out, but all the patient tests are on schedule. I can hardly believe it myself. And everyone's so cooperative. The residents have pitched in and are doing everything we ask them to do."

"Some of the attendings should take lessons from those guys."

"You can say that again. Where do they go wrong? They're okay when they're residents, but sometime after that, they get greedy. What happens?"

"If I knew the answer to that I'd be head of the UN. Let me know if you have any problems."

On the fourth floor, he ran into Joe Goldman.

"Joe, we've got to get rid of Al Robinson. He's got to go."

"I heard about the nurses."

"Yeah, well the word's bound to get around, but it's not just the nurses. Joe, he can't do the job."

"What do you want me to do? I'll help any way I can."

"It's got to be done through the Medical Staff Board. Otherwise, it won't stick. Can you call an emergency meeting of the executive committee?"

"I can get them together for lunch today. They're all here. No one's on vacation this week. But I think it's a waste of time. They'll protect him."

"We've got to give it a try. I'll see if I can get Stan to attend."

Doug went directly to Stan's office. His door was shut.

"Liz, is Stan in?"

"Yes. I'll ask him to buzz you when he's free."

"Who's in there with him?"

"No one. He's not to be disturbed. He's going over plans."

"The hell with that." Doug opened the door.

Stan jumped in surprise. "Well, why don't you come in?"

Doug shut the door behind himself.

Putting down his pen, Stan glared. "Do you have everything under control? Are the nurses back?"

"Yes." Doug expected the astonished look and continued, "There's an emergency meeting of the executive committee of the Medical Staff Board at noon today. We'll be discussing Al Robinson. Stan, he can't continue to practice anesthesiology here."

"You handle it with them. Leave me out of it."

"You should be there."

"I'll be out of the building. And don't you tell me what to do. I know what's best, and right now what's best is not to cross the medical staff." He shook his head in disbelief. "I'd think you had enough on your hands right now without taking on the doctors. But if that's what you want to do, go ahead. It's your ass, not mine." He shook his head again. "You're in the middle of a strike. The nurses are unstable, and now you're going to pick on the doctors. I just want you to know if you screw this up, I'll ask for your resignation."

Thoroughly disgusted, Doug made to leave, saying, "I'll talk to you later. But just for your information, I didn't pick this time. Robinson killed a patient. You don't wait until a convenient time to correct that kind of problem." He closed the door firmly. *Bastard. Maybe I should go to the Hospital Board. But they really don't know what's going on in the first place, and if they did, they don't have to deal with it.* That was just the problem. They wouldn't believe it. They'd think he was trying to promote himself. It would just stir things up more. He remembered a sign he had seen on a small bridge in the Everglades. PLEASE DON'T AGGRAVATE THE ALLIGATORS. *Yeah, right.*

"Dr. Goldman wants you to call him," said Ann as he walked past her desk.

"I just left him." Doug dialed and Joe picked up the phone before the first ring finished. "Are you trying to hatch that thing?"

"No, I was just reaching for it to call another one of our courageous officers of the medical staff. Gutless wonders."

"What's happening?"

"I've just talked to three of them and they refuse to even meet to discuss Robinson. And Jack Apple's next on the list, and I already know how he feels. So that'll make four. We need another game plan."

"Tell them if they don't meet to discuss it, I'll go see the Chairman of the Board of Trustees. It's better if they police their own mess instead of having the Board come down on top of them. See what reaction you get."

"Worth a try. I'll let you know."

The lunch meeting was set up in a small conference room next to Joe's office. Doug was early, but the rest had beat him there.

"Sit over here," Joe motioned with his pen. "I chose this room because of the round table—no head. I want this to be an open discussion. We are all peers in the health business, and we have a problem that affects the hospital."

Doug sat between Joe and Jack Apple, who didn't look up from his coleslaw. Across the circle sat Elmo Bunting, who had once been Chair of Surgery but had grown weary of it after three years. He had reached that pinnacle late in life and didn't have the energy to sustain it. His head was bowed over his plate, where he was teasing the food with a fork. He slowly raised his eyes to look at Doug. No change of expression. No acknowledgment.

To Elmo's left, plate already empty, Bert Allen sat with his arms folded across his chest. Eyes like black marbles, he examined Doug. Bert was the youngest member of the executive committee. He was an internist noted for his excellent diagnostic ability and his explosive temper.

To Elmo's right, the Chair of Dermatology, Jasper Gunderson, a straw-blond giant, sat hunched over his plate, chewing. His watery blue eyes focused on Doug as he nodded his head slightly then looked beyond at Joe.

Doug glanced at the plate in front of him, a small mountain of shrimp. He wondered who had prepared it with so little help in the kitchen. He looked at Joe, who seemed to read his mind.

"I asked them to send the simplest thing they could, and this was it. The dietitians figured it would be a morale booster for everyone stuck in the building. They said they have two tons and we should ask for seconds."

Doug felt guilty that he would think Joe could do anything that smacked as special treatment for the doctors. "You never know, it might help."

"Let's get on with the meeting," said Jack Apple, still looking at his food.

Joe shifted in his chair and leaned forward, folding his large hands on the table. "Al Robinson has an alcohol problem. There was an incident in the delivery room, which you all know about. Out of concern for Al, and for the patients and the hospital, we've got to take protective action."

"Action to protect who from what?" asked Bert.

"Action to protect Al from himself," said Joe. "Action to protect patients from Al's problem—"

"From what I hear, it could have been an equipment malfunction," interrupted Bert, who sat with his arms still folded across his chest. "Until there's proof, we can't do anything."

Elmo laid down his fork and addressed Doug, "This meeting is an imposition. If you want to go to the Chair of the Board of Trustees, do it. That's your decision. Our decision will be to go to the Chair of the Board of Trustees and ask for your termination. Why don't you just run the hospital and let us practice medicine?" With that he smacked and sucked air through his teeth.

Doug wasn't surprised by this comment. "You're right. I'm not qualified to practice medicine, but I am qualified to exercise administrative judgment. Eight days ago, Al had to be relieved in the middle of a procedure. He had been drinking. No one was hurt. It wasn't the first time. We don't need to go through all that. But, yesterday was different—"

"Shit fire!" Bert slammed his fist on the table as he jumped up. "You *don't know* what happened yesterday!"

Joe put his hand on Bert's arm. "He's an alcoholic, Bert. We've got to face it."

Bert jerked his arm away. "He's a fine physician, and I'm not going to allow him to be railroaded. No way. You conduct a careful study to show who was really at fault, and we'll meet when we have something to meet about."

"Jack, you're a surgeon and have more contact with him. What's your feeling?" asked Joe.

"This meeting is a damned waste of time."

"Has he worked with you?"

"Yes, and he's never been drunk."

"Elmo?"

"I've never had a problem with him."

"Then why are we here?" asked Bert.

Joe held up his hand like a traffic cop. "Wait. I know he's a fine anesthesiologist. He does regionals better than anyone in the city. And he's a fine person. But I'm worried."

"Oh, for fuck's sake!" Bert flung himself back in his chair.

"Bert," insisted Joe, "there's reason for concern."

"Conduct an investigation," proposed Jack Apple. "Set up an ad hoc committee, Joe, and have them report their findings to the Medical Staff Board. I'll volunteer to chair it."

"That sounds reasonable," mumbled Jasper, still hunched over his food. "If anyone's to investigate a physician, it should be another physician."

"Okay, can we go now?" Bert asked impatiently.

Doug looked at Bert, then Elmo, then Jasper. Jack was staring at his empty plate. "Joe, I can agree to that approach on one condition: that Al not be scheduled for any procedures until it's resolved."

"No way." Bert crossed and recrossed his arms as if flagging down a semi. "We've no grounds to suspend him."

"I'll agree to there being no suspension. Just don't schedule him. We'll conduct a thorough investigation. If he's an alcoholic, we'll give him a leave of absence to get himself straightened out."

"Are we agreed?" asked Joe.

There was silence for a few moments.

"Jack, how long will it take to conduct an investigation?" asked Elmo.

"Right now, with the strike going on, a day or two. I've got nothing else to do, except for a few post-ops."

"Jack, I want to ask several others to work with you," said Joe.

"Fine. You name them."

"Elmo?"

"Alright."

"Doug? We'll need your help getting records. Incident reports. Okay?"

"I'll find the time whenever you need it."

"I want to work with you also." Joe wanted this to be even and impartial.

"So," said Jack, "what do we do to get started?"

"Doug, can we get started with the incident reports?"

"Where do you want them delivered?"

Doug headed for his office. Jack Apple had volunteered as a ploy to appease Doug. *Jackass Apple. He'll try to clear Al, but Joe will make whitewashing difficult.*

Images of Jean Daniels invaded his mind. He had never seen her, or her two redheaded girls, or her husband. But he pictured her and the family, and a third redheaded urchin, all of them happily chattering away in some fairyland.

And he pictured the father holding two little redheaded cherubs, their tear-streaked faces looking at a casket. There lay Jean Daniels, undisturbed by the sobs above her, the heartache around her.

Ann looked up as he zipped past her desk. "Henry Sims just called. According to the morning news, the union's claiming the hospital is seeing an abnormally high death rate since the strike started."

"Damn. We can't win. We can't announce it was already high, and we can't deny it."

"There's also good news. Bess called. She's being discharged."

CHAPTER SEVENTEEN

Bess gazed out the car window as they passed through Solstory. Doug watched her from the corner of his eye. She looked like the goddess of springtime. He worried about what they would see when they got home.

"It always makes me sad to drive through this part of the city," said Bess. "Aside from the bad memories, there's so much poverty and depression. So much hurt and want."

"Hurt, want, and hate, lashing out because life has rejected them, although some of them are doing the rejecting."

Bess gazed as though she had forgotten where they were going. "I look at this area and imagine people who've been here for years with no hope, shells of what they could've been. I always think of Vachel Lindsay's poem about the world's one big failure. 'Its poor are ox-like, limp and leaden-eyed.'"

Limp and leaden-eyed. That's how Doug had seen Bess in his nightmares about losing his job. A bag lady. "They blame their poverty on whites. Not white bigots. Whites. Bigotry is the problem, but there are as many black bigots as white. I hate bigots, black or white."

Bess put her hand on his arm. He knew she didn't like this kind of talk.

"Maybe this is where Simba's from. Maybe she thinks I let Solstory down because I didn't care. Maybe she thinks I'm a white bigot. After all, I am white, and I am from the South."

They pulled to the curb in front of the house. The security guard leaned down to the car window. "Been awful quiet around here." He had a wide bucktooth grin. "How you feeling, Mrs. Carpenter?" His face grew somber. "Don't know what the world's coming to."

She hesitated a moment, looking at the house. "Let's just say we've had a growing experience."

"That might be, but folks oughtn't do such things."

Everything looked normal from the front of the house, but then they opened the front door. Paint fumes pushed them back, stinging their eyes.

"Ahhgghh," yelled Doug, putting his arm around her. "Problems sure as hell don't go away if you ignore them."

They stepped into the living room and stopped. Doug bundled Bess tight in his arms to protect her from the sight.

"Oh, no! My beautiful house!" she exclaimed.

Red paint was splayed in a fan-shape path across the tan rug and up the opposite wall. "Oh, Doug." She buried her face in the side of his neck.

He gently rubbed her back, concern for her outweighing his anger.

Bess turned and looked again at their living room, wiping her eyes with the back of her hand. "Somehow, I'd thought of only the dining room." She tiptoed across the rug.

Doug followed, the paint smack-smacking under his shoes.

She picked up an object from the rug by an end table, cradling it. When she turned to Doug, her eyes were brimming with tears. "It's the little bear Janey made for me when she was five." She held out the papier-mâché figure with the lopsided ears. "It's covered with paint." Clutching it to her chest, she sobbed, "She . . ."

Doug pulled her to him. Her shoulders shook.

"She made it in . . . she . . . she made it in kindergarten." Bess cried her hurt into the little figure in her hands. "She . . . she was so excited. She . . ."

But she couldn't go on. Bess seemed to grow smaller as she leaned into him, his arms a secure cocoon of unconditional love.

After a few minutes, she stopped and straightened her back, saying, "Talk . . . talk about a catharsis." Bess took a deep breath before turning and placing the little bear on the table. Leaning against Doug, she seemed to be memorizing it. Finally, she looked toward the wall.

Doug followed her gaze. Even the pictures were covered. The lampshade was splattered, but still stood in place.

"The upholstered chair will have to go," she whispered.

Then they faced the dining room opening. It was a different world, like peeping inside an inferno. Except where the glass in the double French doors had been replaced by plywood, the room was blotched with red—walls, ceiling, floor, and furniture. They stood inside a painting of hell.

"It's still wet." Doug pointed to the carpet and his now red shoes. "We'll have to take our shoes off to walk into the kitchen."

They stared, trying to absorb the chaos.

"Oh," moaned Bess, her heart aching with each beat.

"There's one hell of a message here," said Doug, opening windows.

He called the contractor, who agreed to come out and give an estimate on everything except the furniture.

"That'll give me something to do," said Bess, who tried to smile, although her lips were quivering. "I'll make a list of the furniture that has to be refinished or replaced."

"Eastern will pay for it."

Doug hung around, not wanting to leave, but knowing he must. At last, he did, but first hugged her tight again.

Bess would be all right.

Crossing the narrow Woodside Bridge and gliding through Solstory, he made his way to Eastern, past the picketers, and into the parking deck.

Patient census was below normal. Rescue squads were bringing in fewer emergencies. *Maybe I should restrict elective admissions.* He called Kay.

"Doug, we're doing okay in Nursing. We have the staff for a full patient load. I don't know how it will be after you talk to the night shift. Please reconsider."

Doug was beyond irritated at this point. "I'm doing what I have to do, and I'm being open about it. That's more than you've been with me."

"Right now, I'm not so sure I want you to be open with me. I might be better off not knowing."

Doug put a clamp on his feelings and wandered around the building talking to everybody.

Pharmacy was having the biggest problem, run only by supervisors. Crazy that pharmacists should belong to a union. He asked the director if they could keep up the pace. They were under strain, filling prescriptions with so few of them to do it, but knowing he would curtail admissions if they wanted him to, they said they could keep up the pace. They worried about errors, not about being tired.

Henry Sims called. "Two of my clerks who are members of

the union came in and said they wanted to work. The labor pool assigned them to help on the patient units where the morale is higher than ever. In two hours, they were back on the street. I'm sure they're spreading word morale is high inside."

"Stroke of genius, putting them on the patient units. Actually, morale is high everywhere. It seems to be catching."

Doug ate a sandwich at his desk. Morale and adrenalin were high and everyone was running full tilt, but that couldn't last. Simba would be making rounds outside, giving pep talks. But being on the outside when things were going well on the inside was a bummer. The union would call to schedule a meeting soon. If they didn't, he'd consider Street's idea to permanently replace them. He would wait another day.

Ann came in from running errands around the building. "Boy, the A-Team is working. It's like work has become a party."

Henry Sims walked in. "I've got some disturbing news. I'm getting calls from the media wanting to know about an accidental death in the delivery room."

"Damn. How much do they know?"

"Apparently just that. They don't even know the name of the patient."

Doug thought for a moment, then told Ann, "Check with the delivery room and see what they listed as the cause of death for Mrs. Jean Daniels. Oh, and get the husband's name."

She was out of the room before he finished the sentence.

"There's no PR to answer this," said Henry.

"Henry, if they know there was a death, they'll get the name. Tell them you don't know of any accident."

"They're going to want more. We've got to give something to satisfy their curiosity or they'll just keep digging, especially since the union's claiming the death rate's going up."

"I know, but I don't want to lie to them. On the death rate, if they bring it up, tell them that's absolutely untrue. It has not gone up."

"Doug," called Ann from the outer office, "it's David Daniels and the cause was listed as cardiac arrest."

Doug was stunned. "I don't believe this bunch." He paused. "Okay, Henry, if they manage to get the name, you tell them the cause of death as listed. You don't know anything else." Cliff Toliver knocked on the doorjamb. "The placards outside are reading *Hospital Under-Staffed*, *Death in the Delivery Room*. That's going to make the news."

"It already has."

"Okay, Henry, stress the fact that care is of the same high quality. Patient-related activities haven't been affected by the strike." He added, "It's too bad if we hand them the spurt they need. Maybe it'll die where it is."

"Doug," called Ann, "Joe Goldman's on the line."

"Yes, Joe."

"Jack Apple and Elmo Bunting have completed phase one of what they call a thorough study and have exonerated Al Robinson."

"Joe, that's so blatant I'm surprised even they would have the nerve."

"They didn't even call a meeting. Said it wasn't necessary since they represented a majority."

"The Medical Staff Board meets in a week, right?"

"Yes, and by then phase two will be completed."

"What's phase two?"

"They're going to check the equipment to see if that could've been the culprit."

"Joe, they called it a cardiac arrest? Can you believe that?"

"Well, her heart stopped."

"That was the result of something else, not the cause of death."

"I guess you see the direction things are going."

"At least we've got a week before Robinson performs again. I'll think of something."

He needed to be alone to think, or feel. He sat in his office with the lights out, looking out the window across the west lawn. He had to review and arrange his thoughts. *If you're going to dedicate yourself to something, you want it to serve a purpose other than some jackass lining his pockets.* He wasn't clean. He wasn't stopping it. He wasn't making a difference. He focused on the night shift meeting coming up in a few hours. He tried, but Jean Daniels kept interrupting him.

Cannon Hall was jammed packed as Doug entered. He expected to find only the first few rows of seats filled with night shift nurses, but the auditorium was full. Evening, night, and day shift nurses had all come. They became quiet as Doug took the stage. Doug realized the supervisors and head nurses were holding down the fort on the units but wanted to make this a quick meeting nonetheless.

Kay was standing behind the podium, waiting. She looked apprehensive as she addressed the nurses. "Ladies and gentlemen, Mr. Carpenter asked me to schedule this meeting because there are things he feels must be said. We've all been going through rough times but none more than Doug Carpenter. We are all affected by what's happening, but he seems to catch the brunt of it." She stepped aside and sat in a chair a few feet to the rear of the podium.

Doug studied the faces; most were expectant, with a mixture of quizzical and hopeful expressions.

"We're all catching the brunt of it," he said. "What happens in this hospital happens to each of us." He scanned the room, making direct eye contact with those toward the front. "All of us want the same thing to happen here. We want good care."

He paused for a moment, calculating his words. "But that's not easy. I'm not going to talk about the politics of this organization or the vested interests. I'm just going to talk about our roles: yours and mine." He glanced at Kay, who was smiling nervously. "Kay is afraid I am going to de-motivate you with what I am about to say." A few faces became apprehensive. "She's afraid I'm going to make things worse than they already are. So am I, but it's a risk I've got to take."

Doug looked down at the podium as though gathering his thoughts, but he knew what he was going to say next.

"I don't know if I should allow the night shift to come back to work."

There was a gasp throughout the auditorium.

"That's the reaction I expected. You're entitled to know why I'm struggling with this."

Angry faces peered back at him.

"I understand your reasons for the walkout. I share your concerns. But there's not one of you that can't understand it's self-defeating to abandon the patient because of an incident of poor care."

Almost all the nurses stood and shouted at the same time.

"We didn't abandon the patients!"

"The patients were cared for!"

"We do our jobs. It's the doctors who don't give a damn!"

Some of the nurses in the back were making motions toward the exits and Doug was glad those in front hadn't seen. He pointed to a particularly angry nurse in the front.

"You made a comment. Would you state it again, louder so everyone can hear?"

"What the hell is your role in all this?"

Cheers and claps exploded around her.

"Could all of you hear her question?"

"No," came a chorus from the rear.

"She asked what the hell my role is in all this."

This time cheers and claps erupted from the whole auditorium. Before he could answer, Kay came up beside him and pulled the microphone over to her.

"This is the last guy you should ask that question of. The fact he's not as headstrong as we are doesn't mean he doesn't feel the way we do. I could get into trouble for saying this, but I want you to know Doug Carpenter's role is to work his ass off against the politics to make this the hospital we want."

Kay returned to her chair and sat, and when she sat, everyone else sat.

"I know, now, that when you walked off, you made sure the patients would all be cared for. I was on the patient units and saw you rushing around. The night shift came on early and the evening shift stayed on late." He gripped the sides of the podium so tight his fingers ached. "And I know more about the planning than you suspect I know." He breathed deeply to calm his nerves. "I was angry and upset because I knew you cared. You are givers, and I love every one of you."

He leaned forward over the podium, and now, they were quiet.

"So, even though you appeared to, you didn't abandon the patient." He let go of the podium and put his hands on top of it. "But you can't even give the appearance of abandoning the patient. It tells others they can."

Some of the faces were almost pleading.

"We have to agree to always do the right thing regardless of what others do. That way, despite others, we can form a conscience that keeps the others in line."

They were listening, but some looked like they were expecting the worst.

"The hospital's conscience can never appear non-caring. So now you know my frustration. Now you understand the question running through my mind. Should I allow the night shift to come back?"

Anxious concern took the place of anger on their faces.

"If I do, should I pay them? The answers keep evading me. There's a broader concern. The nurses are the conscience of the hospital, but I have to steer, whether or not I have a rudder. How do we work together to reach our destination?"

Doug examined the faces deliberately, carefully, one by one, letting the silence hang like a weight.

"I'm going to answer those questions." He turned to Kay. "We take the night shift back *and we pay them.*"

Everyone in the room stood and cheered. He motioned for them to sit and after a few attempts they did.

"We must agree, however, that even in anger, our actions can never give the appearance of not caring. There are things you can do instead of walking out. Our pact is that you will think of such things and that we will work together. There has to be openness between us."

One of the nurses in the rear who had been motioning toward the door before yelled out, "What are you going to do about Dr. Robinson?"

"I would've been surprised if that hadn't been asked. Today, Dr. Goldman appointed a committee to make recommendations to the Medical Staff Board. Neither he nor I will accept a whitewash. If you don't like the results of their findings, give some thought to what you are going to do about it. Discuss it among yourselves. In the meantime, Dr. Robinson will not be scheduled for any procedures."

Doug could see there was disappointment with the answer, so he added, "Conscience makes quick decisions. Correcting problems takes longer. The issue will not be dropped. I make that promise to you for the things you've already done for Eastern."

Kay stood up. Her energy had returned. "We can't meet much longer because we have patients to take care of, but I don't have the chance to talk to you all together very often, so stay a few minutes."

She thanked Doug. The nurses clapped as he left the stage and some of them even stood.

He was thankful. He could've lost them. He headed toward his office, exhausted and anxious to go home to be with Bess. Instead, he called her.

"I'll be home soon. I've got to get myself together. It's been a crazy day."

"Why don't you stay there? I'm okay."

"No, I need to get out of here."

He wasn't aware of how long he had sat in the chair beside his desk, staring at his reflection in the night mirror of the window. A tap on the door and Kay walked in.

"I owe you an apology. That was good, but you are going to have to do something about Robinson."

"Count on it. I'll get him out even if it costs me my job."

"Costs your job? Do you mean that?"

"I'm fed up. It's not worth it. Nothing is."

"If you go, I go. And if I go, the nurses go. So go get him."

"I can count on you that far?"

"You're damn right."

"Let's hope it doesn't come to that."

"Let's hope. In the meantime, let me give you something else to worry about." She sat and shook her head. "I think we've got a serious problem. We had two more deaths, and this time, one wasn't terminal, just suffering, but no likelihood of death."

"Two more. It's getting worse, not better. Maybe Simba's right. Would this have happened with the full staff?"

"I'm afraid. These patients didn't die from lack of care. It happened during the meeting, and all the head nurses and supervisors were on duty. Doug, something's going on. Jeep says someone tampered with the narcotic drip. They overdosed."

"Jeep's patients again?"

"One of them, but they were both in the same room."

"You're right. We've got a problem."

CHAPTER EIGHTEEN

Simba stared her challenge toward Frank Street. She ignored Doug.

"We want a guarantee that no employee will lose his or her job because of any efficiency moves."

Before Frank could talk, Doug nudged him under the table. Frank remained quiet.

"No," said Doug. "The hospital reserves the right to make any changes in work methods and procedures and to change, reduce, or eliminate jobs as necessary for effective operation."

Simba waited until Doug had finished and resumed. "All established work breaks will continue unless addressed in the contract." She looked straight at Frank.

"Agreed."

"Parking privileges will remain the same. Spaces in the lot will not be taken from union members for other employees."

"Agreed."

"In addition," said Simba, still talking to Frank, "we want TV sets in all employee lounges."

"No. Those lounges with sets will continue to have them, but the hospital won't guarantee repairs if they break down. It will not be a high priority item."

"We want agreement on all these items before we continue the agenda."

Frank shifted in his chair. "The hospital reserves the right to change job content and hours worked," he said, his face blotched, anger-red.

Doug knew Frank would have compromised to keep the salaries lower, and was delighted.

"The TV sets currently in lounges will remain as is unless they break down. There will be no guarantees." Frank bit off the last word. "We agree on the work breaks and parking." Each word was punctuated as though he were swearing. His face had become even more flushed, matching the color of his orange-red hair.

Doug knew Simba couldn't have failed to notice his displeasure, despite the fact she hadn't looked directly at him.

"For negotiations to continue," she said, "we will need job guarantees in the event of efficiency moves."

"We would be happy to continue the negotiations, but we're feeling no pressure. The hospital is functioning well with your people out on the street. The hospital reserves the right to make job changes to operate effectively. It's not a point we will give in on. Not now. Not ever." He slapped the table and even Simba blinked.

Her words seethed with anger. "The white master has spoken. His puppet sits on his ass waiting for permission to speak. I see no evidence that management is prepared to bargain in good faith."

Simba stood and leaned over the table toward Frank. "Somebody told me you were a tough bargaining bastard, but you're just a puppet's puppet." She straightened like a stick and looked down at him. "Are you ready to bargain or do we adjourn? We can carry this strike on until you're run into the ground, in spite of what the doctor's pimp here says."

"She has me pegged, Frank."

This time Simba focused her full attention on Doug. "It's hard not to notice one so smug and self-righteous. You have instant answers to control the lives and futures of good people. You control their food, shelter, clothing, education. Well, those days are coming to an end."

She gathered her papers and her team stood up. "Let me know if you want to bargain in good faith. Otherwise, don't bother." They marched out of the room.

Doug and Frank sat in silence for a few moments.

"I didn't exactly enjoy that," admitted Frank.

"You made that apparent. But I don't think she'll handle it the same way again."

"We can give in on the job guarantees." Frank stood, flipping his file folder shut.

"No. Not now. Not ever. I meant that. You would give in on that because you don't have to run the hospital. You'd keep the salaries low because that would make you look good." They stood and locked eyes. "The job guarantee isn't even an item for negotiation. Management reserves the right to manage."

"Shit," was all Frank could say.

When Doug passed through the hotel lobby, Simba sat at the far side, watching. He ignored her.

Ann buzzed. "Kay's here."

Kay stepped in and closed the door before Doug could answer the buzz.

"Bull knows someone we could call in undercover to check what's going on."

"Bull?"

"We talked about it last night. I called him at home. It's okay, he'll keep his mouth shut."

"Is this one of his police buddies?"

"Yes, it's—"

"Don't tell me. I want you to be the only one to know who he is. Make it real undercover. Have you told anyone else about this?"

"No, but—"

"Don't tell anyone on your staff. Tell nobody. You take him down to Personnel to the labor pool and tell them he's a friend of yours who's volunteered to help out in Nursing during the strike."

"Okay."

"Any more deaths?"

"So far, so good."

"Simba's going to pin us to the wall on this."

Two nights later, the Medical Staff Board met to discuss Al Robinson.

"We've done a thorough study," shared Jack Apple. "The monitoring equipment in the delivery room should be replaced. Only a magician could function with that antiquated system. Al is waiting in my office and I think we ought to tell him he's exonerated and apologize for not scheduling him."

There was a moment of silence. A few physicians squirmed in their seats but said nothing. Joe Goldman folded his hands on the table and bowed his head. He looked up as Doug raised his hand.

"Doug?"

Doug stood because he wanted to be sure everyone heard him. Stan Boswell looked annoyed.

"Some of you will not be surprised to hear that that suggestion disturbs me."

Charles Smith leaned back and examined the ceiling. Ed Whyte, still in pajamas and robe, looked a question at Stan and pointed to Doug. Jack Apple waited like a martyr, looking straight ahead.

"There's no problem with the equipment. No other anesthesiologist has had a problem with it. Al needs help. He's an alcoholic. We've had one death and some near misses." He hesitated. "You cannot ignore this problem. As physicians, you are responsible for keeping standards of practice at an acceptable level—"

"That's right," interrupted Jack Apple, "and that's just—"

Joe Goldman slammed the gavel on the table hard enough to leave a crater. "Doug has the floor and I want to hear him."

Apple stared at the wall.

Doug continued. "The study is unacceptable. This is serious—"

"Oh, come on," said Charles Smith. "Let's get on with the meeting. We don't need this."

"I agree," piped in Ed Whyte. "Let's call Al in and apologize."

"Wait," came a voice from the other end of the table. Josh Feldman, Chair of Radiology. "I want to know why Doug finds the study unacceptable."

"Damnit, Josh, really?" shouted Jack. "He finds it unacceptable because he doesn't agree with it."

"Listen, Josh," Ed Whyte spoke with authority, "I work with Al Robinson and you don't. If he couldn't do the job, I'd know it. I make a motion we call him in here and apologize."

"I second!" Charles raised his hand.

"I call for the question," Apple said.

Joe Goldman looked helpless. "I need a second on the call for the question."

"I already did second," said Charles.

"I need a second on the call for the *question*," Joe patiently stated. "We're going by Roberts' Rules. A call for the question means voting without further discussion. If I don't get a second, the floor is open for discussion."

"I second whatever." Charles threw up his hands.

"All in favor?" asked Joe.

Nine hands raised.

"Opposed?"

Two hands.

"Looks like a few abstentions. The motion carries. Now we can vote on the issue itself. All in favor?"

"What the hell!" exclaimed Ed Whyte. "We already voted once."

"Ed, I know you have a problem understanding Roberts' Rules, but you'll just have to trust me. You haven't voted on the issue yet. All in favor."

The same nine hands went up again.

Even though it was summer and the days were long, Doug pulled up in front of the house after dark. He slammed the car door and plodded up the steps and into the living room.

"Hi, sweetie," Bess greeted him. "How about a cup of herb tea with honey? It's good for what ails you."

He followed her through the rubble of the dining room renovations and into the kitchen.

"The eleven o'clock news will be on soon." She poured while she talked. "Workmen have been crawling all over the place today. The rug man told me he wouldn't carry the old rugs away. Told me I'd have to get someone else to haul them off."

"Then, freakin' get someone else."

"I . . ." she abruptly stopped in her tracks. "I . . . already did." Her voice dropped.

Bess poured a second cup. Doug moved into the living room. He sat in the new easy chair. He gulped the tea and set the cup on the floor by the chair.

Bess came in. "Maybe you'd like a warm shower. It might help you relax." She sat on the other side of the room. "How do you like the new chair?"

"It's okay."

"I think it's a beaut. I love it." She paused to laugh at herself, to try to change the subject and lighten the mood. "If I don't think about it much, it almost makes it all worthwhile."

"I liked the other one better," he said, just to be opposing, and carried his cup to the kitchen. He stared out the window over the sink, only it was dark and more like a mirror.

Bess came in behind him and leaned against the archway, shaking her head, doing her best to make things better. "Okay, tell me what happened at the hospital today."

"Just more of the damned same." He watched her as she bowed her head. She seemed smaller. "I don't know why the hell I bother with the place."

"Maybe you care too much."

"Oh, how can you care too much?"

She turned and disappeared through the dining room. He heard something get knocked over, felt completely rotten, but didn't go after her, just squeezed the edges of the sink and stared at himself in the window. He pushed himself away. *There must be a better way to make a living.*

In the living room, he found Bess sitting in the new chair, crying. "The other one was more comfortable," she agreed, ever so timidly.

Doug could barely breathe. He had squashed the one person who mattered when nothing else did. "Bess?"

"What?"

"The chair's okay."

She leaned forward, cupped her head in her hands, and cried like a child.

Doug came in late the next morning and walked straight into his office without the usual chitchat.

Ann buzzed him. "Mr. Boswell wants to see you."

He slowly walked around the desk just as a nurse rushed into his office. He recognized her as one who had stood in the auditorium motioning others to leave.

"Mr. Carpenter, Dr. Robinson is drunk again. He almost killed a patient in the OR. Dr. Apple was the surgeon. I just told them both I was going to the newspapers and expose him."

"Are you?"

"If I have to. I've had it. I couldn't believe it when he walked into the OR this morning. You could smell it on his breath. The nurse-anesthetist took over. He's sitting in a drunken stupor in the doctor's lounge."

"What happened exactly?"

"He lost control. The patient was already out and he kept on pushing and pushing that plunger. When the nurse-anesthetist moved in, he hit her, and she fell to the floor. The patient's okay, but no thanks to him."

"Will you write your incident report just that way?"

"I'll go get it. It's already done." She headed toward the door.

"Who else was there? Will you have each of them come see me right now?"

"They'll be on the way."

"Doug, Mr. Boswell's on the line."

"Stan," said Doug into the phone, "I'll get back to you." He dropped the phone into the cradle.

"Ann, get Toliver up here. Tell him to run and to bring one of his security officers with him."

Doug called Joe Goldman only to find he was in surgery.

"Ann what's the name of the nurse who was here before?"

"Ollie Silverman."

He dialed Kay O'Connell. "Kay, all hell's about to break loose. Ollie Silverman was just here and—"

"I know all about it and you're about to receive a delegation."

"Good. I think you should come, too."

Stan Boswell stalked into Doug's office. "I wanted to see you."

Cliff Toliver came running in, out of breath, a security officer right behind him.

"I want you to go the doctor's lounge in the OR. Escort Dr. Al Robinson out of the building. Tell him he is being escorted out by my order. Don't stop for anything else. Call me when he's out."

The two men turned and ran like mice.

"What the hell are you doing?"

"Something I should've done one Jean Daniels ago . . . and something you don't have the guts to do. Robinson's never going to kill another patient in this hospital."

Stan started to run after Toliver. Doug grabbed him by the arm and yanked him back. "Let it go, Stan. It's done. He's drunk again."

Doug released him just as six nurses from the OR came in.

"Sit down," commanded Doug. "We need to get the record straight."

Stan stuttered something, peering out into Ann's office. He stepped out, then back in, and then left.

"I want each of you to write what happened this morning and also any other incidents with Robinson."

"It's already done," said one of them, and they each handed him several reports.

Ann buzzed. "Stan wants to speak to you on the phone."

"Tell him I'll call him."

"He said to tell you to answer the phone no matter what."

Doug sighed and picked up the phone. "What is it, Stan?"

"I want you to cancel that directive. I am ordering you."

"No way. By now, Robinson has been escorted out of the building—for good."

The nurses all stood, just as Kay O'Connell came in. "I heard that," she said. "We're with you."

"Doug," said Stan, "maybe you didn't hear what *I* said. I am ordering you to bring Robinson back in here. Do you want me to fire you?"

"Stan, you can fire me if you want to, but the order stands."

Kay grabbed the phone out of Doug's hand. "You'll have to fire me, too. And all the nurses. If Robinson comes back, we go." She slammed the phone in the cradle. "There. That's putting my money where my mouth is."

Doug could see Stan as if he were burning in front of him. "It had to happen sooner or later."

Ann buzzed again. "Cliff Toliver's on the line."

"Mr. Carpenter, we escorted him out, but he was so drunk, one of my men had to drive him home."

"I want that documented, too. Have the full report in my office within thirty minutes."

Jack Apple appeared in the doorway, still in his scrubs. "What the hell are you doing?"

Charles Smith was with him. "You've overstepped this time, Doug."

"It had to be done. You guys wouldn't do it. You know where Stan's office is."

They left, then it occurred to him he should let the Chairman of the Board know what he had done. "Ann, get Walter Bass on the phone . . . and find Joe Goldman."

Stan Boswell stuck his head in the doorway and motioned for Doug to follow him, ignoring Kay and her nurses. "I think you might want to come over to my office."

Ann buzzed. "He's on."

"Walter?"

Stan's eyes opened with surprise and disbelief.

"You may recall my expressing concern about Al Robinson, Chair of Anesthesiology."

"Yes, Doug."

"Last night, the Medical Staff Board exonerated him. It was ludicrous. Today he was so drunk in the OR one of the security guards had to drive him home."

"Maybe the Medical Staff Board will reconsider."

"I doubt it, Walter. I've barred him from the hospital. I'm trying to track down Joe Goldman. Incidentally, Joe was upset with last night's decision."

"Looks to me like it was a long time coming. He's had every opportunity."

"Thank you, Walter. Given the nature of my action, I'll give you a very detailed report." When Doug hung up, he looked at Stan without a word.

"Was that Walter Bass?" asked Stan.

"It was."

"You shouldn't go around me."

The nurses were as quiet as a jury. Stan fidgeted as they watched him.

"Joe Goldman's on the line," called Ann.

Doug hadn't taken his eyes off of Stan. "I've already talked to Jack and Charles. I don't need to talk with them again. I know what they have to say." He picked up the phone. "Joe?"

"I heard already. Congratulations. You have my support. What about Stan?"

"He's standing here trying to decide whether or not to fire me."

Stan bit his lip, turned, eyes forward, and left.

That was the nurses' cue to disperse. They had plenty to do.

Doug called the delivery room nurses and had them prepare written statements. He wanted to add them to the reports from the operating room nurses. He compiled a report consisting of a chronological listing of events.

He thought of Bess. Since he had laid his job and their security on the line, the least he could do would be to let her know. Anyhow, he felt drawn to talk to her because of his temper last night. But Frank Street called.

"Simba has called and we are on again this evening. You want to be there or shall I handle it?"

"I'll be there."

Ann appeared in the door. "Harry Bradour from Channel 3 is here to see you."

"Tell him to see Henry Sims."

"I would like to talk to you, sir," said Bradour, pushing into the office. He had a camera operator with him.

"Mr. Sims is fully informed about the strike. He can tell you more than I can. I'll tell you we are meeting again with the union this evening." He moved toward the door with Bradour.

"It's about a death in your delivery room, sir."

"Henry Sims will dig out whatever information you want. I'm not able to give you the time."

"Is it true, Mr. Carpenter, that the death in the delivery room was accidental?" It sounded like a guess to Doug.

"There've been no reports of any accidental deaths. Now, please excuse me. There is nothing I can tell you." He was guiding the reporter through the doorway. "Ann, call Henry and tell him Mr. Bradour is here."

He stepped back into his office and shut the door.

"Damn," he whispered. "Jean Daniels' family has a right to know."

CHAPTER NINETEEN

Simba and her crew didn't show. Doug and Frank waited an hour past the appointment, had coffee, but said little to each other. Maybe that's what Simba wanted. No dumbbell.

The weekend lasted forever. Doug wanted to go home, but with everything happening, he couldn't. He agonized over what he had done to Bess. He had wounded her. He let the tension get the best of him, and it wasn't getting better. *Bess.* The sweetest person he had ever known. She sat in the new chair and cried like a child. *The other one was more comfortable* gnawed at his heart.

Long halls, institutional colors, and an office prison—no outside air, no sky, no trees. Greed and thirst for power filled the corners like dust and he was letting it clog his mind. They were beating him. Boswell and the takers. It was Solstory all over again. Vultures picking on bones of the sick. He couldn't lead them any more than he could teach a rock to swim.

Monday morning. Time to be fresh, not stale and dried out. He had to get out, almost ran to the parking garage. In his car, he felt some return to privacy, but at the exit to the parking garage, picketers pounded on his car. They were like an exclamation point to all the problems. He drove to a diner, well out of the center city area, and ordered bacon, waffles, and coffee. He breathed non-hospital air. He watched other people eat. He watched people walk past on the sidewalk. People from the normal world.

He wanted a normal life for Bess. He was failing her most of all. The waitress came over and took his empty plates, a message he should leave so someone else could take the booth. He ordered more coffee.

Finally, he cleared out and drove mechanically back to the parking lot. The picketers moved out of the way in slow motion. Then he saw her—the big aide from the fourth floor, the one who had brutalized Jean DeVries and Isabel Eaves. Kay had gotten her name for him. Clinker. Clinker Pottard. He had wondered if Clinker was a nickname. Hard name to forget. Here she stood in the middle of the drive, bumping her hip at him with her eyes half shut. She didn't know how glad he was to see her. She rumbled and inched aside to the laughs and claps of the others. She bumped her huge behind at him when he drove past.

Doug ran all the way to the security office. Cliff was there.

"Get the police. Clinker Pottard's in the parking lot. Jean DeVries and Isabel Eaves will press charges. So will the hospital." Then, as Cliff was dialing, "Tell them to bring big guys. She'll give them a hard time."

He trotted down the hall and called back, "Let me know what happens."

His pace suddenly slowed as though the sounds and odors were solid things that had to be pushed aside. The odors, some from medications, ranged from obnoxious to gagging. In the laboratories, smells attacked. At some stretches of the hallway, he held his breath to smother the fire in his nose.

Odors had permanent addresses in the building. Supplies in the central sterile area smelled of glue, Housekeeping with its cleaning compounds, the paint shop's linseed oil, the plumbing shop's solder, the carpenter shop's raw wood, the laundry's steam ironing and pungent dirty sorting area. Only in dietary were there welcome odors.

In his office, Doug glanced at the census report. Eighty-three percent. Higher than normal. He called the pharmacy.

"Pharmacy," came a harried voice.

"This is Doug Carpenter. Is Mort Klieber there?"

"Mort's out delivering unit doses. This is Andy. Can I help?"

Doug recognized the assistant director's voice. "How are you guys doing? The census is up."

"Keep it that way. We're busting our butts, but we want to bust the union. If it gets too bad, we'll yell."

He had just settled behind his desk when Ann called. "Doug, Frank wants to know if you can meet with the union at one o'clock."

"Tell him yes. We'll try again."

"I'm glad to hear that." Mrs. Tevisina Urqhart, President of the Central Eastern Community Association, stalked into his office. "Maybe you gentlemen can settle and get things back to normal."

"I'd settle today if the demands were reasonable."

"Just settle. Give a little."

"A little is no problem. A lot is a problem. They're asking too much, Tevisina. A lot of the service employees live in this community. Why don't you talk to them?"

"We're telling them to settle. It's hurting the entire community. But what I'm hearing is you haven't even discussed money. You're arguing on the little stuff."

She was a short, heavy woman who always wore bright

flowered dresses. She wore a black straw hat that matched her hair, eyes, and skin—a study of sameness and contrast. She sat, her back straight as cement.

This lady was an absolute influence in the community. She had a hand in every event. She sang in the Baptist Gospel Choir and was the first woman elder in her church.

"Do you know Simba?" he asked.

"Everybody knows Simba."

"Can you talk to her and get her to drop some of her demands?"

"Simba's not going to drop any demand good for our people. Simba is a good person."

Doug remembered Simba's naked body modeling in this same office. The contrast with Tevisina Urqhart was dramatic. "She doesn't do the good you do. You're a community foundation."

Her eyes gave no response. "She wants what's good."

"And I have to be concerned with what's good for the hospital because that's good for them, too. I won't give away everything that keeps this hospital alive to help the employees. That would be feeding them their own flesh. The hospital has to exist for them to have jobs."

"They just want respect, decent pay, job security, and the assurance . . ." she leaned forward and tapped her finger on the desk, "that they aren't being used to make somebody else rich."

"Tevisina, I'm not interested in making others rich. Simba has made me out to be the heavy. I hope you know that's not true."

"You may be the unwitting tool. As President of the Community Association, I am a member of your Board."

"Yes, I know."

"I'm going to the Board to express my concerns."

"I think you should."

"It doesn't matter what I say to Simba." She stood up. "You listen to what I say to you." She walked out of the office.

Doug followed her into the outer office and watched as she exited into the hall.

"I bet even Simba listens to her," said Ann, then in the same breath added, "Mr. Boswell asked for you to come over when Mrs. Urqhart left." She frowned.

When Doug walked through Liz Racoda's office, she smiled. "Good morning, Doug," she said.

Saccharine.

Stan was waiting, standing behind his table. He handed Doug a neatly typed memorandum.

"Please read this."

Doug read it without sitting.

This is a formal reprimand for your impulsive and inappropriate behavior resulting in extreme embarrassment to our Chair of Anesthesiology, Alan Robinson, MD, and to the hospital in general.

At a time when unity is needed, you have provided division instead of leadership. I hereby, officially, ask for your resignation.

Doug folded the letter and placed it in his inside coat pocket. "Stan, as far as I'm concerned, you can stick it in your ear. I've no intention of resigning. If you want me out, fire me. And I guarantee I'll make it rough on you. So you do what you have to do, and I'll do what I have to do."

"What do you mean 'you'll make it rough on me?' Never mind." He waved his hands and shook his head as though to clear it. "The fact is you've mishandled everything. We're in a strike. The medical staff is unhappy. The community is unhappy. Contract negotiations are going nowhere. The general operation of the hospital is poor, and you're causing problems for me. You—"

Doug could listen to no more. "Save all this for public consumption. Some of them will believe it. But right now, it's just you and me, and both of us know those charges are just crap. You know what the real issues are."

Doug leaned forward, almost nose-to-nose with Stan, who looked startled. "Don't forget, you have to keep the doctors on your side for their support in building a new hospital. And you'll promise them *anything* to get it. You're a whore. You're a damn whore. Fire me or get off my back." He leaned so far forward he almost lost his balance.

Stan's mouth began to twitch. One part of Doug wanted Stan to fire him. He wanted to shout out what had happened to Jean Daniels and Jerry Brownstein. He wanted to tell people to stay away from the hospital. There were doctors here who would kill them.

Stan dropped back into his chair, hate virtually seeping out of his pores. His hands clenched the chair arms.

Doug squared his back. "Stan, what'll it be?"

Stan unfolded and hunched forward. His face was beet red. "It's not time to fire you . . . yet."

Doug turned and left the room.

He was vibrating with anger when he reached his office.

"Cliff wants you to call him, and Bess is on the line."

He grabbed the phone.

"Guess who's here?" she asked. "Sammy and Janey. They came home for spring break. Why don't you come home for lunch?"

Doug wrestled with the giants of anger churning through his body. He wanted to lock them in a box. The kids were home. He had thought and hoped they would come home. He sat. "I can't. I want to, but I can't. Got a negotiating meeting with the union. Can't trust Frank to do it alone. He'd give away the store." Doug felt limp. He needed that lunch.

"How about if we come in there and meet you for lunch?"

He thought of the picketers. "I'll tell you what, I'll get out of here early and we'll all go out for dinner."

He didn't tell her about Stan's reprimand and threat to fire him.

"Okay."

"I'll call when I'm out of the meeting and we'll make plans." He wondered what Cliff had to report. "I'm glad the kids are home. I've have to run. Take care. I'll call later. And, Bess, I'm sorry."

"Okay."

"Bess, I love you."

He called Security. "Cliff? What happened?"

"The police just walked up, cuffed her, and took her. She didn't even resist. Good thing. She's one big mother."

Doug called Ann. "Put together everything on Clinker Pottard, incident reports, medical records on DeVries and Eaves, personnel file, everything. Get ahold of our general counsel, Ralph Bacon. Tell him we're pressing charges. Let DeVries and Eaves know."

"Okay, and Joe Goldman wants you to call."

"Damn! Now what?"

He grabbed the phone and dialed.

"Doug, there's a special meeting called for the Medical Staff Board at two o'clock this afternoon. Six members petitioned for it and the subject is for the hospital to give in to the union demands so we can get back to normal. I'm sorry, but the bylaws say I have to call it."

"Tomorrow's the regular meeting. Can't it wait 'til then?"

"When it's an emergency matter, the bylaws don't give me any room."

"Son-of-a-bitch. It's a case of being in two places at one time, but I'll try to make it. They'll make their recommendation to the Board of Trustees, right?"

"Right. And the same group is petitioning for a meeting of the trustees today or early tomorrow."

"Nothing to do but go with it."

He hung up and Kay tapped on his door.

"We've had another death."

"Another Jeep patient?"

"Yes, but this one's different. This was not a terminal patient and her suffering was temporary."

"What was the cause of death?"

"We don't know yet. She was in her late seventies, but in good health."

"You better get that cop in here."

"He's already on the job."

"You didn't waste any time."

"This is serious. Something's going on."

The meeting with the union was at one o'clock. Simba and her group came in ten minutes late.

They remained standing.

"I understand you had one of our members arrested this morning. There can be no negotiation with this harassment. Drop the charges or we cancel this meeting."

Frank turned to Doug. "I think we need to have the meeting."

"The charges remain. She's under arrest for damn near killing two people."

Simba turned her back to the two men and leaned against the wall as though deep in thought, then faced them again. "In an organizing effort, things happen in the heat of the moment. We are trying to put all of that behind us. If you are interested in bargaining in good faith, you'll drop the charges."

"The medical records clearly indicate this 'heat of the moment' was more like a volcano. If you're interested in negotiating, drop the subject. The charges *will not* be dropped."

"Isn't it curious that it's whites charging a black, and it's the blacks that are being put upon?"

"It's not a black-white issue."

"Well," interjected Frank, "if it is, it's because the union's making it one."

"Honey, what do you want? The whites have it all and the blacks have nothing. Of course it's a black-white issue."

"Aren't you supposed to represent whites, too?" asked Doug.

"We represent everybody who needs us and the blacks need us the most—both black employees and the black community."

Doug stood up. "The charges are not racial, and the charges *will not* be dropped."

Simba turned and left, her team moving as though one with her.

In the silence, they could hear Simba's heels plunging down the hall.

"Doug, we need a third person on our team so when we disagree, we can resolve it. I can't beat these spear chuckers with you sitting here."

"We don't need a third person. We need a labor negotiator who's not a self-serving bigot. Keep your filthy racist slurs to yourself. I don't want to hear them anymore."

Frank smiled. "Everybody makes racist comments, the blacks included."

"That's true, but yours are the kind that keep it all going. I don't want to hear any more of it." He left the room.

Doug got back just in time for the medical staff meeting. Not a big turnout. He counted the ones he knew would vote for capitulation. There was Jack Apple, Charles Smith, Ed Whyte, with his nose bandaged and his face swollen lopsided, Jasper Gunderson, Bert Allen, and Elmo Bunting. Probably the six who called for the meeting.

There was Joe Goldman, but as chair of the meeting, he didn't vote unless it was a tie. There was Josh Feldman, a good thinker, and Garland Riggely, who could be counted on to keep a cool head. *Damn. I haven't been keeping a cool head myself the last few days.* Harvey Shocks came in. Hard to tell which way he would vote. Julia Best was a question mark. It didn't look good.

Joe called the meeting to order. Before he could even state the purpose, Jack Apple was on his feet.

"I move that the hospital meet all the demands of the union so we can get back to normal and provide the care a hospital's supposed to provide."

"I second the motion," chirped Elmo Bunting.

"I call for the question," said Ed Whyte, through bruised and swollen lips.

"Nonsense!" shouted Joe. "There's been no discussion. This is a serious issue."

"The question's been called for, and by Robert's Rules, you have to take a vote," said Ed.

Joe showed his disgust. "Those in favor of voting on the motion."

Six hands shot up. The six Doug had expected.

"Okay. A two-thirds majority wants to vote without discussion. This is disgusting. All those in favor of the motion."

The same six hands went up.

"I move this motion be presented to the Board of Trustees this evening," said Jack. "They've already agreed to an emergency meeting if we approve the motion."

"I second the motion!" Elmo Bunting shouted.

"I call for the question," demanded Ed Whyte.

"I guess this is what's called a railroad," said Joe. "All in favor."

Six hands once more went up.

Doug stood. "Before you adjourn the meeting, Joe, I'd like to make a comment for the record. First of all, the union hasn't even given us all of their demands. So you just voted to sign a blank check. Secondly, their first demands are always excessive, so you just voted to give away the store. And thirdly, you wanted to get things back to normal. If we do what you just voted, things will never be back to normal. You can kiss life as you know it in this hospital goodbye."

He sat down and folded his arms.

After a moment, Garland Riggely shook his head and chuckled. "I don't believe what you guys just did. I mean, you've done some dumb things before, but this was dumb-stupid."

"I'm embarrassed someone might think I voted for this. Can the record show who voted in favor of it?" Josh Feldman asked.

"Since the vote wasn't by secret ballot, I see no reason why not," explained Joe.

"I object!" yelled Charles.

"Are you ashamed of your vote?" asked Josh.

"No, I just don't think it's appropriate."

"Doug," asked Julia Best, "what is the progress?"

"We had a short meeting early this afternoon. The union refused to negotiate unless we dropped criminal charges against one of their members who savagely beat two of our nurses." Doug looked at Ed. "We haven't found the goon that beat you, but this one was stupid enough to appear again on the picket line."

Ed shifted in his chair.

"Ed, do you want us to drop the charges?" Julia asked, quite uncertainly.

"They're not going to find the goon that beat me anyhow. After all, I'm only a doctor."

"Should we drop the charges?" persisted Julia.

"It's not the same thing," snapped Ed.

Harvey was next in line. "Doug, what's your best prediction as to how much longer the strike will last?"

"Tough to say, Harvey. My guess is if we hang tough, they won't last another week. But there are a lot of variables. Right now, we are showing a lot of solidarity, and they're worried."

Josh nearly jumped from his chair. "I move that we reconsider the previous vote and not vote in favor of giving in to the union."

"I second the motion," shouted an excited Julia.

"We can't do that!" countered Jack, all piss and vinegar.

"He's right," said Joe, somewhat deflated. "By Robert's Rules we voted to take a vote without discussion. Technically, all this debate is a moot point."

"What the hell? We'll just vote it down anyhow. Go ahead and vote." Ed could barely breathe through his swollen nostrils and sounded underwater but made his voice heard.

"I'll accept that as a motion by one who voted with the prevailing side. All those in favor?"

Five hands went up, Bert Allen's included. He had changed his vote. There would be only five opposed.

"All opposed."

Five hands went up.

"In case of a tie, the chair casts the deciding vote. I vote not to give in to the union demands. Meeting's adjourned."

"Wait just a minute," Ed huffed, face red. "That was an illegal vote. It doesn't count."

Joe gathered his papers. "The Board can decide that for themselves. They'll get the entire minutes to consider before they call a meeting." He left the room.

Bert Allen was right behind him. The adhesive five continued to sit after everybody else left. Doug felt washed with relief.

"I didn't expect to see you so soon. How did it go?" asked Ann.

"We won. It was close, but thank God something has gone right today."

"I hope that sets a trend. Henry Sims wants you to call. Says it's important."

"Get him, and we'll find out."

"Doug," said Henry, "the good news is the newspapers haven't picked up on Al Robinson yet. The bad news is Simba Agiza has."

"Oh, no."

"Oh, yes. And she called to schedule a meeting with us in a neutral place, outside the hospital and off the record."

"She wants to meet with both of us?"

"That's what she said."

"Set it up for tomorrow afternoon. That'll buy time."

"She said tonight at the latest."

"Damn-it-to-hell." *She may have the trump card.* "How much does she know?"

"She said she wants to talk to you about how Dr. Robinson killed Mrs. Daniels, and your subsequent action barring him from the hospital."

"I guess that couldn't be clearer." He sighed and scratched his head. "Schedule it at the Parkside Inn. That's neutral enough for the negotiations."

Kay tapped on the door. "Doug, we need to talk."

"Talking's easy. What's up?"

Kay looked truly wretched. "We found a pattern on the deaths. A lot of people come in contact with patients, but in the cases with questionable deaths, there were only two who came in contact with all of them. Dr. Jeep was one. The other was Juanita."

CHAPTER TWENTY

"Doug, Mr. Lou Pickero from the State Division of Licensing is here to see you."

"This early?" At first Doug's heart raced, then he realized he had plenty of time. "The survey team isn't due for another couple of weeks. Okay, show him in."

Ann opened the door and Lou squeezed past her. He grabbed Doug's hand and shook it hard.

"Good to see you again, Doug." But his eyes remained on Ann until she closed the door.

"Surprised to see you this week. Where's the rest of your team?"

"I'm not here for the scheduled survey." His smile looked like a toothpaste ad. "I've been asked to review the circumstances leading to the death of one of your patients, Mrs. Jean Daniels."

Doug felt his pulse surge. "Have a seat. Why are you interested in that particular death?"

"Deaths in the delivery room always get caught in the first review. OB patients aren't sick patients. And being in her twenties with two previous children and no history of illness of any kind"—he waved his hand—"we thought we'd fill in the gaps so we could close the file." His smile broke into an easy laugh. "It's routine for this kind of death."

Has someone put him on to it? Just as well. There'll be no cover-up. "What do you want to see?"

"I want to see the complete medical record, documentation, including the delivery room schedule, incident reports, quality assurance committee minutes, and special study reports related to the death." He paused. "You might've already collected them since this wasn't a routine death."

Doug nodded.

"I'll want to interview everyone who was there, the obstetrician, anesthesiologist, nurses, everybody. I thought I'd drop by this afternoon since I got into town before quitting time. That way, you can get things lined up for me to start tomorrow morning. If material is available, I could read this evening. By tomorrow evening, I'll be gone."

"You'll find it interesting material." Doug picked up the phone. "Ann, bring in a copy of the report on Jean Daniels I wrote for Walter Bass, with all the attachments."

"Okay," she answered insecurely, knowing what it was.

Lou stood when she came in. His smile seemed poised on the edge of some great statement. She handed the report to Doug.

"Will you schedule Mr. Pickero with Dr. Salerno and the nurse anesthetist that assisted Dr. Robinson?" requested Doug. "And also the nurses. Oh, and Dr. Apple, since he chaired the ad hoc review team. While you're at it, see if you can get Robinson to come in."

Doug handed the report to Lou who continued to watch Ann until she left the room. Then he sat again.

"Nice-looking girl."

"You remember Ann from previous trips here, don't you?"

"Oh, yes."

Doug smiled at the lack of subtlety. "That report you have in your hands is self-contained. In the appendix are copies of the medical record, various incident reports, and the report of the ad hoc review team chaired by Jack Apple, Chair of Surgery. My own commentary, while explicit, is nothing you wouldn't decide for yourself."

Ann interrupted and once more Lou stood.

"Dr. Salerno can see you any time before ten tomorrow morning. What's your preference?"

"Any time you say. I'm putty in your hands."

Doug laughed out loud.

"I'll set it up for nine." She gratefully closed the door.

"Lou, I've a feeling you won't need any other documentation. If you do, let me know." Doug paused a moment, noting Lou was thumbing through the report. "Will the regular survey be taking place as scheduled?" He was anxious for Lou to leave so he could let Joe and Stan know what was happening, as well as Walter Bass.

"Yep. We'll be here as scheduled. We received your drawing showing the installation of the fire partitions above the ceilings." He looked at the packet in his hands. "This is a pretty comprehensive report."

"The drawing?"

Ann came in again. "Dr. Apple says come up now if you have time."

"I'll make the time. Can you show me how to get there?"

"I'll walk you to the elevator and tell you the way from there."

Doug felt like he had been hit by a stun gun. *Stan must have sent in doctored drawings. How could I possibly expose Stan without exposing the hospital? And when the fabrications are discovered, where will that put me?*

"Oh, by the way"—Lou stepped back in—"I'll see you tomorrow before I leave."

Doug dialed Joe Goldman.

"Doug, someone put them onto us. The question is who?"

Doug then suddenly remembered to call Bess.

"I have a meeting this evening. Simba's found out about Robinson."

"Oh, what a shame. The hospital's bound to get hurt, but maybe it's time it got out, Doug. You've done everything you could. Does this mean we won't have dinner together?"

"I guess we'll have to put it off. I'll make it up to you and the kids."

Doug met Henry in the hotel lobby.

"Conference Room A," Henry announced.

"Same as the negotiations."

Simba was waiting. She smiled at Henry. "Henry, would you mind letting Doug and me talk alone?"

"She's being sweet, Henry. Don't go too far."

"I'll stay within calling distance. Just scream if you need help."

"I'm sure he won't need help, honey. You run along now." She shooed him away with her manicured tentacles, then eased the door closed behind him.

"Doug, it's time to fish or cut bait."

"You called the meeting."

"And I'm going to call the shots. I know Dr. Robinson was drunk and killed Mrs. Daniels and her unborn child. And there's some question about the competence of Dr. Salerno. But you grew balls and barred Robinson. At least this time you didn't kiss ass with the medical staff. I've been wondering what it would take to bring you to life. Too bad it had to be murder."

"So now what?"

"So you've not exactly announced it to the world, honey . . . but I'm going to if you don't sign the labor agreement I brought with me." She slid a file folder across the table.

Doug slid it back. "No."

She looked shocked. "No? Do you know I can blow you out of the water?"

"You can try. The state is already conducting an investigation of Mrs. Daniels' death. I've provided them with a full and factual report of the incident. So, as I say, you can try, but you'll fail."

Simba turned sideways in her chair, assessing Doug.

"The fact is," Doug continued, "you can't hurt me, but you can hurt the hospital. You can give it bad publicity and, without a doubt, cut admissions. You can send some patients to other hospitals for years into the future."

"Wouldn't it bother you if I did?"

"Yes, but not enough to sign away the hospital to excessive demands."

Simba pushed away from the table. "There's nothing left for us to discuss. I leave here and go to the newspapers. You are one stupid white man."

"That's exactly what I expected from you." Doug didn't budge. "I know you're smart enough to know there's a direct relationship between the number of admissions and the number of jobs in the hospital. Go to the newspapers, and you'll be destroying jobs for the people you claim to be helping. You fooled them, but not this stupid white man."

Simba held the file folder on her lap. She stared at the wall clock as though memorizing the hands. "Damn you, Carpenter," she whispered. "You bastard."

He sat for a few moments, looking at the tabletop. Then, he stood and left. He had talked her out of it but felt rotten. It seemed as though everybody knew but Jean Daniels' family. The husband was so trusting or grief-stricken, the idea of foul play hadn't entered his mind. And the hospital owed him and the children. He would talk to Walter Bass about it tomorrow morning.

A few minutes before nine a.m., Doug was surprised to see Lou Pickero walk in.

"Know how to get to Salerno's office?" asked Doug.

"Yes, I have directions. I just wanted Ann to know she didn't need to set up anything with Robinson." He managed a pained smile. "I saw him last night."

"Oh, did Dr. Apple set things up?" asked Ann.

"Yes."

"What did you think of the report?" asked Doug.

"Very in-depth."

Doug sensed Lou's reaction didn't quite fit. "Let me know if you need anything else. I think Ann will have the interviews with the nurses ready. Drop back by."

Lou looked surprised. "Oh, right. I'll come by as soon as I've met with Salerno. Thanks."

Doug felt a vague sense of uneasiness. Ann looked puzzled, too.

"That's the first time he didn't drill me with his laser eyes."

Doug called Walter Bass about Jean Daniels.

"I agree, Doug. We've got to let Mr. Daniels know. Let's meet with Herb Cline since he handles the hospital's malpractice litigation."

Doug felt better but knew he should've discussed it with Stan. *What the hell. Stan would have disagreed anyway.*

By ten, Lou had begun interviews with the delivery room nurses. Three in all. Doug had debated about including the OR nurses, but Lou had only asked for the delivery room. It was an investigation of one incident, not an inquisition.

By ten-thirty, though, the interviews were over.

"Thanks a lot, Doug. I'll see you with the survey."

"Wait a minute. Come on in. What's the conclusion?"

"I haven't written the report yet. I'll have it done in a few weeks."

"A few weeks. I don't get it."

At that moment, Jack Apple dropped in. He handed a large manila envelope to Lou.

"That's the additional material I said I'd get you." He smiled directly at Doug.

Jack left and Doug pulled Lou into his office. "You and I need to talk."

"I wish I could, but I've got to run."

Doug slammed the door. "Sit down."

Lou did. The envelope was too big to fit in his coat pocket. He slid it half inside the coat and held it like it might get away.

"We've got an anesthesiologist I've barred from the hospital because he's an alcoholic. He killed Mrs. Daniels. It's simple. What do you mean you haven't written the report yet? You know your conclusion. What is it?"

"I don't want to jump to conclusions."

Doug stared in disbelief as Lou, still clutching the envelope, stood to go.

"I don't believe this. What's going on?" *The envelope. It has some bearing.* Doug snatched it and pushed Lou into the seat.

Lou resisted, yelping, "No!"

As Doug ripped it open, Lou sank into the chair, limp.

Doug stared at a full glossy photograph. Lou, naked except for his socks, lying on top of Jack Apple's secretary and looking over his shoulder in surprise.

"I'll be damned." Doug stepped over to his desk and pressed the intercom. "Ann, get Jack Apple on the phone." He placed the photograph in the center desk drawer, slowly closing it. All the while, Lou hadn't blinked.

"Doug, I'll be ruined if I find against Robinson."

"You'll be ruined if you whitewash it. Jack found your weakness. Your gonads."

"He's on the line," buzzed Ann.

"Jack, I'm here with Lou Pickero . . . and I have the photograph. Your secretary, Patricia, is definitely more photogenic on her back than any other way. You use this photograph against Lou, and I'll use it against you. You tried to blackmail him into a lie. I'll deliver it to Walter Bass myself. Blackmail is against the law, Jack. I knew you were stupid, but I didn't know you were a total moron." He slammed the receiver without waiting for a response. "What's your conclusion on Robinson?"

Lou hesitated, but for only a moment. "Worst case, manslaughter. At best, malpractice. I doubt if there'll be manslaughter charges because there were no tests to determine the amount of alcohol in his blood." He smiled, half-giggled, and shook his head. "The way you handled that . . . I just had no idea it could be that easy. I owe you." He leaned forward and studied his hands for a moment. "I'd sure feel better about it if I had the negative. You don't suppose . . ." He gestured with his hands.

"Lou, that's between you and Jack. I don't know if there's anything he can do with it, but I don't know that I'd go ask him for it either." Doug leaned back in his chair.

"You're right." He stood slowly and made for the door, eyes glued to Doug's desk. "I'll give you a confirmation in a few days." He opened the door to leave, paused, and closed it again. "That Patricia . . . Boy, can she put out!"

The Medical Staff Board had its meeting that night. The usual menu that ran the spectrum between hors d'oeuvres and aperitifs preceded it. For Doug, this was a duty meeting. The display of near-decadence served as a reminder the doctors were the elitists of the health field and many expected to be served. The Quality Assurance Committee's recommendation that Doug and Kay be censured was on the agenda. Worse yet, he would be expected to sit there and say nothing. The doctors spoke at these meetings, others only if asked.

Damn good thing there were some decent human beings among them. It would be easy to become a doctor-hater. It had happened to a number of administrators, making it difficult for them to function. In some hospitals, the bad doctors came close to outnumbering the good ones, and they were so aggressive and demanding they appeared to be everywhere, like cockroaches.

When the Quality Assurance Committee recommendation came up, Joe Goldman presented the facts.

"There were three people voting on this issue." He held up three fingers. "Two voted for it." He held up two fingers. "And by the vote of these two people, you have to decide whether or not to censure Doug and Kay for the handling of the Brownstein case. Personally, I'm appalled to present it, but I must. It's your decision."

Julia Best raised her hand and was recognized by Joe, but before she could speak, Ed Whyte stood to read a statement.

"This hospital has suffered from inadequate nursing care and poor administration for—"

Joe Goldman slammed his gavel. "The chair has recognized Dr. Best. Dr. Whyte, you may have the floor next."

"I just wanted to comment," Julia stood, "that it's inappropriate to cast blame in this case. Dr. Afton could not have predicted the suicide. And it would not have been in the interest of good patient care to have the patient transferred to the Psych Unit." She paused, evidently gathering her thoughts.

"It would, however," interrupted Charles Smith, "have been

appropriate for good administration and nursing care to be rendered regardless of which unit the patient was in."

"Please continue, Julia," said Joe, giving both Whyte and Smith "I dare you" looks.

"I think Doug and Kay do their jobs well. I can't censure them. None of the things that happened were predictable. Doug is very concerned about it. We've met about it. He's set up a review team to try to prevent something like this from ever happening again."

"How many times has the review team met?" asked Charles.

"There hasn't been a meeting yet."

"Charles," interjected Joe, "you might recall that in the meantime there's been a strike. Things are not normal."

"Things are never *normal*. Administration always has a good reason to fail."

"Ed," Joe nodded in his direction, "you have the floor."

Whyte stood again.

"This hospital has suffered from inadequate nursing care and poor administration for too many years. The medical staff has been patient for too long. We have an obligation to the sick people who come here for medical care to correct this—"

"Stop right there, Ed," interrupted Josh Feldman. "We're here to discuss one case, not your historical perspective of the way this hospital has been run in the last hundred years. What happened in the Brownstein case that warrants this extreme action of censoring Doug and Kay?"

"Poor nursing care is ultimately caused by poor administration. The medical—"

"Joe, must we? Really?" Josh gestured in despair.

"The medical staff," read Ed more loudly, "is obligated to point out poor practices to the Board of Trustees, who are, in turn, obligated to correct such deficiencies."

"Great!" shouted Josh. "What are the specific poor practices we are to point out?"

"The carpenter di-didn't dri-drive the nails in fa-r . . . far enough," sputtered Ed.

"I move we buy the carpenter a bigger hammer!" exclaimed Josh.

"The chair recognizes Garland Riggely."

"What kind of committee is this Quality Assurance Committee? This has got to be the dumbest recommendation I ever heard!" Garland, indignant and disgusted, peered into each person's eyes.

Joe looked at Ed and Charles. "Do either of the two that voted for this want to answer the question?"

"It's just typical," Charles jumped to answer, "of how things are handled by Administration."

Jack Apple sat staring at his folded hands.

"Are we ready for a vote?" asked Joe, trying to hurry things along.

Garland pounded the table once and yelled, "I call for the dumb question, and I hope the Quality Assurance Committee won't insult our intelligence again."

The recommendation was defeated by a vote of seven to four. Doug's neck and shoulder muscles loosened.

On the way to their offices, Stan was silent until they reached the hallway. "You're a constant source of embarrassment. Have you made your decision?"

"What decision?" Doug stopped to look him directly in the face.

"Why, I asked for your resignation, that's what," he said, acting surprised.

"I gave you my answer. The ball is in your court." With that, Doug went home.

CHAPTER TWENTY-ONE

Frank Street peered over his cup of coffee, hate flashing like a neon sign. "Doug, ninety percent of what you say is full of shit."

"Why do you think we're having this meeting?"

"I want to hold them to a three percent pay increase."

"I know, but what you want doesn't matter. What matters is what's good for the hospital. If our salaries are below average, we'll lose good employees. Five percent would be right. Three percent next year."

"I'm not going to give those niggers five percent."

Doug slowly stirred his coffee. "You will if you're going to be part of this team. You want me to let the president of the university know you can't work on behalf of the hospital, that you're more interested in making yourself look good by keeping the salaries lower than they should be?"

"Shit."

"And another thing, I told you I don't want to hear any more of your racist slurs."

"It's a nigger union."

"Even if it were a black union it wouldn't matter. The fact is ninety-one percent of our service employees voted for this union—fifty-two percent are black, forty-eight percent are white.

That's balanced. How can you deal with blacks if you hate them so much?"

"Doug, shove it. I deal with them to beat their black asses."

"I guess a bigot's a bigot. Five percent minimum. No past-practice restrictions. We can compromise on most anything else. I'll see you at four o'clock."

Frank unfolded himself from the chair and left the office without glancing back.

Ann popped in through the door. "In case you're interested, several ward clerks snuck in last night. They wanted to know how they can get back to work. They said everybody wants to come back. They've got bills to pay."

"If they ask again, tell them all they have to do is report to work. We'll accept them anytime."

"Morale's low on the street. Joy said they even miss the smells."

"Joy's one of them? I'm glad to hear that."

The phone rang. "The day's beginning," Ann announced as she slipped into her office. In a moment, she called Doug. "Al Robinson's in the security office. He wants to come see you."

Robinson sat in the chair by the window. He looked older than his forty-five years—the alcohol—eyes glazed. He looked around the room and out the window, stood, and sat again. He jerked constantly, as though every joint were spring-loaded, thin, almost anorexic, as though he had given up eating. He kept brushing back his thick, black hair, which poked in all directions despite his efforts.

"Doug, I've tried to quit drinking." He leaned forward, running his fingers through his hair, nervously twitching. "My head is about to come off."

Doug closed the door.

"I could use a drink. But I've got to stop." His face was apple red. He jumped up and strode over to the window again, but he shielded his eyes from the light.

"I've got some coffee," Doug offered.

"Maybe if it's black."

Doug poured and handed him the mug.

Robinson grasped it with both hands and, even so, shook so hard he spilled some on his shirt without noticing. He held it to his mouth as though it had reached a safe place and took a large gulp, disregarding the heat, and set it on the table by the window, then flung himself into the chair again.

He fixed on Doug, his brown eyes wide and wet. "I don't know what to do. You were right to bar me." With his hands cupping his forehead, he leaned forward and propped his elbows on his knees. "I wish you'd done it sooner." He picked up the cup and tried to get it to his lips again, but succeeded in spilling it on his trousers. With great effort he managed to set it on the table. "Doug, please help me."

"If you're serious, there's an alcohol rehab program in Maryland I can recommend. But only if you're sure."

"I'm sure. I mean it. I have a problem." He covered his face with his hands. His shoulders shook and his voice squeaked out like a thin whistle. "I killed her, Doug. I killed her. I can't get her out of my mind. I see her all the time. She's everywhere." He hunched over, face cupped in hands, and cried. "Please call them. Please get me in. Please."

"I'll make all the arrangements. I know the administrator. When can you leave?"

"Today. Now."

"Is your wife home?"

"She left." His voice was almost a whisper. "Sh-she left me. Gone."

Doug sat beside him in the extra chair. Robinson leaned over and laid his head on Doug's shoulder.

"If you're sure you want to do this, I'll have someone from Social Service go home with you. I think you need help getting packed. I'm sure they can take you unless they're having an unusual year. I'll call them right now."

Robinson sprawled out in the chair and stared at the ceiling.

"Al," Doug picked up the phone and dialed, "I'll recommend a leave of absence for you, and I'm sure the medical staff will appoint an acting chair until you get squared away."

"We better talk about it some other time. I don't know what I want. I don't know if I'm fit." He sat up and wiped his eyes with his fingers.

"Sylvia Hamilton, please," requested Doug.

At a quarter to twelve, Doug went out to Main Street to look around. The picketers had almost disappeared, with only three on the whole street. The area was clean of leaflets and trash.

Cliff Toliver spotted him and came over. "The rumor is the union members are shirking picket duty because they want to come back."

"Good news if it's true."

Back in his office, Doug called Joe Goldman.

"Joe, two things. I just wanted you to know Stan has asked for my resignation. He's not going to get it, of course, but he's asked for it and has threatened to fire me."

"Doug, what can I do to help?"

"Nothing. I just wanted you to know. It's just part of the continuing saga. Kinda fits in with the patchwork of crazy things that go on here all the time."

"I hadn't heard. I'm not one of the people he confides in. But I'm glad you told me. You have my support."

"That's good to know. The other thing. Al Robinson is on his way to an alcohol rehab center in Maryland. He asked for my help, and I think he's serious about facing the problem. He was in bad shape this morning. I'll fill you in later, but we need to appoint someone as acting Chair of Anesthesiology."

The meeting with Walter Bass and Herb Cline was scheduled in the boardroom. Herb liked space to lay things out.

"How are contract negotiations going, Doug?" asked Walter. He folded his big square hands on the table in front of him.

"From all indications, the session scheduled this afternoon could be conclusive."

"You remember our board meeting is this evening. I assume you're planning to be there."

"Yes. If necessary, I'll recess the negotiations and schedule them for tomorrow."

"You might want to let someone else handle it. That's too important to put off. By the way, where is Stan? Isn't he coming?"

"He pretty much leaves operations to me, Walter. He's involved with the new building."

Walter sat like a statue, his black hair framing his square face and black eyes. "You did ask him, though."

"No." Doug felt uncomfortable. "Experience tells me he wouldn't want to be bothered."

"Why don't you call him?" Walter motioned toward the phone at the end of the room.

Doug tried to think of a reason not to but dialed Stan's number.

"Liz, let me speak to Stan."

"He's out. I'll tell him you called."

"When do you expect him?"

"He didn't say."

"Is he out of the building?"

"I believe so."

When Doug hung up, Walter grabbed the phone. "What's his number?"

"Two-three-eight-two."

"Miss Racoda, this is Walter Bass. Is Stan in?"

"Just a moment."

"Hi, Walter. How are you?"

"I'm fine. Can you come to the boardroom?"

A few minutes later when Stan walked in, he looked surprised to see Doug and Herb there and was obviously puzzled by the summons.

"Sit down, Stan." Walter had the appearance and objectivity of a judge. All he lacked was a black robe. "You're aware of the death of Mrs. Daniels and that Dr. Robinson was the direct cause of it?"

"I'm aware of her death, but I think the medical staff exonerated Dr. Robinson."

"If you aren't aware that Dr. Robinson caused her death, you're the only person in this building who isn't."

Stan looked shocked and darted a quick glance toward Doug.

"To the discerning eye it would have been obvious weeks ago he was going to kill somebody." He paused. "I won't involve Herb with all this. We want to discuss settlement with Mr. Daniels. That's why Herb is here. We want to keep it out of court, and we want to be fair. Herb, what does your experience suggest our most logical approach to be?"

"I suggest we contact Mr. Daniels and tell him the hospital feels some responsibility for his wife's death and that we want to discuss it with him."

"All right. Then what?"

"We lay it bare. Tell him what happened," said Herb.

"In the meeting, you mean."

"Yes, in the meeting."

"Do we offer anything as restitution?"

"Depending on his frame of mind, it could go anywhere from $200,000 to $2,000,000. He could get whatever he asked for if he sued."

"Offer him $200,000 to help raise his children. I think we should set up the meeting as soon as possible."

"Walter," said Doug, "the state conducted its own investigation yesterday. It would be best if we met before their conclusions were made known. Our sincerity could be questioned, otherwise."

Stan piped up, "My understanding was the state agreed with the medical staff investigation."

"Apparently Jack Apple hasn't filled you in on the latest," Doug interjected. "The state's only question will be whether it was malpractice or manslaughter."

"Probably malpractice," responded Herb. "Tougher proving manslaughter. Unless someone ran tests on Robinson."

"No. He disappeared."

"Herb, use Doug or Stan's office and set it up. I want to talk to these two gentlemen. Let us know when it is."

When Herb left, Walter resumed, "Stan, apparently you haven't been kept fully informed, but I'm not so sure you've wanted to be."

"What makes you say that?"

"A few moments ago, you were in your office when Doug called. Miss Racoda said you were out. Was that by your instruction, or has she overstepped her bounds?"

"I gave her instructions I didn't want to be bothered. Naturally, she'd make an exception for the Chairman of the Board."

"But not for your own administrator."

"No, not really." Stan couldn't hide his discomfort. "I can see him anytime."

"Just for my edification, what were you working on that was too important to be interrupted by your administrator?"

This startled Stan so, he actually answered honestly. "I was working on the building plans."

"The building plans. And that's such a short-range rush project you had to do it today. Is that right?"

"It is important, Walter."

"Then you don't have time to be here right now, do you?"

Stan sputtered as though he had run out of gas. "I-I said, I'd dr-drop anything for you."

"I'll let you decide whether or not you should stay."

During the entire meeting, Walter hadn't changed posture, expression, or tone of voice.

"A last-minute item has been placed on the agenda for this evening's meeting. I thought we three should discuss it. It is simply this. The vice president for Health Services and the hospital administrator do not work as a team. Indeed, they do not even communicate. I've seen prime examples this afternoon. Knowing your building design is pressing you, I'll excuse you from the meeting, Stan."

"No, I think I'd better stay."

"Are you sure you can put the design off until tomorrow?"

"Yes. Yes. I can put it off."

"Then why didn't you talk to Doug before?"

Stan struggled but brought forth no words.

Walter's eyes never left him.

"Walter," Doug finally broke the trance, "could I ask how this came to be an agenda item?"

"Fair question. A group of doctors asked it be discussed."

"Was one of them Jack Apple?"

Walter suppressed a smile. "It's funny you should ask. He was the only one that asked his name not be disclosed. I frown on anonymous accusations and told him so. Do you know why he wanted it that way?"

"Yes." Doug walked over and phoned his secretary. "Ann, in my middle desk drawer there's a large envelope. It's taped shut. Don't open it. Just bring it over to the boardroom."

Doug registered fear on Stan's face for one short instant but it was replaced by a look of nervous interest.

"When Ann gets here, I'll show you the content of the envelope, but I want to summarize the background information." Doug returned to his chair. "I've been using every legitimate means I could think of to get Al Robinson out of this hospital. Stan didn't want to get involved. He wanted the doctors on his side so they would support his building plans. The doctors, no matter what Joe Goldman said, whitewashed the whole Robinson situation."

"And Jack Apple chaired the ad hoc review team."

"Yes."

Ann came in with the envelope and handed it to Doug.

"Thanks, Ann. Please shut the door behind you." Turning his attention back to Walter, he continued, "When I barred Al from the hospital, Stan gave me an official reprimand and asked for my resignation."

Stan laid his hands flat on the table and seemed to be studying each fingernail, shaking his head.

"Excuse me, Doug. Stan, if any of this isn't factual, please break in at any time."

Stan made no comment but nodded his head.

"Go ahead, Doug."

"When Mr. Pickero arrived from the state for the investigation, I figured it would be settled once and for all." Doug paused for a moment. "I wondered if someone hadn't called him."

Walter interrupted. "It wasn't you, was it, Doug?"

"No. But as I've reflected on it, I might be able to pick out who did. But I don't want to say until I know for sure."

"You'll let me know when you find out?"

"Yes, sir. Anyhow, I gave Mr. Pickero a copy of the report I prepared for you. That should've clinched it. The last I saw of him, he was off to see Jack Apple. The next morning, Pickero hedged and I knew he was going to exonerate Al. Then Apple had the stupidity to send—no, to hand-deliver this envelope to Pickero while he was in my office. From the way he behaved—Pickero, that is—my instincts told me the key was here."

Doug held up the envelope. "It's a photograph of Pickero and Jack Apple's secretary." He slid it across the table to Walter.

Walter removed the tape and opened the envelope, pulled the photograph out and examined it for a long time. There was no change in expression. He glanced at Doug. "You've seen the photograph, Stan?"

"No."

Walter shoved it to him. "You've been missing a lot."

Stan studied the photograph as though he didn't know whether to put it down or stare at it. He handed it to Walter, whose eyes bore holes through him.

"The latest information you had about Pickero's findings when you came into this meeting was that he was going to exonerate Dr. Robinson. Did you know about the photograph?"

"No. No. I didn't know anything about the photograph."

Walter continued to study Stan as he handed the photograph to Doug. For a moment, the room was quiet.

Walter shifted his attention to Doug. "Bring it with you tonight. I doubt you'll need it, but have it handy. I'll see you two gentlemen tonight. Reception at six, dinner at seven, meeting at eight."

As they emerged from the boardroom, Herb Cline was coming down the hall.

"Mr. Daniels will call my office later. I'll let you know then."

On the way to their offices, Stan lowered his head and walked rapidly ahead of Doug. Doug let him gain distance. He could think of a lot of terms from the vernacular that described Stan. Piece of work. Spare parts. Certifiable. The employees must have been struggling to respect an Administration headed by him. Now Doug knew for sure who had called the state. The OB nurses. He could never prove it. But he would never want to, either.

CHAPTER TWENTY-TWO

Kay O'Connell and Juanita were waiting for him. "We need to talk."

Kay closed the door behind them. "The medical examiner has done an autopsy."

"On who?"

"Mrs. Ramirez. The lady we think was killed," said Kay.

"I figured that would happen. We reported it as a death with unknown cause."

"Yeah. Technically, she died from an electrolyte imbalance. But the cause for that is unknown, and they say foul play." Kay shook her head. "We were pretty sure it was. Their toxicologist is reviewing it. They think it was a poison of some sort but haven't found any traces yet."

"Did she just up and die, just like that?" he asked, snapping his fingers.

"It wasn't quick. She had a high fever and vomiting. She was really sick. She had septicemia, became violent and was extremely confused. They had to restrain her. Kept shouting in Spanish. Juanita was there."

Juanita struggled to hold back tears. "It was pretty awful. I never saw her like that. She was always so in control, you know?

She kept shouting things like 'Watch out! Duck!' 'Sell the business.' 'Take him out of my will.' I couldn't tell who she was talking about."

"Did she have a business? Did she have anything to leave to anyone? Most people in Solstory are too poor to even have a will."

"She and her son started a retread business and they made money. She was the brains. But she never moved out of Solstory. She stayed and everybody loved her."

"Was her son there when she died?"

"No, he was there the night before, but she died at eight a.m. He got there too late. Her temperature dropped, suddenly. Her blood pressure dropped. But her pulse increased to 160 a minute. I couldn't believe it."

"Doug," added Kay, "the lab said her white blood count was triple the normal rate."

"What's going on in this hospital?" He ran his fingers through his hair.

"I know her son," said Juanita. "When he got here, I thought we were going to have to sedate him."

"Where was Jeep during all this?"

"He was in and out. He didn't know what to do. I wish she had a different doctor. A good internist."

"Hell, if she was poisoned, it probably wouldn't do any good. I don't remember her from Solstory, but I didn't get to know everybody there. Are the police conducting an investigation?"

"Yes," Kay answered, "including our undercover man." At Doug's reaction, she added, "I had to tell Juanita when he started questioning her."

"Kinda blew his cover, didn't he?

"Evidently he felt it was serious enough."

"We've got a serious problem and we need to get to the bottom of it. But why Juanita?"

"He questioned other people, too."

Juanita bit her lip and tried to smile. "It makes me feel strange."

Doug felt sorry for her. "Juanita, there are a lot of people in the hospital who could have done whatever was done. They're just looking for motives now."

Kay nodded. "I told her she could expect it to get worse."

"I'll help as much as possible. I want to see whoever did this get caught." Juanita's hands turned into fists. "Have any ideas who it might be?"

"No. I don't even think Jeep would do that." Doug pushed the thought out of his mind that she could have had anything to do with it. An angel, she was pure innocence and truth.

Juanita wiped her eyes. "I don't know if I'm in the right place. A higher death rate than normal, Jean Daniels, Mrs. Ramirez. People are supposed to come here to get well, not get killed."

Senior RN Sharon Smith called from the ER. "I've got a problem I need to talk to you about, but not over the phone. Can I see you for a few minutes?"

She brought the ER resident, Dr. Samuel Smallwood, with her. Normally good-natured and energetic, he looked worried. He closed the door quietly but firmly, pushing against it even after it was latched.

Sharon was the epitome of the professional nurse, everything an ER nurse ought to be: precise, crisp, but not brusque. She was uneasy. Didn't sit. Brushed back her blond hair. "The problem is we have an orderly who's a drug pusher."

"And that's not all," interjected Sam Smallwood. "He intimidates the other orderlies, the clerks, and even the physician assistants. Of course, they're all on strike, but I guess I'm afraid of him myself."

"Isn't he on strike?"

"No," Sharon replied. "He keeps coming in. When I asked him how come he wasn't on strike, he said, 'I don't need the bleepin' union,' and he doesn't."

"What makes you think he's a pusher?"

"We can't prove it. He's street smart. But others have told us. And we're missing narcotics."

"We can't dismiss him on the basis of what others say," explained Doug, "unless they're willing to testify. Can you build a case with the missing narcotics?"

"No, that's the thing. You see, they're missing from all three shifts and also his days off. But he lives in the neighborhood and he's in here all times of the day and night."

"What's his name?"

"J.C. Urqhart."

"Tevisina Urqhart's son?"

"Is she on the Board? He's always saying his mother is on the Board."

"Oh, no!" said Doug.

"He doesn't follow orders," Sam told him. "He just does his own thing."

"That's something you can get him on. Insubordination."

"I'm not afraid of him." Sharon squared her shoulders. "I'll write him up if you'll back us when he goes to his mother."

"I'll back you. Post a notice that employees are to be there only when they are on duty and no other time."

"That's going to be difficult because he brings patients in, like a local godfather."

"For the time being, let him know he can come as far as the waiting room, but not into the ER itself."

"Okay. I can do that. I had a run-in with him earlier today when he told a volunteer to transport a patient that had been assigned to him. I think I'll write him up on that. I'll make it a formal warning."

"Sam, you be with her when it's discussed. There has to always be a witness."

Doug was about to leave for his meeting with Frank Street and Simba when a hulk of an orderly with pitch black features contrasted against his white lab coat appeared in the outer doorway. He scowled at Doug. "I need to see you about a warning I just got from that ER nurse."

"You must be J.C. Urqhart."

"You knowed about it, didn't you," he said accusatively, bowing out his back.

"Yes, they discussed it with me."

"Then you as guilty as them."

"What it means is you have to learn to do as you are told. If you want to talk about it, in deference to your mother, I have just five minutes. I'm on my way to a meeting."

"No. I don't want to talk with you. I'll talk with your Board." Urqhart stormed out.

"Holy smokes!" exclaimed Ann with a *whew!* "I knew there was trouble when he walked in. That's Mrs. Urqhart's son, and he's bad news. She protects him, says he's the community advocate."

"Some advocate." But his impression of Tevisina was suddenly quite different. He didn't think she would be pleased with her son's true role. He wondered how much she knew. "What will be, will be. Just kind of fits in with this whole week."

CHAPTER TWENTY-THREE

Four o'clock. Doug and Frank waited for Simba. Frank had brought his assistant, Harold Garner, to observe. He was a wrinkled miniature of a man with a few brown strands of hair plastered forward in a failed attempt to cover a shiny head. His shirt was tie-dyed in gray that matched his baggy suit.

"Frank," said Doug, ignoring Garner. "Things might be about to break."

"What makes you think so?"

"Word from the picket line is there's some dissatisfaction."

"Hell," Garner said, "that's why they're there in the first place." His speech was slurred, making Doug concentrate on to each word.

Frank guffawed. "Doug thinks they're out there to get a suntan."

"Let's have an understanding," Doug looked at Garner, "you're here to listen. You won't be participating in the negotiations. Do you understand?"

"Yes. I know to keep my mouth shut. I've sat in on a lot of these."

"Then you're not here to learn."

"No."

"Why are you here?"

"He's here so he can give me feedback," said Frank.

Doug let it fester.

They sat for a while, Frank and Garner making useless conversation. At half past, Doug suggested Frank make a phone call to see if there had been a mix-up, but right then Simba came in with her crew.

"Good. Are you ready to start?" Doug asked.

"If you are."

"Let's start where we left off last time. We've agreed on check-off, existing work breaks, parking privileges, existing TV sets—but no guarantee on repairs—and a lot of boilerplate stuff. We won't agree to restriction on efficiency moves, and we haven't discussed wages. Does that sum it up?"

"You failed to mention Clinker. Are you dropping charges?"

"No."

"Prosecuting her is worth more to you than letting the employees return to work?"

"As far as I'm concerned, it's not an either/or situation."

Frank interjected, "We're ready to bargain. But charges have been brought against Clinker Pottard and they won't be dropped. You tell us. Do we negotiate or not?" Frank sneered. He was obviously daring her to walk out.

"The reason we came was to negotiate, but we don't want to see an employee suffer who got carried away in the spirit of things. After all, if the hospital had been fair to its employees, the union wouldn't have even been needed." Simba's voice rose as though she were in a pulpit. "The fact that the union is needed should be enough for you to drop all charges against any employee who, in good faith, overreacted."

"I watched her overreact from my office window. The fact those two nurses aren't dead is a miracle. She tried to either kill or maim. Overreaction is an understatement. You can't justify attempted murder."

"This lady is a good Christian lady. She goes to church, sings in the choir, and shouts the praises of God."

"I don't care if she's a saint," stated Doug. "She's going to jail."

"Simba," asked Frank, "are you going to hang these negotiations because Clinker Pottard is an instrument of God?"

Simba narrowed her eyes, clearly waiting for his follow-up remark.

"I mean, if you make this a religious issue, we're going to be here a *long* time."

"You have a smart mouth."

"Hey, you mentioned she's a good Christian, that she goes to church and sings the gospel. Well, me, too. I'm a damn good Christian. I go to church every lousy Sunday and I sing my ass off." Watching her lean back in her chair, he went on. "I mean, come on, what do you want? You're a good Christian. She's a good Christian. I'm a good Christian. We're even. What the hell? We'll even write into the contract Clinker Pottard is a good Christian. It won't mean she's not going to jail." He flashed his teeth, pleased with himself.

"We will take a short recess." Simba left, her team following.

"I think this could be a long night," said Doug.

"They'll drop Clinker."

"I bet they'll be out 'til five." Doug checked his watch, feeling pressured. He could miss the Board reception, but he didn't want to leave negotiations in Frank's hands if things dragged on past then.

They returned at about a minute past five.

"We drop our demand that Clinker Pottard not be charged if you agree to set aside one holiday a year in her name."

"Clinker Pottard Day?!" exclaimed Doug.

"Right. It's the least you can do."

Frank crossed his arms and leaned over toward Doug. "You could take one of the two personal days and make it a holiday."

"No way. That's the dumbest idea I've ever heard. If there is to be a holiday, let's name it after the two nurses she mauled—"

"I've got it!" Frank squealed. "Why doesn't the union set up a scholarship fund in her honor?"

"Will you make an annual contribution of $10,000 toward it?" she countered.

"What the hell," said Doug, "name it the Clinker Pottard Nonviolence Scholarship Fund, and we'll give $5,000 a year to it, dumb idea and all."

"Eight thousand. Not a penny less."

Doug thought about it. *What's $3,000 more?* "Okay, $8,000."

"Now, regarding efficiency changes that eliminate jobs, *gentlemen*," she minced her words, "we would like to arrive at an amicable solution, but we cannot allow thoughtless, archaic practices. Employees are not furniture you discard."

"That's why the hospital pays unemployment compensation," Frank explained.

"That is not enough. In this day and age, finding a new job isn't easy."

"I'll tell you what," offered Doug, "we would be willing to help retrain any employee whose job was eliminated due to efficiency changes."

"How much help?" asked Simba, clutching the idea.

"To an amount not to exceed one-half the annual wage of the employee."

"If you gentlemen will excuse us, we will have a short caucus in the hallway." They left the room.

"We're making progress, Doug. Don't get impatient." Frank, all ego, patted his colleague on the back.

"I guess they'll be out deliberating this for another half hour." He looked at his watch. Ten past five.

At 5:45 p.m., he was ready to call it quits, but Simba returned.

"Look," he said, "you're making this a marathon. If you're going to require a thirty-minute recess after every item, we'll never get done."

"We want to be sure we are doing the right thing, Mr. Carpenter. After all, employee livelihoods are at stake. It's not something to rush."

Doug wondered if she knew about the Board meeting.

"What's your decision?" asked Frank.

"We want to make a minor change in the wording. The required training will not be less than one-half the annual wage of the employee."

"You know," countered Doug, "I thought that was a generous offer. You're screwing around with it to see what else you can bleed from the hospital."

"Mr. Carpenter, it's not going to cost you that much more. An employee's job can mean his life."

"If I agree, will it take you another thirty minutes to accept it?"

"No, honey," she smiled. "I'll accept it right now."

"Agreed," said Doug.

"The wage increase," Simba pushed on. "We are willing to accept seventeen percent per year if you agree to a three-year contract."

"Ha." Frank slapped his hand down on the table.

"We have come down from our original demand, but you haven't budged from yours."

"Simba," Doug reminded, "we are agreeable to five percent instead of four. A twenty-five percent increase over our initial offer. Your seventeen percent is unrealistic. You might as well ask for a hundred and seventeen. Our offer is in good faith. In today's economy, it's a reasonable offer. If you're not able to see that, we might as well recess until you do see it."

Simba looked at her watch. "We'll think about your offer while we have dinner. We'll meet you here at seven o'clock." She stood up but so did Doug.

"Look, to hell with dinner. Let's sit here until it's done. We are almost finished."

"Your offer has to be discussed. We will think it over while we eat." They left the room.

"It's happy hour," said Frank. "Let's go to the bar and see what we can get. Buffalo wings and a beer sound good."

"I'd think you'd want to keep a clear head."

"What the hell for? You just gave away the store. Five percent. She didn't even work for it."

"That's the amount on the table. You're going to have to finish things off. I've a Board meeting to go to." *Damn. It would have been better to finish it off. But at this point, Frank can't screw it up much.*

Doug got to the reception at 6:15. Stan was already there, wearing his congenial front. He acted as though the meeting earlier in the afternoon hadn't occurred. He didn't seem to see Doug. Joe Goldman did and came right over.

"Everything okay?" he asked.

"Yeah. Just came from the union contract negotiation session."

"Get anything accomplished?"

"Yes. But not as much as I wanted."

"Come on. Let me pour you a glass of wine." Joe put his arm around Doug's shoulder and pulled him over to the bar. "How are things between you and Stan?"

"It's bad and it'll get worse. Did you know that's an agenda item tonight?"

"No way."

"It's okay. I think Walter will handle it. If anybody can, he can."

"Did Stan ask for that?"

"No. Some good physician friends whom we both know."

"One of them wouldn't be something-something-something the third, would it?"

"You got it," said Doug. "You and I need to talk. There are things you need to know about. If they don't all come out in this meeting, let's have breakfast."

"Let's have breakfast anyhow. If seven o'clock isn't too early, we can meet in the cafeteria tomorrow morning."

Charles Smith strolled in, leaving a wake of tobacco stench.

"You know," Joe commented in his most sarcastic manner, "that guy's on so many boards, he's a detriment to organized society."

"He's been creating hazards around here for a long time, too."

"Don't worry. You have more friends than you think."

The dinner put every five-star restaurant to shame, but Doug didn't begrudge it for the Board. The members received no pay for their services. It was the least the hospital could do. Tevisina Urqhart came in just as the meal was being served. Her face and eyes gleamed with anger

Walter Bass tapped Doug on the shoulder. "Glad you were able to work it out to be here." That simple gesture by Walter gave Doug encouragement, like he had a guardian angel.

Walter ushered everyone into the boardroom at eight o'clock.

Doug carried the envelope with the photograph and wondered if he would have to use it. Walter tapped the table with his gavel. "There's a late item for the agenda, and I want to place it first because it's unpleasant and it's best to get unpleasant things resolved."

Charles leaned forward to speak, but Walter held his hand up. "I'll call on you in a moment, Charles. First, a few introductory comments. The subject has to do with the fact that the vice president for Health Services and the hospital administrator do not function as a team and, in fact, communicate poorly. It's essential they function as a team. I was asked to place this on the agenda by doctors Smith, Whyte, and Apple."

Charles Smith looked surprised at the mention of Apple's name. "Actually, Dr. Apple wasn't the one who suggested it."

"Yes, Apple did suggest it, and asked for anonymity, which I did not guarantee him, nor does he deserve, as it turns out."

Charles looked at Stan. Obviously, Stan had failed him by not filling him in on what happened earlier.

"This afternoon, I met with Stan and Doug to discuss the matter."

Charles, again, looked at Stan, who avoided eye contact by studying his fingers knuckle by knuckle.

"It's true the two are not communicating, and it appears Stan has placed a wall between them. I will ask Stan if he wants to comment. But first I want to cite a short case study that typifies the relationship and also indicates what Jack Apple's ulterior motive was in asking that this item be placed on the agenda."

He restated the events regarding Al Robinson and Lou Pickero in Doug's own words.

"I asked Doug to bring the photograph of Mr. Pickero enjoying Jack Apple's secretary in the event you would want to see it, but I don't recommend pornography. If Dr. Smith would like it presented, we'll oblige him."

Charles, through all this, had slouched further and further into his chair. His face had turned from red to ashen.

"Before I turn to Dr. Smith, does anyone want to add any other pertinent comment?"

Doug raised his hand and Walter called on him.

"Only that Al Robinson came to see me today. He was trying

to withdraw from the alcohol, was in a terrible state, and asked for my help. He's on his way to an alcohol rehab program in Maryland. I talked to the administrator there myself. He'll be there no less than thirty days. He isn't sure what he wants to do when he returns, but it would be my suggestion to Joe," he looked over at Joe and nodded, "someone be appointed acting chair until Al decides about his future."

Walter looked at Charles. "Dr. Smith?"

Charles straightened his back but slumped again. He mumbled at his hands clasped on the table. "It seems the chair has looked into the matter. I have nothing to add."

"I hope there are others among you who have something else to add. I don't think it's a matter to be dropped. Stan, do you have something?"

"No. I've left the running of the hospital to Doug. I've been involved in getting the new building designed to meet everyone's needs. I think you all know this is the single most important project before us. And it was your charge to me."

"Yes, that was our charge to you but not our only charge to you."

"I want to go on record," Joe Goldman raised his hand, "as being totally impressed by the way Doug handled this Robinson incident. Roadblocks were thrown in his way continually. If the medical staff had shown a more responsible reaction, Mrs. Daniels would be alive today. And in my experience, Doug has always acted in the best interest of the hospital. He's a fine administrator."

"There are some members of the medical staff who don't agree," declared Charles. "Some of you have been on this Board as long as I have and know my interest is in patient care. I've looked in vain for Administration to provide a better setting for that."

"Is that a new opinion?" Walter opened to the floor.

"I'd like to make a comment," interjected Tevisina. "I don't think Mr. Carpenter shows the respect he should to the community, and I feel the strike should have been settled long ago."

Walter waited, but there was no other comment. "We would all like to see the strike settled. I'll ask Doug to comment on that later. The issue brought to the table was one of teamwork between Doug and Stan. I'm going to give each of you a chance to make a comment or a recommendation." Walter folded his hands and waited. No one wanted to be first.

Dean Shocks broke the silence. "Obviously, communication is poor between them. I don't know how they can run things if they don't let each know what the other's doing."

After another long pause, Joe Goldman volunteered, "I'd think Stan would make sure they communicate every day."

"It's up to the chief executive to ensure teamwork." Charles was obviously irked.

Stan's left eyelid was twitching.

Dean Shocks added, "As far as I can see, though, things are running pretty well."

"Mr. Daniels might not think so," Joe stated.

"Oh, yeah."

Charles leaned back in his chair. "There seems to be no leadership at the very top."

After a round of crickets chirping, Joe spoke up again. "I don't know about the rest of you, but I think the Robinson-Daniels events are unacceptable and so is the fact that Doug had to go to extreme measures to resolve it."

"I agree," said Tevisina, all huffy, "but he didn't get it resolved quick enough to prevent a death."

"I think it's just typical of hospital administration in general," said Charles.

"Some of you seem to be uncomfortable discussing this," Walter pointed out.

Charles raised his arm and thrust it forward. "This administration is an imposition on every patient who comes here and every employee who works here."

Walter shook his head. "Since some of you aren't participating, I'll just say it outright. I think we need to do something about it and it has to start at the top. Stan, you deserve censure. I expected better of you, and I question if you are the man for the job."

Stan was folded in his chair, holding his breath so nobody would see him.

Charles wasted no time. "I agree with censure. Maybe we should censure them both and give them a time frame to straighten out their act."

At this point, Joe almost burst an artery in anger, face red, clenching his hands. "I spoke before of Doug's ability, and it's even more remarkable in light of the limited support he receives. He doesn't deserve censure. He deserves thanks."

Dean Shocks shouted and pointed his finger at Stan. "I feel we should censure Stan and give him three months to demonstrate his leadership."

"And I feel we should reprimand Doug because there's always two sides to an argument," Tevisina reminded them all.

"All right," Walter conceded. "I'd be happier if there was more participation, but I'll entertain motions, and I ask that you handle each of them separately."

Tevisina aggressively spoke up. "I motion that Stan Boswell be censured and given three months to demonstrate if he is the right person for the job of vice president of Health Services."

"I second the motion," said Charles, his anger darting at Stan.

"All those in favor raise your hands . . . It looks unanimous."

"I motion," said Tevisina once more, "that Doug Carpenter be reprimanded by this Board."

"I second the motion," pounced Charles, who could not wait for this moment.

"Before you vote," Walter cautioned, "I want you to know that if you reprimand Doug, I will hand over the gavel and resign from this Board. All those in favor, raise your hands."

Not one hand was raised.

Charles boldly chastised the Chairman of the Board, "Mr. Chairman, with all due respect, that was a little high-handed."

"Agreed. But the idea of an official reprimand to one who fought against all odds seemed like an unjust reward."

"How about an unofficial reprimand?"

"I don't know what an unofficial reprimand is, but I don't guess I'd resign over it."

"In that case, I move Doug Carpenter be unofficially reprimanded by this Board." Charles crossed his arms smugly and with great satisfaction.

"I second the motion," Tevisina raised her hand quickly. "I think he needs to know we are not happy over the death of Mrs. Daniels."

"This is ridiculous!" Joe raised his voice stood. "Doug wasn't in the delivery room. He wasn't the one administering the anesthesia."

"Any other comments before we vote? All those in favor?" Walter counted. "Seven in favor. Opposed?" He counted again. "Six opposed. There are seven abstentions. Since this is an unofficial reprimand, it will not be graced by any vestige of officialness and will not be included in the minutes. I'm disappointed the motion was made. The seven votes in favor disturb me. But the seven abstentions leave me at a loss for words. On the other hand, maybe seven people felt it didn't deserve the dignity a vote would give it. Maybe that's why so few of you participated. I'll get on with the regular agenda."

"Walter, could I be excused," asked Doug, "to return to the bargaining table?"

"Yes, but would you give a short report on how things are going?"

"When I left, just before six o'clock, we were coming close to resolving the final issue, wage increases. There have been rumors all day the rank-and-file members want to return to work. I'm optimistic, but I don't know what has happened since I left."

"Good luck, and keep up the good work."

Doug found the hotel conference room empty. No Frank or Simba anywhere. After checking the lobby and the restaurant, he drove to the hospital. No picketers anywhere.

Cliff called out as he passed the security office, "Congratulations. I hear they're voting on the contract tomorrow morning."

"I'll be damned. I miss one hour and they settle. Where did you hear it?"

"Henry Sims."

Doug half ran to the office and found Ann and a half dozen nurses, Mary Jane McCarthy, and Mort Klieber sitting around talking and drinking coffee.

"We heard you settled," said Ann. "Does that mean we can all go home to sleep tonight?"

"I missed the last hour for the Board meeting. What have you heard?"

"The only thing we've heard is three and a half percent."

"Three and a half percent?"

Doug ducked into his office and called Henry Sims. "Where did you hear it from?"

"Frank Street called."

"Any details other than three and a half percent?"

"Only that it's a three-year contract."

Doug called Street's office and found him still there. "How did you get it down to three and a half percent?"

"It was easy. We made concessions that before any changes in methods and procedures were made, we would review it with them and get their approval."

"We can't do that."

"That's what I agreed to and the union is happy as a punch bowl full of turds. If you want to reverse it, be my guest, but I think you'll get your ass singed. It's your problem. I've done my job." He hung up.

Doug stared out the window. He knew he could reject the offer. He also knew he couldn't. He was defeated. *If I could only have been in two places at once.*

The intercom buzzed. His watch showed almost midnight. "Mrs. Urqhart and her son are here to see you," said Ann.

"You don't need to be hanging around if you don't want to."

"Won't be for much longer."

"Send her in. I guess I've got to face her."

Tevisina stormed in followed by her son. "You know my son, J.C. I want to know why you are persecuting him." She sat, barely getting her ample bottom in the chair, and folded her arms, waiting for an answer.

J.C. shut the door and leaned against it. He was wearing a black shirt unbuttoned enough to show his chest and a gold cross on a gold chain around his neck.

"What did he tell you?" asked Doug, working to stay calm.

"Doesn't matter what he told me. What matters is what you tell me. You saw at the Board meeting what happens when you don't behave."

Doug pondered for a moment. *A tough one. Can't make any unfounded accusations. But she's no fool. Can't believe she doesn't already know or suspect something.*

"All right, I'll tell you since you're on the Board. You have a right to know. And I think I owe you because of your work in the community."

Tevisina glared at him and bit off each word, gritting her teeth. "He is a righteous man. He does good things."

"We have good reason to believe he's pushing dope."

J.C. straightened with indignation, preparing for a confrontation.

"We have begun our investigation." Doug figured he would make the bluff come true by actually doing it. "We'll have it wrapped up in another two days. You'll be informed as we go. I'll keep it in the quiet of this room. And if we're wrong, I'll give you an apology. But I don't believe we are."

While Doug talked, Tevisina turned her gaze upon her son, who leaned against the door.

He shrugged. "You ain't gonna believe no white man, are you?"

"Tevisina, I'm sorry. The insubordination warning and other restrictions, while justified, are simply because we know about his other activity, and we're closing in on him."

J.C. guffawed and crossed his arms, showing his large biceps. "You can't prove nothin'. Can't nobody prove nothin'."

Tevisina looked at her knees and raised her hands to cover her face.

"We've enough proof, but we're going to firm up a couple more witnesses—"

J.C. stepped toward Doug shouting, "Ain't nobody gonna testify against me! Nobody dare!"

Tevisina jumped to her feet, raising her hands above her head to the Lord, and let out a loud cry, "I dare!"

J.C.'s breath caught and his jaw dropped. "He bluffin'. He don't know nothin', Momma."

"I know! That's who knows! I know! And you promised never to do that again! Get out! Get out! Get out!"

J.C., shocked, opened the door and stepped out backward.

Ann, Mary Jane, Mort, and the nurses looked ready to run.

Tevisina moved to close the door, bowed her head, and sat. She wrapped her arms around her chest and rocked to and fro. "I told him if he did it again, I'd call the police." A tear dropped on her arm from an anguish filled face.

"He's done this before?" Doug asked quietly.

"He promised me." She continued to rock, taking a handkerchief from her sleeve and wiping her eyes and face. "I know what I have to do." Her whole body trembled as she started to stand, but fell back. She gathered her strength once more and pushed herself to her feet, slowly. "He won't bother you anymore." Wiping her eyes, she squared her back, jerked her arms against her sides, and left.

CHAPTER TWENTY-FOUR

At seven o'clock, Doug pushed his tray along the cafeteria railing. Joe sat in the far corner with a couple of residents. He ate and gestured, reviewing patient cases. The residents grabbed each word.

Doug carried his tray over and Joe closed a folder. "Okay, you guys, scram. I've got to talk to the administrator."

The two residents said their good mornings to Doug and carried off their trays.

"They've heard enough from me for one morning." Joe flipped his hand in a shooing manner. "You missed some additional fireworks last night." He took a bite of toast and drained a glass of orange juice. "Now for the morning luxury, I get to sip a cup of coffee."

"Are you going to tell me about the fireworks or are you going to let me simmer in my own juice?"

"Wow!" He chuckled and shook his head.

"Anyhow, you're a happy man this morning."

"I'm sorry. It's a crazy world. They did a number on Jack Apple."

"What? What? Are you going to tell me?"

"Jack is no longer Chair of Surgery." He leaned forward, confiding, "There's no way Charles hasn't already told him, but I'm supposed to inform him this morning. That's what's so funny. As President of the Medical Staff, I've certain 'powers' I can exercise over him, but as Chair of Surgery, he's my boss. I'm instructed to tell him he's acting chair and I'm chair of the search committee to find his replacement."

"You're kidding. There is a divine providence after all."

"Hey, this only happens in the movies. They don't call him Jackass Apple for nothing."

"Will you take the job?"

"No, no. I want to practice medicine. I'm a neurosurgeon, not a politician. I'd hate the job and hate myself for taking it. I can't wait until my term as president is over. Not me. No way." He shook his head. "End of discussion. By the way, you should be on the search committee."

"Okay, but you ought to consider the position."

"Nope. Nope."

"Let me just point out a few things. You believe in good teaching programs. You could set the mold for others. You believe in quality care. You could set the standards. Your reputation would be a draw for better surgical residents—"

"Doug, no, no." He waved his hands. "Never in a million years. Not this life. Not the next. Nope. Nix. Nein. I love this place, but it's secondary to my practice, and when you're chair, that's primary. I'm not willing to do it. Fini."

Doug finished his scrambled egg. "Would it be correct to assume you're not interested in the job?"

"Damn. You administrative types are astute."

"Joe, we have an opportunity. We're looking for chairs of both Pathology and Surgery. If we get individuals who aren't power mongers, we have a chance to change things."

"That Board meeting might have been a milestone for this hospital."

"Sorry I had to miss it."

"You brought it about. And Walter Bass made a comment to Stan. Let's see. I want to get this right. 'A hospital isn't a building, it's the people in it.'"

"A perceptive gentleman."

"He made another comment you should know. He said he and the Board have to be more aware of what's going on in the hospital. And, quote, 'Doug has been hung out to dry.' Stan sat there with his mouth shut and his squinty little eyes, too."

"Damn. Thanks for telling me."

"My pleasure. What's with the union? There are no picketers, and the word is they've settled."

"They vote at ten o'clock this morning. We'll know by noon if the members accept the contract. I've no doubt they will."

Mort Klieber came over. "I apologize for interrupting this high-level meeting, but the pharm techs want to come back to work. Can we let 'em?"

"Why not? But the strike plan is still in effect until we get the official word."

"Oh." He gave a resigned smile. "That means supervisors can't go home to sleep yet?"

"Stand them in a closet somewhere."

Mort meandered out of the cafeteria totally depressed.

"I'm not happy with the contract. While I was at the Board meeting, Frank Street changed the game plan. He gave them less salary increase and tied management's hands when it comes to making operational improvements. We can't make changes that would affect work hours and our pay will be below average within a year."

"How did this Simba character let that happen?"

"Two things. Street's a damn good negotiator. He knows how to dig into people. And the union wanted job security in preference to higher wages."

"So if I'm reading it correctly," Joe tried to wrap it around his brain, "we'll have poorer paid employees, meaning the better ones will go elsewhere, and we won't be able to get rid of anyone who does a lousy job."

"Pretty close. We can still get rid of people who are problems, but if we eliminate a useless job, the union has to agree. And when you improve operations, you sometimes need to eliminate antiquated jobs."

"We save money in the short range and lose it all in the long."

"Just another problem to overcome. We'll find a way."

"I'll stick to medicine."

The two men stood, disposed of their trays, and headed out out of the cafeteria.

"We've got to meet this way more often." Joe pushed the elevator button, more content than he'd been in months.

The union membership voted by a heavy majority to accept the contract, and by the following day, work schedules were normal. But some members expressed dissatisfaction with the three and a half percent increase, especially since they were locked into it for three years.

Employees who hadn't struck criticized those who had for whatever reason. Animosity washed like a wave over everything.

The census dropped. Jack Apple stopped admitting patients. He had privileges with at least one other hospital and was admitting elsewhere to show his dissatisfaction. In checking the printouts, Doug discovered Ed Whyte wasn't admitting either. It was like Jeep and Solstory all over again. But Charles was still admitting. He was on the Board and wanted to maintain his power base. Doug knew the others would start admitting again after they had made their point.

* * *

Doug, Herb Cline, and Walter Bass sat at a round table with Mr. Daniels and his attorney, Mr. Dante Bosco, at Bosco's office.

"Mr. Daniels," said Walter, "you have been devastated by your wife's death, but I'm afraid we are going have to reopen the wound. I'm sorry."

David Daniels nodded, eyes dull and red. Doug imagined the shock when, waiting to hear if it was a boy or girl, the man learned his wife and baby were both dead. Gone. A young family ripped apart.

"We would like to hear what you have to tell us," said Mr. Bosco. "I don't think we'll reach any decisions today."

"I understand," Walter said sympathetically. "I'm going to ask Mr. Carpenter to explain what happened. He is the most informed."

Doug couldn't remember an unhappier job. "There's no way I can tell you this without it being a blow. She died as a result of the anesthesia. The anesthesiologist misjudged and gave her too much. He put her too far under. And they couldn't save her."

David Daniels' shoulders sagged, his eyes brimming, chin trembling. He was losing her all over again, and struggled to focus watery eyes on Doug, stunned, as though the words were worming their way into his mind. His head dropped and silence was broken by his sobs.

Doug's throat tightened. Walter's eyes closed for a long moment.

"What about the baby?" asked Mr. Bosco.

Doug leaned forward and respectfully stated, "They attempted to save her. But it was the same for both the mother and the baby."

"But the baby was otherwise normal?"

"In all respects."

"Will you send me a copy of the medical record and any incident reports?"

"I'll see that you get them."

"Mr. Daniels," explained Walter, "we wanted no cover-up on this. We conducted our own study, and the reason we called you in was to inform you and express both our deep sympathy and our desire to make whatever restitution we can."

David Daniels stopped sobbing and leaned back in his chair, drained.

"We are all sorry." Walter placed his hand on David's arm, and David lifted his hand in response but let it fall again.

"Thank you for your openness," Mr. Bosco nodded. "We'll be in touch after Mr. Daniels and I have talked." He extended his hand, in turn, to each of them. "I'll call you," he addressed Herb Cline.

In the downstairs lobby, Doug, Walter, and Herb hovered near the front entrance before going their own ways.

"I don't know what's going to come of this," said Herb, "but I feel better about making a clean sweep of it."

Doug dug in his pockets. "The fact is they would have found out about it anyhow. Aside from it being the right thing to do, it is the smart thing to do."

"True," agreed Walter. "Anyhow, I think we should always do the right thing. No lies. No cover-ups. If you can't make it straight in this life, you have no right making it."

Driving to the hospital, Doug replayed Walter's words. *'If you can't make it straight.'* Stan had manipulated him into collusion on false drawings for the state. Stan had placed him in the middle, and the only way out was to expose him to the licensure team, something he didn't want to do.

* * *

Upon Doug's return, Sharon Smith called from the emergency room. "I thought you'd like to know J.C. just walked in and handed me his resignation. It was all typed out and everything. I guess we were effective after all."

"I suspect his mother had something to do with it." Doug wondered what she had said to him.

Doug came into the office on Monday after nine o'clock and found Lou Pickero talking to Ann.

"Didn't expect you before ten o'clock. The rest of the team here?"

"No, thought I'd get here early and discuss the fire partitions."

Doug moved into his office wishing he hadn't heard Lou, who followed him in and closed the door.

"Doug," he searched for the right words, "I want you to know how much I appreciate your getting me off the hook with Jack Apple." He paused but plunged ahead. "The photograph. Do you think I could get my hands on it?"

"To protect yourself or to fantasize over?"

"I've learned my lesson. I just want to make sure there are none floating around."

"The best thing you could do would be to forget it. I want to hold on to the one I have because I can always use it as a reminder to Jack, or any of his disciples, that he is a miserable human being. But you could confront him and tell him you want the negative."

Lou thought about it less than a nanosecond. "No, I guess not. Anyhow, thanks for getting me off the hook." He reached into his satchel. "I've reviewed the drawings for the fire partitions, and find them acceptable." He slid them in front of Doug. The top drawing was stamped approved and signed by Lou.

Doug forced himself to look.

"When the team gets here, we'll divide three ways and get done by the end of the day. I'll review the medical records and medical staff bylaws. Miss Pinker will visit the nursing office and do some spot-checking on some of the floors. Mrs. Bloom will be checking the laboratories for the usual things, quality control and the like."

"Who's going to check the physical plant?"

"Nobody. It's done. I looked at your drawings and they meet the criteria."

Damn. If I had ratted on Stan, I'd be accused of not being a team player. The drawings have been accepted. Let sleeping dogs lie? It's all done. But why do I feel like the loser?

He swallowed. "Ann has reserved the boardroom for your use the whole day. Whatever you want, she'll either get it herself or have the right person bring it. When you need me, she'll drag me there. And there's coffee, tea, and the like. So give a yell if you need anything. By the way," he added. "Jack Apple is no longer Chief of Surgery. The Board didn't think he was suitable for the job." He didn't think Lou needed to know the word was out about him and Patricia.

Ann buzzed. "I thought you'd want to know. Mr. Boswell's mother died. He just got a call from the nursing home."

Doug stepped out into the hall just as Stan came by. He didn't look up, but Doug could see the pain on his face. A shock. There was no arrogance there. No hate. Just human pain. Doug wanted to reach out and tell him he was sorry, but the moment passed as Stan passed.

At two o'clock, Ann called from the boardroom to let Doug know there would be a summation conference at three.

"Ask Lou if he can break away from staring at you long enough to drop by up here. I need to discuss something with him."

"Thank you very much. I certainly will."

When Lou came in, Doug had him sit by the west window and pulled a chair over to him.

"Lou, there's a lot of monkey business in this world."

"Doug, I'm sorry about that whole thing with Patricia."

"I'm not talking about your shortcomings, Lou. I'm talking about something else."

Lou looked at him without understanding.

"The drawings of the fire partitions, they're fakes. The job's not been done."

Lou was shocked. "Come on."

"I'm not kidding. I won't go into the details that led to their manufacture, but both you and the state deserve better treatment. So do our patients." Doug shook his head. "I'm sorry this happened, but I guarantee the partitions will be installed."

"Doug, whatever you say is good enough for me. We'll change these to proposals. I approve them. All I need from you is an anticipated date of completion."

"Six months."

CHAPTER TWENTY-FIVE

Talking to Stan was like reasoning with a braying jackass, but he had to tell him about the plans for the fire partitions. He'd be angry, but honesty was a strong weapon.

Liz was polite this time and told him to go on in.

Doug sat across from Stan and expounded the details. "The fire partitions are going to cost forty thousand. The entire project is to be completed in six months, and I'm putting it out to bid. We might be able to get it done for less than forty days."

Stan placed his fingers on his temples and closed his eyes. "How did the state catch on?"

"Evidently, you think everybody is a fool but you."

Stan ignored the comment. "Where's the money coming from?"

"You're controlling the capital expenditures. You decide. We either do this or the hospital closes. You're planning the renovation of several doctors' offices. You've spent that much on one in the past."

"Those projects have to move forward. The doctors have been promised. What else?" He dropped his hands on the desk, palms down.

"I suggest you talk to those doctors to see what they think is most important, delay their offices or close the hospital."

Stan clenched and unclenched his left fist. "I can't do that."

"Then, you'll have to let me know where the money's coming from. In the meantime, I'm proceeding."

"Look, Doug. I want to get along with you, but you're going to have to play ball, too. We're a team, remember?"

"That would be nice, Stan, but to be a team means having some rational exchange. And what just happened wasn't rational. I offered a workable way. If you reject that, fine, but suggest an alternative. That's how a team works."

"Get started. I'll think of something." Stan swiveled his chair around, his back to Doug.

"Okay. I want to let you know something else I'm thinking about. We've had patient after patient abused by HMO rejections, delays, and substitute treatments to the point that some action has to be taken. We can't just sit back and say it's the patient's responsibility or the doctor's problem. We have to be the patient's advocate. We have to stop the abuse."

"Wait, Doug. You know there's nothing we can do to control the insurance companies. Don't you have enough problems? You have the medical staff breathing down your neck—"

"Hold it. *You* have the medical staff breathing down my neck—the greedy ones—but that's changing. Jack Apple's out—"

"No, you hold it. I'm still your boss and I'm calling the shots."

"You know, I'd think under the circumstances you'd want to prove yourself. You're not going to do it standing in the way of patient care."

"I'm not going to let you fritter away your time on some cockamamie project to tell insurance companies what to do. You think they're going to listen to you? Forget it. Do your job."

"Patient care *is* my job. And I'm not going to forget it. We can't forget the patient. And by the way, this is something the medical staff will agree with."

"What I hear is they're upset about the way Administration is operating in this hospital."

"That's crap. That's just some of your friends upset because they don't get free rein."

"Okay, smartass, cut to the quick. What's your plan?"

"It's complicated and still formative, so bear with me."

"No, have a plan or don't start."

"I have a plan, and it involves cooperation—no, *participation* by the medical staff, the Medical Society, the other hospitals, and the Hospital Council. We're going to go after them from a legal point of view and from a moral point of view. We'll pull in the Chamber of Commerce and the business community so pressure can be applied by the people signing the contracts. We'll work with consumer groups to get the patients directly involved. Somewhere in the process, we'll include the churches and the mayor's office. Then we go to the governor and get the other cities in the state into the act. We need to establish a model for others to follow. Then we'll pull in the AHA and the AMA. Everybody's sick of these bastards."

Stan had buried his face in his hands during all this. When Doug stopped, he looked up. "Okay, write it out and then review it with me."

"The idea is to have the medical staff work with me to develop it."

"No, prepare it ahead of time and get my approval before starting."

"Stan, do you want to be a leader or an obstructionist?"

"Damn. You're right. Okay. Leave it in my hands. I'll get with the medical staff. You run the hospital. That's your job. I'm Mr. Outside. You're Mr. Inside. Right? I'll do my job. You do yours."

"Really? And when do you plan to call that meeting?"

"Pretty soon. I'll let you know all about it. We're a team."

"I know the other administrators in the city. I'll deal with them. I tell you what. I'll let you know when we need you. I think it would be good if you came along when we go to the mayor and the Medical Society. In the meantime, I'll discuss the goal with the medical staff and we'll develop a working plan."

Doug stood up. So did Stan, who looked as though he was about to spring across the desk.

"Thanks for your support, Stan. We're a team." He reached across to shake his hand but was denied the effort.

Doug was halfway through the door when Stan called out, "I want to work on this."

"Your approval is appreciated and we will definitely be calling on you. It's good to know you're in favor of it."

He shut the door and strolled past Liz Racoda.

Before he got out of her office, Stan opened his door and yelled, "I want to see your plan!"

"We'll share it with you from the first draft on," Doug answered him, cool as a cucumber.

In Ann's office, Juanita was waiting for him. "Can you give me just a minute?"

"Sure. Come on in."

He closed the door and waved her to a seat.

"I can't sit. I'll only take a moment."

"If this is about the investigation, Juanita, you know you have nothing to worry about."

"I know, and thanks. I know I have your support, and I would do anything for you. And I mean that." She waited a moment then sat anyhow. "I'm hoping you'll help with the nursing home watch program. In fact, I don't think it will go far without you. I don't want an answer now, but you can influence some of the other hospitals. Nursing homes that abuse patients need to be exposed. If the hospitals inform Medicare or Medicaid or the state licensure group every time it happens, the nursing homes will have to clean up their act. Please think about it. That's all I ask."

Doug sat on the edge of his desk. "Yes."

"You'll think about it?"

"No, I'll do it."

"Really?" She leaped forward and kissed him on the cheek. "Thank you. I'll let you get back to your work." She was out the door but called back, "Thank you. We will make a difference."

He wondered what he had gotten himself into, but realized it really was important. He had seen too many patients abused by nursing homes. The state system just didn't have the teeth or commitment to penalize the offenders. He thought about how he could approach the other administrators on both the nursing home problem and the HMOs. He walked to the window and looked out over the hundreds of cherry trees. The blossoms were all gone now, but somehow he could still see them. He shook his head and walked back to his desk.

Doug called Marge Mills at Community Hospital.

"I don't know, Doug. With the nursing homes, it seems to me you'd be biting the hand that feeds you."

"If all hospitals in the city join in, the nursing homes can't single you out."

"If you get all of them to agree, I'll support the program."

"That's all I need to know. Now on the HMOs . . ."

"That's a different matter. If we all stick together, we can force them, but all it takes is one or two to break rank and their census soars and ours drops."

"If we pull the Medical Society with the medical staffs to back the boycott, we can make it work and it will improve patient care."

"I'm with you on that, but there has to be close to full commitment from everybody or it won't work."

"Just as long as I know you're on board. I'll set up a meeting with everybody."

"I'm on board, but only if you get strong support."

He called Herman Stortzman at Highland Hospital who also agreed to a meeting of all the administrators, although reluctantly. Then administrators of Riverview, South Side, and Center City all agreed to meet, but Dr. Loreno, who owned Main Street Hospital, wouldn't consider it, saying, "We have had a lot of nursing home admissions and had yet to see one that had been abused." Also, he thought HMOs were fine.

Six out of seven, counting Eastern, wasn't bad, and Main Street was small and second rate anyhow. There were twenty-six hospitals in the city, some small and some proprietary or investor-owned, and all had to be pulled in.

He called Sarah Fulton, Director of the Hospital Council.

"Yes, Doug. We'll sponsor it if you'll chair the program. And our office will arrange the meeting."

It was shaping up. Juanita would be dancing. But then there was Stan. He was going to be mad as hell, but that was his problem. He needed to get with the medical staff.

Herb Cline called. "I just got a call from Dante Bosco. David Daniels is willing to settle for two hundred thousand. Bosco isn't happy with that amount. He thinks they could get more. He's right. I say we settle. What do you say?"

"Yes. Call Walter and get his blessing."

"I did, and he did, and he said to do the same with you."

"Then settle. I'll let Stan know."

Ann buzzed. "The hearing for Clinker is scheduled for Friday. It's on your schedule for ten in the morning. You're a witness as well as a plaintiff."

"Okay. Do Jean DeVries and Isabel Eaves know?"

"They'll be there. They're both on the job. One look at Jean, and you'd never know she'd been hurt."

"Heck, they're both in their twenties. That's what it's like to have young bodies. If that'd happened to me, I'd still be unconscious. When did all that happen? Weeks ago? Damn. Seems more like a couple of days."

The next morning, Doug came in at seven and found Joe Goldman in the cafeteria. "You here every morning at seven, Joe?"

"Like clockwork. Saturdays and Sundays included."

"Are you punishing yourself?"

"It's the food. I just can't get enough of it."

Doug told him about the HMO and nursing home programs.

"Glad to see that. I don't get many of those nursing home patients, but I've had a few on consults. And the HMO thing is past due. How are you and Stan doing?"

Doug told him about the firewalls and Stan's frustration.

Joe nodded. "He's promised a few people some expensive equipment that could be delayed. He just has to decide which of his political allies to offend. It'll be old 'Whip-It-Out Apple.' He's lost power."

"Whip-It-Out?"

"You never heard that? He's known in the OR for his favorite saying, 'When in doubt, whip it out.' Breast, uterus, colon. He doesn't always have the patience to wait for pathology reports, therefore, lots of healthy organs and tissues have been disposed of. But Snowden and the Tissue Committee got on him, so for the last year or so, he's behaved. Except for the census, I'd just as soon see him use a different hospital. Main Street has a rubber-stamp Tissue Committee. He'd love that place. A mastectomy a day keeps the doctor in hay."

"If I could, I'd do a number on some of these bastards."

"Ah," Joe gathered his tray, "you run for that office and I'll vote for you."

Charles Smith strolled into Doug's office unannounced, dumped his pipe tobacco in Doug's bin, looked at the pipe, and pushed it into his coat pocket. Then he finally sat, crossed his legs, and actually looked at Doug. "We need to talk."

Doug waited.

"We've got to stop being enemies."

Could it be he's switching alliances? Stan let him down at the Board meeting. "I've never been in favor of us being enemies."

"We need to team up against a common enemy. The HMOs."

"I'm glad to hear you say that. I was going to call you about joint action by the hospital and the medical staff to tackle it. I've some ideas. I thought you felt it was something I should control. I hope I'm wrong."

"You're wrong. I know I've given you that impression. We need to work together."

Maybe Stan had told him about the dumb idea and now he wanted to go against Stan. But the motive didn't matter as long as he cooperated. "There are actually two matters, Charles, but the other won't require medical staff participation." He told him about the nursing home watch program.

"This nursing home thing is a bad idea. I think you should forget it. There're enough regulations already. You'll just make it worse for the good nursing homes."

"The same way the bad doctors make things worse for the good doctors?" He was immediately sorry he said it, but it was out.

Smith moved not one muscle. "We shouldn't always be on opposite sides."

"Hard not to be when you want different things."

"I just think it's a bad idea."

"Afraid of losing some admissions?"

"Doug, you know the hospital can't afford to lose admissions. The docs don't get paid that much for these patients. Personally, I'd just as soon not see them at all."

"Does it worry you that they're being abused?"

"I've seen no evidence of it."

"In the future, when they come in, I'll make sure you're called to take a look."

"That's just going to be another imposition. We should be working against the HMOs. They're cutting physician fees and hospital fees. We ought to be joining forces to find ways to fight *them*, not ourselves." He leaned forward as though to get up, but continued to lean, looking at the floor. Then he stood and started to leave.

"Charles. You have a point on the HMOs. But if the hospital and medical staff did anything together, we'd have to have common goals. And if we take money from the HMOs, it's got to be for the patient first, not the doctors. Some of our staff have practiced fee-driven medicine so long they live fee-driven lives." Smith was still listening, so he continued. "We're pumping up our census projections for additional beds to the point of no return. Fake statistics equals fake revenue, and fake revenue doesn't pay off real expenses, real wages." As Smith turned to leave, Doug added, "Some of my predecessors may have cried wolf a few times to the doctors about controlling costs. I don't do that."

Smith nodded but didn't change expression.

"Charles, just out of curiosity, did you discuss the HMO threat with Stan?"

"No. I think you're the one to talk to. We'll talk again." He strolled out just as he had strolled in.

Ann leaned in through the door.

"Sorry about that. He just walked through."

"It's okay. It was close to a rational conversation."

CHAPTER TWENTY-SIX

On Friday morning, Doug made his way to the courthouse. The Pottard preliminary hearing was being held on the third floor. Ralph Bacon was counsel for Jean, Isabel, and the hospital. Walter Bass had said he wanted the best lawyer in town for his people and had personally picked him. Clinker Pottard was charged with aggravated assault and battery. Doug was surprised to see her case being handled by Mr. Wichard, the union's labor attorney.

On the right side of the small courtroom, Clinker sat behind a table with Wichard. They looked like a mountain and a molehill. Doug took his place with Ralph Bacon on his right and Jean and Isabel to his left.

Judge Cordova was a young man with sharp features, birdquick eyes, and a crew cut so close it was hard to tell if his hair was black or brown, and he had a nervous twitch at the right corner of his mouth.

The bailiff, an oak tree in a blue uniform, announced, "Case of Eastern College Hospital, Jean DeVries, and Isabel Eaves versus Clinker Pottard."

"How does the defendant plead?"

"Guilty, your Honor," said Mr. Wichard.

"We could have saved time if you'd just said so earlier."

"Your Honor, extenuating circumstances compelled my client to extreme measures."

"Case remanded to court June 1. Bail set at twenty thousand. Next case." The gavel fell.

"That was short and sweet. What'd we come here for?" Doug asked a little sarcastically.

"If you hadn't," said Ralph, "the case might've been dismissed." From the other side of the room came an angry voice.

"What do you mean you're not gonna pay my bail?"

A hush fell over the whole courtroom, and Judge Cordova started to raise the gavel to gain control.

Mr. Wichard was speaking almost in a whisper, "I'll speak to the union about it—"

Clinker arose like a volcano and brushed Wichard and his chair over like a bowling pin, then stepped over him and trudged toward Isabel and Jean. Hovering over the table, she grabbed Isabel by the throat, squeezing her neck, bending it like a straw. Isabel frantically grabbed the huge hand like a moth fluttering on a piece of granite. She couldn't make a sound. Ralph and Doug both reached out for Isabel at the same time.

The bailiff had moved to the back of the room. But before he could reach them, Jean jumped on top of the table and jabbed her fingers into Clinker's eyes. Clinker yelled and dropped Isabel on the table. Jean brought her knee up like a sledgehammer under Clinker's chin. The big woman crashed backward to the floor, but Jean was off the table, straddling her, slamming fists one after another into her temples. The bailiff grabbed her and pulled her off, kicking as she went.

"Damn you!" screamed Jean.

Doug cradled Isabel with his left arm, her head on his shoulder as he carefully touched her throat.

She croaked, "I think I'll be all right."

"No matter, you will be checked out in the ER."

Clinker was struggling to get to her feet, but the bailiff was sitting on her.

"Guards," he called, but they were already there with handcuffs.

Ralph led Jean to the far end of the table, but she had regained her control.

"I'll have no such outbursts in this court!" Cordova was furious.

"Your Honor," said Ralph, "the defendant attacked my client *again*."

"I saw it. Bail is set at two hundred thousand. Next case." He slammed the gavel once more.

Even on her knees, Clinker was almost as tall as Jean. When they walked past, Jean sneered at her. The big woman didn't change expression.

Isabel, shaking all over and distraught, held her neck with both hands, the pain thudding with every heartbeat.

"Damn," Doug commended Jean, "I'd like to hire you to be my bodyguard."

"If it's to protect you from Clinker, I'll do it for nothing. Damn, I bruised my knee." She wrapped her arms around her chest and held her ribs that had been damaged before.

"You had a cracked rib or two, didn't you?"

"Yeah, and I'd like to have them taped again." But her grin said it was worth it.

Doug had been in his office for only a few minutes when Ann buzzed.

"Simba Agiza is here and would like to see you."

Doug made no response. He walked around the desk. Simba posed in the outer doorway.

"May I come in?"

Doug waved her in. She sat by the window and smiled when he left the door open. "Now that the union business is settled, I want to ask for your help."

"About the contract?"

"No. About providing free care for the poor in the community."

"We do that now, through Medicaid."

She gave Doug an indulgent expression. "There's a lot Medicaid doesn't cover."

"We provide outpatient services over and above Medicaid."

She crossed her arms and surveyed him. "You know that unless you're poverty level you don't get Medicaid. Those that work hardest get the least. That needs to be changed."

"I didn't write the Medicaid laws. I agree some of them are dumb. That's the way the lawmakers dump the problem."

Simba gazed at Doug, and he began to get uncomfortable.

"Isn't it the job of the hospital to meet the needs of the community?"

"Yes, to the extent possible."

"Do you know what the needs of the community are?" she asked.

"We try to meet them, whatever they are."

"Has anybody ever listed what they are?"

Doug thought for a moment. "I suspect it's just been done by trial and error, on a need basis. There are no services that aren't being used."

"There are none that aren't making money," said Simba. "And that's the real problem. You've decided you have to get your money out of it."

"That's a stupid statement."

"*That's a stupid statement.* That's a stupid statement? You're telling me you don't work it out so you make money off the sick?"

"We make enough to make ends meet. That's about it."

Simba had a look of resigned disbelief. "How can an intelligent man like you stand for all the shit these doctors dump on the poor so they can have big homes with swimming pools?"

"How can an intelligent woman be so blind to the real world?"

"You want to talk about the real world, honey, let me tell you about the real world." She pointed. "There are people within walking distance of your hospital who are dying from lack of care. You call me blind? You don't even know what's going on in your community."

He started to shout back at her, but somewhere in his head, a question echoed, *Within walking distance?* "You'd have to show me. Besides, you have no idea what goes on here. You don't know how a hospital is run. You can't judge what we can do for the community. Things don't happen by a snap of the finger and an order to do it. Why am I talking to you?"

"I thought I could talk to you about the care needed by this community."

"What do you know about care?"

Simba walked over to Doug's desk, jabbing her finger while she talked. "I know needs, honey. I grew up with needs. I've seen a momma die while rocking her baby. I've seen a grand-momma die while praying to God for money for her daughter to see a doctor."

"Damn it!" he roared, leaning across the desk. "Who said there isn't suffering in the world? Hospitals can't take on all the problems."

Simba took a step back. "You can at least learn the needs."

"Damn. I think I hear an echo in here. I'll learn the community needs if you'll learn the hospital needs."

"I could show you, but you wouldn't learn. You wouldn't even take the time."

"I don't have time to waste, but if you show me what you're talking about, I'll show you why hospitals operate the way they do."

Doug was surprised by his own outburst, but he could envision how to do it. "But there are a couple of conditions. You'd have to agree that if I go to this trouble, you'll stick it out to the bitter end, because it won't be easy. And you'd have to agree to educate some of your unior leaders. They think we're a bank."

"Honey, you're going to feel like quitting after the first half-hour because you're going to want to heave your guts right out on the street. You don't know what suffering is. You think you can take it?"

"When do you want to start?"

"Give me a few days to pick the right places to turn your stomach and I think I might be able to reach a white man, even one that could be a bigot. If I come back next Wednesday, can you be ready?"

Doug checked his calendar. "Wednesday afternoon at two o'clock. But I'm not sure I can get through to an anti-management racist."

"I'll see you at that time on that date, honey." She moved toward the doorway and paused. Doug was sure she was going to bump her rear end at him. She smiled.

He wondered what he had gotten himself into, but his instincts told him to do it.

On Monday morning, Doug got a call from the deputy for Nursing Home Administration of the State Health Department, Mr. James Flanagan. He had received a flood of letters about nursing home problems and phone calls from senators and representatives because of sudden interest by their constituency.

Flanagan had learned in talking to Sarah Fulton of the Hospital Council that Doug was chairing the committee of administrators interested in developing a monitoring system. Could Doug suggest some approaches?

"We're meeting within the next several weeks. We plan to draft a proposal. Maybe we can try it out on you. We like the idea of making the monitoring a joint state and volunteer process including church, community, and consumer interest groups."

"Would you agree to be on a special task force to study this problem?"

"Yes, but we have a nurse on our staff who should be part of this. You say when."

"Include anyone you want to."

He thought about it carefully and then called Juanita to let her know where her idea was leading.

"Oh, I knew you would come through. I was right about you at Solstory. You're not a bottom-line freak. You're a people person."

"Hard not to come through on this issue. And, actually, I'm probably a combination of bottom-line freak and people freak."

"Where do we go from here?"

"The committee of administrators will be gathering to draft a proposal. I'd be glad to take any of your ideas to the meeting. After that, Flanagan will be calling a meeting that we ought to both go to."

At five o'clock, Doug was still answering his mail for the day.

Ann stepped in. "I'm leaving. Mrs. Urqhart is here to see you."

"Show her in." Doug stood to greet her.

But Tevisina was already coming through the door. "I'll only be a moment," she said and sat in the chair across from him, her back straight, hands folded in her lap, and chin jutting out.

Doug initiated, "I hear your son resigned."

"He has, and now . . . he has gone away. He will never work here again." Her accusing eyes focused squarely on Doug as if she were putting a pin in a butterfly's wing.

"Where? Where has he gone?"

"I don't know," she groaned. "I went with him, and he turned himself in.

"The district attorney says he'll tell who his suppliers are or he'll go to jail. He'll tell. But he won't live around here anymore. They'll kill him if he does. Police gave him a new name and moved him someplace else." Her chin quivered, but she didn't cry. "This is the son I wanted to be a preacher. This is the son I wanted to help other people. This the son I wanted to be strong and fine."

"Tevisina, maybe he will be now."

She gazed at her clenched hands in her lap and leaned forward. She remained that way for a few moments, then raised her face, unblinking eyes with a chin like a rock. "I want you to know, sometimes we have to do things. Sometimes we have to do things we don't like. Sometimes we have to hurt ourselves to do the right thing." Her voice broke, but she retained her forbearance. "I want you to think about that."

She pushed herself out of the chair, turned toward the door, and straightened her back.

"Tevisina, maybe now your son will be strong and fine. Maybe he will help other people. Maybe he will become a minister."

She didn't turn around, just squared her shoulders and left.

CHAPTER TWENTY-SEVEN

"This is the dumbest thing you've done yet," announced Stan. "I can't figure out if you're a hospital administrator or a damn social worker. Simba Agiza?"

Stan pushed away from the table, cradled his forehead between his thumb and forefinger and massaged his temples. "Doug, she made you look like a horse's ass during the strike. Now she's going to prove you're a complete fool."

Doug knew Stan needed to let his chain of thoughts rattle out before he could listen. *Patience.*

"This is stupid. Putting you on parade like her captive." He swiveled his chair and faced the wall and then swiveled again. "And for what, for Pete's sake?"

He held his hands in a why position. "What in the hell do you hope to gain from this? I don't understand, Doug. What the hell is this about? And who's going to run the hospital while you're running around with that bimbo black lion? Would you tell me that?"

"Come on, Stan. We've got good department heads, and you know I'll be running the hospital. I'll never be far away. We're talking about the immediate community."

"You call this ghetto a community?"

"It's our primary catchment area, Stan."

"And none of them has a pot to piss in, and they'll piss in your pot if you let them."

Doug took a deep breath to steady his patience. "Look, I understand this could be a mistake."

Stan crossed his arms and peered at Doug in defiance.

Doug continued. "I'm acting half out of instinct and half on faith. I will tell you this, I'll know if it's a mistake early on, and if it is, I'll put an end to it. I'm taking a gamble, but I think it's worth it."

"All gamblers think it's worth it." Stan's smugness reeked. "Doug, you and I have to be a team. Right?"

Doug waited.

"Am I right?" he repeated when Doug just sat there.

"That's right! You want to go with us?"

"No. I'll stay here and guard the fort, and I'll be ready to pay the ransom if you get held hostage." Stan spun a pencil in and out his fingers. "So, now you see, I won't stand in your way. I don't think it's a good idea, but I'm not saying no. But I do want to be kept informed. I'd like a written report each week. A written progress report."

Doug detected the sarcasm in Stan's use of the word *progress*.

"Fine. I'll keep you informed. And if I decide it's all a mistake, I suppose you'd like that documented, too."

"Of course, the stupid along with the brilliant. Keep me informed." He walked around to the door and ushered Doug out.

Doug walked the short distance to his office. *Bastard*, he thought. *All of a sudden, he's happy I'm doing this because he thinks I'll make a fool of myself and he can expose me. He may be right.*

James Flanagan from the State Health Department called. "Doug, I got a copy of your nursing home watch agenda, and we're excited about it. You'll be getting a notice for our task force meeting within a few days, but I wanted to let you know right away it's scheduled for next Friday. Can you be here at nine in the morning?"

Doug glanced at his schedule. "Yes, I can move things around to be there. I'll check with Juanita, the nurse I mentioned."

"I also wanted to let you know the governor is going to attend. He's anxious to meet you."

"I'm glad he's interested. I hope the task force will come up with some options. It's a serious problem."

He dialed Juanita. "Are you free Friday to go to the State Health Department for a meeting with the Nursing Home Watch Task Force? You'd have to take off for the day."

"Are you going? Can we go together?"

"We can take the seven a.m. train."

At the dinner table, he told Bess about the agreement with Simba.

She smiled. "Simba Agiza is going to learn hospital administration? You better watch out. She may be after your job." The imp behind her eyes danced. Then she seemed to think about it. "It might be good for her to know some of the problems hospitals face if she can believe anything you tell her."

"It's different worlds coming together. I don't know what's going to happen."

"You think she'll try to seduce you again?" asked Bess. "You taking a bodyguard?" Her joking might have been covering legitimate concern.

"No, that's a failed tactic, and seducing me at this point wouldn't gain her anything."

"I still think the cap to the whole thing was the Clinker Pottard Nonviolence Scholarship Fund. How could any of you keep a straight face?"

"At the time, it was easy. Anyhow, judgment tells me this thing with Simba is right. But no bottom-line manager would do it."

"That's because to them watching the bottom line is the same as watching their ass." She grinned and lifted her cup as though toasting.

"Guess I won't need to worry about that. There'll be enough other people watching my ass. But there was a brighter side to my day." He told her about the call from James Flanagan.

"Honey, it doesn't hurt if the governor's interested in you. Take it as a compliment."

"Unfortunately, he doesn't swing any weight at Eastern. As far as he's concerned, I'm just one more grain of sand on the beach."

"Then why's he interested in meeting you?"

"Politics. Just pure politics. He has to glad-hand everybody."

Simba arrived promptly on Wednesday at two p.m. carrying a grocery bag. Even though her skirt was short, she was wearing a pinstriped suit. He felt relief. No embarrassment being with her.

"Come on in." He motioned her to have a seat. "We need to set our agenda."

She set the bag on the chair instead. "That's right. And I hear you have all kinds of people involved to brainwash me—finance, nursing, personnel, and a half-dozen others, including people from the Hospital Council."

"Good grapevine."

"I've done the same thing. You're going to meet people you never heard of. But I'm going to be there, too, and I hope you plan to be in the sessions you've set up for me. After all, it's what's in your head that counts."

"I'll be there. I just don't want you saying the hospital's decisions are the result of a southern bigot."

"All right, let's split the week. On Monday and Tuesday, I'll take you out on the street to see what's happening in the real world. On Thursday and Friday, you try to brainwash me, and on Wednesday, we catch up on our own work."

"Okay, except we'll have to cut those to half days even if it means more weeks. I can't give this four days a week. It'll be hard enough giving it four half days. Only next Thursday, we'll go the whole day because Friday I've got a meeting out of town."

Simba leaned against the wall, arms folded in front of her.

"All right, Doug, but it's important enough for four days a week. You're about to get an education that will change your life. I mean all of you white administrators need to know what's happening out there." She pushed away from the wall as though accepting the conditions. "But I do have something I want you to see today. It may help you to change your mind and give it more time."

"The rest of the day is yours."

The sun was baking everything outdoors when Doug and Simba walked through the emergency room exit and onto Berry Street, heading east. Her stride picked up and he had to push to stay with her. At the corner of Berry and Trowbridge, she stopped abruptly and he almost went past her.

"Part of what I want to show you is the area. We're going to walk up Trowbridge. You've never been on this street, and some of the people you're going to see may be beyond help. But not all, and you'll see one in particular."

He peered at the debris-littered yards and sidewalk. Stripped cars lying on their axles lined the curbs and blocked the narrow street. He wanted to stay where he was.

Simba read his face. "Without wheels it's harder for the city to tow them off before they're picked clean. The city stays off this street. When they want to arrest somebody, they come in large numbers. You still willing?"

"If it's part of the tour, let's go."

They stepped over trash and crunched through broken glass, mostly from car windows.

"Street diamonds," Simba translated.

"No small children play *here*." Doug imparted the obvious, kicking the top half of a beer bottle off the sidewalk.

Simba glanced at him from the corner of her eye, but she was intent on where she stepped. "Not even the larger ones exactly *play* here. More like they work here or fight here. And some just stay off the street, except to go or come."

A beer bottle crashed to the pavement in front of them, shooting glass in all directions.

"Hey, momma," came a voice like an empty drum from a second story window, "you gonna be okay, but that cracker might be in for trouble."

Simba called back and motioned for Doug to keep moving. "You gonna have to go on faith, baby. He's no cracker, and I'm no momma. Trust me. And keep the glass up there."

"I got a long list of things for you, sugar, but trusting you ain't on it."

Doug could hear laughter from the room beyond. Another bottle hit the sidewalk. Doug felt closed in by boarded-up houses. He sensed eyes everywhere, and out of there was a long way off.

Simba kept her voice down. "He has to act out his macho somehow, and breaking glass is fine with me. He can spend the rest of the day breaking bottles for all I care, and it might be enough to keep his little mind going. Don't step in the garbage." She tugged Doug's arm to help him avoid a bag split open, spilling soggy trash in the path. "Lots of hungry dogs around here. Even the garbage is poor."

"Hey, momma." A different voice.

Straddling a porch railing sat a man in his early twenties. No shirt, beer bottle in one hand, eyes unfocused. He kept grabbing the post in front of him to catch his balance and smiled as though everything in the air was funny.

"You get a lot of that noise around here," Simba told him. "One thing you don't do on this street is look around. You just go."

"I guess someday I'll thank you for this," said Doug warily.

He could hear her muffled laugh.

Two-thirds into the second block Simba motioned Doug to a house on their left with a porch but no front steps. It had to be deserted, but then all the houses were shells with no signs of life. Without even pausing, Simba hiked her skirt, planted her left foot on the edge of the porch, grabbed a post, and pulled herself up, pinstriped suit, grocery bag, and all.

"Every man for himself," she said.

Doug followed, but the flooring almost gave way under his weight. "Does someone actually live here?"

"If you can call it that." She walked to the far end of the porch, reached around the corner, and pulled on a string.

Doug could hear a bell ringing upstairs.

"Mrs. Stallings, it's Simba. I've brought the man I told you about. Come let us in." She waited in the center of the porch.

In a minute, Doug heard a chain loosen on the door. He realized the door was still a door, even though it had boards nailed to it. A bolt slid, and then another. The massive gate of a door swung open revealing an elf of a woman with watery blue eyes and quivering chin. She wore a faded blue housedress and ragged, mismatched slippers that had long since lost all color. Her face wasn't in use. No expression, no relief, no pleasure, no fear, nothing but dirt and dirty gray hair plastered over what had been a person.

"Are you coming?"

He realized Simba was talking to him from inside, waiting. He stepped in quickly.

"Mrs. Stallings, would you please take us upstairs," asked Simba, closing and bolting the door. They started up the steps. "You seem shocked, honey. Is it because she's white?"

But Doug couldn't answer. The downstairs was filled with trash, a million flies, and a gagging stench. He blinked to cut the burning in his eyes and tried not to breathe. It didn't seem to bother Simba.

He remembered an expression his father used to describe a bad odor, *Enough to drive a buzzard off a gut wagon.* This would kill the buzzard.

"Upstairs, it's better. There's a window not boarded up all the way. There's some air."

But upstairs wasn't any better.

"Is there any plumbing in this house?" The stench sunk into his stomach and was trying to come back out.

"Oh, you noticed the odor." They stepped over some old boards to get through an open doorway. "As for plumbing, there used to be, but some of the locals salvaged it."

Doug looked around. They stood in litter up to their knees.

Simba handed Mrs. Stallings the bag of groceries. The tiny woman set it on a skinny table that rocked, the only piece of furniture in the room, and began to unpack the contents. She took out each can, bottle, and box. She examined each and tunneled it under the litter as though that was where she always kept that item.

"Makes you wonder what else is under there, doesn't it, Doug?"

Mrs. Stallings tore up the grocery bag and sprinkled it like confetti near the window, then she lay down on it, like it was a feather bed, and sunk into it almost out of sight.

"Clean paper for her bed."

"Is her bathroom in here, too?"

"Oh, no. That's down the hall to the rear of the house. Why don't you go take a look." Doug stepped out into the hall and began to pick his way toward the rear.

"Just follow your nose," called Simba.

"My lord," Doug whispered, though he was trying to hold his breath. The odor was like a wall rolling over him. He couldn't go any farther. He turned back, eyes burning.

"Bet you never thought the air in here could smell so sweet."

"One match and this place would go like a volcano. Mrs. Stallings, how do you feel?" His nose and throat felt like steaming lava.

She turned her head but made no comment.

"She doesn't have much to say anymore, Doug. As far as her health is concerned, she's seen better days. She suffers a few rat bites every now and then. But, mainly, they stay near the other wall, where she hides her food." Simba pointed. "I think she and the rats reached an agreement. She's not been bit for at least six months."

"Good grief." Doug shuffled his feet in the litter. "I think she may have joined them." *It's like a big nest.* He was sure he could hear rustling under the paper. "How long has she been here?"

"Three or four years."

"Where'd she come from? How did she get here?"

"She was one of the street-people, a bag lady."

"Dumped by the mental institutions?"

"Not that I could make out. Just dumped by the system. Her husband died or left. Her children couldn't afford to keep her or got lost. She wound up on the street. Nothing new about that. Been that way since the caveman."

"But why here?"

"The guy that used to live in this house took pity on her one cold night when she was trying not to freeze. Big Ernie. He used her as a maid. Got sent off to jail. She stayed."

Doug gazed at Mrs. Stallings, who had turned her face toward the partially boarded window.

"How does she survive? How does she get food?"

"Old Mrs. Crutchfield across the street brings her food and bottles of water."

Doug wondered what would happen if old Mrs. Crutchfield died.

"She is used to staying here, so she just stays. Nobody's going to bother her. She has nothing anybody wants." Simba paused to look at all that nobody wanted. "There are close to a hundred people like her, mostly black, within a ten-block radius of the hospital. Cliff dwellers. They hole up anywhere there's a cave above ground. Abandoned houses. Abandoned people."

"Simba, this isn't a health as much as a social problem."

"It's both. Don't kid yourself. She and the others are part of your community. What are their health needs? How do you or anybody else meet those needs? Or do you just forget them because they're a social problem?"

"No. No, we can't do that."

"I'm glad to hear you say that because some of them have real physical problems. Mrs. Stallings has deep mental health problems brought about by her social situation. She can't get back to normal without psychiatric help."

"Living here she must have health problems." He felt as though the stench was forming a crust all over him and he wanted to scrape it off.

"It's your community, and you have a Social Service Department. You like a challenge? Here's one every city hospital in the country has ignored."

273

"That may or may not be, but we might be able to do something. Some may be candidates for nursing homes, but getting patients into good nursing homes isn't easy these days."

"Honey, you might be the one that's going to make some of them better, or else close them. Anyhow, there are enough empty beds to take them in at Eastern."

He wondered where she had heard about the nursing home program. "It doesn't work that way. But we might be able to get something started. I'll need to know who and where they are."

Simba pulled an envelope from her inside coat pocket. "Here's a list of eighty-six. We'll add more as we search them out. There are a hundred empty beds. Why can't you take them?"

"I just made a change on your education program. The first item to be addressed is your question. In the meantime, I'll give you a short answer. We can't make them permanent residents. We treat them and release them to nursing homes. Also, they have to have a medical problem. We can't just go out and round up every abandoned person."

"You're beginning to sound like all the other CYA administrators."

"I'll agree to take in the ten with the worst problems first. Next week we'll talk about the next step."

"I'll get my committee to work on it." She turned to the litter-bed. "Mrs. Stallings, come lock up. We're leaving."

Simba walked over to help her, but she was already scrambling to her feet.

Doug was so glad to get outside to breathe, he wasn't upset that there were six black men standing at the end of the walkway waiting for them.

Simba called the biggest one. "Come here!"

He strutted over while the others all mumbled, "All right, man." "Yeah." "Uh-huh."

"Help me down." She put her hands on his shoulders, jumped down and pushed him.

"You the one throwing all the bottles?" she accused.

"No. Wasn't me." He backed away.

The men on the street were calling out.

"Hey, man." "Let's go." "What'sa matter, man."

"Then I'm telling you," she jabbed him with her finger, "keep everything just the way Big Ernie wants it. You got that?"

Doug stepped down off the porch.

"Okay. I keep it that way." He strutted toward the others. "Git out the way."

"Big Ernie coming?" asked one in obvious disbelief.

"She say so, didn't she?"

"Shit."

They turned and ambled down the street.

Simba watched them for a moment, then turned to Doug. "We'll go to the next corner and head over to the hospital. It's shorter."

"And a lot faster."

"Especially a lot faster."

Ann was just putting down the phone as Doug walked in. "That was Lou Pickero. He wanted to talk to you about the death rate. Shall I call him back?"

"Might as well. Had to happen sooner or later." Pickero was becoming omnipresent. So were the deaths. He was surprised it hadn't come up during the survey. Maybe they just noticed it in reviewing the stats they had gathered.

"He's on," she called.

"Doug, I wanted to alert you that we were pulling up Eastern's file for weekly monitoring of deaths reported."

"We're aware it's higher than average."

"There's nothing for you to be doing other than what you would do under the circumstances anyhow, but I just thought I'd alert you."

"Will you be coming in for a review?"

"Not yet. If it continues, then we'll have to conclude it's more than just an anomaly."

Doug called Kay. "Maybe you better come down here. I just got a call from Pickero and the state is now monitoring us on a weekly basis because of the death rate. We need to review the status and plan what we're going to do about it. We need to do some special monitoring ourselves."

"Let me bring Juanita with me. She's very upset. I'll explain why when we get there."

When they came in, Doug could see a change in Juanita. She was pale, but more than that, she looked tired, absolutely drained.

Kay put her arm around her. "It'll work out."

"What's the problem?" He knew something else had happened.

"We've been informed that there were some names listed in the Ramirez will that might narrow down the suspect list."

Doug waited, holding his breath.

"Her son isn't the only one in her will."

"Who else?"

"Jeep."

"Holy shit! And why would she even put him in her will? Was she incompetent?"

"No," answered Juanita. "She felt he was the best doctor in Solstory. You said yourself that the Hispanic doctors were weak."

"Yeah, that's true. They kinda laid down and stopped being human beings. They let Jeep walk on them. But, still . . ."

"I didn't agree with her, but she felt he had helped some of her neighbors. Feelings were mixed. But he and her son weren't the only ones in the will." Juanita hesitated. "I'm listed, too."

Doug nodded at the implication. "Well, that I can understand."

"Yes, but it does complicate matters, from a police perspective," Kay pointed out. "The three people in her will were all with her some time before she became violently ill and died." Kay pulled Juanita tighter, and Juanita bowed her head.

"I didn't even know I was in her will. What'll I do?"

"Do nothing, sweetie. You have nothing to worry about."

"There's nothing you can do, but don't worry. We all know you. Kay, we've got to take some action, even if it's to monitor every terminal patient every thirty minutes around the clock. We have to get a handle on it. By the way, what about our undercover man? What's his name? Has he come up with anything else?"

"Gregg. Marvin Gregg. He's working with the police, and he said 'Don't muddy up the water.'"

"Meaning what?"

"Meaning they'll do the investigating."

"They can investigate all they want to. We have to prevent any more. Figure out how you're going to monitor and let me know."

Doug's instincts told him Jeep had done it, not the son and especially not Juanita. *Or am I denying she could do it because I like her? But Jeep is devious and dishonest.* He disagreed with Juanita. He was sure Jeep could do it.

Juanita went back to her floor, leaving Kay and Doug to discuss things.

"Is Gregg still around here today?"

"I don't know. He's not working for us as a volunteer anymore."

"Do you know how to get in touch with him? Through Bull, maybe?"

"I'll call the precinct office. He may be there. Why?"

"I'd like to meet with him. I've got to know they're doing something."

Kay made a couple of calls and then shared her findings. "He said he'll talk to you, but wants to wait a couple days."

"Did he say why?"

"I asked, and he said 'Trust me.' He'll call you."

"'Trust me.' It sounds like he's the one who doesn't trust."

"It's his job not to trust."

CHAPTER TWENTY-EIGHT

Doug was relieved to be in the hospital, in a safe area. He thought of Mrs. Stallings and that crazy broken glass street. It was a lost world.

In the hallway, Amy Heil, Director of Social Services, came rushing around a corner and bumped into him, scattering her papers on the floor.

"Oh, Doug, I'm so sorry." She was already on her knees, scrambling the papers together.

"I'll survive." Doug knelt to help. "I wanted to see you, anyhow."

She looked up at him, her amber hair wired with gray. Doug figured when she was younger she must have set hearts racing.

"Really?" she asked, gathering herself back to her feet. "Not this way, I'll bet."

He told her about the agreement with Simba.

"Oh, how wonderful. Thank you for being a caring person." She clutched her papers to her chest. "What can I do to help?"

"We'll need to determine if they're eligible for Medicare or Medicaid, and look for nursing homes to take them." He wondered if the nursing homes would be an improvement over the caves.

"That's great, Doug. The credit office can determine their eligibility and file the Medicaid applications for them. It'll take some searching, but we'll find nursing home beds. Oh, this is wonderful." She worked one hand free to reach out and touch his shoulder and squeeze. "Let me have the list Simba gave you. I might be able to add a few names to it."

Doug handed her the envelope and she started toward her office, then turned back.

"Do you mind if I call Simba? I have her number. I've always liked her except for those horrible things she said about you."

Doug called after her. "No, feel free to call her. Think about which medical residents we should pull into this, too."

On Friday, Doug met with Marvin Gregg and Kay O'Connell.

"I didn't want to meet with you earlier because we were in the middle of something I couldn't talk about."

"I understand that, but you have to understand we have a hospital to run."

"I have some interesting news for you. Have you seen Dr. Jiparmalanaron lately?"

"Jeep? Can't say I have, but then I don't see him that often."

"We think he may have skipped town. We got a search warrant to go through his clinic and home yesterday morning. We told him not to leave town, but he's gone. We think there's an underground movement of East Indians and he may have used it to get out."

"Makes it look like he has a reason to run."

"He does, we think. We found a poison at his clinic that could have been the one used on Mrs. Ramirez—ricin. It's a derivative of the castor bean and hundreds of times more toxic than arsenic or cyanide. It only takes a pinch. Only problem is, we can't prove it. The body's natural protein-making cells break ricin down leaving no trace."

"But the fact that he's running is almost an admission."

"Yeah, but that's circumstantial, and the D.A. will want something more substantial. Fortunately, Jeep, as you call him, doesn't know that. Or he wouldn't be running. When we catch him, we may be able to get him to confess, especially if we promise no death penalty."

"Doug," Kay added, "the symptoms are identical to what she had. It causes the red blood cells to agglutinate and then attack other body cells. And the medical examiner says that that appears to be the case."

Gregg picked up the thread. "In addition, they found a small red spot on her arm that shows an injection of something. Again, typical of an injection of ricin. Frankly, I never heard of the stuff until the M.E. described it to me. He says it's the only poison with these particular symptoms, but if we can't find a trace of the stuff, it's still circumstantial."

"Looks like you have to find him in order to get a plea bargain, if that's what it is. I've probably seen too many TV shows."

"That's more or less what it is."

"Does this let Juanita off the hook?"

"Pretty much. In fact, it's likely he might be responsible for other deaths as well. We'll only know that if he confesses. With nothing to lose, he might clear that up. Anyhow, we're searching for him, and we're not considering her a suspect at this time."

"'At this time.' You mean after all this, you could still suspect her?"

"We have to be sure."

"I never considered her a suspect from the beginning, and I certainly don't now."

"Neither do I," said Kay.

"I guess it's okay to tell her." Gregg didn't seem sure.

"You guys keep on suspecting right up to proof positive, don't you."

"We have to, Mr. Carpenter." He shrugged. "It's our job."

"Kay, Jeep's patients—"

"I'm ahead of you. I'll let Smith know, and he can assign a resident."

Doug felt relieved. Juanita was clear. Jeep did it. He felt a little guilty. It took Jeep's obvious guilt for him to feel relief. He had known all along she wasn't guilty, but still, he hadn't come right out and declared her innocent. *Subconsciously, did I really think she could possibly have done it? No matter. She's innocent. And now she'll collect from Mrs. Ramirez's will. She deserves it.*

On Saturday morning, Doug stayed away from the office. He mowed the grass behind the house with a hand mower—no motor. It worked the tension out of his shoulder muscles. The sun seeped through his skin. He watched the woods. Birds and squirrels were flitting in a busy carnival of motion. It was a day to be outside. There was no indication that his house had been damaged or that this peace had ever been violated.

That evening, he and Bess went to a classic film festival at the library. They saw *The Red Shoes* for the sixth time. The first time they saw it was at the Ritz in Pittsburgh when he was an undergraduate student at the university. He felt as though he was visiting a world he had left. He was glad to be back, even if for just a few hours.

On Monday morning, ten disoriented cliff dwellers came by ambulance after ambulance into the emergency room. Among them was Mrs. Stallings. The residents felt her confusion was due to imbalances in her system, the result of diet, viruses from rat bites, and who knows what else.

Simba arrived at Doug's office at one p.m., and they left immediately.

"We've got a lot of ground to cover in four hours, Doug."

"You're not taking me to Trowbridge, are you?"

"Yes, honey, but we'll be heading the other direction unless you want to go back and meet with our friends."

He gave her a look for an answer. "What's it going to be this time, dead cats and rabid bats?"

"I just love your southern sayings."

The first house she selected was on the corner of Berry and Trowbridge, the closest they came to the previous tour.

An old lady, heavy and bent to one side, came to the door.

"Mrs. Bessie May, I want you to meet Mr. Doug Carpenter, the administrator at Eastern." Doug remembered the talk show and the things Simba said about him. He wondered what Mrs. May had heard or thought of him.

"It's nice to meet you, Mrs. May," he said as they moved into the house.

Mrs. May glanced around the room as though checking it out. "Well," she said, as though no choice remained, "come in. Sit yourself down."

She pointed to two wooden chairs next to the door while she limped across the small room to an upholstered chair with the stuffing falling out. She brushed off some fallen plaster. "Excuse me for taking the good seat, but my body can't take those hard things." She laughed nervously. "I don't think they could take my body, neither."

Doug, grateful for the wooden chair, took one look at the greasy upholstering. It warned him of bedbugs, lice, ticks, and all manner of crawling and biting things.

"Mary Ann," Mrs. May called. "You and the children come on in here."

A young girl, about eighteen, came in carrying a baby on one arm and holding a toddler with her free hand. The girl hovered by the massive chair. There was no other place to sit. In fact, the only other furniture was a playpen with half the flooring gone.

"Mrs. May," said Simba. "Mr. Carpenter is interested in learning about health care needs in the neighborhood, and I thought maybe you could tell him about some of the things you would like from Eastern."

"I sure can. When they tore down all the houses on Main Street to build that hospital, they told us we would all get free care. But every time we go there, they ask for a card or a number or a check or something, so I just don't go no more. And, oh yes, I got this thing on my side so I can't hardly walk no more. Can't even straighten up."

"Does it hurt?" asked Doug.

"When I move, it does."

"Has anybody looked at it?"

"Mary Ann here has, but that don't help none."

"I mean, have any of the doctors seen it?"

"No, because I don't go there no more."

"Is the reason you don't go because they want to see a Medicaid card?"

"Yes. And they ain't supposed to make no money off us. They said it was going to be free for us to give up our homes so they could use the ground for the new building. That ain't right."

"Mrs. May, is Mr. May home?"

"There ain't no Mr. May. Just us and Cheryl, the younger girl. She in school. Mary Ann stay home to take care of her children."

"Is Mary Ann's husband home?"

"She ain't got no husband. He just a no-good, like all the boys around here. He get her pregnant and brag about it."

"Where did she have her babies?"

"Right here in this house. Her older sister come and help."

"You're just blocks from the emergency room. She could've

gone there, had the prenatal classes, gotten the best of care, Medicaid or not."

"Shoot. She got everything here she would've got there, and it cost nothing. Besides, that big doctor look down on us. He think we nothing."

"The obstetrician, Dr. Whyte?"

"Yeah, that the one. I thought they call him that because he so white. Didn't know that was his name."

"What does he do that you don't like?"

"He yell at us. He don't like nothing we do."

Simba interrupted the interview. "Mrs. May, tell Mr. Carpenter how you hurt your side."

Mrs. May remained mute for a moment, just gazed at the opposite wall as though looking through it. "Man cut me."

Doug leaned forward. "Someone cut you? With a knife?"

"With a butcher-knife, right in the side."

"A man did that? What man?"

"My man. He gone now. Won't be coming back."

"How long ago?"

"Oh, must be two years ago. Raymond here wasn't born yet."

"Did the doctors do anything for it?"

"Shoot no. Didn't see no doctor."

"You're telling me you got stabbed and you didn't go to the hospital? As much as it's bothering you?"

"Bothering me more than it used to. Been thinking of going, but can't stay in no hospital. Have to watch out for her boyfriend. If I left, she be pregnant again tomorrow." Mary Ann smiled and looked sideways at Doug.

"There is such a thing as free birth control," he said.

The girl replied, "Tommy don't like that."

Simba nodded. "Thank you, Mrs. May. We have to move on."

"Mrs. May, you have to come in and have that checked out."

Mrs. May struggled to her feet. "Thank you for coming."

On the street, Doug said, "We're talking about some basic education."

"It's a community need, Doug. You know how many there are like her?"

Simba had obviously planned the afternoon to prove that point. None of the women they talked to understood what a hospital could do for them other than the basic and obvious patching-up type things, and they weren't even taking advantage of that because they thought it should be free.

They visited eight homes. In none were there fathers. In all but two, there were pregnant, unmarried teenage daughters, and in the other two, the teenage daughters had already had children. In one case, the infant was brain-damaged. That might have been avoided in the hospital delivery room, or discovered and prevented during prenatal testing, or avoided through prenatal education.

One of the girls was so bright. Doug pictured her as a candy striper, not a mother. *If she had been part of that program, would she be pregnant?*

Tired, they walked back to the hospital. "Simba, if you can get Mrs. May to come into the hospital for help, I'll tell them not to ask for her Medicaid card. But one of the things you're going to hear about this week is why we have to ask for those cards, regardless of foolish promises made in the past."

Tuesday afternoon. Simba and Doug walked south on Main Street and east on Dogwood Street.

"What are we going to see today?"

No reply.

He tried to sense her mood, solemn, temperamental, angry, sad. "What are we going to see?" he repeated.

After a while, she answered. "Something bad."

They walked a few blocks and turned right on Church Street, a name the surroundings seemed to mock. They turned in at the first house. Five young men sitting on the front steps quietly moved aside. Doug didn't worry, not with Simba.

The door opened as they stepped on the porch. The woman holding the door just eyed them like the plague. Simba walked past and up the stairs to the second floor. He followed. In a back bedroom, a sixteen-year-old boy lay on a bed staring into the air. Simba passed her hand in front of his eyes. They were like glass. No reaction.

"He's been like this for three weeks."

Metallic noises and shouting brought the outside into the room. Doug glanced out the window but saw nothing.

"Those are the usual sounds here, Doug. Don't worry about it."

"What happened to him?"

"Probably an overdose. Might've been done to him instead of by him."

"Why isn't he in the hospital?"

"Combination of reasons. The police want to question him about something, and his friends can't guard him in the hospital."

Simba took a dropper from a glass next to the bed and placed a tiny trickle of water on the boy's tongue.

"Seen enough?" she asked.

"Let's go."

At the second stop, no guards, only a mother with eyes swollen from crying and a face hiding hurt.

"He's still here," she told Simba. "But it hasn't been easy."

She led them to the kitchen. Leaning against the back door, or guarding it, was a teenage girl, about sixteen. Seated at a table was a ten-year-old boy.

When Simba walked in, he jumped to his feet and hollered, "Hey, this the momma we been waiting for? Hey, sister, I'm glad I waited. You okay." He looked her over, then he spotted Doug. "But who's the white dude? He in the wrong place."

Doug could see the swollen nose tissues and unfocused eyes.

There were just three chairs. Simba sat and motioned to Doug, who followed suit. "Sit for just a minute, Samuel."

The boy did.

"I was here Sunday. You don't remember, do you?"

"Sure, sister. I couldn't forget you now, could I?"

Simba stepped behind Samuel's chair. She put her hands on the sides of his face, pointing him straight ahead. "What am I wearing, Samuel?"

"You're wearing the prettiest purple dress I've ever seen, but on your body, anything would be pretty, even a brown paper bag."

The boy's mother left the room crying.

Simba sat again, but Samuel didn't seem to notice the pinstriped suit.

"You told me you sniff coke because it makes you a man. Is that right?"

"Hey, that's right, sister. And now I got places to go and things to do. Sorry I can't stay to show you how much a man I am." He rose and left the room, slamming the front door.

Simba turned to the girl. "Susan, do drugs affect you the same way they do Samuel? Do you feel more like a woman?"

"No, ma'am. He just don't know he's hooked."

"Why do you take drugs?"

"It makes me feel good."

"Are you hooked?"

"Uh-uh. I can quit any time I want to."

"Drugs are expensive. How can you afford them?"

"You know, men like me. I can get as much money as I want. I give to the pusher. The pusher gives to me."

"Aren't you afraid of getting pregnant?"

"I haven't yet."

"Susan," asked Doug, "what would you do if you got pregnant?"

Susan raised her voice, "That won't happen to me."

Simba tilted her head in disbelief. "Why not? You think those sperm all die the second they get inside you?"

The girl crossed her arms. She tilted her face toward the ceiling. "Won't happen." She squeezed her arms and swayed back and forth. "Won't." She bit her lip and closed her eyes, clearly trying to keep a tear in.

"Won't, huh?"

"Leave me alone!" she screamed, running from the room. The front door slammed again. Simba glanced at Doug as the mother came in, heavy-footed. She collapsed in the empty chair. She looked worn by age, but Doug knew she couldn't be more than thirty-five.

"I don't know what I'm going to do," she said to the room. "Both my little ones are on drugs. They different children since taking drugs. They was good and smart. And they was loving. We was all loving."

Slowly, she folded her hands and began to cry. "But no more. I want what's good for my children, but there's pushers all over the neighborhood." She bowed her head and sobbed. "My girl, my boy, they hooked. I can't get them back. I wisht I was dead."

Simba slid her chair over and put her arms around the woman. "Mrs. Lamar, you pray to Father. Pray hard. We'll try to help, but we can't make promises."

The mother leaned her head on Simba's arm for a long time. She lifted her head as though listening to something outside. She struggled to her feet. "I got to go. I got to look for them." In the doorway, she turned apologetically. "Thank you for coming, anyway."

The rest of the afternoon was more of the same. Eight distraught mothers. Overwhelming. Their sobs blended into a symphony of sorrow. Exhausting. He was ready when Simba suggested they stop in a corner cafe for coffee. It didn't matter that it was as ramshackle as any of the houses they had been in all day.

They sat at a small table that rocked when they touched it and ordered coffee from a black man wearing an apron and whose eyes reflected what looked like hate or anger. Doug felt as though he were sitting on somebody's closed-in front porch. The plank flooring was petrified with age and exposure. An old sink and refrigerator filled one corner, a stove another, shelves along the clapboard wall between with a scarred table in place of a counter, three other small tables, all different, and a mixture of chairs, but everything was clean.

What the hell? What could they do to coffee besides make it taste bad?

Doug felt the owner's eyes. Then he recognized Simba and moved faster. The coffee came in thick mugs with no glaze left.

"You look tired, Douglas. Is this too hard on you?"

"Not too hard. Just different. Very different. How about you?"

"This is lull-time for me."

"Where are you from, Simba?"

"The jungle."

"Yeah, I know. That's what you told the reporters. Which jungle?"

"It's not something I talk about." She held her coffee mug with both hands. "You can't do anything about the past."

"Except prevent it from happening again."

He lifted his mug and studied it. The outside, including the rim, was sticky. The remains of a thin green line running around the outside were partially concealed by coffee stains.

Simba watched him. She sipped her coffee. "I grew up in Elizabeth City, North Carolina. My mother died while I was sucking her tit. My grandmother told me. She raised me. Was that what you wanted to know?"

"I didn't mean to pry. You don't sound like you're from the South."

"You mean I don't sound black."

"I mean you don't sound like you came from the South."

"I don't want to sound like I came from the South. And I don't want to sound black. If someone says they want to ax me a question, I tell them to go out to the woodpile and ax some wood, and when they're ready to ask me a question, to come in and ask, but not ax."

"So you got a law degree at Yale. What was your degree in at Carolina? Elocution?"

"That was my husband. Philology, to be exact. My degree was in government. Feel intimidated sitting with an educated black woman?"

"You forget. I work with dozens of doctors, a whole hospital full of gods. Not much intimidates me anymore. I didn't realize you were married."

"I'm not anymore. He was killed in an automobile accident. A drunk driver hit us on the Baltimore-Washington Expressway. I was pregnant and lost my baby. That's all about me. Does the neighborhood intimidate you?"

He hunched over his mug. "Good lord. You have had a time of it. Okay, today was the worst day. You know how to make a point. Yesterday, it was ignorance, today it was drugs."

"What do you think?"

"We might be able to do something about the ignorance if you can get the Community Association involved. But we can't clean the pushers off the street. We're not the police."

"How about a Detox Unit for children?"

"What would they come back out to?"

"Lord Jesus! Just when I thought you were getting smart." Simba gazed at him with forced patience. "It's my fault. I didn't tell you our plans. We're starting a community watch program in cooperation with the police."

"Have the police agreed to that?"

"They're going to."

The owner was sitting quietly, listening to their conversation. There was a man at the larger table, gazing into a cup of coffee, as though studying the future.

Doug thought about her idea. "If you can do that, we might be able to form a Detox Unit as an adjunct to our Psych Unit. But how are you going to pull this community together to clean the place up?"

"Through the Community Association. Through the churches. Don't underestimate the power of righteous people. We'll get it done, but we need help from you."

"Simba, how's this community going to do anything? We've been in and out of homes in the last two days. We've seen nothing but despair and defeat. Family problems, infections, pregnant teenagers, women working their asses off and physically sick from worry. Nowhere did I see any sign of hope. And nowhere did I see any sign of a husband. Is this the community you say is going to correct its problems?"

"Hey." The owner leaned over Doug and glared. "You just shut up an' listen. There's plenty of good people in this community. And in my family, there's a father. Me. I care about my children."

"Maybe so, but you must be the only one."

"You don't know what you're talking about. I know lots of fathers that care for their children."

"Care for them. Fine. Do they live with them or support them?"

"Can't nobody support no family these days."

"Do you live with your family?"

"Yes. I live with my family, but I don't make enough money to support my family. I work from six in the morning to nine in the evening, and my wife works from seven to three, and I don't make enough in this dump to buy her lunch."

"But you spend time with your family, right?"

"You know how that makes me feel? She makes ten times what I make and I work seven days a week. I'm a cook. I should be making better than this. Between her and me, we don't make nothing compared to you. All them new cars. Look at this place." He waved his hand toward the walls.

"See what your damn propaganda's done?" Doug asked Simba.

"Excuse me, honey. Your two-year-old car is new to anybody in this community."

"But you do spend time with your family, don't you?" Doug pursued.

The man pulled a chair over and sat across from him. "Yeah, yeah, I spend time with my family. I heard your question. My family's important to me. Okay? Now, let's get down to the real problem." He held his hands out in front of him as though he were measuring something. "A man got to have a job. If he going to be with his family, he got to have a job. I'm a cook. Why don't your hospital hire me?"

"Don't bullshit me. I'll leave if you do. Maybe you want a job, but how many of the men in this community do?" They sat, eyes locked. "Tell me what you really think the answer to that question is."

The man studied his hands for a moment.

"By the way"—Doug held out his hand—"I don't know your name. I'm Doug Carpenter."

The man glanced at Doug then Simba. His chest heaved as he took a deep breath, relaxed, and shook his hand. "I'm Robin Jefferson." He traced doodles on the table with his finger. He seemed to be processing thoughts. Then he put them to words, honesty pushing out hate from his eyes. "Okay, a lot of them don't want to work, but those that do can't get work. So there you are. If you black, you can't get work."

"There are lots of unemployed whites, too."

"You don't know what it's like. You don't know what it's like to be turned down for a job you can do because you're black."

"I'm sure that happens, but not everywhere."

"It happened at your hospital."

Doug shook his head no.

"Yes, it did. I know. I know 'cause I applied for cook there, four years ago. They was looking, and my wife's a nurse there, LPN. She told me about it. The head cook didn't want no black cook. He hired a white man got hardly any experience. Still there. Head cook still there, too. See, that's the problem."

Doug felt the man's sincerity. He didn't want to believe him, but he did.

Robin Jefferson continued. "You support the community by giving jobs here, and the community support the hospital. That's the way it work." He scraped his chair back from the table. "I didn't mean to mouth off, but I just had to get that out because I love my family." His lip trembled for just a moment.

The man at the large table shuffled toward the door. "Well, I got to go home to my fambly, because they needs me."

"Get out of here, man. You got no family."

Doug remembered the coffee mug sitting in front of him. "Mr. Jefferson, would you give a cup like this to a patient in our hospital?"

Mr. Jefferson grabbed the mug and exclaimed without examining it, "No! It's dirty!"

"Why did you give it to me?"

"It was good enough for some white dude in a suit coming in here with a black girl. You want a clean one?"

"The coffee any good?"

"Made it myself."

On the way back to the hospital, they walked down Rush Street. The houses were neat and painted. The grass in the small plots was trim. Flowers bloomed. The sidewalks were clean. Simba stopped in front of one house. "This is as far as I go. I'm visiting someone here."

Doug examined the house. "Not on the tour?"

"No, Douglas. It's one of the community leaders who's going to help build the neighborhood watch."

Doug nodded. "I'll see you later this week. It's your turn to learn."

"Did you learn today?"

He had started to walk away but stopped. "Yes, Simba. I did learn today. I confess. You opened my eyes, just like you said you would."

He turned to leave again, and, once more, stopped. She waited.

"I admit something else." He hesitated but went ahead. "I damn near cried when Mrs. Lamar came back in that kitchen."

Simba reached out and touched Doug's arm. "I bawled like a baby on my first visit."

CHAPTER TWENTY-NINE

Doug knew the community drug situation was bad, but seeing it firsthand had filled him with a sense of urgency. Something had to be done. And the hospital had done nothing. Of course, Stan, Whyte, and Smith didn't consider it a community. He had trouble dealing with that himself. But he could see Mrs. Stallings, Mrs. May, little Samuel, Susan, their red-eyed mother, and a host of others.

Mr. Jefferson reminded Doug of a face he hadn't seen for over thirty years—the janitor in his grade school—Willis. Everybody called him Willis. The teachers and the children. He was a big man, a kind man, and an image of something right. A voice always of reason. He remembered Willis better than most of the teachers who just filled space, not minds.

The hospital had a responsibility. Here he was, worried about nursing homes, and look what was at the back door: drug dealers and despair and beer bottles crashing on the sidewalk. Some of them didn't deserve care. Not true. At some point, they all deserve care. They never lost that right, even if they lost their spirits or selves or inner lights. *And who am I to judge, anyhow? Who was anyone to judge?*

Julia Best didn't think much of a Detox Unit for children. "Let the children's hospitals take care of children."

But the senior resident in Psychiatry thought it was a great idea. "It's all around us in our own backyard. Why shouldn't we be on the cutting edge? Anyhow, the children's hospitals *aren't* doing it."

Stan was obviously prepared to put down anything Doug came up with from Simba's tour. "Bringing those flea-bitten, stinking cave people into the hospital is an imposition on everybody—nurses, doctors, and patients. Nothing we do is going to help them anyhow."

"It will if we get them stabilized and place them in a nursing home."

"They'd rather live in their caves. They're where they are because that's where they want to be."

"I guess we'll just have to play it out and see."

His reaction to the children's Detox Unit was the same. "Who would pay for it?" Stan waved the idea aside.

Doug knew he had to find a way to support it. He also knew the community had to help. They had to help or it wouldn't get better. Stan was hoping he would fail, that he would compromise an already weak bottom line so he could jump on him and put himself in a more favorable light with the Board. He knew what he had to do and knew it was right, but he also knew, in spite of a few things that had gone his way, he could lose Bass and the Board and his job.

Cliff Toliver called some of his friends at the police station to see how bad the drug problem was from their view. It was rampant. Pushers overran the schools. They gave free drugs to the children to hook them, especially the girls. They could lead them into prostitution and use them for their own pleasure and to make money.

The City Health Department said there was no problem. Sometimes it takes a volcano to reveal a mountain. He would have to ignite them, and Simba would help.

On Wednesday, Simba brought Mrs. May, limping, into the emergency room. She had a serious staph infection in the unhealed gash in her side. Her entire right side was swollen and inflamed. They found pockets of pus, and all the flesh around the cut was red from cellulitis. In addition, the knife had slashed through the abdominal wall, resulting in a severe hernia.

The nurses and residents were amazed that she was able to move and that she hadn't developed gangrene. The Med/Surg resident wanted to admit her to the hospital, but she refused. She had to stay home and watch her daughter to keep her from getting pregnant again.

Sharon Masters, the head nurse, nearly got into a fight with her. "Mrs. May, if you don't let us treat you, you're going to die, and then who's going to watch your daughter?"

"I ain't gonna die. If I was gonna die, I'd a'done it already."

"You're half dead now and don't know it. In another month, you won't be able to move, and her boyfriend can come in and do it anytime he wants, right in front of you, and you won't be able to stop him."

"Just give me some pills and let me go home."

"Then you're going to die and she'll get pregnant every nine months. Is that what you want?"

"I want to go home." She pushed at Sharon and fell on the litter in pain.

"Mrs. May," Simba tried to convince the woman, "she's right. There's no medicine you can take home that will cure you. You let the hospital take care of you, and I'll see to it Mary Ann behaves. I'll get somebody to stay with her."

Mrs. May moaned, "He most likely there doing it right now."

* * *

Lucien Samuelson presented the new building proposal to the Medical Staff Board. The statistics were slanted, but Doug had helped the planning group in its preparation for the presentation to the state.

"Mr. Bass," Lucien said, "will lead off, discussing the role the hospital plays in the community, as only he can. He'll stress the need for a variety of services and beds to support education in a medical school hospital. I'll follow with the slideshow many of you have already seen, showing trends and statistics that support the proposal. Mr. Boswell will cover program issues."

Stan smiled and glanced around the room but frowned when his eyes met Doug's.

"Dr. Goldman will discuss medical needs associated with new services, highlighting problems caused by antiquated facilities. Mr. Carpenter will give an overview of all the operational problems with the old facility, stressing deficiencies found by the Joint Commission and State Health Department. He'll introduce the architects, who will unveil the plan for the new building."

"Are we still asking for an increase of five hundred beds?" asked Garland Riggely.

"Yes."

"Is that the total gist of it?" asked Charles Smith.

"That's it."

"There's one more thing. We need to add a doctors' office building to the plan."

Doug waited for Stan to remind Charles this idea had been discussed and rejected because it was financially unsound . . . but Stan was mute.

Joe Goldman pointed it out. "Can't, Charles. The hospital wouldn't be able to pay back the bonds on it."

"There's another way to do it that the hospital can afford." Charles tapped the burnt pipe tobacco into an ashtray. "A group of us are forming a corporation of physicians, and we'll put up the building ourselves and lease it to the hospital." He carefully put the pipe into his inside coat pocket. He folded his hands in front of him. "The hospital can allow its physicians to use the space, charge them a bare token, and the hospital wouldn't be using capital dollars. It would all come out of operating expense."

Doug wondered what it would take to get through to this crowd. "Regardless of which way you do it, it comes out of the same pot that pays the salaries, and we're struggling against a layoff as it is. The census continues to drop—"

"Oh, come on," complained Charles. "We've heard this before."

"Charles," Joe once more reminded, "it's a fact, like it or not."

"It is a lot of crap." Ed Whyte sat erect in his chair and took the floor. "Everybody overreacts to Medicare payment changes. Administration tries to con us into thinking things are tight and concocts a 'cry-wolf' story every year. Stan, you're going to have to do something about it. We want that building. It's necessary if we want the right patients in this hospital. I know you can work it out. You've told me. So tell Doug to stop arguing. Can't you control him?"

Stan's face turned a deep red. "My perception of it is," he said, watching his folded hands, "we will be able to manage it."

"Stan, there's no way we can afford it—" Doug was cut off by Ed.

"Here we go again." Whyte sounded like a wounded animal.

Doug continued. "In addition, who's going to pay for all the new furniture and interior decorating? I know you fellows aren't going to move your old furniture over."

Charles did not even respond to Doug but to Stan. "Stan, I'm going to answer the question and then I hope we can get to the business of the day. The hospital pays for it and recaptures it by charging the doctors rent. Those doctors not on our staff pay a larger amount to cover for our own physicians. It's simple."

"I understand now." Doug adjusted his posture. "And if there are no doctors or other hospital staff who want their offices all the way over here, we'll still charge a nominal token to our own physicians. Is that right?"

"There he goes again." Whyte was about to lose it. "He's the most negative person in the world. Nothing will work. You owe this to the doctors. Who brings all the patients and the revenue into the hospital, anyhow?" He pounded the table, garnering some astounded looks.

"Hold on a minute. This is getting out of hand. This was to be a short meeting. Let's discuss that later." Joe gave each person a glance to make sure they heard.

"No!" Charles refused to move on. "We need to settle it. There will be a doctors' office building, designed by the doctors, including a doctors' dining room, a rest and relaxation area, maybe even an exercise room. We'll design it, and the hospital will pay for it, either directly or by leasing it from us, or there will be no new hospital, and then you can find out what hard times are really like."

"No worries, Charles"—Stan waved him down—"you've got it. I'll see to it. You just get the Medical Staff Board to endorse it, and I'll present it to the Board of Trustees. It will be done. End of discussion."

Doug slapped his hands on the table. "This is irresponsible. I can't believe this is even being discussed. Stan, the money's not there." *Should I go straight to the trustees? Who would they believe? Whose side would they take?* Stan had lost credibility, but the Board wanted the building. Even with Joe Goldman's support, it was him against Stan and Charles Smith, who still had credibility. With the state hearing coming soon, there had to be another way.

Stan avoided eye contact and didn't seem to notice the knowing smirks.

"One of the reasons for our problems"—Doug would not let this go—"is the number of physicians who still ignore the length-of-stay requirements for Medicare patients. The HMOs are another problem that we will have to face up to, but with Medicare alone we have a high number of days disallowed and lose ninety-five thousand a month. It's got to—"

"Doug," barked Whyte, "if you were a doctor, and God has blessed us you aren't, I would hope you would not send a patient home before he was ready. There is such a thing as quality care. Doctors save patients while administrators save paper clips."

"You know and I know many patients are kept in longer than necessary. If you didn't keep getting paid by the insurance companies for those extra days, you can bet they would be out of here on time. That's one of the practices brought about the HMOs. One of these days, we are going to have to get a real quality assurance committee to monitor you."

"I don't have to take that! I won't sit in a meeting with him anymore."

"You crossed the line, Doug," said Charles.

Whyte and Charles moved toward the door. The other members of their departments followed. Charles stepped back into the room. "The hell with your HMO plans. We're not going to bust our butts to improve hospital reimbursement. We're going to focus on getting our own control back. Hospital problems are your problem. You're on your own." This time he slammed the door behind him.

Lucien announced, "Just a reminder, the presentation is one month from today."

Joe closed his folder and stood. "It looks as though we've covered everything we could here today. And just for the record, I agree with Doug." With that, Joe also left the room.

Stan sat in silence, watching Doug through narrow slits.

Doug leaned toward him as though confiding. "You are going to leave a legacy of bankruptcy for your successor." He left without waiting for a response.

CHAPTER THIRTY

Thursday morning. Simba arrived early, all business. Wesley Mills, the hospital finance officer, attended the meeting with his budget officer. So did George Rodabush, Finance Officer of the Eastern Hospital Council. The Hospital Council, excited about what Doug was doing, felt it would help all the hospitals.

Doug explained the hospital organization to Simba. "There's a Medical Staff Board and a Hospital Board. The Hospital Board is the final authority on all matters and is concerned about policy, quality care, finances, and general management. The Medical Staff Board reports to the Hospital Board. The Medical Staff Board is concerned about physician matters and medical care. In many hospitals, the Medical Staff Board sometimes gets wrapped around its own axle on personal matters. There are two physician members on the Hospital Board. Right now, they are Charles Smith and Joe Goldman."

Simba sat through the flip charts and slides showing hospital expenses and insurance company payments. Doug always felt any finance officer could talk a monkey into a coma, but Simba drilled them on every detail.

"So the doctors aren't employees of the hospital." Simba tried to wrap her mind around it all. "And they don't get paid by the hospital. They get paid by the insurance companies. The longer the patient's in the hospital, the more the doctor can charge, even for visits that are ten seconds long."

"That's right, but with the HMO patients, they go to the opposite extreme. For those, they get paid a flat rate. That's a different set of problems. Instead of giving too much care for too much money, the HMOs provide too little care and pay too little, but the doctors and some hospitals brought it on by their own behavior with excessive fees."

"So if it's not an HMO patient, the doctor doesn't discharge the patient and can keep getting booty by just popping his head in the room."

"For the non-HMO patient, yes."

"Then they're raping the system. They're raping the hospital. They're raping the employee, *and* they're raping the patient."

Doug faked a smile. "You have to remember, these guys paid a lot to get through med school. They sacrificed."

She was ready to lift off the ground. "Come on! Are you going to continue to be their whore?" Then she realized he was kidding. "How can anyone run a damn hospital?"

During the noon break, Wesley Mills came to Doug.

"I sure didn't want to mention this to Simba, but we are having one hell of a shortfall. If it continues, we'll have to talk layoffs before the end of the month."

"Don't mention layoffs, but do mention the financial condition this afternoon. She'll find out sooner or later. Be sure you discuss the free care given to members of this community who haven't applied for Medicare and Medicaid, and how many jobs that lost money could pay for."

"Okay." Wesley nodded his head in compliment. "She has a good brain. We won't have to draw a picture."

The session became even more technical.

Simba asked, "Are you saying if the people in this community paid nothing but gave their Medicare or Medicaid numbers, enough revenue would be generated to pay for thirty-five jobs?" This was her suggestion at the end of the session. "If you're forced to reduce staffing because of the shortfall, cut everybody's hours and cut everybody's pay. No layoffs."

"There are a couple of problems with that," Doug explained. "The people with seniority will think they shouldn't be cut, and everybody will say they're working fewer hours so they should do less work."

"The second problem you'd have anyhow," Simba replied. "Layoffs are immoral. Those people were loyal and helped you become what you are. How can a hospital expect its employees to be loyal if management isn't? Hospitals are getting as bad as corporations. Corporations have the sorry excuse that they are putting stockholder dividends before loyalty. So they can screw the workers who made the profits for them in the first place. You don't even have that excuse. Employees are not disposables, honey."

She stopped to take a breath and would have run on, but Doug shocked her by saying, "You're right."

"You white guys do let a body go on, don't you."

"No way to stop you short of a two-by-four upside the head."

"If you agree, what's holding you up?"

"I guess I'm just not sure the employees would ever agree to it."

"I can guarantee a uniform cutback will maintain the same workload. I'll talk to the employees with seniority and they'll agree. And there'll be a lot of appreciation for your fairness. It'll build loyalty in your organization. A layoff won't."

"You may be right." The wheels and cogs were turning in Doug's brain. "I'll think about it. I hate layoffs. I see it as a failure of management." And to Wesley, "When will you give me your recommendations?"

"In a week. Two max."

"How many positions?" asked Simba.

"Maybe a hundred. I don't know for sure. I'd have to calculate it out."

"Doug, there's just one thing." Simba sounded serious. "With a cutback in salaries, everybody has to be cut, from top management down, or I can't make any guarantees. And I promise to educate the community so they agree to give card numbers when they come into the hospital."

"Would you agree that those who don't have cards will be urged to apply for them through our credit office?"

"Doug, I can't agree unless you give me a few things."

"Like what?"

"If I feel specific salaries are low, you'll agree to negotiate."

This chick has some big kahunas.

"It sounds like an equal exchange to me. Besides, it'll show both of us are concerned about the employees." She smiled so assuredly.

"No need to amend the contracts. A handshake will do, and either of us can break the agreement."

"Agreed, but I don't intend to break it."

"Neither do I."

Doug dictated a memo to Stan listing the highlights of Simba's tours, the finance session, and the agreements. He also sent a copy to Walter Bass.

On Friday morning, Doug and Juanita took a train to the capital. On the way, they reviewed notes on the nursing homes.

In the Health Department conference room, James Flanagan talked about the pressures to place quality controls on the nursing homes, and how this was spreading across the state.

"A thousand letters a week are pouring into the department and the governor's office. I know Doug can give us some background regarding some of the concerns and approaches. Doug, fill us in."

Doug nodded. "People have become aware. They realize abuse is taking place. Those of us in the hospitals have seen it and want it to stop."

He listed the concerns: dehydration, malnutrition, comatose conditions, evidence of physical abuse.

"Juanita has been working with some of the churches in our area to set up unscheduled visits to nursing home residents."

He outlined legislation requiring that abuse be reported. The governor played an active role in the discussion.

"Doug, we will be drafting legislation within the next two weeks. We'll count on you to get it to the Hospital Council for input."

"Fine. And I've got a favor to ask on a different subject. We have a serious health crisis in our community because of rampant drug abuse. The City Health Department doesn't seem to agree. Do you think you could suggest they take a closer look?"

"Done."

Over the weekend, Doug took a pile of correspondence home with him. He decided there'd be no more Saturdays or Sundays spent at the hospital. He might be thinking business at home, but he would be where he wanted to be, and he could stop anytime to be with Bess.

On Monday morning, ten more cliff dwellers came in.

Stan was obviously attempting to be tactful. "We really can't handle all these long-term free patients in here."

"Stan, most of them are eligible for either Medicare or Medicaid, so they're not free. And they're filling empty beds. They'll be discharged or transferred in reasonable time. And Simba will get the community to use Medicare or Medicaid and we'll begin to fill even more beds."

Doug leaned over Stan's table and fixed his gaze on Stan's eyes. "Without these additional patients, I don't see how we can keep the number of beds we have, let alone convince the state we need more. This arrangement could be the bridge between you and the new hospital building."

Stan had no comeback. "Do it, and don't bother me."

"I'm glad to see our teamwork is paying off." Doug strolled to the door. "You're going to have to face the fact we can't justify everything in that building proposal."

He left the room, but Stan called after him, "You can't change it, Doug. It's the way it's going to be."

Stan's phrase kept repeating in his head. *It's the way it's going to be.* Like a rooster crowing in the morning. *It probably is the way it's going to be, and I'm not going to be able to change it, but I can do my best to do the right thing.*

There was a tap on the door and Ann ushered in Al Robinson.

"I'll be damned!" Doug jumped up. "You're back. And you look good!"

"I just got in, Doug. I wanted to come directly here to thank you."

"How was it?"

"Doug, I owe my life to those people and you. They made me take a good look at myself, and I didn't like me. I don't know what I'm going to do yet, but it's wrong for me to just walk back in here. I've got to do penance or something for the damage I did to that family and to this hospital." He leaned forward putting his fists on the desk. "Maybe some kind of community service?"

The answer sprang to Doug. "How about helping us set up a children's Detox Unit for this area? The community needs it desperately."

"Yes! When do I start? That's it. I don't know if I'll ever go to anesthesiology again."

"You won't be making the same bucks, you know."

"Doug, believe me. Dollars don't interest me anymore. I graduated from that class."

"Okay. Go home and get yourself squared away and be back tomorrow. We'll do some planning. How good do you think you are at setting fires under people?"

"Watch my smoke." Robinson grabbed Doug's hand and shook it.

CHAPTER THIRTY-ONE

Doug and Simba were alternating between hospital education and community education, or "the real education," as Simba called it. Simba took Doug to every corner of the run-down community. He talked to mothers, merchants, community leaders, and ministers. Among the community leaders was Tevisina Urqhart.

"I want to remind you that I am the Community Association's representative on the Hospital Board."

"Yes, Mrs. Urqhart, I certainly remember that."

"You just listen to what Simba tells you, and you'll be all right."

"We all do what we have to do," said Doug.

"Yes, some do what they have to do. And some talk about what they have to do." Tevisina winked.

Doug took Simba through all of the hospital departments and allowed her to interview the department heads. Resting over a cup of coffee in the cafeteria, Simba told Doug, "It surprised me that your managers were saying a lot of the same things I was saying, only they weren't blaming you. But you know you're wrong if you give in to the doctors' rotten demands."

"One thing you have to understand, Simba, doctors don't work for hospitals. They work for themselves. Administrators don't control them."

"I don't know, Doug. Your job doesn't sound all that difficult to me. You just need to knock some heads."

"There's more to it than that. Even if Stan Boswell and I agreed on everything, I can't just control. There are problems you haven't even dreamed of."

"Like what?"

"That death rate for one thing. Terminal patients dying off much sooner than normal."

"What's causing it?"

"Not sparse staffing like you guys tried to claim."

"Well then, what? You got an angel of mercy?"

"For a while I wondered, but it wasn't that."

"Wasn't?"

"Wasn't. The police figured it out, along with the medical examiner. It was a doctor. We don't know what motivated him in all cases, but in one, he was listed in her will. That's what tipped them off. But he's disappeared; ran as soon as they searched his clinic."

"I'll be damned. What else goes on here that the public doesn't get to know?"

"A hell of a lot that I'm not going to tell *you*, of all people. You'll do a TV show and be called glamorous."

"Now, Douglas, don't be jealous."

"I have to admit, you know how to wrap dumb TV hosts around your pinky." He stretched. "Damn, I'm tired. That's all the news from Lake Wobegon today."

"Right. I've got to be running along, too."

They placed their cups on the cafeteria conveyor belt by the exit. "By the way, Doug. I'm beginning to like you."

"You're not going to seduce me, are you?"

"You should be so lucky. Besides, you had your chance, white boy."

Doug and Kay made rounds for the first time in several weeks.

"Can't fall behind on this again," said Doug. "It's always an eye-opener. Want to go talk to a few patients?"

"Yeah. We need to exchange news more often than once a week at the staff meeting. Now that you're going steady with Simba Agiza, I never get to see you."

"You're still my favorite director of nursing named Kayo."

"Well, Kayo this. Juanita has given me her notice. She's resigned to go to Riverview Hospital as a nurse supervisor."

"Even in a small hospital, that's a step up. I'll miss her."

"We'll all miss her. It's a step up, but that's not the reason she's leaving. The Hispanic admissions have dropped because Jeep was admitting most of them. The Hispanic doctors all admit to Riverview and that's where she thinks she can do the most good. The director of nursing there is a friend. She felt guilty, stealing her away, and called to see if I was still speaking to her."

"I assume you still are."

"I told her I wanted weekly progress reports."

"That poor girl just can't get away from you."

Doug called a meeting with Lucien and the Planning Committee for a final review of the presentation to the state.

"Lucien, do you think they'll buy our projections?"

"No, but it's a good strategy with these folks to ask for more than you expect to get. They cut arbitrarily anyhow. The fact is, there isn't anyone there smart enough to pick us apart."

"If you were still with the state, what would you take exception with?"

Ed Whyte leaned forward, face turning red. "Are we going to waste time, again?"

"No, Ed," said Doug. "It's just good to know where you're vulnerable."

"We can support anything we've stated."

"Maybe, but there could be someone there with the idea that for one-third the cost of the proposal, we could do extensive renovation on the existing structure, convert some of the empty beds to office space, and not place an impossible debt burden on the hospital."

"Let's get on with it," said Smith impatiently.

"Go on, Lucien, tell us where we have to shore up our statistics."

Lucien began. "For starters, Obstetrics, Psych, and Med."

Doug smiled. "We're going to make it easier. We're reviewing community needs and have identified an average of ten admissions a week in Med/Surg, with a few admits in OB."

"If you're talking about filling our beds with patients from around here, forget it," Whyte barked. "My better patients won't tolerate it. They'll leave, and you'll turn this into a charity hospital."

"We don't have any choice. Even these additional admissions won't bring the statistics up enough."

"If my patients leave, you'll lose paying patients, and that's what keeps the doors open."

"Ed, it's time we stopped tolerating prejudice in the hospital. Let's leave that to the country clubs. This is a place people come to for care, not catering."

"If those twelve-year-old girls come in for abortions so they can keep on doing it, I'll treat them like the filth they are, and so will my residents."

"You're right, Ed," piped in Stan, who had kept out of the discussion. "It's up to you how you handle those patients, or even *if* you handle them, but we can use the statistics, Doug."

Doug doodled on his scratch pad. No matter which way he twisted to get to the right approach, they all twisted with him. *Maybe I should just shut up and go along.* "Check with me later, Lucien. I'll give you the figures."

Charles Smith had to have his say. "Doug, my census isn't dropping. My admits are still the same."

"When the admissions stay the same but the length of stay decreases, the census decreases," recited Doug.

Smith nodded.

Whyte uttered, "Oh, bullshit."

Doug remembered how easy it was for Simba to understand everything. It wasn't difficult. But for some reason, Ed Whyte couldn't get it.

"You better decide what you want us to do," said Charles. "One day you tell us to cut the length of stay, and then you complain because the census drops."

There was no point arguing. When the meeting ended, Doug made his way to his office. Wesley Mills was waiting for him.

"Just about to leave," said Wesley.

"Doug," Ann got his attention, "Simba Agiza called about an hour ago. Wants you to call."

Wesley winced. "She won't like what I'm about to recommend. We need to cut by the equivalent of a hundred and twenty people."

"A hundred and twenty?"

"Yep. The census has continued to drop."

Stan walked into the office.

Doug plunged in. "We were just discussing the need for a layoff or cutback. It was inevitable with reimbursement tightened by the Feds and the HMOs. In addition, Stan, with the drop in patient census, we'll have to close a few patient wings."

This revelation put Stan in a tizzy. "In view of the upcoming state presentation, keep it in this room. That could queer our hopes of ever getting the new building."

What gall! "Stan, that presentation's a week away, and they won't approve it that night. They'll schedule a meeting here and tour the facilities in about thirty days, and they could take another thirty to sixty days to make their decision."

"Get Lucien to grease the skids. If you need to borrow money, do it. We have a credit line. Nothing is to screw up that proposal."

"I better go take care of payroll." Wesley sought an escape and scooted out the door.

"Doug, I have the architects working on the additional drawings. We're adding a large outpatient facility on the eastern edge of the hospital for the local community."

"You sure your architects didn't have them done months ago, before your doctor friends even brought it up?"

Stan ignored the question. "The doctors will cooperate. It'll be their clinic, and if a patient can't meet the fees, we'll pick them up."

"Now it comes out." Doug had put the puzzle pieces together. "We pay the doctors off to see those patients so we can swell the census, give the doctors some additional revenue, and keep those patients out of their private offices."

"That's right!" Stan was grinning ear to ear. "And *you* gave me the idea."

Doug had no counter-strategy. He just couldn't get past the wall of greed.

As Stan waltzed out, Juanita stepped in.

"I had to see you." She was sniffling and trying to hold back an overflow. "I know Kayo told you I'm leaving."

"She did, and I'm surprised. You'll be missed."

"I want you to know I'll always miss you and be grateful for everything you've done."

And she was out the door, almost running, when the dam broke.

He was jolted by her tears and wanted to call her back, but Simba came in unannounced, looking over her shoulder after Juanita.

"Since I was over here to see my delegates, I figured I'd stop in to see you."

"Give me a chance to catch my breath."

"That pretty nurse running out of here have anything to do with your condition? Or are you just getting old?"

"Some things catch me by surprise. All day I've been dumped on, and it never seems to end."

"Are we feeling sorry for ourselves?"

"Nothing I won't get over. What's on your mind?"

"Douglas, I want to let you know something I'm doing because I don't want to mess up our relationship."

"Sounds serious."

"It's something you should be doing but since you aren't . . . I'm opposing the new hospital building. It's dropping jobs to pay for bricks. You can't pay for new real estate and still pay the salaries. I thought I'd alert you before I go to the press. That state hearing will have a few more people than normal."

"I guess we'll have to let the chips fall where they may. I wish this could all be done in a constructive way."

"I got to tell you, baby. You're the only one that can do it. I'm from the outside. I have to attack."

"You're right, Simba. But I must tell you, I've done about everything I can, and it's not been good enough. Maybe it'll take the frontal assault you'll give it."

"You going to fight me?" she asked, burrs up.

"It's like in the union drive. We each have our jobs to do."

CHAPTER THIRTY-TWO

Once again, Simba appeared on local talk shows. One interview was filmed with the hospital in the background. She called the doctors fat rats. She cried that the new hospital building would serve no purpose but to increase costs.

In addition, layoffs would follow because the hospital couldn't absorb the increase in expense. She was knowledgeable *and* convincing.

I trained her, thought Doug.

Stan Boswell, his face streaked with anger, charged into Doug's office, followed by Ed Whyte. "You've been tutoring that Simba bitch to sabotage our plan."

Doug pressed his back against his chair. "Nonsense. Now, I have work to do to counter her arguments."

Both turned and huffed out, on a mission.

Whyte could be heard all the way down the hallway. "You have to get rid of him."

Doug set about documenting why the new building would reduce expenses. He calculated how much would be saved in house-keeping because a new structure is easier to clean. He calculated the reduction in maintenance costs as compared to the old building.

He determined the savings in utilities. Some departments would save through efficiencies created by more space and new equipment. He compiled a feasibility study to counter Simba's claims.

Simba questioned quality. The morning paper carried the headline: "Is Eastern Biting Off Too Much?" She appeared on the same talk show that had roasted Doug before.

Stan, Doug, and Henry watched in Henry's office.

"With the expense of a new building," she stated, "and the losses in revenue hospitals are experiencing due to low census, how can Eastern even pray to maintain staff for quality care?"

"Simba," said the host, "I said it before, and I say it now. You would make a great hospital administrator. Why doesn't Eastern fire Doug Carpenter and make you the administrator?"

Stan shook his head and sing-songed, "I told you so."

Simba looked thoughtful, and Doug quietly acknowledged she was one hell of a performer.

"I think Mr. Carpenter is a good administrator. I think he's stymied by his boss, vice president in charge of health care, Mr. Stan Boswell. He's the one that should be fired."

Stan jumped up and screamed, "Damn you, Carpenter, you've gone too far!" Henry stiffened.

Doug stifled a laugh. "She has a mind of her own, Stan."

"You told her to do this. You two are trying to destroy this hospital. You're trying to destroy me." Stan ran from one side of the room to the other, a man on the edge.

Henry turned off the television set.

Stan pressed his forehead against the wall, his fists clenched above his head. Doug had never seen him so out of control, a lunatic making animal sounds.

Henry gave Doug a "what-now?" look.

Stan turned around and pointed. "You're fired, Carpenter. I want you out of my hospital."

"Fine. I'll call Walter Bass and tell him you've gone berserk because Simba turned the spotlight on you."

"The operative word is 'fired,' Carpenter." Stan ran out of the room and down the hall. "Clear out," he screamed.

"Where's he going?" asked Henry.

Doug grabbed the phone and dialed Walter Bass. To his relief, he was in.

"Glad you called, Doug. I was just watching Simba tear us apart, again. This time she zinged old Stan." He laughed heartily.

"Yes, we were watching. And old Stan isn't laughing. In fact, he just accused me of arranging the whole thing and then fired me."

"Is he out of his mind? Does he think you arranged for her to hammer you, too? I'll call him. Are you ready for the presentation?"

"Yes, I'm ready."

"You're still not a hundred percent with this proposal, are you?"

"No. In fact, that's an understatement."

"I wish I could be there, but I learned this morning I'll have to be in Washington at a Justice Department meeting. If it weren't on an issue of national concern, I wouldn't go. I want you to lead off in my place. I'll send over my presentation. Change it any way you see fit."

"I think you better let Stan know." He replaced the phone. "Talk about a vote of confidence."

"Are you fired?" asked Henry.

"No." Doug kept heading for the door. "Just status quo."

"Thank God."

Doug had no sooner walked into his office than Stan came running in behind him.

Following him were Cliff Toliver and one of his sergeants.

Stan pointed at Doug. "I want you two to escort Carpenter out of this building, and he's never to set foot on the premises again."

The two men looked confused.

"You've just been overruled by the Chairman of the Board. If you'd been to your office, you'd know he just called you. You two fellows go on about your business." The two men looked relieved and scurried out of the way.

Doug dialed Walter's number and handed Stan the phone.

"I'll use my own damn phone." Stan brushed past him.

Doug hung up and Ann came in carrying a file.

"Here's the finished copy of the feasibility study. If you approve it as is, I'll make copies."

"I approve."

After dinner, Doug helped Bess with the dishes.

"You don't have to do this, sweetheart." She took the dish cloth from him. "After that scene with Stan today, you could use a rest."

"Don't have time." He needed to talk to her, the person who never passed judgment. "I've got the big presentation tomorrow morning at ten. Walter sent his opening remarks over and they're eloquent. He's convinced we need the new building. Hell, he almost convinced me."

"But not quite."

"No, not quite."

"So what are you going to do?"

"I don't know that I have much choice."

"We always have choices."

"All of my choices are non-choices. I can make the presentation and the hospital gets the new building and a legacy of debt.

Or, I can say I can't, in good conscience, do it and that'll be the same as a resignation, and someone else will do it anyhow."

"You also have to worry about what it does to you. If you didn't do it, at least your conscience would be clean. And you'd get something else. Or at least we have to think so." She forced a thin smile.

"A clean conscience and an empty bank account or a dirty conscience and a full bank account. I wonder how far that correlation goes."

"Do you want me to come to the meeting?"

"No. If I do the right thing, I won't be there. If I do the wrong thing, I don't want you to watch."

Doug, Stan, Lucien, and the architects arrived at the chambers of the state office building at 9:45 a.m. The auditorium was already two-thirds full. Normally, there'd only be a few rows filled. Simba's friend, the talk show host, came over to Doug, poked a microphone in his face and asked if he thought the hospital could justify the new building, given Simba's findings.

"Our presentation will address that issue." Doug brushed by the man.

"Damn fool," the man said under his breath.

Sitting in the front row was Simba, and sitting next to her was Tevisina Urqhart, jaw pushed forward, eyes still numbed by pain. He remembered her in his office after her son turned himself in. *Some of us do what we have to do.*

"We're going to have a full house," Lucien observed.

Joe Goldman, who was sitting on the far end of the first row, motioned Doug over. "Congratulations, I hear you won a victory yesterday. There's talk you are going to take Stan's place."

"That's flattering, but it might be better for everyone if Stan won."

"No way." Joe patted Doug on the shoulder in confidence. Doug said hello to Simba.

"So you're going to go through with it." She searched his face. "Yep."

"Humph," Tevisina imparted her wisdom to whom would hear, "some folks do what's right and some don't." She stuck her chin out further. "Some do until it hurts." Her eyes watered. "And some do for themselves. I worked all my life for this community."

Doug suddenly felt rotten and remembered another quote. *You are what you do.* And Tevisina was. She was the community. She was what was good in the community. She represented its hope.

A coterie of doctors, led by Charles Smith and Ed Whyte, sat in the rest of the front row.

The director of the State Licensure Office, Mrs. Pickett, directed Stan and his group to sit at the presenters' table up to the left. There was a table on the right for the state examiners. The room was now filled and people were standing in the back.

Doug unpacked his briefcase and took out the remarks Walter Bass had sent. In the margins, Doug had penciled notes, mainly that he endorsed each comment the chair had made. Mrs. Pickett asked Stan who would speak first. Stan frowned and pointed at Doug. She stood at the microphone like a sentinel until the audience became quiet.

"I want to welcome this unusually large group of citizens to today's hospital expansion presentations. We have a full agenda today, the first being Eastern College Hospital's request . . ." She was drowned out by feet stomping in unison to a chorus chanting, "Jobs, not bricks. Jobs, not bricks." Mrs. Pickett spoke loudly into the microphone, ". . . for a new building. And I will clear this room if I must."

Doug felt a flood of anxiety.

The noise subsided, and Mrs. Pickett continued. "I repeat. I will clear this room. The scheduled presentations will be made." She glared like a bailiff for a full minute to make her point. "All right," her stainless-steel eyes still riveted on the gathering, she measured each word, "I introduce Mr. Douglas Carpenter, Administrator of Eastern College Hospital."

The room was quiet as Doug stepped to the podium.

"Mr. Walter Bass, Chairman of the Board at Eastern, was called to Washington to attend a meeting at the Justice Department. He regrets he is unable to be here."

Doug glanced at Tevisina again. He remembered the tears on her old cheek as she sacrificed for the right thing. He lost his place for a moment.

"The condition of the hospital building at Eastern College Hospital, and the ability of its staff to serve its public . . ."

He was unable to keep from looking at her again. She stared straight ahead. Her chin quivered for just a moment.

"Its ability to serve the public is in jeopardy."

Tevisina turned her face toward him, the same funeral eyes that had seen her son go to jail, eyes that shadowed pain and knew right from wrong and made tough choices. It was as though she had become his conscience. At the very least, she summoned his conscience to push him in the right direction.

Doug tried to say something else. He looked at the papers on the podium. He picked them up. He turned them face-down. He took a deep breath and looked at the crowd.

"There is no need for more hospital beds in an already over-bedded community. These modifications would cost more than we could bear. Some physicians muddied the plans for their own self-interests. Sometimes the caretakers outnumber the caregivers."

Out of the corner of his eye, Doug could see Stan and the others sitting as though frozen.

"We have some outstanding physicians, but the greedy behavior of a few chairpersons makes them all look bad."

Stan came to life and stumbled to his feet.

Doug continued, "The request for more beds is based on some legitimate need, but a large portion of it is for selfish reasons on the part of some members of the medical staff."

Stan lunged and tried to grab the microphone, but Doug held on.

"Others in my party will disagree, but I can refute their facts because I'm the one who put them together."

Some of the audience began applauding. Stan was lying across the podium, trying to get the microphone from Doug.

"Let me introduce Mr. Stanley Boswell, Vice President of Health Services at Eastern College Hospital."

Tevisina jumped up and praised Him, "Glory be to God!"

Doug handed the microphone to Stan. Stomping and chanting shook the building. Screams and cheers drowned out the futile shouts of Whyte to fire Carpenter. Smith stayed in his chair, his face chiseled in granite.

Stan held the microphone and tried to talk but couldn't be heard over the noise. Mrs. Pickett just watched in disgust.

Doug put his papers into his briefcase, saying, "Sorry about that, Lucien."

"Sorry, hell. You've got guts." He reached out and shook Doug's hand just as a camera flashed.

Doug made his way up the aisle through the crowd, feeling hands on his shoulders. He couldn't tell what was being said, except for Ed Whyte.

"You bastard!"

Stan was shouting over the microphone, "Eastern will reschedule its presentation."

On the outside, a reporter came through loud and clear, "Mr. Carpenter, does this mean you're resigning from Eastern?"

"I'll do what's best."

Doug walked to the parking lot surrounded by a group of reporters asking questions and unlocked his car. "I'll meet with you and answer questions at a time arranged by our PR Department. Until then, there's one other thing to say. Eastern needs to update its facility. It's just that the wrong things were being asked for."

He got in his car, slammed the door, and started the motor. He figured the rest of his party would find their own rides. He forced himself to drive slowly, savoring the aloneness in the car. He felt clean. Something had swung shut behind him. He was sorry Bess hadn't been there, after all. It was a turning point for both of them.

CHAPTER THIRTY-THREE

From his office, Doug called Bess. "I'd like to have lunch with my favorite wife in a quiet place out of town."

"How about Imirie's, north of the city? That's one of my favorite spots in the whole world."

"Good. How about a quarter of twelve?"

"How was the presentation?"

"Short and to the point. See you there?"

"Right," she sang.

"Ann," he called, "get Walter Bass's secretary on the phone."

"Gretchen, I know Walter's in Washington and probably in a meeting, but get hold of him and tell him to call me either this afternoon after two in my office, or this evening at home."

"Are you in your office, now?"

"Yes."

He no sooner put down the phone than Stan rushed in. "What the hell are you doing here?"

"Preparing for the real presentation for Eastern. What the hell are you doing here?"

Stan sputtered, "You're not preparing anything. Get out."

"Only if Walter or the Board says to, and I'm waiting for Walter's call now. You can wait or you can go."

Stan rushed out. "I'll call him myself."

Doug called Henry.

"Henry, you'll be getting calls from the media about a press conference. When you do, tell them you've received no instruction as to when it'll be. Tell them you'll notify them when the time is set."

"Okay, but what's this all about?"

Doug told him.

"Geez, I didn't know anybody had that kind of guts."

Jack Apple rushed into the office and out again.

"What's going on?" asked Ann.

"I sabotaged the new building presentation is what's going on."

"After all the work you did?"

"You know enough to realize we don't need that new building."

The phone rang. Walter Bass.

"Stan insisted I be pulled out of my meeting and Gretchen told me you called first. It sounds urgent. What's going on?"

"In a fit of conscience, I scuttled the building presentation. We're asking for the wrong things for the wrong reasons. I'm sorry, but it was the only way to do it. I'm sure it appears high-handed, and there'll be a lot of people on the Board who'll want my scalp. You may be among them, but I want you to listen to all sides before deciding."

"Fair enough, but I'll have to admit to some displeasure. I'll be getting in too late this evening. Set tomorrow morning aside. Now I'll call Stan."

When Doug got to Imirie's, Bess was there, waiting.

"Tell me what happened!" She leaned forward to accept his kiss. "On the car radio coming over, I heard there was a near riot at the hearings this morning, and you agreed with Simba that the new hospital wasn't needed."

"Big-mouthed media. I'll tell you about it after we've ordered. The excitement has made me hungry."

After lunch, they continued to talk about possible options over coffee.

"I want to stay on at Eastern, but as vice president. Hell, I might not be given the option of staying at all. I'll have a better feel for that tomorrow."

"What if you don't stay?"

"There'll be other jobs. Also, I've considered starting my own consulting business before. I just might have the courage to do it, if I don't have a job to resign from anyhow."

Kay O'Connell and Ann were talking when Doug came in.

"We didn't know if we'd see you again or not," said Kay.

"Tomorrow morning after the meeting with Walter Bass, we'll all know."

Kay wrapped her arms around him and hugged him tight. "If you go, I go."

"Don't say that out loud. You want to be able to make your own decision."

"They just don't know how much you've done here and how much everybody loves you."

"Especially Stan and Smith and Whyte and Apple."

"Those jerks. They are terminally stupid."

"Dangerous to be terminal anything at Eastern."

"You'll be glad to know that at least that's back to normal. There've been no unexpected deaths since Jeep left."

"At least we got rid of him, but at what price? Still no sign of him?"

"Gregg says he's either in Mexico, Canada, or Cuba."

"That narrows it down to three haystacks."

"Gregg also mentioned India. Lots of little villages where he could hide."

"I don't think so. He needs to be where he can earn money."

"And the other possibility is he will come back under a different name and start over. But they'll keep looking. They've now formally charged him with murder."

The evening newspaper carried the story about the hearing on the front page with a picture of Lucien shaking hands with Doug. The caption under the picture read, "Not everyone at Eastern disagrees with Carpenter."

"I sure hope that doesn't hurt Lucien," said Doug.

The story was flattering:

"Mr. Carpenter, who feels a strong commitment, both to Eastern and the community, made his point in no uncertain terms. An unofficial comment from one of the state officials indicates Eastern's request would have been denied anyway because the increase in the number of beds was unjustifiable."

Mrs. Pickett commented that the state would welcome any alternative plan presented by Doug. 'I have nothing but admiration for Mr. Carpenter.'"

The paper quoted Simba Agiza. "If all administrators were like Mr. Carpenter, hospitals in this country would be the best in the world."

"For a change," said Ann, "you didn't come off too bad."

"Tune in tomorrow."

Doug and Stan met with Walter at eight the next morning. It was a short meeting.

"I've read the newspaper accounts from last night and this morning," said Walter. "I've caught several newscasts. You came off looking good, Doug, if one can believe the media."

"They've made some kind of folk hero out of him," complained Stan.

"If only Eastern had come off looking as good. Doug, why

didn't you let me know you were going to do this when we talked the day before?"

"When you and I talked, *I* didn't know I was going to do it."

Stan arched his eyebrows.

"You had no idea you were going to do it?"

"I saw two options. One was to resign. The other was to go through with it. And the fact that I was there meant I had decided to go through with it. Maybe because I didn't have the courage to do otherwise."

"What changed your mind?" Walter sat, eyes locked on Doug.

Doug hesitated. "When I saw others there who had sacrificed so much, especially one."

Stan lunged forward, nose to nose with Doug. "Simba Agiza."

"Simba Agiza?" asked Walter.

Doug did not flinch. "No. Tevisina. She has the guts to do what's right. She even turned her own son in for pushing dope. She fights for this community."

Walter sat like a rock, his gaze fixed on Doug. "We'll have a special board meeting tonight. You two gentlemen be there."

Throughout the morning, Doug's phone was busy. Every department head called. While one was talking to him, another would be waiting on the other line. They just wanted to thank him. As soon as he would hang up, Ann would buzz and there would be another.

At around eleven, Simba called.

"It wouldn't be PC for us to have lunch today or I'd take you to the biggest, most expensive lunch of your life. Guess you'll just have to settle for a thank you. Thanks for what you did yesterday. And I'll see you at the board meeting tonight."

"What?" cried Doug. "How did you find out about that?"

"You know I have spies all over that building."

"Can you hold on a minute?" asked Doug. Another phone light had just gone on. Putting down the phone, he walked to the door and peered out at Ann just as she finished dialing. Surprised, she dropped the phone, quickly.

"Hi, there." She smiled pleasantly, leaning over her desk. "Been busy?"

"Yeah. What's going on?"

"Just a lot of phone calls." She shrugged, genuinely puzzled. "Seems like everyone wants to talk to you."

"You wouldn't have anything to do with that would you?"

She folded her hands and squirmed a little. "I'm just sitting here minding my own business, and that's the truth."

Doug walked back to his desk and picked up the phone.

"Okay, Simba. I know how you found out. What are you planning?"

"If I told you, white-ass, that'd make you guilty of collusion."

"Look, Simba. That's going to be an important meeting. And it's not politic to crash it."

"Tell me about it, honey." She hung up.

Ann buzzed him.

The meeting was scheduled for eight that evening. By seven-thirty, the building was surrounded by employees and people from the neighborhood. They stood silently, staring at the building. The hallway leading to the boardroom was lined on both sides with department heads, employees, and more neighbors. They were linked, arms across shoulders, along the walls, being careful not to block the way.

At least two hundred people jammed in. Except for their breathing, there wasn't a sound.

Across the far end of the hall there was a large sign taped to the wall. *Doug Carpenter—Vice President.* And another, *Doug Gives Until It Helps.*

Doug was stunned. The hall was full of banners and a wave of faces, all turned toward him, all smiling. He started down the hall, saw Ann to his left, and stopped again.

She said, "Hi, there."

Across from the door to the boardroom stood Simba.

Walter Bass entered the hall and registered surprise. He regained his composure and walked slowly down the hall, looking at the signs, and all the people. When he entered the boardroom, he said, "With that crowd outside and then this, I feel as though I just passed through the hall of truth."

Behind him came Joe Goldman, who clasped his hands above his head and shook them all the way to the door. At the boardroom door, he asked Doug, "How much did this cost you?"

"A lot of sleep."

From out in the hall, Stan's voice could be heard. "What the hell is this? What are you people doing here? I want you out of here. I'll have security put you out. All of you."

Walter stepped out into the hall. "Stan."

Stan looked around at him, hurried through, head down, and followed Walter into the room.

Charles Smith came through, followed by two physicians from his department. For a man whose expression rarely changed, Charles's face was comical. He frowned, then smiled, then went to non-committal.

Simba stepped across the hall. "Mr. Bass, some of those men are not members of the Board. Does that mean this is an open meeting?"

"No, it is not. They are physicians on our staff, and I suspect they have something pertinent to say."

"Sir, shouldn't they clear that with you?"

Walter paused for a moment. "You are quite right, Miss Agiza."

"Because," Simba continued, "there are some of us here who have something to say, also. Tevisina is on the Board to represent the community. I would like to represent the union. There is someone here who would like to represent the department heads, and there is someone else who would like to speak on behalf of all the other employees."

Walter stepped out of the doorway and walked slowly up the hallway. He stopped and turned around, then spoke in a low voice, but it could be heard from one end of the hall to the other, "You people have made it obvious that your intent here is constructive. Miss Agiza, I would be pleased if you and the two others you mentioned would attend this board meeting as my guests."

Walter ushered in Simba, Mary Jane McCarthy, and Joy Coleman. Simba smiled graciously. Mary Jane was intent and serious. Doug could almost see Joy's heart knocking. They all sat together at one side of the large table.

In the hallway, Ed Whyte spit his venom, "You ungrateful tramp!"

Walter and Doug rushed into the hall to see Whyte shaking a frightened girl by the shoulders.

"Just look at her," yelled Whyte. "I gave her an abortion, and in return, she does this to me." He tried to pull her away from the wall, but others held her.

Walter raised his voice. "Dr. Whyte, if you plan to join us in the boardroom, would you do so? If you don't, would you leave?"

As Whyte let go, the poor girl collapsed into those holding her up.

Suddenly, Whyte seemed to see the others for the first time. He walked, fists clenched white, contrasting with the red of his face and neck. Someone started to hum "We Shall Overcome" and others joined in. Walter was the last to re-enter the room.

Walter stood at the end of the table. "In the last few weeks, some individuals have shown sides of their personalities I didn't know existed."

When the music got a little louder, he asked, "Doug, would you step out there and ask the Eastern Tabernacle Choir to take a break?"

Doug stepped out and the hall erupted into loud singing and clapping. He put up his hands and they sang louder. It was like a release for him, too. His throat grew tight. He put his finger to his lips and walked part way up the hall. A few "shh's" and the music subsided, leaving one beautiful voice singing solo the last three words, "we shall overcome." She held it for an extra few seconds. Doug turned and went back into the room. But outdoors, they had heard, and the song was picked up.

Walter addressed the Board. "We've had the prelude and the background music. Let's get to the serious business. This meeting was called because of the explosive hearing yesterday, which you all know about if you can hear or see. A few of you were there. It's a serious issue because some important plans for the hospital have gone astray." He turned to Doug. "I'm going to ask Doug to explain why he did what he did, and when he's done, I'll elicit comments from each of you. Since this may become an emotional issue, I'll reiterate the words, 'when he's done.' Please save us all time and trouble by refraining from interruptions. Doug?"

"To those serving on the planning committee, this will sound familiar," Doug began.

Whyte gestured, palms up, and sighed. Charles remained motionless.

"Those few will have to hear it again."

He could see Whyte, in particular, turning red.

"I'll keep this as concise as possible, but I'll pull no punches. The proposal was wrong. All the way through the process, we had to manipulate and create statistics to support our plans. This hospital neither needs more beds nor can it support more beds. We can't support the beds we have. We are facing a layoff of one hundred and twenty people or an equivalent cut in salaries. By Stan's order, we are holding off action on it until after state approval and are borrowing money to meet the payroll."

Doug looked at Stan who stared at his pencil. "We do need new construction. But more than anything else, we need to renovate what we already have. Not only would the new building be an anchor, the physicians concocted a scheme to increase their own revenues—"

"That's a lie!" bellowed Whyte, who appeared to be about to stroke out.

Walter slammed the gavel so hard he broke the handle. The mallet skittered off the table and onto the floor. "I will escort you out if you do that again."

Whyte's mouth hung open, fish-like.

Walter motioned to Doug.

"Their plan was to build a new office building, lease it to the hospital for an exorbitant amount, and be charged a token amount for rent, services, new furniture, equipment for their private practices, food service, a private dining hall, and a recreation center, for starters. There has been no concern shown by Stan, Dr. Whyte, Dr. Smith, and a number of others for the financial well-being of the hospital, its employees, or its patients."

Stan, Ed Whyte, and Charles Smith shook their heads in unison, as though they had practiced synchronized shaking.

"The hospital has a need for and could support a renovated structure and some new construction. The doctors' plans for a new office building could be feasible if divested of their private greed.

"I've taken a copy of the proposal and written next to every statistic what the real projection should be, and in many cases they aren't even half what is stated. I'll pass it on to you, Walter." He slid it across the table. "I went to that meeting intending not only to present the plan but to successfully present it. I had given up winning the argument with Stan, Ed, and Charles. They had beaten me. But when I got there, some good people shamed me into doing the right thing. And to them, I apologize for having come so close to breaking their trust."

He nodded to Tevisina and Simba.

"For the record, I also offer an apology to this Board for my process. I kept hoping—although without much conviction— we would not be making that proposal." Doug relaxed and took a deep breath. "Thank you, Walter."

Not a word. Walter looked from face to face, stopping at Whyte. "You were anxious to talk before. What do you have to say?"

Whyte's mouth spewed anger. "For all the work we do, we should be compensated. And this man," he pointed at Doug, "this man has thrown roadblocks and regulations in our way."

In the moments that followed, Walter's gaze covered Whyte, who looked up and down as though movement counted as words. Walter shifted to Charles, who waved his hand and shook his head no.

"Stan," said Walter, "this project was your charge. Anything to add?"

Stan was bent forward, elbows on the table, fingers in his hair. He waved one hand. "Nothing. Nothing. I tried to do what had to be done. I just wish we could have had more teamwork."

Walter looked around the room. "Any other Board member?"

Tevisina lifted her hand. "Yes." Tears rolled down her leathery cheeks. "Thank you, Doug."

"Would any of our guests like to make a comment?"

As though on cue, the singing outside the building stopped. It was replaced by clapping of many hands in unison. It wasn't loud, almost muffled, but persistent.

Mary Jane McCarthy stood. "I'd like to say that without any exceptions, the department heads fully endorse what Doug says and stands for. He has made better managers of us, and he has made Eastern a better hospital." She sat down and smiled at Doug.

Joy Coleman stood. Her fingers fidgeted, but she plunged ahead. "The employees think he's fair. They'll do anything he asks them to do." She sat then stood, "And *I* mean it." Some of the Board members murmured as she sat down.

Then Simba took her turn. "I want to thank Mr. Bass for inviting me to this meeting as his guest. I consider that an honor." She paused. "I want to apologize to Doug Carpenter for all the rotten things I said about him during the union organizing effort. Although that was a situation that sometimes calls for derogatory comments, in his case, there was no justification. I want to say as long as he's at Eastern, this union will work with him." She stopped for a moment and looked at Doug, then faced Walter Bass and struggled for words. "I want to add that I never expected a white man to become a role model for me."

She sat, and Doug could see that her embarrassment matched his own.

Walter glanced toward a window and listened to the clapping. "Those were impressive testimonials. I want this Board to consider several issues. One is the fact that our top management team is not a workable match. The other is we have to do something fast regarding building plans. The management team is the top issue. Comment?"

Everyone waited for someone else to start.

Finally, Joe Goldman stood. "I just want to make a statement for all of you Board members to consider. As a physician who cares not only for the health of his patients but also for their financial well-being and their quality of life, I thank God for Doug Carpenter."

Tevisina stood up and spoke slowly, emphasizing each word, "I am proud to be on this Board with Doug Carpenter."

Stan looked like a plaster of Paris statue, leaning forward looking at his folded hands.

"We need to do something, ladies and gentleman," urged Walter. "What are your wishes?"

Charles Smith cleared his throat. "It's obvious we need to do something. I agree. And I also agree . . ." He searched for words. "I also agree that our demands were somewhat excessive." He looked at Doug. "I don't agree with everything you said, but you're right about some things. I don't agree with you about mixing classes of people. It's just an accident that it goes down racial lines."

"Charles, you can't stereotype people," stated Doug.

"I don't think I am, but we can talk about it."

Walter nodded to acknowledge Charles' concession. The rhythmic clapping continued outside.

"Walter," Stan mumbled, still in the same petrified position, "I think it might relieve pressure if I tendered my resignation effective six months from now." He glanced at Walter and then the tabletop.

Tevisina cleared her throat and spoke firmly. "I don't think we *want* you here for the next six months."

Walter made the command decision, "Unless I hear to the contrary, the Board accepts your resignation effective six months from now, but you will be relieved of all duties effective immediately."

No one made a sound. Stan continued to stare at the table.

"I want to get a consensus from this group, including our guests, as to whether or not to proceed with a modified building program."

"We need to renovate with some new construction, but not everything we were asking for," said Charles Smith.

"Definitely, we need to do *something*," Joe Goldman emphasized. "The older parts of the hospital are falling down around us."

A few more comments dragged out, but it was apparent the group felt nothing else needed to be said.

Walter gave them time by removing his glasses and cleaning them. "I take it the consensus is we should proceed. Any comment to the contrary?"

No comments.

"I'll adjourn this meeting, asking the executive committee to remain behind. You, too, please, Doug. Stan, this meeting was your last official act. I want to thank our guests for coming and for their participation."

Stan sat for a moment then gathered his papers together. Outside, the hall was still lined. When Simba, Mary Jane, and Joy appeared in the doorway, their smiles conveyed the message. Stan pushed through the hall in the midst of cheers and a lot of happy talk.

When all had left except for the executive committee, Walter walked out into the hall and lowered his hands. The group immediately became hushed. Then he came back in and closed the door.

Walter did the talking.

CHAPTER THIRTY-FOUR

"Doug, we made a mistake selecting Stan over you for the vice president job. You've had a hard time of it, and I could rationalize and justify your every action." He paused, as though deciding how to proceed.

"But?" questioned Doug.

"But you displayed dirty linen best left in our laundry. What's done is done. But the fact is, you can't be the facilitator you were."

"What are you saying?" asked Tevisina.

"I'm saying Doug should act as vice president, get our building program on the right track, but start looking for another job."

"We can't fire Doug," she said adamantly.

"Of course we can't fire him. But Doug, you're smart enough to know you can't be effective working with these physicians. It's going to become more and more unpleasant, and, eventually, we'll have to fire you."

Doug felt the air go out of his lungs. He hadn't won after all. "I'm not happy with that. But I guess I half expected it."

Tevisina moaned it again. "We can't fire Doug."

"I'm not questioning your motives." Walter put his hand on Doug's arm. "That's not the issue."

"I didn't expect the public to make a folk hero out of me, but, right or wrong, Eastern can capitalize on it."

"Yes, we can and we shall. You owe us that. And we owe you. I'm saying your useful days are numbered. I want you to acknowledge that and agree you will resign and give us a future date."

"There's a lot I can get done because of the circumstances. I'd like to think about it and let you know."

"Not good enough. I know there's an astounding bond between you and the employees, the department heads, the union, and the community. But you can't make it with the doctors."

"With a large number of them, I have no problem. But the only person who could make it with the more miserable part of this medical staff"—Doug looked at Charles—"would be a cross between a jellyfish and a shark."

"Walter," interjected Joe, "Doug is right. This job will never win a popularity contest with the medical staff."

"Joe, credibility is gone. We can't just squelch the selfish doctors. There are too many. We have to draw them into a world of decency. Doug, I repeat, you've done a good job. You've laid the groundwork for someone else to carry on."

"Okay, I'll give you my resignation effective in twelve months." He was sick of saying it.

"It can't be twelve."

"Okay!" he cried. "I'll agree it won't be twelve, but that's the notice I'm giving."

"Walter," Joe looked him in the eye, "in all the time I've served on this Board with you, I've never disagreed with you until now."

"I'm not happy about this either. I like Doug. I think he's a fine administrator, but he *must* have the trust of the doctors."

"We need him," repeated Joe, "contrary to some of some of these lousy physicians he can't get along with. I have trouble with them, too. Maybe it's them we should get rid of."

Charles cleared his throat and stood up. "Wait a minute. Speaking as one of the physicians he's talking about, I want to say I don't agree with everything he does, but he can work with me. He's the first administrator I've met who's not afraid to say what he thinks. I move we make him vice president for Health Services with no resignation time hanging over his head."

Charles didn't look at Doug. And Doug couldn't imagine what had gotten into Charles.

Joe Goldman broke the silence. "I agree with you Charles, for once. And I hope for many times in the future."

Tevisina stood and announced in a loud voice. "I want Doug Carpenter. This community wants Doug Carpenter. It would be wrong, wrong, *wrong*, to fire Doug Carpenter. He's doing the right thing." She sat abruptly.

"Well, for once," Walter contemplated each of them, "I have been overruled. Doug, I'm surprised and pleased. Congratulations."

Tevisina leaned over the table, her head propped in her hands. "Jesus, thank you," she prayed.

"Walter," Doug recaptured his breath, "this has been a fast merry-go-round and I'm still a little dizzy."

"You have a lot of support here, and obviously, you've earned it."

"Then I guess it's not too early to get busy. I want to hire an administrator right away."

"I think you should. And, Doug, if you had needed it, I would have given you a reference that would sing you to the heavens."

"I would have needed it, sir. Not many boards would have trusted me after this."

"Ladies and gentlemen, that concludes this meeting. If you don't mind, I'd like a word with Doug, alone."

Joe shook Doug's hand. "I'll see you tomorrow."

Tevisina put her arms around him and rested her head on his chest for just a moment. Charles smiled for the first time Doug could remember, and then it was just Walter and himself.

Walter eyed him and seemed to relax for the first time that evening. "I want to tell you something before you leave. When I said I would give you a reference that would sing you to the heavens, I meant it. You might like to know, the governor called me today. I think you'll be hearing from him. If my recommendation means anything, you may have a decision to make."

When Doug emerged from the boardroom, the crowd had thinned to only a few—Ann, Joy, and a handful of neighbors.

"I don't know who arranged for the sound effects outside, but it did its job. You can call off the Indian rainmakers and start paddling."

"Simba said she would call you tomorrow." Ann wrapped her arms around his neck and kissed his cheek. "That's from all of us."

"You and Simba," Joy shook her head in disbelief, "this was a beautiful thing."

From his office window, Doug looked out on the lawn, lighted by street lamps. He held a note in his hand that Kay had left on his desk. He had priorities to set: children's detox, the racist hiring, nursing home legislation, HMO control, no layoffs. The next administrator would have it easier. As Walter said, the hospital wasn't a building, it was what went on inside. "The real building program," he said out loud, "people, not bricks." He called Bess, filled her in, and promised to drive slowly.

He unfolded Kay's note and read it again.

"Thought you'd want to know, or maybe not. Just talked to my friend at Riverview Hospital where Juanita is now. Their death rate has jumped. Terminal patients expiring earlier than expected. All Hispanic. Jeep might have killed Ramirez, but I have to wonder about the rest."

He sat, staring at the note.

ABOUT THE AUTHOR

William T. Delamar was born in Durham, North Carolina, in a home full of books, which ignited a love for reading. In high school, he worked part-time at Duke University Press, further increasing his insatiable desire for literature.

He served in the navy as a weatherman, received his bachelor's degree from the University of Pittsburgh, and a master's degree from Antioch University. After thirty-five years' experience in hospital organization and development, ranging from methods and procedures examiner to CEO, Delamar became a founding member of the Hospital Management and Information Society. Under his guidance, it grew from twenty-eight members to thousands internationally.

Delamar was on the board of the Philadelphia Writers' Conference, having served five times as president. His works include: *The Hidden Congregation*, *The Caretakers*, *Patients in Purgatory*, and *The Brother Voice*. He crossed over to join his wife Gloria in 2022.

WILLIAM T. DELAMAR

FROM OPEN ROAD MEDIA

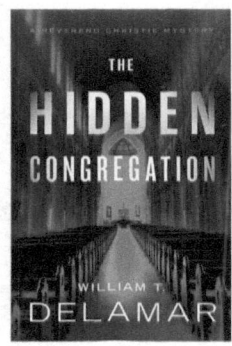
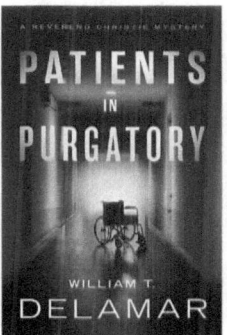
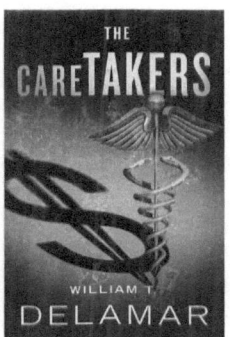

INTEGRATED MEDIA

Find a full list of our authors and
titles at www.openroadmedia.com

FOLLOW US
@OpenRoadMedia